# The Ferret Files

Introducing Ferret

*London's premier detecting consultant*

# The Ferret Files

**Phillip Legard**

# Dedication

For Sue and her unwavering support throughout project Ferret.

Happy significant birthday, lover!

# Chapter Zero: Project XIII

Flamen Dialis bolted upright in the rough wooden sleeping crate he called a bed and let out a gasp of astonishment. Moments earlier, he'd been on the deck of a ship, reaching out to grab his old friend the chemist by the wrists, to pull him to safety. He felt a tightness in his tendons, a burn where their hands had met as he tried to yank the scientist back over the rail, losing his grip at the last moment. Far below, an angry cobalt sea crashed against the steel hull, whipped into a frenzy by an unfriendly squall.

"So real," he tried to say, fat tongue clinging to the roof of his mouth.

Clearly, the gods were speaking to him in their improbable language of signs, showing him something divine. It was to the augurs he must turn, for an official interpretation. In his opinion, although he wasn't formally qualified to comment, the reappearance of his friend after all these years suggested but one thing: a warning.

Someone was prying into the project.

The priest took a long, slow breath.

Good luck with that.

He'd put specific precautions in place to prevent the powers that be from doing such a thing.

And with good reason.

Still half asleep, the old man narrowed his eyes and focused on the glass of water on his dressing table, beyond physical reach. Gently, he caressed the scuffed beaker, fondling atoms of silicon, hydrogen, and oxygen, until each stood to attention.

In his mind he barked an order.

The glass flew through the air and landed in his open hand, perfectly aligned. Flamen nodded in satisfaction and took a long sip of cool liquid. It had taken years of practice to achieve such results, but it was still only a magician's parlour trick.

Flamen rubbed the sleep from the corners of his eyes and began the ritual of baselining his senses, a habit started many years ago while still in the service of his country. Having assured himself that all were functioning optimally, he chanted his daily mantra:

"One must always keep up one's guard."

"Never allow the enemy the space to regroup."

"The Brotherhood comes first."

"Always."

Contented, the old man rocked from side to side. The project was secure, of this he had no doubt. As hard as they might try, a lifetime was not long enough to dismantle the maze of blocks and false trails he'd put in place. The paperwork alone was a great nightmare of a Gordian knot, expertly tied by his own hand.

Discover the inner workings of Project XIII?

What a ridiculous notion.

The chemist's reappearance must mean something else.

In order to be certain, Flamen knew he must seek a second opinion while the details of his vision remained fresh. Pulling himself out of bed, he pushed his feet into a pair of padded woollen slippers. He took a few tentative steps across the cold flagstone floor, making faces at his reflection in the long, plain mirror that occupied one corner of his sleeping quarters. Years of mountain living, regular backbreaking toil, and a sensible diet of home-grown food had honed his body, leaving no sign of fat. Truth be told, he was far older than the image the looking-glass displayed. It was the lack of body hair that threw the eyes into disarray. When confronted with a plucked chicken, ready to be basted, the mind was wont to play all manner of strange tricks.

Flamen washed his face in chilled mountain water and shivered. He pulled on a thick white woollen toga trimmed with royal purple and donned a simple white cap. Below the north tower where he quartered, the world was slowly stirring from its sleep.

A goat maaa'd.

Clanking cow bells whispered through the mist.

Far away to the east, the sun poked its head above the horizon, illuminating the foothills and sending dancing shards of lilac this way and that. The great castle of the Himalayas began here. The low-lying hills were merely its outer battlements; the impregnable central keep lay many days' travel hence. The old man's breath crystallised; he felt the edges of his nostrils tighten.

Pulling the robe tightly about his body, he hurried along the monastery's outer wall, keeping to the heights, mindful of his brothers below. He dare not risk being seen at this time of day, for once spotted, they would call on him to lead a prayer to the new day, an invitation he dare not refuse.

As Jupiter was his deity, so he was Jupiter's representative on earth, the most powerful man in the compound.

Only the Pontifex stood higher.

When he was here.

Flamen descended to the earthen floor, traversing a well-worn stone staircase that offered little protection against the chill. Outside the office of the chief augur, fist raised to strike the wooden door, he came to an abrupt halt.

And sighed.

It was not unknown for the augurs to take two cycles of the moon to respond to a request such as his. Even the simplest interpretation took them forever with their endless meetings and philosophical jibber-jabber, consulting this tome and that in a quest for the ultimate definition of how to phrase the question. Once they decided on the grammar, there was then the wait for an auspicious day.

The old man exhaled hard, his shoulders sagging underneath the robe.

Damn them all!

In order to change the outcome of his vision, he must be there, as foretold.

Instinctively, he turned around and, gathering up the toga, headed resolutely towards the compound's chicken coop, clinging to the shadows, the premonition of his friend's forthcoming accident never far from his thoughts.

A cockerel pecked the ground, finishing off the seed Flamen had dropped, eyeing him with suspicion. It ruffled its feathers and held its head to the sky. Fearing what an alarm call might bring, Flamen drew a circle in the air with his forefinger and pointed to the creature's beak.

"Five minutes."

Unable to make a sound, the bird ran around furiously, its comb erect, head clacking back and forth. Thrice the wild ball of feathers smacked into Flamen, forcing him to glare at it hard. Only then did the cock moodily retire.

The priest entered the coop and collected a wooden carrying cage, into which he thrust one of the girls from the cluster of hens that had stopped laying. She flapped and squawked in confusion until, with a wave of his finger, he silenced her too.

To the haruspex!

To the one member of The Brotherhood trusted with reading signs. He was new to the post, his credentials unproven but his references sound. It was perhaps a little early for a blood ritual, but what choice did he have? Holding the detail of the vision in his mind was becoming increasingly difficult; he had to let it go.

Knowing the haruspex's sleeping habits, Flamen hurried to the stables. The rest of the brothers didn't agree with how the seer carried on. They thought him a little odd. Even the pontifex found it tiresome.

"Do you not know the time?" The shaggy seer tore himself away from a sheep, hay clinging to his matted body hair, voice booming out louder than a foghorn.

"The matter is most urgent."

In contrast to the priest, who despite his thick white robe of office still looked like a skinny polar bear, the seer was as large as a grizzly and quite naked. In public, he consented to a robe, but here, in his own domain, he set the rules. Flamen took a step backwards and craned his neck to catch the man's eye. If he got too close, the haruspex would hug him, as he hugged all living things, leaving a distinct smell of warm, stale livestock about his person.

"I had a vision, and in it, I lost a friend."

"Someone close?"

Flamen nodded.

"Do you bring an offering?"

The priest held out the wooden cage.

The haruspex snatched the cage with one hand. "Undo your spell."

Flamen waved his finger.

The bird flapped its wings, scratching and screeching, causing the sheep to stir and an old grey mule to bray in annoyance. The racket spread throughout the stable. Despite the din, Flamen knew an interruption was unlikely.

Deftly for such a large man, the seer took hold of the bird by its feet, pulling it clear of the cage. He waved it once around his head and, wiping his mouth with the back of his hand, snapped its head clean off, causing a spurt of blood to gush forth.

The stable fell silent.

Blood dripped from the seer's stomach. He inserted a finger into the bird's neck hole, ejecting a mix of blood and mucus. A wing flapped. The giant of a man wiped blood and snot across each of Flamen's cheeks, then his own, letting his fingers come to rest in the bush of his beard.

"Hear me, great Jupiter, whose orbit dictates the energy that flows around and through this world, I say this passing is not in vain." With which the seer pulled the dead bird apart, casting its entrails roughly on the floor, the heart still beating. The bird's gizzards and liver slopped in an elongated heap.

Flamen's nostrils curled with the stench of fresh faeces.

"I see a ship," said the seer, interpreting the patterns left by the innards.

A lump formed in the priest's throat. "Where?"

"Three swords stand guard above a fjord."

Despite the weight of his toga, the priest danced a jig. His premonitions were always a week ahead at least. He had a dozen valid passports, a dozen identities; a dozen disguises to wear.

"I fly to Stavanger."

Why not?

What a jolly jape.

"Oh no you don't."

Flamen sighed.

It was true.

His chain of office was wrought with great responsibility. Only one day, from sunrise until sunset. That was for how long he was allowed to leave the compound.

"This is important," he said. "I must know precisely when."

Closing his eyes, the priest let the vision wash over him, replaying every detail. The fear in his friend's eyes wasn't just the fear of death made manifest, there was more. He was trying to say something. A word hung fresh in his throat, suspended in the air, begging to be heard. Flamen pressed his eyelids tightly together in concentration.

"*Sohn* . . ."

"I see a young man with a large nose and an unruly mop of hair," said the seer, cracking a smile.

Flamen nodded. He'd observed the youth many times from a distance although they'd only formally met once. The priest had tried to open the boy's eyes by lighting a cigar with his thumb, a feat the lad was convinced relied on concealed tubes and a supply of compressed gas. They discussed the possibility that the boy might be mistaken, only to be interrupted by the lad's best friend, who howled in derision at the thought of such tripe.

All that good advice, dismissed as incoherent nonsense.

When he tried to press the case again later that evening, the boy's friend became ever more vocal until the ushers had little choice but to intervene.

In retrospect, thought Flamen, the youth's graduation ceremony was the wrong place to make first contact.

"I see a vault in a green and pleasant land."

"That's hardly important." Flamen waved the seer away.

"It is open."

"That's not . . . possible . . ." The words dripped sourly from the high priest's tongue, reminding him of the taste of curdled cream.

"But true, nonetheless." The seer found a cloth and wiped his hands.

Flamen gulped. In his heart he'd always feared there might be a way to cut through the countermeasures he'd put in place, specifically designed to keep all comers out of the secret underground bunker.

"God forbid." He cradled his head in his hands.

If the vault was open, then whoever was responsible must have access to the official records. If this was so, they knew the nature of the treasure contained within.

The priest's mind raced.

The chemist had sworn to keep their off-piste work secret. Those responsible for the opening were missing vital details.

"I see a dying lion, gored by a dead unicorn," said the haruspex, poking the entrails with a stick.

The priest's heart skipped a beat. Evidently, the realm had a new enemy, stalking the corridors of power, operating within the shadows.

He sighed.

After they had their hands on the treasure, they'd follow the paperwork trail until eventually his name came up. Sadly, he knew such people of old. They'd employ violent scum to do their dirty work, the result being a nasty assault with automatic weapons followed by missing limbs and a long, drawn-out death for each of his brothers. Whatever it took to unearth the secret of secrets.

The priest coughed, spitting out a glistening ball of phlegm which spun through the air, catching a dung fly unaware.

"Now," said the seer, "your authorisation."

"I'll bring it by later."

"Ho! You will not," laughed the seer, a twinkle in his eye. "You know the price for unauthorised advice."

Flamen removed his robe, taking care not to dirty the edges, and hung it on a gleaming metal hook. Sex and magic were always so interlinked. One type of energy morphed into another; this was the way of things. The haruspex wasn't interested in mounting him, the High Priest of Jupiter, oh no. He had an entire stable set aside for such purposes. No, this was a chore of a different kind.

"Assume the position," said Flamen wearily, picking a supple leather strap from an array of interesting instruments.

Thwack!

The vision of his friend came back to haunt him once more.

Thwack!

"Jupiter loves you," said Flamen.

Thwack!

The seer turned his head in time to see the bird's heart stop beating. "Your friend's time is up."

"No!" Flamen gasped for air.

He felt himself detach from his body, watching the spanking of the seer, while the vision unwound in slow motion in time with his blows. In a blink, through the ether he flew, arms outstretched, determined this time to save his friend.

Fingertips met.

Gravity screamed in defiance.

One, two fingers unwound.

The middle one ached.

The god of immutable physics took a bow.

A scream.

And the chemist was gone.

The priest snapped back into his body, eyes stinging, tears streaming down his cheeks in hot rivulets. Of all the deaths he'd been witness to, this one had consequences more far reaching than most.

Flamen saw once more the look of horror on the chemist's face, heard the cry of abject terror.

There was something reflected in his friend's eye, in the very corner of his pupil.

In astonishment, the priest dropped the whip.

It wasn't a something.

It was a someone.

His friend hadn't slipped from the ship's deck.
He was pushed.

Pressing a combination of buttons on an electronic key fob, Ferret unlocked the front door to his home. The seasoned oak door swung open on well-oiled hinges. The consultant wiped his feet on the doormat and whistled three notes in succession, disarming the motion sensors.

Bob Bobson, Ferret's co-worker for the week, took a step backwards and gazed up, surveying the three-storey townhouse towering in front of him. He pinched his hand. "How . . . on . . . earth . . ."

"It's a little larger than the last place," said Ferret with a wink, beckoning the engineer in.

Bob poked his head inside the door. "Perhaps I should stay outside."

"Nonsense! You're as welcome as any of my friends."

Bob dropped an old beaten-up metal toolbox outside the door, unlaced his heavy boots, their steel toecaps protruding through cracked leather, and deposited them on a shoe rack next to the welcome mat. Methodically, he unzipped the faded blue overalls he favoured, making sure not to drop any of the contents of the pockets on the polished black marble floor and stowed the garment atop the boots.

Weird, thought Ferret. He has one bare foot.

Grabbing hold of the grand-banister rail, the consultant set off up the stairs, suit jacket tails billowing behind him, but stopped at the first turning. Bob remained rooted to the spot, mouth agape, staring at the pale-yellow paintwork and the diagonal row of carefully chosen pictures. Begrudgingly, the engineer pulled a carrier bag from his toolbox and, with a look of bewilderment, trudged on up the steps.

"Close sesame!" Ferret clicked his fingers, the noise echoing through the entry hall.

The door did as commanded.

As they ascended, Bob's curiosity got the better of him. "How many rooms?"

"The agent said twenty-six, although I suspect some of them of being cupboards."

"That one?" pointed Bob.

"Bathroom." Ferret held the door ajar.

Nervously, the engineer poked his head inside, nodding at the complementary shades of Italian marble adorning the walls and floor. "And that?"

"The master bedroom," smiled Ferret.

Truth be told, he was rather proud of the wrought iron four-poster bed, feature wall, and walk-in wardrobe, the hanging rails packed with suits for every season. The whole ensemble looked like it belonged in a fashion catalogue, which unsurprisingly, was exactly from whence it came.

"With an en suite?"

Ferret nodded. Getting the colour right had been a nightmare. So many shades of light grey and yet only one that truly matched the brushed aluminium fittings, bringing them to life. At least that's what the designer had said and, being Italian, she should know.

The consultant pressed on, towards a jet-black rectangle with no visible handles, located at the very top of the stairs.

"This is all topsy-turvy," said Bob, scratching his head. "The living room is downstairs; I saw both of them. And I'm sure the kitchen must be too. This layout, it makes me feel all . . ."

"Discombobulated?"

"That's the one."

Ferret pressed a button on the keychain, resulting in a faint click. The door opened just a crack. He pushed it with his index finger, causing it to swing open effortlessly. Loosening his tie, he marched in and flung his suit jacket across the back of an easy chair. Bob followed. With a flourish of the wrist, the consultant introduced the engineer to the massive single-pane picture window that fronted the attic-cum-den, offering a panoramic view of Regent's Park all the way to London Zoo.

"Wow," said Bob. "Nice TV."

Ferret slipped into the adjoining kitchenette and rummaged through the fridge. He withdrew a frosted glass container and poured a measure of clear liquid into a cocktail glass, adding a pair of ice cubes. Wrapping up the operation, he grabbed a bottle of beer, which he handed to Bob. "Welcome to my den."

Bob took the amber nectar.

Clink!

"Is that vodka?"

"Gin martini," said Ferret. "I make them in batches that don't last as long as they should. But how rude of me . . ."

"Beer's fine."

Ferret pointed his colleague at the window. From high above, the park was a sea of mottled green extending far into the distance, punctuated by random flashes of bright blue, yellow, and pink, the battle banners of runners and cyclists.

The consultant wandered over to the nearest recliner and picked up a game controller. "Fancy massacring zombies?"

Bob shook his head, swigging deeply from the bottle.

Ferret polished off the martini and returned to the fridge. "I'm glad the problem with Ted's all sorted."

"He's innocent, and he's not a mad loony," retorted Bob, raising his voice. "There. I said it."

Ferret felt a stirring inside that might be anger, although he wasn't sure.

He shrugged his shoulders, poured a second drink and returned to the lounge. Bob had taken up position in the midpoint of the den, the park behind him, ceiling spots illuminating his squat frame, focusing in on his left eye which was bruised like a battered peach. He looked so innocent, so alone, like he was facing the beak on serious charges of grand larceny, deserted by his friends, the jury against him.

"I had a proper good chat with Ted earlier. I told him you'd do the right thing and get his job back."

"Honestly, Bob, you can be so naïve." Ferret grimaced. "I've already squared the situation away with management. As far as they're concerned, Ted's guilty. They've agreed to pick up the damages tab and pay us in full for all the time you put in. Plus, I negotiated a 'keep quiet' bonus and an extra double-time bonus, provided you finish by Sunday."

In an instant, Bob flew off the handle, jabbing the air with his finger. "You know he's innocent and you don't want to face the truth."

"Explain the hairy wig they found in his locker," said Ferret, parrying the assault.

"It's a stage prop from his wrestling days when he was known as Hairy O'Fairy."

"And the tunnel access panel in his office?"

"Coincidence. They're everywhere on that site, as you well know."

"What about the bag of goodies for those voice-activated attack squirrels?"

"They were ordinary squirrels who were nesting."

Involuntarily, Ferret moved to cover his thighs where his trousers were dotted with small holes ringed with spots of blood. While he'd been underground, chasing whatever it was that had vandalised Bob's work, those damn rodents had set upon him tag-team style, nipping away without remorse. In fact, if he didn't know better, he'd swear the suit had been assembled in a factory that handled nuts.

"Why won't you face the fact that Ted was telling the truth?" said Bob.

The consultant took a sip of martini. "There's no such thing as the little folk and there's certainly no such thing as a Gurp! On the other hand, there is such a thing as dressing up in disguise to sabotage our work. I don't know what Ted's motives were, and quite honestly, I don't care. Management says he's guilty, and that's good enough for me. As for voice-activated attack squirrels, they *do* exist. I've seen them for sale."

"Don't."

"Do."

"Double don't with hundreds and thousands," said Bob, triumphantly.

"Triple do, with hundreds and thousands, syrup and a flake."

"You can't have syrup AND a flake. That's greedy."

"Can."

Bob took a step back. "What is it you're scared of?"

Ferret tensed his shoulders. "I'm not frightened of anything."

"You were a lot nicer when you believed in ghosts and yetis and the Loch Ness monster."

"I've grown up, got real, and got with the program." The consultant sighed, fiddling with the game controller. "Come on, indulge me. Zombie assault."

"Perhaps it's time you regressed, got unreal and stepped off the program," said Bob, ignoring the invitation. "This is a great opportunity to take up paranormal investigating again."

Ferret wandered over to the picture window. A bunch of rowdy gulls flew past, arguing over the remains of a pizza crust. Leaning against the glass, the consultant turned to face his friend. "Let me tell you a story about a successful TV presenter who decided to channel alternative theories. In a matter of months he transformed from respected sports correspondent and Green Party spokesperson to turquoise-wearing nut job, who claims to this day that trans-dimensional lizards are running the planet."

"But that's not you!"

"Bob, I'm building an international consultancy practice from the ground up. My business will not incorporate any kind of strangeness, and I include weird personality-profiling tools." Ferret undid his cufflinks and threw them one by one at the easy chair on which his crumpled suit jacket lay. "The paranormal is a ruthless, self-obsessed predator that seeks out believers and devours them in a single gulp. If I let it anywhere near me, it won't be long before I lose my credibility. In my experience, this is usually followed by the loss of one's residence."

"You're far too clever to let that happen."

Ferret shook his head. He'd thought the same, until things had come to a head at The Consultancy. It was none of Bob's business and hardly relevant to the conversation, but it lodged in Ferret's gut nonetheless. From Golden Boy to Spank Boy to out the door in less than thirty-six hours. All it had taken was turning up late to an important client meeting with the wrong haircut.

Ferret rubbed his left eye, brushing away an imaginary tear. "About these zombies."

"I said no." Bob fiddled with the carrier bag he was clutching and withdrew a padded envelope, handing it on.

The consultant raised an eyebrow. He emptied out the contents of Bob's offering onto a low-slung glass coffee table, revealing a broken video camera with exposed electronics. The lens was missing. He stroked his chin, turning the pile of mangled electronics over. "Is that *the* half-destroyed camera?"

Bob nodded. "Ted told me where he'd hidden it."

"There's no tape." The consultant exhaled hard through his nose, braying like a donkey.

Bob produced a cartridge from his pocket.

Ferret turned to face the window. "Unfortunately, I have no means of playing it."

"I knew you'd say that, which is why I copied it to a disk."

"Sadly, my laptop is in for repair."

"Then it's a good job I brought mine." From out of the carrier bag, Bob produced a portable computer and a tangle of cables. "Prepare to be amazed."

Although the image was off-centre, the location was instantly recognisable. It was clearly Bob's head and shoulders moving in and out of focus, jutting out from a hole in a computer-room floor. Down he ducked. A syrupy radio presenter announced that Brentford had won one-nil the night before. Then Bob reappeared in an explosion of flailing arms and expletives, with a woolly shape clinging to his back, reminiscent of a replete sheep, fully charged with electrickery. Teeth did gnash, drool did fly, claws did snick and snack. Bob fell on his back, grappling bravely. Just as he was winning, the creature stuck its stubby snout into his eye and licked him right around the lips.

Slurp!

Spitting frothy bubbles, Bob kicked out with his foot. The creature bit his boot, entering into an ownership dispute during which Bob frantically untied the lace. Screaming loudly, he shuffled backward on his bum, free foot pumping at the floor, eyes firmly closed. Hackles raised, the creature let go. Bob shot backwards, gasping for air. In a single leap the creature was upon him.

Gurp!

Bob reeled.

In the confusion that followed, the hairy whatever-it-was pulled off his boot and ate his sock.

Slurpagurp!

The thing lolloped back to its hole-cum-lair, snarling and drooling. Bob dared to open an eye. Searching around, his hand located his lunchbox, which he threw at the thing with all his might, striking it on the flank. Distracted, it turned and sniffed the air. Bob curled into a tight ball and lay whimpering, awaiting his fate. The hairy thing collected the trophy in its mouth and dropped it in the hole. Then it saw the camera.

The last frame of film was of its slavering maw; the last sound, clear and unmistakable:

Gurp!

Ferret rewound the last ten seconds of film and watched it again.

"Top prank," he said with a smile. "You almost had me there. Which of your friends is it that looks like a wolfy Saint Bernard with a comedy beard?"

"Ferret!"

"You must have made this first thing this morning, before anyone else was about. Ingenious. I'm really impressed."

The colour of the engineer's face shifted gear from pink through to purple. "Ever since you joined that consultancy you haven't been right.

They went through your head and changed all the best things about you, and now you don't even remember who you are any more."

"Look around you," laughed Ferret, back-peddling. "I'm proud of what I've achieved and unapologetic about the compromises it took."

"When was the last time you spoke to your dad?" Bob asked, covering his mouth with his hand.

"Months ago." Ferret counted to seven on his fingers. "He's an interfering busybody who can't keep his nose out of my affairs."

"That night, then. He was in a right panic when he called me. I came over immediately and found you passed out on the floor."

"Sounds like an average Friday night."

"He said you'd had a blazing row; the worst one yet." Bob rubbed the side of his neck. "You were being so bloody unreasonable, he shot you."

A curly lock of hair sprung to attention aside the consultant's head. "Now you're being melodramatic."

"I thought I'd find blood everywhere." Bob knocked the last of the beer back. "Instead, you were lying in a heap, a sweet smile on your face, sleeping like a babe. Your dad was working away at his desk, like nothing had happened."

The consultant searched through his jacket pocket, producing a mobile phone. He tapped the keys, summoning the requisite number. "So he shot me? If you think the last argument was bad, wait until you hear this one."

"Ferret." Bob's eyes welled.

The consultant held the phone aloft, ready to press 'dial.' "Let me guess. He's back in the Middle East."

"He was on holiday."

"I find that highly unlikely. He's never taken a holiday in his life."

Bob wrung his hands, playing with his thumbs. "There was a terrible accident. I'm really, really sorry."

"He was injured?"

"It's worse than that. He's dead."

"That can't be." Ferret's arm shook so much he was forced to put down the drink. "There's still so much to shout about. Only the other night, I composed a list of names to call him in German next time we meet."

"Sit down," said Bob. "You're as white as a sheet."

Ferret felt sick to the core and yet mentally the news meant nothing at all. He knocked back the remainder of the martini then walked over to the drinks cabinet, rifled through the whisky section and withdrew a bottle of unopened fifteen-year-old single malt scotch and two crystal tumblers. He cracked the foil on the bottle, removed the cork and poured a generous two-finger helping of silky liquid into both of the glasses, handing one to Bob.

"To Wolfgang," he said.

The consultant's world swirled around him.

He was supposed to be sad, dammit.

How could he cry over losing someone he hardly knew, someone who wasn't there from one birthday to the next? As a child, he'd had no idea when he was going to see his father next and when he did, the old scrote was never happy, always sporting a scowl and a criticism, delivered in fluent German.

Ferret wondered what it might feel like to cry, to sob his heart out. He leant on Bob's shoulder. His tear ducts felt like they were made of porcelain, the reservoirs behind as parched as the Atacama Desert at midday during drought season.

"I met him the day before he went away," said Bob. "He was so looking forward to seeing the fjords."

The engineer opened the carrier bag and produced a small package carefully wrapped in brown paper, methodically bound with string. On top, tucked underneath the string, nestled a manila envelope which was decorated with a single word, written in gothic German script.

"He said if anything were to happen, I must give you this. Everything is explained inside."

"When's the funeral?"

"Ferret, I'm really sorry. It was two months ago."

"And you didn't think to tell me before now?"

"I thought you'd know." Bob walked around the den, unable to look Ferret in the eye. "It was in the papers and everything. When you didn't turn up in Salisbury for the burial, I didn't know what to do. I don't have this address, only your old one. And the phone numbers I have didn't work either."

"But you knew where I worked."

"And they told me you'd left. They didn't want to talk about you. It was as if your name was a dirty word."

Ferret and Bob sat in silence, sipping whisky.

The consultant recalled how Bob, in his capacity as family handy-man, used to help him build models as a child. Later, his father would rebuff him because he was too busy on this project or that. Every once in a while Ferret shook his head and readied himself for the tears he was sure would follow. But they never did.

The day it had all gone downhill faster than an Olympic skier greased with weasel spit was the day he announced he'd been headhunted by The Consultancy and earmarked for a star-spangled career as a management consultant. Wolfgang blew his top in spectacular fashion, letting loose a full artillery barrage, coupled with an air strike, peppered with cruise mis-siles.

About what one might expect from a government scientist turned weapons inspector.

"This doesn't change anything as far as Erin Breweries are con-cerned," said Ferret at last. "I know you like Ted, but someone has to take the rap for vandalising your work."

"But the tape."

"The tape doesn't exist. If it did, the Asset Conformance Team would have watched it. Then they'd hide it and blame Ted."

"That's not fair."

"Life isn't fair, Bob. Not unless you happen to have the right connec-tions, a pile of money and a gang of supportive friends. Then, perhaps, it can become too fair."

"About that." The engineer held his nose, then offered his right hand, the middle finger tucked against the palm.

"Well I never!" Bemused, the consultant completed the shake. "To friends."

"To friends," said Bob.

"I've known you how long? You kept your membership very quiet."

Bob blushed. "I didn't know you were in The Network either, until your friend Marcus called. He passed on your details. He said that ever since you'd left that job in the City of London you'd become a hermit and you were avoiding your friends. He asked if I could do something. That's why I offered you a job, managing me, to get you out of the house. I've been trying to say something about your dad all week, but you're all de-fensive and shut off and not right in yourself."

Ferret took a slug of whisky. "Thank you for stepping up."

Bob said his goodbyes, gifted Ferret a four-leaf clover, mumbled something incomprehensible, and let himself out.

Ferret returned to the window, piling into another two-finger salute of whisky. Once he was sure his father's old handyman was two floors down, he switched the TV over to the home security system and skipped through the channels, checking each of the concealed internal camera feeds in turn.

Bob was by the front porch, climbing into his overalls. The consultant skipped to a different camera feed and waited, catching Bob nodding to one of his neighbours, a snooty gent in his mid-fifties, who gave a sneer of disapproval from beneath the brim of a Panama hat.

"Good old Montgomery," chortled Ferret. "Always contemplating a citizen's arrest."

Bob climbed into a grimy grey van parked up in the private road that ran the length of the terrace and fired up the engine, creating a cloud of blue smoke.

Ferret laughed.

The engineer's visit would be reported in the next residents' newsletter. Workmen must use the rear entrance or the tone of the neighbourhood will suffer. Ever since he'd moved in, despite his best efforts, he just couldn't stop collecting acerbic put-downs. The Lord knows he'd tried to fit in, but like the rest of the world, his neighbours were quite alien to him.

The consultant tutted, picking up a game controller. There was nothing quite like a full-on, no-holds-barred Friday night zombie massacre.

At least the undead didn't criticise him.

Unlike his father.

Bob was a member of the same secret club. Now that was a surprise.

The engineer's parting words rankled in his brain.

Ferret put the joystick down, his face screwed up in contemplation.

What had Bob meant exactly when he'd wished him the best of Irish luck at getting his secret powers back?

# Chapter Two: The Consultancy

Of all her attributes, Marianne Lavalle considered there were three that had powered her career all the way to the top.

Well, almost to the top.

Damn those short-sighted New Yorkers, handing her job to a man twelve years her junior with no verifiable experience to his name.

Thumbing through a book that fell neatly under the moniker of "workplace psychology," she glanced at herself in a nearby mirror. She'd inherited those high cheekbones from her father, her thick, wild hair from her mother, and the skinny ankles from the family Jack Russell. The neatly clipped check couture suit with skirt cut just above the knee completed her first attribute: The Look. That was all hers. She'd shed the power shoulders some years ago, which was a shame, as when she dressed in power-pads and full battle armour, they treated her like Darth Vader, cowering away under tables, hiding in cupboards, and gasping for breath when they whispered her name.

Marianne twitched her nose.

Unfortunately, those days were behind her now. As every woman knows, business dress is wont to change with the season, and failing to evolve is route one to a loss of corporate face.

A couple of young office workers drifted into the room, laughing at a private joke. Marianne straightened her back, stood tall and froze, pretending to be a leopard stalking its prey. She curled her lip ever so slightly, bared her teeth, and let her presence expand. The youngsters fell silent and looked at each other, wide-eyed. Deciding they'd got the wrong section, they turned quickly on their heels and fled.

"Still got it at forty-eight," cackled Marianne, checking her pose once more.

A hot flush crept across her breasts. Damn those feelings, mugging her again. It was her fault for forgetting to take her supplements with breakfast coffee. At least she'd had the foresight to make arrangements, just in case. That took balls, which was her second attribute. Thanks to her ex-husband and his secret little club of corporate raiders, her future was secure.

All she had to do was keep her side of the bargain.

Marianne replaced the tiny volume entitled *Inspiration for Leaders* and picked out the number one bestseller from the neuro-linguistic programming section. *The Omniverse* by Barry Albright. Her curiosity had been piqued at a one-day workshop she'd recently attended, and she was determined to discover more about his groundbreaking theory regarding how to communicate pictures and feelings using only vocal tones. The idea of scaring people into doing her bidding without the need for threats intrigued her.

Inevitably, her balls were going to need reinforcing and inflating too, but that was taken care of, in the form of a hired coach.

A loud voice boomed through the adjoining rooms of the labyrinthine Charing Cross Road bookstore, catching her attention. She immediately began walking towards it.

"Cu-Sith? He's an Irish devil dog, like Black Shuck. No, I don't know if he's the same dog; that's why I'm here to purchase a book on the subject."

"Sir, you want the supernatural section, not parapsychology," replied the assistant.

"It was the supernatural section that sent me here." The owner of the voice sighed in frustration.

Marianne's heart beat a little faster. It was her favourite graduate, who she hadn't seen for six months, not since that ill-fated sideways step she'd taken over the pond.

"Ferret," said Marianne, in a measured dusky tone. "How the devil are you?"

"M . . ." The consultant glanced nervously from side to side. "What an unexpected surprise."

"Relax," purred Marianne, letting her jacket fall open. "And call me Marianne."

"I thought you were in the Big Apple," said Ferret, crossing his hands over his private area.

"The promotion went to hell in a handbasket!" laughed Marianne, launching into a well-rehearsed routine. "I realised after three months of hard living that a 24/7 party town was no longer the town for me, and my shrink agreed. He told me to slow down, make some more me time in my packed agenda. So, on his advice, I jacked it all in, came home, and moved out west."

"As in Kensington?"

"Cheltenham."

"Wow. It must be a pretty special project to afford talent like yours."

"I'm acting CEO in a hush-hush merger." Marianne winked.

"Really?"

"Some slowdown, huh?" Marianne moved silently towards her prey. "I'm afraid I can't tell you who I work for, or who we're merging with, as that classes as insider trading. Of course, if the market's still your thing, you could make it worth our while."

"What are you doing in town?" asked Ferret, taking a step to the side.

"I'm here for a long weekend to meet with our lawyers and tie up some of the more unctuous merger details. What about you, Ferret? The last I heard, we were reviewing your record and scratching our heads, trying to figure out what happened to stop our most prominent rising star in his tracks."

"It's a long story."

Marianne put her finger to Ferret's lips. "Tell me over coffee."

It was indeed a long story, one which required several shots of espresso in a nearby Soho coffee bar. From there, they proceeded to a cocktail lounge and set about drinking Champagne on Marianne's expense account. Ferret complained, citing firstly the need for a book on dogs, then a requirement for the entire Sherlock Holmes canon in hardback. Finally, he confessed to taking up computer gaming, using the forthcoming release of a new title as his reason for needing to leave early.

Marianne didn't answer. She simply ordered a round of martinis.

Ferret explained how once she'd left to join The Consultancy's U.S. arm, he'd been reassigned to work for Ross McGyver, a short, balding man of Scottish origin, who, according to the partner rumour mill, was the culprit behind the "cash for balls" scandal, in which money from the office charity tins was replaced with rolled-up silver foil. He'd denied it vehemently, of course. Ferret told a tale in which Ross forced one of the juniors to leave behind a large tip at a restaurant, then pocketed it when her back was turned, laughing at the poor lass for being dumb enough to place notes on the table.

"In his feedback I once wrote: Has the vision of a mole and the kick of mule," smiled Marianne.

Ferret laughed uncomfortably.

Sadly, Ross had sufficient top cover in place to simply shrug it off. Had she still been in the UK, he would have gone for her throat, of this Marianne had no doubt, the resulting fight being both savage and brutal.

Back in the day, the winner was a sure bet. Marianne rolled her eyes. Nowadays, she was no longer confident that the battered body tossed to the crows from the battlements would be his.

"He handed me a string of poison chalices to sup from," said Ferret, slipping from his chair, martini in hand. "Once I'd made myself well and truly ill on the foul-tasting contents of his goblets — not to mention vastly unpopular amongst the people I was ordered to sack — I was unceremoniously shown the tradesman's exit on a charge of poor performance."

"I heard he gave you a verbal warning for turning up to work with pink hair."

"That was just the paperclip that held all the other charges together. If there's one thing I learnt from my resignation, it's that no matter how incompetent you are, if you're in with the in-crowd at the top, you can get away with anything."

"Sad but true." Marianne reached out and clasped Ferret's hand. "Ross was hired as a professional scalp hunter, tasked with hunting down complacent high achievers. The odd firing reminds those who remain not to coast."

"It's all water off a duck's back, under a bridge," said Ferret, using an old consultancy phrase that made them both giggle.

Marianne ordered another round of apple martinis, served with a twist of peel jutting just above the vodka line like a little green piggy tail.

"What happened to you?" she asked.

Ferret raised his left shoulder, dismissing a demon. Marianne saw the cogs whir away in his brain, but once they stopped, the divine light that had so often illuminated their partnership simply wasn't there. Was this really the same senior consultant who they'd awarded consecutive promotions to, year on year?

"What kind of kinky smut am I thinking of?"

"How could I know that?"

Marianne paused for a second, to consider her latest conquest. Something really wasn't right. Ferret used to have this intuitive way of knowing what the opposition was thinking, often before they knew themselves.

"This might sound mad," said Ferret, "but I can't connect with anything that happened before you went away. Not in colour, anyway, and heaven knows I've tried. You remember my thirtieth birthday? Apparently I had a massive argument with my father that night, a right old screamer by all accounts."

"Have you called him?"

"Sadly, he recently passed away."

"I'm sorry to hear that," said Marianne, inviting Ferret to hug her, an invitation he gratefully accepted. "Let me know if there's anything I can do."

"My best friend is out of town and my other best friend is tied up with work, so I can't ask them about his death. They both knew, yet they kept it from me. Why would they do that?"

"Perhaps they were acting in your best interests?"

"I can't see it myself."

Marianne made her excuses and headed towards the washrooms, where she cornered one of the good-looking bartenders she'd secretly made eye contact with earlier. With a wink and a quick squeeze of the bum, she slipped him her business card.

Seductively, he caressed a Champagne glass with a cleaning cloth. "Aren't you?"

Marianne put a finger to her lips, turned on her heels, and, slinking her hips, sidled towards the ladies' room, turning her head at the last and blowing a kiss.

It was such a shame about Ferret.

Somewhere along the line he'd become vulnerable and lost the killer instinct she'd instilled in him. It happened. She'd seen it many times before, most often in women of a certain age, which was why she specialised exclusively in training men. To have it occur to one of her own . . . that was a horrible disappointment.

No wonder he'd resigned.

Except that wasn't quite true, as they both knew only too well.

He'd taken the honourable option and fallen on his own sword before they'd pushed him.

She'd heard that McGyver was livid that morning. Not only had he intended to publicly sack Ferret, he was also determined to bring charges against him for profiteering on confidential information. The Consultancy soon put a stop to that, but not before an external investigation was launched and later contained. Who could blame them? Expose one and you risk contagion, followed by the collapse of the entire house of cards, which wasn't in anyone's interests — especially the partners.

Better to bury the bodies at sea, she thought. That way it wasn't possible for a mass exhumation to take place. Certainly not on the say-so of one nasty, vindictive man, his insides consumed by petty jealousy.

Marianne checked her look in the mirror. Behind her, a couple of young things fell into one of the spare cubicles, legs splayed everywhere, reminding her of a pair of young deer on ice.

She supposed she was a cougar now, not a leopard.

They gave her that nickname when she was the same age as the silly young things in closet A, due to her ability to track men of power, drink with them until the sun came up (her third attribute), and then bed them with ruthless precision.

She rolled her eyes. The current generation really were clueless.

Some of them had The Look and some had balls, but few of them possessed the ability to discover a person's buttons and press them in the correct combination. Sure, they'd connive to bed the boss. That was the easy bit. Getting paid in full, that was trickier. Marianne craned her head, listening in on the two young things scratching away, full of spite and remorse.

"Then he dumped me."

"Tosser."

"I'll get him back online. Just wait 'til I publish those photos."

Marianne laughed privately and finished adjusting her lipstick. These days, they think they're entitled to have it all, just for putting out. When a leopard goes hunting, she must do so with passion, then turn the tables and get what she wants in writing.

She purred inwardly. Sex is his reward for being a good boy.

Believing in promises is for daydreamers, she thought. A mirage littered with the husks of promotions that never were.


"What I can't figure out is why the doors of finance are closed to me," said Ferret upon her return. "I've done everything by the book. I took my contacts with me, set up my own company, had business cards printed, made calls, called in favours, but to be honest, it's like pulling hen's teeth. I've had one job in three months and that was project managing a computer room upgrade. It wasn't even remotely connected to the City."

It was obvious to Marianne what had happened. Unable to turn the screws in an official capacity, that wily bastard McGyver had put the frighteners on half the City, effectively making Ferret unemployable. Unfortunately, there wasn't much she could do about it, except offer him a job.

That option crossed her mind for a millisecond only.

Granted, he was one half of the fighting fuckers, but their dues to each other were long paid off. She smiled, fondly remembering the night they'd gone out to celebrate a minor success, fully aware that bed was the final destination. For two years they'd fought and fucked together, working their way through The Consultancy's acquisitions portfolio, fearlessly trashing the opposition and loving every second of their new-found notoriety.

Hell, it felt like an aeon ago.

Marianne slapped herself.

If she entertained her old star performer now, it might compromise her current activities, and that was strictly *verboten*. No matter how down on his luck Ferret was, she was not about to invite him to Cheltenham.

"What about your secret society friends?"

Ferret's eyes bulged; his cheeks turned bright pink.

"Oops," said Marianne.

The consultant took a slurp of vodka martini. "To be honest, I'm thinking about packing it all in."

"To do what?"

"Investigate the paranormal."

"Are you qualified to do that?"

"Not formally." Ferret played with the tail of apple peel, watching it bob up and down. "All of my business acumen is screaming at me not to be such an idiot, yet I can't get the notion out of my head."

"You've always been impetuous. Why stop now?"

Ferret nodded. "There's something I'd like your advice on. Before my father went on his ill-fated cruise, he left me a letter. On one hand, the instructions seem harmless, but on the other, I hate being told what to do and I can't trust him."

"Is he asking you to do anything illegal?"

The consultant shook his head.

Her pulse racing, Marianne lent slowly over the table, allowing Ferret a flash of cleavage and snogged him hard on the lips. Seconds later, she withdrew. "He's your father. Do what he says and screw the consequences. What's the worst that can happen?"

Later that evening, back in her hotel room near Hyde Park, Marianne reflected on her encounter with the onetime superstar she'd moulded personally to her exacting specification. Ferret was good. No, he was better than good — he was brilliant. And when he was being brilliant, there was a light in his eyes that couldn't be diminished by a mere mortal such as McGyver. That was why Ross had gone for him and savaged him so badly: He knew Ferret's ship was listing. Of all the things he could have done, arming torpedoes and releasing them was by far the cruellest option. That was The Scalp Hunter all over. He'd made his name undermining, shaming, and firing top performers. Boot them hard, boot them often, and then keep on kicking all the way to the door.

Marianne turned her attention to her lover for the night. He was young, he was handsome, and he knew a few tricks — certainly enough to make her squeal. But when all was said and done, he wasn't Ferret. She hoped that whatever it was that had happened to him would unhappen. The idea of bedding her rugby playing fly-half, with his intimate knowledge of all her fantasies made her bum wriggle. She held that thought as she pulled her stud roughly by the hair in a mixture of passion and frustration, determined to make the most of her first Friday night in London for as long as she could remember.

Her lawyers had been taken to a dogfight.

Unlike her, Old Man Cocks wasn't taking it lying down.

"Give it to me," she said, writhing like a hot reptile.

If this boy gave out halfway through, she'd send him home and order another. She was the boss; whatever she wanted, she got. If the Old Man didn't know that by now, he had a deep and long-lasting shock coming his way. Give up willingly and she'd show him some leniency in the compensation department. Otherwise, the big guns were coming. If necessary, she'd fuck his company into the ground, running a procession of assault weapons over the remains.

Then she'd turn the turrets on him.

She gasped, her toes tingling. There was nothing like the thought of tanks on the lawn to get the juices going.

# Chapter Three: Highgate

Ferret sat in his favoured recliner, joystick in hand, staring at the re-claimed Victorian fire surround that occupied one wall of the den. He focused in on the mantelpiece and the carefully wrapped package that Bob had delivered from his recently deceased father.

It had taken plenty of persuasion in the form of three double whiskies and a line of cocaine to open the accompanying letter. He'd hoped to find something soothing inside, an explanation perhaps for why his father had acted so unreasonably. Instead, he found contrite blame. It was Wolfgang, not Ferret, who was the wronged party.

The consultant felt he ought to be really angry and assembled a pile of kindling in the grate, tossing the package on top, striking a match, ready to let it burn. His father had been a bloody nightmare in life and now here he was, prodding away from the afterlife.

It's my fault for entertaining him, he thought, allowing the match to creep all the way down to his thumb.

"Ow!"

The source of ignition petered out and fell to the hearth, granting the package a temporary stay of execution.

Cursing his father's name, the consultant measured out another two lines of cocaine and settled in for a marathon session of Zombie Death Camp, which, although enthralling, was somewhat ironical.

His father was dead. The thought rattled around his brain. Good rid-dance! No, that didn't sit right.

He'd build a memorial, celebrate his father's achievements.

That felt wrong too.

In frustration, he threw the controller at the wall, pulled on a suit from the rack marked "casual," and set out for the West End, intent on buying a couple of books and having a damn good drink. Anything to get away from the gift beyond the grave.

Passing by the bathroom, he paused to dampen down the annoying curl. Looking good, he thought. With luck, he might even come home with a lady.

Many hours later, following an unexpected meeting in a bookshop with Marianne Lavalle, his old consultancy boss, Ferret returned home and settled back into the recliner. Once comfy, he poured another tumbler of whisky and did something he'd spent his entire life priding himself on not doing: thinking. And the more he thought about his father and his childhood, the more he realised none of it felt real. He tried to remember his thirtieth birthday, which remained mostly blank. He thought about the day he'd resigned to the practice head and the distorted look on McGyver's face when he'd discovered he was too late in delivering the fatal blow. He'd watched the spittle run down the Scalp Hunter's chin, foaming as it dripped onto his tie, forming a most splendid stain. He remembered those tiny shrimp-like eyes, black to the core, intent on conveying fear and intimidation as they tried to burrow deep into his skull.

Ferret watched himself laugh at the weird brain-eating crustacean from another planet; he saw everyone else in the open-plan office make themselves busy, pretending not to listen.

He recalled the first of his cock-ups, that horrible affair with the Swiss bond broker. Instead of walking away from the deal, he'd put inappropriate details the way of his friends at exactly the wrong moment. Thanks to his impeccable record, he got away with it.

However, attitudes changed.

His team eyed him with suspicion rather than awe.

He thought about Millfield and his time on the rugby pitch captaining the winning team, the applause from the crowd deafening as he scored the only try in the most important game of his career.

It was horrible.

Instead of being illustrated in colour, all of his favourite memories were faded, transmogrified into dog-eared black and white.

The more he thought about it, the more convinced he became that everything changed on the night Bob collected him from his father's apartment. He tried really hard to remember what had happened, but the more he tried, the less tangible everything became. He tried distraction, deliberately not thinking about it, hoping it might come to him. Then he tried sneaking up on the evening from behind, eyes closed, opening them only at the last.

Nothing.

He abused alcohol to supercharge his memory. Then he added Peruvian flake into the mix, which only served to make him restless for more drink.

Exhausted after a sleepless week of thinking, the consultant took a hot shower followed by a cold bath. Still feeling empty inside, he pulled on a pair of slacks, an England rugby shirt and a tweed jacket, and headed into Camden to try to purchase marijuana from a series of likely looking lads, all of whom insisted on trying to deal him crack for money up-front. Disappointed, he sought refuge in the nearest public house, aptly named The World's End, where he intended to resume drowning his sorrows.

Mixed groups of tourists huddled around a smattering of tables, shopping bags on display, chatting away in Spanish, French, and Japanese. Ferret ordered a double gin and tonic. For a Friday afternoon, the pub was pretty dead. He'd missed the lunchtime crowd; he supposed it was still too early for the party brigade. Turning around, a tiny Asian girl dressed in a tight school uniform caught his eye. Captivated by her costume, he stepped away from the bar and clattered straight into another customer, spilling his drink over her boots and knocking a pint from her hand.

"You clumsy oaf!"

"I'm terribly sorry," said Ferret, offering up a handkerchief. "Let me buy you another."

"Cider. And not the cheap rubbish."

The girl he'd bumped into was in her early twenties, slim, and pallid, with hair the colour of burnished copper. She was dressed in a tight brown corset with bronze fittings and frills, topped off with the most ardent undertaker's hat he'd ever seen. To seal the deal, the hat was decorated with watch cogs and dials, and a nifty attention-grabbing feather.

"I'm Ferret," he said, handing over a replacement pint. "Pleased to make your acquaintance."

"Emily. Before you start with any of that posh-boy chatting-me-up nonsense, you're not my type."

"You're not really mine either. To be honest, I hadn't intended to get drunk. I was trying to buy marijuana, but everyone wanted to sell me crack."

"Voice down," said Emily. "There are plainclothes about. Your business isn't their business."

Ferret apologised again, intending to end the conversation, but his mouth had other ideas. Before he knew it, he'd blurted out that his father was dead, he'd had a run-in with a devil dog, he was no longer sure who he was (except he was going to become a paranormal investigator), and he simply had to get stoned, in order to try and make sense of it all.

"Calm down." Emily shook her head, flicking her hand through long curls. "I've got a friend who may be able to sort you out. Let's sit down and finish our drinks first."

Emily's friend, it transpired, lived in Highgate, but before an introduction was to be made she insisted on having a second drink, to get to know Ferret a little better. To this end, he bought two pints of cider with brandy depth-charges and proposed a race to the bottom. Having drawn the first round, Emily lined them up for a repeat race. Ferret professed he was more of a distance drinker than a speed drinker, and the last time he'd competed in such a race, a hair dye forfeit had cost him his job. Chatting away, their mutual love of over-indulgence soon became apparent. As he predicted, Ferret lost round two.

They finished up with a pair of schnapps chasers, falling out of the pub arm in arm. Pulse racing, the consultant raised his arm to hail a cab. His new friend waved the cab away.

"I'm not taking you anywhere dressed like that." Emily took hold of his hand. "If you want to score drugs, you've got to look the part."

The consultant hadn't thought to ask Emily what she was doing in Camden. He discovered she owned a gothic clothing shop, located just off the high street. Business had been slow, so she'd locked up early and snuck off for a drink. Now she was opening up again for a personal fitting. From the racks, she chose a pair of sharp, black, frosted trousers with laces up the side, some unfeasibly pointy shoes, and a shirt with the most outrageous frills Ferret had ever seen. He flounced in front of the mirror, excited by the new look.

"That's better, my Lord." Emily's face lit up in delight, her hand flitting along a row of purses, eventually settling on a black heart-shaped one. "Let's go."

"Which part of Highgate?" asked Ferret, giggling at the shoes.

"The cemetery."

Lord Ferret flagged down a cab and instructed the cabbie to take them to their destination. Emily stopped the driver before he reached the gates. Ferret paid. His accomplice swore him to silence, on his dead father's grave. Once he'd crossed himself and said the words, Emily told him how she used to come here as a teenager and hang about the West Cemetery, where many a Hammer Horror film was shot. She knew a secret entrance.

Once over the collapsed wall, they fought deep undergrowth and eerie, clinging tree roots, aiming towards a rough path hewn through the ivy. Free of the jungle, they frolicked amongst ancient tombstones and memorials, drinking green chartreuse from a black-and-copper hip flask. Ferret wondered where Emily's friend might be hiding. What did he look like? How much might the merchandise cost? Although he'd heard about the therapeutic qualities of cannabis, he hadn't actually tried it. Would he even know whether it was the real thing?

Arm in arm they walked the Egyptian Avenue, the entrance flanked by mock pylons, borrowed under licence from the Temple of Karnak. Lady Emily showed Lord Ferret the Circle of Lebanon with its ring of cedar trees and stone tombs, packed together as tightly as single-storey Victorian townhouses. She confessed that as a young girl, she'd once sent out party invites to every Hammer Horror monster she knew by name, requesting they meet her here on her birthday. Sadly, none came. In theatrical malaise, she recited a fine soliloquy, paying tribute to the bones of her adored Shelley, who Ferret assumed to be a favourite pet, most likely her dog. In turn, he tried to say positive things about his father, but what started as a eulogy soon turned into a gesture of defiance.

They waltzed among the graves, a whirl of frills, drinking and dancing together. Lady Emily encouraged him to imagine his father's corpse and describe it, growing ever more animated with each sordid image. Lord Ferret learned that his Lady was a fan of steampunk, her costume being one of her own creation. He complimented her on her skills. She pushed him against the trunk of a tree, painting his eyes with thick black eyeliner, darkening his eyebrows and adjusting his cravat for maximum effect. Finally, she handed him her hat, posing him for a ream of sepia photographs against a mausoleum that she'd once identified as the resting place of the Highgate vampire.

In need of a breather, the cute little steamstress sat down, cross-legged, atop a nearby grave.

"Where's your friend?" Ferret was beginning to think the trip one big charade.

Emily blew a kiss.

"Do you intend to mug me when he arrives and make off with my wares?"

"You posh boys can be such dunces." Emily retrieved her hat from his head and from inside the rim produced a roll-up. She motioned him over.

He took a swig from the flask, and then another. Emily warned him to slow down, a suggestion which he, as a seasoned pro, ignored. When she doubly warned him to be careful with the smoke, he ignored this suggestion too. Three or four puffs later, relaxing against the grave's headstone, Ferret felt his head inflate with helium.

"Blowback," said Emily, hastily applying a layer of burgundy lipstick.

"A what?"

"Stay there."

Emily inserted the burning end of the joint inside her mouth, leaving most of the filter protruding from her closed lips. Lifting her dress, she squatted low over his middle, put the filter between his lips, almost touching his mouth with hers, so tantalisingly close, and gently blew, instructing Ferret to suck. He felt a stirring in his pants. They reversed the process. By the time Lady Emily collapsed against him, giggling, he was floating away amongst the clouds.

"This is so naughty," said Emily adjusting her dress and unlacing his fly.

Ferret felt Emily grab hold of his ears. They touched noses. She frotted slowly from side to side, her luscious rear moving in a tight figure eight.

The volume cranked up; Ferret's ears roared.

He heard each note of every bird's individual call.

Perfect.

"Wow." He pulled Emily close, his nose alive with hints of musky perfume.

"You are *so* wasted," she laughed, placing his hand on her breast.

"And horny."

As indeed was she: Her briefs were sopping, a counterpoint to the coffin handle in his trousers.

Emily leaned in and kissed him, her tongue tip brushing his, hair falling in cascades around his neck.

He imagined they were skipping along the edge of a dark passion play, ready to fall into each other.

Why could he not feel the truth of it?

Lord Ferret's peripheral vision played tricks with the light and shade, revealing creepy creatures amongst the graves; colours swirled brightly, amalgamating under the canopy of trees, the dancing shadows a cinematic extravaganza of horror from the early days of film.

Emily adjusted her undies, and taking hold of little ferret, winked.

Ferret braced himself, fingers flexing. Grasping the top of the raised memorial, he gazed deep into her eyes.

He felt the annoying curl on the side of his head spring erect. His stomach growled; tentacles spread out inside him. He felt a surreal Dali octopus fill up his shell, dappled with spots of pink, red, and green.

"Tell me again how your father died," whispered Emily, wriggling her bum up and down.

Ferret gasped. "He drowned."

"Louder."

"Drowned. Lungs . . . exploded . . ."

"Ohh . . . More . . ."

"Eyes . . . popped . . . out . . ." Without warning, he turned his head to the side and threw up, ejecting the meagre contents of his stomach.

"Ohh . . ."

Ferret felt the whole inside of his being rush for the exits. The black-and-white memories of Millfield came first, tumbling out of his mouth, followed by the Scalp Hunter's disdainful grin, spewing forth from his nose. The octopus brought up the rear. His memories mixed in a sorry puddle of puke, soaking into the stained grass. Apologetically, he composed himself. Miraculously, his shirt was unspolit, unlike the moment, which lay dead and buried.

Ferret swung his legs over the side of the raised grave and tried to jump down. Another rush caught him unawares, bowling him over. Wave upon wave of nausea engulfed him, forcing him to his knees. With the past, present, and future colliding around him, he finally realised what was missing from his life: He had no sense of connection between body, mind, and soul.

Emily consoled him.

Attempting to brush away the mess, he caught a trouser lace on the edge of a headstone and ripped a mighty hole in the pants.

Curse words echoed across the graves.


"And people get stoned for fun?" Ferret coughed, wiping himself down in the cemetery's washrooms.

"It doesn't always mix with alcohol," said Emily.

"Where's the fun in that?" Ferret laughed meekly. "If it doesn't mix with alcohol, surely it's no fun at all."

Lord Ferret instructed the cabbie to drop Emily back at The World's End and headed off home, determined not to think any more. Thinking led to complications. What he needed was to get out more, get back in touch with his feelings. Dressing up on a whim, whirling through a cemetery, making up speeches, that was life itself. Steadily, the consultant's thoughts turned to the joys of sex.

Rewind.

He'd abandoned Emily without a second thought.

"Driver. Back to the End."

It was no use. By the time they reached the pub, Emily was long gone. Her final words came back to haunt him: *So long, posh boy. There are worse ways to die.*

"Damn! Damn! Damn!" They were a hot item and Ferret hadn't even realised. He slapped himself. "The Regent's Park."

Lord Ferret watched the world whiz past while he counted the number of times he'd had intercourse between his birthday and the graveyard. He was appalled to discover he needed zero hands on which to do the reckoning.

He shook his head, catching the reflection of his longer-than-average nose in the driver's mirror. His eyes were smeared with makeup, and across his forehead, written in burgundy lipstick, was a single three-letter word:

TIT.

The consultant mooched his way up to the den and slumped down in his favourite recliner to read his father's letter one more time. The instructions were quite specific. He was to make himself familiar with the files contained on the enclosed memory stick, taking care to keep the contents private. And then . . .

Unable to bear it any longer, he ripped the package open and undid the catch on a small wooden box contained within. He removed the glass phial to which the letter referred, holding it up to the light, observing how the liquid moved when he sloshed it gently from side to side.

Was he really going to do as his father asked?

Perhaps later, he thought. Or perhaps not at all. No, he'd had enough of feeling disconnected from the world.

Ferret removed the stopper from the phial, closed his eyes, and with a nervous gulp, let the ritual begin.

Salinger's of Bloomsbury was really Marcus's club, reflected Cyrano, from the comfort of a great wing-back chair that hugged the edge of a scuffed and threadbare rectangular carpet; it had been scored by dozens of burning embers spat from the grate of the grand old fireplace it fronted. Marcus sat opposite, in an equally ancient cracked olive leather chair, thumbing through a copy of *Country Life*, tweed jacket slung over the chair back. A third mismatched chair, located between the two friends, was being eyed hungrily by a number of uniformed veterans.

Inwardly, Cyrano smiled.

Their consultant friend was late again, he thought. Assuming he deigned to appear at all. Since his dismissal from The Consultancy, Ferret had locked himself away in his den, refusing to come out. No doubt he was busy shooting imaginary zombies despite a promise he'd made to the contrary.

One of the vets shook a tin in the Frenchman's face. He reached into his pocket, produced a folded fifty and stuffed it into the slot, making sure that the recipient saw the colour of his money.

"Sir," said the veteran, with a salute. Hastily, the old-timer directed a stray serviceman away from the free chair.

Cyrano recalled how Marcus had badgered them for days to come and visit his new discovery, in that oddly effeminate way of his, fawning over this detail and that. Whilst he was intrigued to see how the upper classes lived a hundred years ago, the Frenchman was already comfortable with their regular Sunday haunt and went to great pains to remind his two friends that Simpson's-in-the-Strand, which arguably served the best roast beef in town, was far more illustrious than mouldy old Salinger's. Ferret, who'd been Cyrano's friend since junior school, sided with Marcus until it was pointed out that the great detective Sherlock Holmes once frequented Simpson's, whereas he'd never been anywhere near Salinger's.

That put a cat squarely amongst Marcus's pigeons.

Marcus, who worked for the government specialising in intelligence, had countered that Holmes and Watson were merely fictional detectives, causing Ferret to hit the roof and swear he'd never eat roast beef in any establishment but Simpson's ever again.

Over the next few weeks, Marcus slowly wheedled his way back into Ferret's affections. Then came the bribe: a bottle of Chateaux Margaux, if only they'd join him for lunch the following Sunday. And here they were, two years later, surrounded by oak panels and dusty chandeliers, immersed in the scent of ancient leather mingled with spicy colonial pipe tobacco, staring wide-eyed through an opaque screen into the final years of Victorian Britain, when the Empire stalwartly ruled the waves with ironclad and cannon.

The Frenchman eyed his timepiece, tapping the dial.

Marcus glared over the top of his reading spectacles. "He promised he'd make it this time. He swore he wouldn't be late."

On cue, their friend the consultant burst into the tight circle of chairs, beaming wildly from ear to ear. "Are you absolutely positive that Holmes and Watson didn't eat here?"

Cyrano's jaw dropped.

It had been a while since Ferret had pulled that particular trick.

At least he looked well, certainly better than the last time they'd met. Shaved. Groomed. Shirt ironed. Shoes polished. And a twinkle of copulation in the eye.

"I'm a single gent about town; it was Saturday night," said his consultant friend with a wink.

"Who was she?" asked the Frenchman. "I demand details."

Marcus stared hard, firstly at Ferret, then Cyrano, before returning to the magazine.

The Frenchman and his friend shared a moment, bursting into a fit of giggles.

Cyrano unleashed a micro-smile, aimed at his friend. "Are you straight, dear boy, because I'd swear there's a tell-tale sparkle about you."

"Completely." Ferret plonked his derriere into the vacant chair, fluttering his eyelashes. "And yet I feel so alive!"

Cyrano raised an eyebrow. The boy was likely doped up on louder powder. The signs were all there.

"Whatever it is you're about to discuss, I can't know about it," said Marcus, stuffing his fingers into his ears. "I signed forms to say I wouldn't do anything illegal, unless instructed by my superiors, but that's different because that's legally illegal."

How typical, thought Cyrano. Not that it mattered; it was Ferret he was here to see. Marcus was a latter add-on, their sensible chaperone, there to keep the reputation of The Network intact. The Frenchman wasn't sure if Marcus, as their official sponsor, had any legal claim over the pair. He'd studied the rules they'd agreed to abide by before committing their signatures in blood, and formally, a *beneficiarius* had no rights over a legionnaire. However, he knew from experience that when push came to shove, written rules counted for squat.

"Come," said Cyrano, poking Ferret in the ribs. "Tell all."

"Her name was Cristina. She was a raven-haired seductress, extremely lewd and very filthy, exactly as she promised to be. I could feel it in the way she was leaning against the bar. All it required was mention of the hot tub and the chiller full of Champagne."

"And the new flake I left in the usual place?"

"Nice."

The Frenchman thought about his time on the Peruvian Express, heading up into the Andes with nothing between him and a cloudless, star-spangled sky but pure powder-white mountain tops. From there, it was two day's travel down into the Amazon basin and a further day after that to the world's most exclusive coca farm. It had taken him nearly ten years to track it down. He'd had to exploit every contact in his thick black book to make the right connections. The first consignment proper was due any day, and one word was all his friend had to say about the free sample.

"You insult me!"

"You're obsessed."

"Blah, blah, blah," said Marcus.

"If there's one thing I take pride in, my boy," said Cyrano, "it's my encyclopaedic knowledge of cocaine hydrochloride. What you call 'nice' has six-star reviews the length of the Côte d'Azur."

"On condition of anonymity, my opinion is officially upgraded to 'good.'"

"Good!" exclaimed the Frenchman, delighted at the form shown by his old sparring partner. "I give the boy Premier Cru Charles from the world's finest estate and the only description he can formulate is 'good.'"

"Good with a hint of mellow."

"How about stunning with a hint of barbaric Inca sacrifice?"

"Blah."

"Well, Cristina certainly found it stunning. I still can't believe she came Veuve Cliquot in the way she did. Never in all my years have I witnessed such a trick."

"At last, the boy gives me a review worthy of the product."

"It's Cristina's pleasure, I'm sure."

Cyrano made a mental note to track down filthy Cristina, then settled quickly into the ritual of Sunday lunch, which was bound by a strict set of protocols. Arrival time was set at 12:30 p.m. sharp, with aperitifs served fifteen minutes later, on the dot. The grand clock, which as Cyrano had noted on many previous occasions, was one of the few things in the club that actually worked, pointed to twelve forty-two.

"Blah . . . is it safe yet?"

Cyrano shook his head. "Do you want to hear about France?"

"So that's where you were," said Ferret.

It had been a particularly good month for the Frenchman. He'd spent two weeks flitting between Monaco and Nice, where he'd been introduced to a pair of rich Russians, who, like most Russians abroad, knew how to throw a party. They'd also claimed to know a thing or two about marching powder, and although they were initially dismissive of his claim of unmatched quality, they soon realised, as Dimitri had so eloquently phrased it, that he was a purveyor of "some wicked shit." Their complimentary samples were eagerly devoured. Once the twitches kicked in, Cyrano made a call to his delivery people. Thirty minutes later, the deal was done. As far as his clients were concerned, he was just another salesman. Dimitri's relationship was now with François, unless he was throwing a party, in which case Cyrano would make a personal appearance to fuss over the client. Later, he'd do some sampling of his own . . . of the leggy Russian model variety.

"I expect you spent the entire time peddling dope out of brown paper bags, exchanging sullied notes in French latrines," said Ferret, cracking a smile.

Cyrano flicked his nose. "The yachts I conduct my business on have solid-gold urinals and diamond-encrusted automated paper dispensers."

"I'm sure so." Ferret fingered his jaw. "I'm still banging away at the City, waiting for a break. In the meantime I've been project managing computer room upgrades."

"How terribly exciting," said Cyrano mockingly.

"Oh, it was. It changed who I am, possibly forever."

The Frenchman motioned to Marcus to remove his fingers from his ears. "You need to hear this. The boy's had an epiphany."

"An apostrophe?" said Marcus quizzically. "Oh, to hell with it, order me one anyway. I love a surprise."

Cyrano signalled to Beauleigh, the retainer, who he knew to be a veteran of two wars, neither of which was a World War, although looking at him, one wouldn't know it. Truth be told, he was fascinated by how the retainer managed to look so ancient, and was determined to ask him one day what kind of lard he moisturised with.

"Three apostrophes, please. And don't scrimp on the gin."

"Will that be all, sir?"

"I'd like a date for later."

Marcus lowered his head in shame. "Ever since I discovered this place and invited you along, you've ordered a high-class call girl with your aperitif. Don't you ever tire of the same old game?"

Cyrano shrugged his shoulders.

Beauleigh returned in an instant. Ferret, as poison taster, gratefully accepted a cocktail glass by the stem and took a sip. "Gin martini. What a pleasant surprise."

Cyrano and Marcus each took a glass.

The Frenchman opened the accompanying special menu and scanned it quickly. "I've had all of these," he said grumpily. "Some of them twice."

"What is it with you and prostitutes?" asked Marcus, furrowing his brow.

"I'm simply sticking to the three 'Fs' rule."

"Enlighten us," said Marcus.

"If it flies, floats, or fucks, rent it. Didn't your expensive education teach you anything?"

Bong!

On cue, a variety of uniformed pensioners in various states of mobility assembled in the great room, which was separated from the lounge by a grand arched doorway, decorated with coloured-glass panels. Judging by the overpainted screw marks left in the jamb, the doors had been removed at some point in the distant past and not replaced again.

Cyrano was convinced he'd seen them once, stacked up in a storage area beneath the club. Without a working light bulb, he couldn't be entirely sure, but the arched tops and cut glass certainly felt right. Then he stumbled and put his hand down on something metallic and rusty, which he was sure was an ammunition box. His friends had both laughed at his discovery, dismissing him as paranoid, but he still got the shivers when he thought about one of the regulars flailing around blind in a cellar packed with unstable munitions. He thought about the padlock on the cellar door. He'd checked it on the way in, and again when he nipped off to the gents.

One could never be too sure.

The veterans arranged themselves in a long line. With the arrival of the impressively moustached colonel, swagger stick under his arm, they stood promptly to attention. Everything that could be polished, be it leather or metal, had been finished to a degree of perfection found only in those whose careers involved the military.

"Cyrano," said Ferret quietly, "you've hung out with shamans in the jungles of the New World. In your travels, did you ever run into the little folk?"

"Shush!" said Marcus.

"You mean dwarves?" Cyrano grinned. "I've certainly supplied a few. There was this one chap at the Cannes film festival . . ."

"I'm thinking more leprechaun-shaped."

"Myth and nonsense!" The Frenchman pushed his friend in the shoulder. "Elves don't exist, not outside of Tolkien. And you know what a waste of time I think he is. Now, dwarves on the other hand . . ."

"A friend of mine recently passed me some video footage he took."

Cyrano tried not to bite, but already it was too late. The fluid inside his cranial cavity reached boiling point in a flash, frying his brain.

"Who is this friend?" he snapped.

"I'm not at liberty to say."

"We're both members of an organisation that has no secrets. Name him now."

Ferret laughed. "There's no need to be a rules-Nazi."

Marcus glared, slapping both friends across their wrists in annoyance.

Cyrano turned around in his chair, fuming on the inside.

By now the immaculately presented Colonel was a third of the way down the line, working his way through shoes and laces, which were checked for signs of wear and tear. Next came hair, measured with a ruler, marked in imperial inches. Buttons he inspected front and back, along with medals. Content that the platoon was up to scratch, the Colonel cleared his throat.

"Jones of the Royal Welsh Fusiliers will lead the trooping of the stag."

An intense wailing noise filled the long corridor. From an adjoining room, Corporal Freddie McShanter, the official club piper, appeared in full tartan, blowpipe in mouth, piping away on the kaba gaidi, a unique wind instrument related to the bagpipes.

The Frenchman smiled.

In the presence of Cyril, it was impossible to be annoyed.

Many years ago, so the story went, Salinger's adopted an official mascot, who, upon examination, was declared too old for active duty. The billeting of Cyril the regimental goat had not been without issue, mainly due to his propensity for chewing anything within the radius of his rope, which for a brief period included the Major's prize blooms. It was to the relief of all concerned when Cyril passed away suddenly, under mysterious circumstances. There was a brief move to have him stuffed, until the Corporal intervened, ensuring the hapless goat would serve the club in a way he never did in life. The blowpipe was constructed inside one of Cyril's front legs, while the sound pipe came out of his mouth. Although not a traditional instrument of the British Armed Forces, the club voted to overlook this minor detail on the grounds that Freddie was a fully qualified Scotsman and a jolly dab hand with the pipe.

Jones led the parade from the front, holding a massive silver platter on which was impaled a huge side of venison. The smell of roast meat engulfed the friends, causing Cyrano to salivate, despite a lack of hunger signals from his stomach. The line of boredom cocaine he'd had as a pre-lunch *amuse-nez* was still doing its job. The bearer was followed by the rest of the rag-tag regiment.

The three friends stood, downed the dregs of their martinis, and joined the end of the line, marching in single file towards their favoured table, with Freddie bringing up the rear.


"Afternoon, Colonel," winked Cyrano as the group circumnavigated the great room, which contained at its very centre an antique brass globe of the world, some four feet in diameter, mounted on a dark marble plinth inscribed with the names of the club's founders.

"Afternoon, what?" replied the Colonel. "I hear those blessed Zulus are on the rise again, threatening the stability of the Cape. I need some good men with fire in their bellies to help put the blighters down."

"Jolly good slab of stag," replied Cyrano, changing the subject.

"Shot him myself in the Highlands, just the other week."

"An excellent choice of target, sir."

By the time Cyrano prised himself away from the Colonel, the carvers had already set to creating a neat array of thickly sliced melt-in-the-mouth floppy segments, burgundy red in colour. The Frenchman's appetite was lacklustre at best, but then he'd been here many times before.

If necessary, he'd force it down.

No point in wasting perfectly good venison.

At the table, Marcus and Ferret were engaged in animated discussion. The Frenchman took a seat next to his government friend, across from his consultant friend, and pulled up his sleeves, flashing a pair of gold pointed cufflinks, allowing cut stone to catch the light. The consultant stopped mid-sentence, drawn in by the unmistakable sparkle of diamond. Cyrano showed off the full-gold rectangle, finely engraved with what the uneducated might construe to be a decorative logo, consisting of a row of six ionic columns, supporting a triangular roof, inset with a precious stone.

"How elegant," said Marcus.

Cyrano twisted his wrist to reveal the fastener: a golden eagle, wings spread, its eye a ruby. Ferret eyed the jewellery lasciviously.

"They're a reward from our banking friend for the quantity of goods I put through the books this month. You can have a pair too." The Frenchman paused for effect. "Just as soon as you prise yourself away from that stupid game and start earning again."

"For one of my friends," said Ferret, "you're an ass of the highest order."

"Ladies!" Marcus leant back to allow one of the waiters to place a plate of meat in the space in front of him. "Curtail the squabbling this instant and let us lunch in peace."

Once the roast was behind them, the three friends retired to the lounge to digest, each taking up their favoured position around the fireplace.

"Now the pleasantries are over," said Ferret, stretching his arms. "I have one word: Wolfgang."

Cyrano felt an uncontrollable scowl overtake his face. He'd known for some time that this conversation was coming. He and Marcus had discussed the situation to death, involving all the other members of their decuria. After the initial hush-up, which had them all on tenterhooks until the funeral was well and truly over, they'd agreed to tell Ferret, en masse, just as soon as he came out of hiding.

"I'm so sorry you had to find out the way you did," consoled Marcus.

"How fortunate you didn't get on with him." Cyrano flicked his nose.

"That's not the point," said Ferret. "You had no right to keep his death from me."

"After you locked yourself away, we acted in what we thought was your best interest," said Marcus softly.

"On that point I have no doubt, but when all's said and done, he was still my father. I've been thinking long and hard about our relationship, and while I'm really hurt that he had the audacity to shuffle off this mortal coil before we were able to resolve our differences, I now think I was rather hasty when I said I didn't want anything to do with him ever again."

"But you've always been so intractable in your anti-father views," said Marcus.

Cyrano found himself nodding.

"However, I have a problem," said Ferret, "which is this: If I recant and let my father off, that makes me soft. If I stick to my guns and continue to hate him, I'll end up bitter and twisted. What am I to do?"

Cyrano knew the predicament his friend was in only too well. His personal feud was an ongoing war of attrition, the outcome currently unresolved. The fact that his papa had chosen to accept a teaching post in Paris made it easy to live with. It was a situation that suited them both.

He'd tried really hard to follow in his papa's footsteps and become an economist, even taking a lucrative advisory post at the treasury. It turned out to be the longest, most tedious week of his life. Bored senseless by the routine, he'd handed in his notice on Friday and flown to Mexico on Saturday to sit on a pyramid and have a long, hard think about the future.

Beauleigh appeared, brandishing a tray filled with three large balloons of brandy, accompanied by three lengthy Cuban cigars.

Cyrano took one of the Montecristos and sniffed it lengthways, the spiced aroma of quality tobacco wafting him all the way back to his favourite island haunt. The Frenchman relaxed, allowing the old retainer to clip the cigar. Whatever his initial misgivings, the level of good old-fashioned quality attention offered by the club was second to none.

The retainer produced a desktop lighter. Cyrano puffed away until ignition ensued. One by one, the friends followed suit.

"I've decided on number fourteen," said Cyrano. "Three thirty, please."

"Very good, sir." With which, Beauleigh was off.

"How does he do that?" asked Ferret. "They say he has shrapnel in both legs."

"And bullet fragments in one shoulder," added Marcus.

"Must play merry hell with the airport scanners." Cyrano exhaled a thick plume of smoke from the side of his mouth, expertly aimed at his consultant friend's nose.

"My crisis," said Ferret, coughing heartily.

"Tell me all about it," said Marcus.

The Frenchman inhaled once more, holding cigar smoke in his mouth until the edges of his tongue tingled. Only then did he exhale, taking the brandy to his lips, swilling it around, allowing the alcohol to partially evaporate, contemplating the complex notes of oak.

His consultant friend, he reminded himself, was certainly high maintenance.

Fortunately, his government friend was up to the task of setting Ferret right, despite his own unresolved family differences, which began on the day he joined the civil service instead of the armed forces, a move which Marcus Senior claimed diminished the family's honour. Even though their government friend was in his mid-forties, he was still reminded on a regular basis how valiant in comparison his brothers were, risking all for Queen and country. The only consolation, apparently, was that the middle son had retained enough common sense to continue voting for the Conservative Party.

Cyrano chortled to himself.

Rebellion was one thing, but the loss of one's inheritance was inexcusable folly.

The Frenchman listened with one ear to the ongoing conversation, which had moved onto their armaments friend Rusty and his team of hired guns, currently causing trouble in a small African principality he'd never heard of. Rusty's papa had not so much forgiven him as given up completely.

"I wish my father had done the same," said Ferret.

Cyrano nodded. "He was a stubborn old bugger, refusing to concede to any of your choices."

"Bloody academics," agreed Marcus. "I have several working for me, and I find them most inflexible to new ideas that aren't their own."

"Has Ferret ever told you about the time his papa sabotaged our summer trip to Falmouth?"

The consultant's cheeks turned bright pink.

Scenting the opportunity to score points, the Frenchman told the tale. Rather than let his son have his freedom, Wolfgang had hired a campervan and dragged Ferret off to sit in a field instead, watching the skies for flying saucers, surrounded by a merry band of middle-aged men with homemade UFO detectors. The trip culminated with an outbreak of wigs and false beards, a change of vehicle, and a midnight chase across the Home Counties.

Ferret filled in the details, telling Marcus how he purposefully befriended a bunch of grade-A lunatics, giving them far more credence than they deserved in order to get free booze, something his father had strictly prohibited. Once inebriated, he'd accidentally blurted his father's government connections, which resulted in an instant transfer of interest, as the loonies became convinced Wolfgang knew all the darkest secrets of Porton Down.

"Do you remember what the group was called?" asked Marcus.

"'The Conspiracy Co-operative'."

Marcus tutted. "Cheltenham has a special unit for the CCO. They're bound by a pathological need to break into top-secret government establishments and harass scientists."

"They chased us for hours." Ferret shuddered.

"It's no wonder you're determined to not let your father off." Marcus put his hand on Ferret's forearm.

The Frenchman sloshed brandy from side to side. "In my opinion, dear boy, your papa was just too German to engage in the traditional British pastime of fighting you and losing, thus handing on the baton to the next generation. As far as I'm concerned, the moment he cashed in his chips, life declared you the winner."

"Hear, hear," said Marcus, proposing a toast. "To Ferret, the winner."

"Why thank you," said the consultant, a weight dropping from his shoulders. "That's a resolution I can live with. For the purposes of closure, I must divulge that I've been in contact with the family solicitor. There are some files, apparently, that I'm obligated to read."

"I understand," consoled Marcus.

Cyrano glared at his friend. "Your father was an unreasonable control freak who had no time for you at all. If that's all he left you, I say burn the lot and curse his name forever. That's how we do closure in my family."

For a long while the group sat staring into space, sloshing and inhaling god's own brandy, enjoying three wonderful cigars. Every thirty seconds or so, Ferret adjusted his posture. Cyrano found his agitation levels increase with each fidget; he wanted to yell at his friend, to drum some sense of decorum into him. Not that any good would come from such a rant, when what he really needed was a toot of Charles.

Eventually, the consultant broke the silence. "I have a proposal to run past you both."

"Go ahead," said Marcus.

Inwardly, the Frenchman cursed.

The correct answer was to dig a rabbit hole and lead Ferret down it, not pander to his whims.

"Given my lack of progress with the City of London, I'm contemplating investigating the paranormal in my spare time."

Cyrano's heart sank all the way down to his bile duct, where it became immersed in green sludge before slowly making its way back up to his chest cavity. His annoyance steadily rose with each passing beat.

"I strongly advise you against such action," said Marcus sternly.

"It's only a stop-gap." Ferret smiled.

"You swore an oath to me many years ago never to entertain the paranormal, the supernatural, or the occult ever again, as our friend here will attest." Cyrano thumped the chair. "I'm inclined to report you for even thinking about it."

"That won't be necessary," said Marcus soothingly. "Ferret is about to change his mind."

"Actually," said Ferret, "I'd rather hoped for your support in this endeavour."

"You're asking me to keep a secret from our other friends?" Cyrano coughed, stubbing out the remains of his cigar in the ashtray, flattening a smokeable inch of fine tobacco. "I think not."

Grabbing his jacket, he headed for the door, turning at the last to see a wide-eyed Ferret, reminding him of a bush baby on lysergic acid.

"My boy, when I made my commitment to honour Plutus, the god of wealth, pledging my eternal allegiance to the One, I was deadly serious. It seems you were not. Good day to you, Marcus. Ferret, you'll be hearing from the authorities in due course."

Cyrano stormed past the bathroom, checked the lock on the cellar twice and once again for luck, then headed out of the club, carefully closing the battered gloss vermilion doors behind him. A pair of polished brass knockers, wrought into the shape of lion's heads, roared their goodbyes. The Frenchman slipped into a waiting taxi, where a gorgeous blonde greeted him, draped in fur and pearls. Stella tried to sooth her man with erotic suggestions, but he was too infuriated, his ears turned off.

What was his friend thinking?

This was by far the most scatterbrained, ill-conceived, crackpot notion he'd heard in a long time. Give up a position working in the Square Mile worth millions of pounds a year in discreet deals, for what? Ectoplasm detectors and . . . Cyrano had no idea what went with an ectoplasm detector, and he didn't care to find out.

Not now, not ever.

After all, The Network was their family.

The Frenchman produced a small silver container from an inner suit pocket, and with the aid of a dainty spoon, nourished his nostrils.

While Stella fiddled with his fly zipper, Cyrano smiled and lay back, hands behind his head.

*Vive la Légion!*

*Vive Plutus.*

*Vive Rome.*

Ferret's plan had to be stamped on, before he embarrassed the decuria. And he was the man for the job.

Marcus sensed trouble the moment Ferret mentioned filling his spare time with the investigation of strange goings-on. As their *beneficiarius*, he'd profiled Cyrano and Ferret in their final year at university, confident of what kind of members they'd become. Certainly the Frenchman liked his rules. On the other hand, Ferret, who was ostensibly German, wouldn't touch anything that came in list form with a bargepole. Marcus had concluded over the years that Cyrano, whose papa was French, had inherited his penchant for following rules to the letter from his German *Mutter*, whereas Ferret, whose *Vater* was German, inherited his flippancy and disregard for convention from his socialist French mama.

He chuckled at this little nugget.

It was one of those ironies that made life bearable.

As expected, Cyrano had made a furious call to Tom Tom, their *decanus*, tearing him off a strip for mishandling Wolfgang's death. Once he had Tom Tom's attention, a few choice words were issued regarding Ferret's blatant disrespect for a sworn oath. Tom Tom did his best to be diplomatic, but the Frenchman stuck to his guns, demanding direct action. As a consequence, Marcus and Tom Tom were sitting in the back of a cab, heading to Regent's Park for a meeting with the accused.

"This won't be easy," said Tom Tom, busily working himself into a lather.

"I spoke with our consultant friend last night. He was quite apologetic."

"I know him. He won't accept the punishment."

Tom Tom was not the most inspirational of men, mused Marcus. An excellent art dealer and purveyor of fine objects he may be, but a leader of people he was not. Given the lack of eligible candidates, what else was the *decuria* to do? The Frenchman had his foreign business interests, Blair was forever in and out of various institutions, Rusty was busy fighting African warlords, and Rajesh and Philip were only in their second year. That left himself and Ferret who, as the previous incumbent freshly fallen from grace and ruthlessly dismissed by their banking friend, was hardly trustworthy. Such a shame. It had been a joy to watch him climb through the ranks.

"In my experience," said Marcus, thinking out loud, "our consultant friend isn't going to forget about an idea just because our French friend has objected to it."

"But we can't let him go ahead with his plan."

"At the same time, we can't stop him. If you read him the riot act, Ferret will simply down periscope again. We must be seen to take his side."

"But paranormal investigator?" Tom Tom winced visibly at the thought. "He'll become the laughing stock of the legion."

"We live in an age of misdirection," said Marcus solemnly. "So misdirect we will. Watch and learn."

The balding art dealer mopped his brow with a handkerchief, looking increasingly uncomfortable in the muggy London heat.

"And our French friend's pound of flesh?"

"Have faith. The plan we put together will do the job nicely."

The two legionnaires exited the cab alongside the park and walked along the front of the terrace, past a pair of Mercedes, three BMWs, and a lone Bentley. They climbed the front steps to Ferret's home, passing underneath a grand stone archway that supported a veranda running the length of the complex and, finding the door ajar, let themselves in, making their way up the stairs to the den at the top. Marcus made a point of poking his head into the master bedroom, noting that although the sheets had been stripped, the mattress was still in need of attention. Spotting an upturned bottle of Champagne in an ice bucket, he chortled to himself.

On entering the den, they found their consultant friend rampaging around the floor.

Rip!

Tear!

"Damn packaging," squawked Ferret. "Why do magazines always insist on making it impossible to open goods they give away on the cover? Being free, you'd expect every expense possible to be spared on glue, but no. Apparently that's not how it works."

"Good morning," said Tom Tom.

"You're asking for it!" Ferret waved a large, unfriendly Sabatier knife deadly enough to fillet a pig at the art dealer and, with a skilful flick of the wrist, skinned the magazine.

Tom Tom gulped.

Marcus motioned to Ferret to put the glossy down and pay attention, terms to which the consultant reluctantly agreed. Under normal circumstances, Marcus would be in there with Ferret, assisting him to get the free CD off the cover. Today, he couldn't afford to send out any mixed messages.

"Can't we just do small talk?" asked Ferret, knife in hand. "I ask you how the decuria are doing and you give me an update. You tell me our friend with the freckles is in prison again, Angola this time, for selling arms he didn't have to the wrong side in an attempted coup. Our psychiatric friend has been setting fires, except this time it was more than a tool shed he burnt down. Our banking friend . . . I forgot Tristan."

"He's embroiled in some rather ugly litigation," said Tom Tom, rolling his eyes. "He chose not to promote one of his senior managers up the banking hierarchy, despite assurances he allegedly made whilst the two of them were *in flagrante delicto*."

"Let's move on to the weather. Today looks like a scorcher."

The chords in Tom Tom's neck stood taut. He cast a quick glance in Marcus's direction. "We're here to have a chat with you regarding some serious allegations raised by our French friend."

"He's hardly a friend of mine," snapped the consultant, brandishing the blade.

"Yes he is," said Marcus, moving between the art dealer and the consultant.

"Our French friend accepts that he insulted you regarding your rights to read your late father's files," said Tom Tom, seizing the situation, exactly as rehearsed. "You have our blessing to act as you see fit in this department. I realise this is a little late, but the decuria sends its condolences."

Ferret smiled. "Thank you."

"Secondly, there is the matter of the paranormal, the supernatural, and flying saucers. You swore a solemn oath to our French friend, with our government friend here as witness, that you would not engage in the pursuit of any of these subjects in a serious manner ever again."

"I may have been a little hasty there," said Ferret.

Marcus stepped into the breach. "As your *adiutor*, my advice to you is this: Treat all of those subjects with the disrespect they deserve. Especially conspiracies that involve your own government."

"That's a command," said Tom Tom. "From now on, when in polite circles, you will speak of all that jazz only in jest."

"Not a problem," said Ferret, lowering the kitchen knife.

"Now," said Tom Tom, "this nonsense about becoming a paranormal investigator: It ends today."

Ferret sunk his chin into his chest and sighed.

"It's the 'paranormal' word," said Marcus. "It sends out entirely the wrong message. You're a management consultant. If you want to be an investigator in your time off, give yourself a suitably flowery job title."

"Oh." Ferret lightened up.

"One final point," said Marcus, stepping backwards. "Our French friend demands compensation for the insult to his *dignitas*."

"In line with our organisation's rules governing such matters, we're setting you a task," said the art dealer, mopping his brow. "Do you remember my older brother Tim Tim?

"How could I ever forget such belligerence?" replied Ferret.

"He has a problem with the theft of intellectual copyright. Your mission is to play dumb and catch the perpetrator."

Ferret raised an eyebrow. "Isn't your brother an Old Boy?"

"That's why it's imperative you wear a disguise."

"Let me get this right," said Ferret, putting down the knife. "As *castigatio* I'm to investigate a mystery by going undercover?"

"Think of it as your first case," said Tom Tom.

Ferret's face lit up like Buckingham Palace on the queen's official birthday.

"Thank our *adiutor*, not me." Tom Tom shook his head. "In my opinion, you'll never make it as a detective. This is simply your opportunity to prove me right."

To Marcus's trained eye, his consultant friend was genuinely delighted at the outcome. Naturally, there was a twist, which they'd come to later.

"This assignment has no fees attached," said Tom Tom. "It comes out of your pocket. Once you're in, you're quite entitled to pull your usual consultancy tricks, but be warned: If you scam Tim Tim and he discovers you're not even a lesser Old Boy, there will be repercussions."

"Overcharge for my services?" Ferret grinned from ear to ear. "The thought never even crossed my mind."

Later that evening, Marcus headed back to Regent's Park.

He stopped the cab near Baker Street station, paid the fare and climbed out, opting to take a brisk walk around the park's outer ring road to Ferret's spacious townhouse. For the occasion, he'd chosen beige slacks and a light-blue summer shirt with short sleeves trimmed in brilliant white, tan moccasins, and a dark-blue blazer adorned with gold buttons, which he slung over his left shoulder. He walked slowly, a swagger to his step, pulling a heavy black suitcase on wheels behind him, eyeing the hectic commuters and confused tourists for any signs of an opening. Stopping a young man in his early twenties, Marcus asked for directions to the nearest blowjob in broken Russian, raising an appropriate eyebrow where it was inappropriate. Apologetically, the youth shrugged his shoulders and carried on his way.

Marcus continued with the ruse of being lost, smiling at the youngsters having fun, but not that young, heaven forbid! Not a single one of them understood his extracurricular offer, which was a shame. Determined to raise the flag to at least half mast, the intelligence man minced past the Holmes museum, only to discover a gaggle of girls outside, all members of the same club.

The Baker Street Babes, indeed!

Marcus wiggled his head, raised his chin to the sky and with a dismissive huff, marched off.

It was an impossible task, he reflected, being a friend and *adiutor*. His professional relationship with Ferret required distance, whereas his personal relationship required closeness, and that compromised any fairness he might try to wield. He dare not get too close to his friend, as that would require lowering all of his barriers, and as soon as he did that, Ferret would do that thing of his.

There was little doubt that Ferret's talent had served The Network well over the years, earning the decuria a substantial fortune and the consultant a handsome cut. And given how The Network had changed since the millennium reforms, Ferret was definitely an asset to the organisation. He just needed to start earning again. When Tom Tom brought this up earlier, Ferret had responded enthusiastically, claiming he had a lead he was working on that their banking friend could readily exploit.

It was about time.


The *adiutor* was familiar enough with Ferret's home to let himself in, something which he'd done every few days for the last three months, leaving provisions just inside the front door. Each time he returned, they were gone. Once or twice, out of curiosity, he'd even climbed the stairs to Ferret's den, getting no farther than the featureless door that was always shut. Today, out of politeness, he pressed the buzzer using a tell-tale pattern and, upon hearing the lock click, marched right on up the stairs, suitcase in hand. The government man patted his pocket and smiled. Their French friend had been badgering for a key for the last six months but still didn't have one. On the second floor, Marcus poked his head into the master bedroom and giggled again at the empty Champagne bottle still lingering on its side. Then he grabbed hold of all of his feelings, stuffed them in a box, tied it firmly shut with a pink ribbon and, in his mind, hid it firmly behind a billowing black curtain.

The door to the den was ajar. The sounds of moaning echoed forth from dozens of hungry zombies tearing away at the inside of the TV screen.

"Good evening!" shouted Marcus over the clamour of ravenous undead.

Ferret smiled and handed him the game controller, heading to the kitchenette.

Marcus took the controller, his eyes distracted by a new addition to the coffee table: a hardback volume entitled *The Sign of the Four* by Arthur Conan Doyle.

In his head, a light switched on.

That was the moment he knew his friend's new job title.

He'd need an image to go with it.

Perhaps a hat.

The *adiutor* pulled himself together just in time to skewer a zombie through the ear with a pickaxe. "I'm no detective, but I'd say from the number of magazines scattered around the floor that you're taking the release of DeathWorld: Apocalypse a little obsessively."

"Surely not." Ferret reappeared with two large glasses of white wine. "Petit Chablis?"

"Absolutely." Marcus paused the game, put down the controller, took the glass, and toasted his friend. "Chin chin, old chap."

"Chin, chin," said Ferret. "Good day at the office?"

Marcus shuddered. "You know I can't discuss work until I'm drunk."

Truth be told, he didn't want to think about the day he'd had at City Intelligence — the department of the security services for whom he worked. His day had involved the near termination of a ten-year-old boy who was packing a replica handgun in a spare sock. The crowded minimart in which he chose to show it off to his friend had a spasm as customers hit the floor and flew out of every orifice. Fortunately, the off-duty officer queuing for cigarettes missed, seven times in a row, taking out a casket of melons in a flurry of lead.

A shut-up payment to the mother kept the incident out of the news and off the front page of the *Evening Standard*, saving face for the department. Once the incident was hushed up, all that remained was to reassign the officer from SO17 to another unit. After all, there was no point in having an undercover enforcer who can't shoot straight on the books.

The intelligence man flipped one of the magazines over. "How fortuitous our decanus didn't think to check what you were reading."

"I managed two days this time before I cracked."

Marcus laughed politely.

Giving up the stick of joy was something he'd tried to do himself, on numerous occasions, only to be overtaken by the twitches at an inappropriate moment, forcing him to scarper to the nearest washroom for a quick fix on a concealed mobile device. The withdrawal pangs were horrible, like having a ball of hungry rats in his stomach gnawing away, trying to hollow him out from the inside.

Today had been particularly intolerable. Adverts for DeathWorld began taunting him from the minicab radio on his way to collect their art dealer friend, then from advertising hoardings en route to Ferret's home, and finally from a double-page spread in one of the more serious broadsheets.

Marcus touched his friend's hand. "I understand your pain. However, this is special. It's the most exciting games release of the decade."

"Never mind decade. They say the launch party will be the event of the century."

The two friends continued to speculate wildly about DW:A, until the last of the rumour Ferret had accumulated was spent, bar the best bit, which he kept back until last. One of the RockSlut developers had leaked the existence of a revolutionary new user interface, which had the games world in knots. Shortly afterwards, a particularly abrasive journalist had discovered a box in a public house marked 'DW:A — Top Secret' and, in desperation to be the first with an inside scoop, had published details of what turned out to be a reputation-damaging decoy.

Marcus raised his glass. "Have you taken delivery of your father's files yet?"

Ferret shook his head. "Following the rumpus at Salinger's, I have forsaken all interest."

"I know you better than that." Marcus scanned the den, searching for a stack of mouldy old paper. Although he'd only met Wolfgang once, being a man of science of a certain age, Marcus had anticipated him having boxes and boxes of disorderly junk.

So where were they?

The *adiutor* felt a lump in his throat.

At some point he was going to have to discuss the details of Wolfgang's demise with his friend. Not the reports of drowning that had appeared in the papers, which were cursory at most, but the department report he'd used the privilege of position to accrue. Ex-government weapons inspectors, he reminded himself, don't fall from cruise ships every day, only to be chewed to pieces on the propellers of a fishing smack operating illegally in foreign waters.

The consultant emptied his glass and cracked open a second bottle of wine. After he'd topped them both up, he produced a small, black, rubberised rectangle, which he waved with a wink and a smirk.

"Is that a cache of really exciting pornography?" asked Marcus.

"My father's files. 1974 to the present day, all typed up and neatly formatted, which is a step into the light, but sadly they're lacking any sort of catalogue system."

"And the muscular young men?"

Ferret looked at Marcus quizzically.

"Oh my god!" squealed Marcus. "I just outed myself!"

"For about the tenth time."

"Well, thank you for your understanding." Marcus stuck his bottom lip out. "Coming out is supposed to be a wonderfully intimate act, to be shared with allies and close friends. You're so matter-of-fact, it's hardly any fun at all. In fact, this is the worst coming out ever. There. I hope you're happy."

"I'm sorry. Next time, I promise I'll do better."

"Good." Marcus took a glug of wine. "Make sure you do."

Inwardly, the *adiutor* let out a sigh of relief.

Keeping up the pretence of being straight in front of his dearest friends was something he detested. If only he'd been born twenty years later, to a poorer family. As it was, his inclinations were a secret he still kept from his father. His mother had known, bless her dear departed soul; she'd kept his secret all the way to the grave. As long as he acted responsibly, keeping his man-bits in his pants in public, the family name and his inheritance were safe. It was when he tried to leave his man-bits in someone else's pants that the trouble started. That was a long time ago. He hadn't had a fancy-youth for years.

His superiors at City Intelligence knew all about that particular string of encounters, as did those in The Network to whom he informally reported the decuria's gossip.

Marcus winced.

He didn't like to think about the spilling of secrets, the naming of names. Those confessions were the most difficult tasks he'd ever undertaken in his life, far more intimate than any government interview he'd ever had to attend.

It was little wonder so few members ever crossed The Network.


"What's in the suitcase?" asked Ferret inquisitively.

"Your new best friend." Marcus pulled the case onto his lap and fiddled with its dual combination locks. "It's part of your disguise kit."

"Do we have to?"

With a wave of the wrist, the *adiutor* reminded his friend that he was bound by the terms of *pecuniaria multa* and, following their French friend's acceptance of the formal apology, punishment was now due.

"Meet the SniffPhreak Two Thousand Government Issue, or SP2K-GI for short," he said. "It's slightly out of date, having been superseded by the SP2K7-GI+, which is why I'm able to borrow it without having to complete any uncomfortable forms."

"I want the new one!" exclaimed Ferret, taking a seat.

"We couldn't possibly allow a member of the public to wander around unescorted with state-of-the-art dark hardware."

"It's still pretty sexy." Ferret reached out to stroke one of the SniffPhreak's matt black dials.

"Naughty." Marcus slapped the consultant's wrist. "You haven't been trained yet."

The *adiutor* opened a pocket on the inside of the case and produced a wad of documentation, explaining that for this particular mission his friend was now known as Ferret the Nerd. The consultant took possession of a passport, flicking through the pages, only to recoil in horror at the picture he found.

Marcus smiled. "I had the yearbook photo that our French friend supplied doctored, adding in some wild hair and a pair of rather ghastly glasses."

"I look disgusting."

"There's more. Your new social networking pages are being typed up by one of my juniors as we speak. Incidentally, you have a first from a minor Cambridge college, in computer sciences."

"Such detail really isn't necessary."

Marcus wrung his hands. "Our French friend thinks it is, and, as your *adiutor*, I find myself siding with him for once. He's invested considerable time and effort into your disguise kit. You must wear every element of it — no matter how much discomfort it causes — until you've solved the case."

Ferret shuffled uncomfortably. "But the ladies . . ."

"That, my friend, is the whole point." Marcus giggled, picking up a wig. "Once the Chablis is done, we must take photographs for the Album of Shame."

"I have a very large cellar. We can drink for weeks."

"On this occasion, sadly not."

Mentally, Marcus checked his to-do list. Toy: delivered. Hairpiece: delivered. Instruction to make sure Ferret is tucked into bed nice and early: superfluous. Prohibition on drinking: already broken beyond repair.

"What time do I start?" asked Ferret.

"Ten o'clock sharp. Cyrano will be here shortly with your costume. If he finds us killing zombies, there'll be trouble." Marcus picked up the game controller. "So, quickly, multiplayer game."

The consultant located a second controller, then donned the wig. "If I have to look ridiculous for the next two days, I might as well get started."

"Attaboy," said Marcus, feeling his ardour diminish. It was quite impossible to fancy his consultant friend when he looked so blatantly unfashionable. Why, it was even more effective than bromide.

Finally able to relax, the *adiutor* felt his internal curtain fall to the ground, letting loose his thoughts and feelings.

"Oh," said Ferret, "I like that idea very much. Detecting consultant Ferret. Outstanding! It's going on my business cards first thing tomorrow. Now all I need is something fashionable to cover my head."

Eight hundred and fifty-eight was a number long burnt into the matrix of Flamen's brain. It was the figure quoted on the Order in Council put into place to protect the contents of the bunker from misappropriation, appearing on the inventory list that fell onto his desk once a year, every year, until the time of his hurried departure from the shores of his homeland.

The priest crouched low in the short grass, listening to dogs howl in the distance. German shepherds were clever; they were able to sense him in a way that other animals could not. He had perhaps ten minutes until the rock apes manning the main gate figured out their hounds were onto something and possibly ten more while their superiors vacillated as to what to do about it. Flamen rubbed his backside where a piece of razor wire had cut through camouflage fatigues, raking soft flesh. Fortunately, the wound was not deep, just bloody.

Still, it stung like a jar of Jupiter's piss in a hailstorm.

The priest glanced up to his right, catching sight of a hoarding on which a yellow-and-black triangular warning sign was displayed. The symbol, formed from three interlocking partial circles gave no indication of what classification of biological material was once tested here in Compound-13. The official documentation claimed it was type A; he'd signed it off as such. If they discovered him in an area supposedly contaminated with toxins hazardous to mammals, he faced mandatory isolation for the next three months.

Though if he was caught, isolation was the least of his worries.

Shuffling along on his knees and elbows, the priest made for a stubby concrete structure that lay almost equidistant from each of four surrounding high mesh fences, designed specifically to keep out the inquisitive. By the light of the quarter moon, it was just possible to make out the old concrete access path that led from the northwest gate to the buried store. Following years of neglect, it was now overgrown, split open along its length by a combination of couch grass and comfrey.

From inside the science park, a searchlight beam cut open the night sky.

Flamen drew a pair of short breaths and pulled himself up into a crouching position, counted to five, then ran as fast as he was able straight towards the bunker. Huffing from his exertion, yet not daring to rest, he felt his way around the hard concrete slabs in a clockwise direction, until he came to a set of wide steps that led down to a pair of thick steel blast doors. Quickly he descended, one step at a time, until he reached the platform at the bottom.

He smiled.

Finally.

The circular green-and-red metal signs attached to each of the doors promised a cocktail of chemical death within. These signs at least told a partial truth.

Flamen's heart beat furiously.

While he was sure there were no motion sensors or cameras in the compound, there was still a chance they'd detect the holes in the fences.

Away to the east, the howling of alert pooches reached fever pitch. The priest poked his head above the ledge and listened. He counted five distressed canines in total, each exciting the others to ever greater levels of anxiety. A second searchlight beam cut through the darkened sky. In the cool, still night he heard voices carried on the wind, then boots on metal, and finally the sound of a weapon being cocked.

"Jupiter's shaven ballsack."

It was April 1978 when he was last here, to personally supervise the sealing shut of the great blast doors, burying a priceless treasure within. He hadn't intended to leave the prize alone so long, but events conspired against him, pulling him this way and that, preventing him from returning. By the time his order was enshrined in law, the team of twelve had long been disbanded, returned to their units.

One of their number had later been killed in action and three had died from natural causes. Now there was one more to add to the inventory of corpses: his old friend the chemist.

Following his vision, the priest read every single newspaper report he'd been able to get his hands on regarding the unfortunate demise of his scientist friend. None of the imported British newspapers told him what he needed to know, namely who the chemist was working for at the time of the accident. The broadsheets devoted mere inches to the death of the ex-weapons inspector, never once mentioning his family.

Flamen had approached the Ministry of Defence, hoping to find a few giveaway details in their official statement.

He came away unfulfilled.

The priest rested black-painted hands on the right-hand blast door, feeling the mechanism of the great lock concealed inside the riveted frame. He counted the steel pins in his mind, exercised their springs, and commanded them to align. With a twist of his wrist, the lock sprung open. The pins were not as resistant to movement as he expected; they'd been pushed into position fairly recently, certainly within the last two years.

Summoning all of his strength, Flamen took hold of a brass handle with both hands and pulled. The door slid to one side, grating angrily on its runners, throwing up a shower of sparks. The sound of his exertion echoed out into the night.

Eight hundred and fifty-eight.

In the distance, an engine coughed into life; a rotor blade swooshed, quickly finding its idle speed.

The priest wiped his forehead, taking care not to smear the green and black camouflage paint, and ducked inside the bunker, activating a torch. He shone the tight beam in the direction of a storage tank. It was all still there, exactly as he remembered it. From the storage tank, he followed a series of interlocking pipes past various flow valves, all the way to the immersion tank where Lewis's body was found one morning, stark naked, a ghoulish grin upon its taut lips.

Did that count as a natural death or an unnatural death?

There had been calls to close down Project XIII after that. Instead, he used his influence to assign his friend Wolfgang to the vacant post of chief scientist. Flamen knew that somewhere in the depths of Porton Down, Lewis's body was still held in a freezer. Equally, somewhere in the Midlands, his coffin was still filled with thirteen stones of sandbags. Then, as now, the military doesn't like to surrender its experimental dead, just in case they accidentally fall into the hands of a foreign power.

Fumbling in the dark, the priest kicked a bucket, filling the room with reverberating sound.

"Jupiter's codpiece!"

He picked up the steel container and headed towards the main storage tank, where he stuffed the container underneath a nozzle and turned the tap forty-five degrees, then another forty-five.

Nothing.

Not a single drop.

Quickly, he closed the valve, returning it to its original position and headed for the door. A helicopter circled low on the horizon, its search beam flashing against the ground. The dogs were silent. Flamen pushed the door closed. As he reached the top step, off to the northwest a party of men with flashlights came into view.

A vehicle engine spluttered.

Then another.

Without warning, the sky lit up a bright candy red.

Flamen stopped dead in his tracks, curiosity getting the better of him, as he interpreted what he was seeing. Where the old concrete path met the steps down to the bunker, it was possible to make out the outline of an irregular stain, a giant Rorschach inkblot. Within its perimeter nothing grew, not a single blade of grass.

Eight hundred and fifty-eight.

The priest turned and ran for the inner perimeter fence, his mind racing. There'd been a spillage. How wasteful. His fingers located the severed links where he'd cut his way in. He parted the wire and squeezed through, losing his beanie.

Dog bark.

No time to think.

Fixing his eye line, he ran towards the second fence and freedom. The skies turned dark again, momentarily confusing him.

Where was the damn hole?

His ears danced to the sounds of rotor blades.

A searchlight picked him out.

A bullhorn crackled. "Put your hands above your head."

Flamen realised he'd gone the wrong way along the fence. Caught in the helicopter's downdraft, he dropped to his knees, felt his way to the gap and slipped through. A warning shot zipped past, burying itself in the soft earth. That was the only time the soldier would miss on purpose. The priest tore the camouflage netting from his carefully concealed transport, jumped into the saddle, hurriedly turned the key and set off as fast as the throttle allowed, steering the quad bike towards the tree line, zigzagging from side to side to avoid the beam of light from above.

From inside the science park, a siren blared.

"Jupiter's gnarly gonads!"

Swerving this way and that, high on adrenaline, the priest relaxed into the ride. Oh, how he loved the body's own natural drugs. Racing across the darkened plain, weaving an evasive pattern with a Land Rover in hot pursuit, he found himself drifting back in time. Flouting the law was his thing; running wild without restraint his opium; getting paid to do it his just reward. What a life he'd led, before his body gave out and they forcibly pensioned him off. The other business: His reason for leaving the country . . . he didn't want to think about The Brotherhood right now.

Ahead, the woods loomed.

What he really needed was a stolen sports car, capable of rapid acceleration. They'd never expect that. In the sky above, the helicopter was having trouble staying with the bike.

It overshot, doubled back, then hovered, searching for clues.

Away from the cauldron with the sounds of his pursuers fading, the priest let his mind wander. What fun they'd had all those years ago when Project XIII was finally given the green light. There was the pompous munitions expert from the Army who knew all about modern armour and insisted on having his own personal orderly, the flying ace from the Air Force who crashed his way through more test planes in a year than they made and, of course, his submersible counterpart from the Navy, whose real expertise lay in escaping from depth in a pressure suit. The ministry had added a mandatory bean counter to measure progress and also a defender of the realm, whose speciality was psychological warfare and whose absurd theories about the nature of the universe gave them all a bloody good laugh. Finally, there was the chemist, whom nobody trusted. They all figured he must be a plant, out to report on their activities to military intelligence.

A nice theory, but wrong.

Lewis was intelligence's secret bitch, until he took to the tank and ended up on the mortician's slab, his chest cavity pinned open, organs assigned to numbered jars stacked neatly in a row alongside those of his ape ancestors.

Fourteen thousand four hundred and forty-nine. At the time, it seemed like a massive quantity of liquid, more than any of them knew what to do with, until they realised the figure was in litres not gallons. That was the Germans for you, always measuring in the wrong set of units. The Navy and the Air Force soon lost interest and pulled out their men, reassigning them to more profitable clandestine projects. Like Wolfgang and the Army man, the psychology expert refused to give up on his pursuits, right to the bitter end. It was thanks to Sir Edward that they were able to continue as long as they did. With his crazy sideburns and tumbleweed ginger hair, the group wildcard cut quite the figure in Whitehall, although his insistence on wearing a deerstalker around Main Building wore the patience thin.

Five hundred and seventy-five litres.

By the horny helmet of Jupiter, that man had excelled in the twin skills of bribery and corruption.

So which of the team had sold out the project?

While Flamen mulled over the possibilities in his mind, a deer ran out in front of him. Reacting on instinct, the priest crashed into a low wooden fence, throwing himself from the bike. He sailed through the air, landing roughly in a ditch in a crumpled heap.

"Jupiter's slippery salami!"

He staggered to his feet, a searing pain in his ankle, the taste of blood in his mouth.

He wasn't out of the woods yet.

While he was far from happy with the new wardrobe, Ferret couldn't deny that his French friend had an eye for detail. As promised, the costume was delivered before midnight in a fanfare of cackles. Once Cyrano was ensconced in the den, it had taken a further two bottles of quality wine to prise him out again. Undoubtedly, as part of the costume assembly, an establishment specialising in vintage clothing had been looted, although how his friend had guessed the sizes so accurately remained a mystery. To be pernickety, the pastel-blue nylon trousers were too tight, the brown corduroy jacket had frayed cuffs and missing buttons. The pillar-box red viscose shirt, with its wide, round collar, fit just right. His French friend had taken the liberty of smearing tomato sauce on the shirt pocket in a ghastly display of poor personal hygiene, which was also reflected in the mayonnaise stains on the crotch of the pants. Thoughtfully, the Frenchman had supplied a battered aluminium tool case, replete with foam lining, which contained a mangled toolset, leaving just enough room for the SniffPhreak to nestle comfortably between a pair of bent spanners. A sticker on the case front proudly declared 'I heart 7 of 9'.

When travelling in London, Ferret had a preference for taxis. As a geek, he was compelled to take the tube. In the crowd he felt conspicuous; everyone was watching him. The conspicuous feeling was followed by a period of conspicuous and sweaty, and finally, just sweaty.

During the journey from Baker Street to Soho Square, Ferret took the opportunity to test his intuition by finding some real-life geeks. Steve the sound engineer was first. Ferret felt that Steve had an unhealthy obsession with dials and switches, sound envelopes, and waveforms. He wasn't sure that Steve was actually called Steve, he just felt like a Steve, with his six foot two frame and hands like spatulas. Intuitively, the consultant found himself standing in Steve's shoes, wishing that girls wouldn't point at his hands and giggle. Out of curiosity, Ferret imagined what Steve's soft bits felt like and was surprised to discover that the girls were correct. Steve should be shouting about his *Wurst* from the rooftops, not considering surgery to reduce the size of it.

A smartly dressed Sikh accidently kicked Ferret's case. The chap mumbled an apology. His name jumped into the consultant's head. Intuitively, he knew that Mani was a programmer, knee-deep in commands and subroutines, a walking encyclopaedia of barely concealed coding expertise, confident in the depth of his knowledge. Ferret felt reassured, knowing everything about anything technical.

The third and final geek he spotted was Alekz. Intuitively, Ferret knew she was obsessed with cats. She loved her Siamese, Janeway, who would one day pilot her own starship. Cats. There was enough knowledge concerning feline habituation contained in Alekz's brain to write a full-length novel and a sequel.

Ferret exited the tube train at Tottenham Court Road. It was an amazing feeling, gathering up the secret habits of others, he thought. But if he did it all the time, he'd soon forget who he was and became a geek himself, obsessed with the details of other peoples' lives.

He pressed the record button on his phone and said a few words: "Detecting Consultant Ferret. The Case of the Missing Ideas. Nine fifty-eight. Soho Square. Grrr! Communications beckons. Let's hope the Old Boys aren't biting today."

How fortuitous, he mused. As long as he didn't take the paranormal seriously, this was his new life. The only obstacle was his banking friend. Somehow, in order to satisfy Tristan, he had to find a way to get paid vast sums of money for solving crimes.

"Grrr!" Tim Tim growled, hands aloft mimicking a set of claws.

"Grrr!" replied Ferret, mirroring the Old Boy. His eyes wandered this way and that, scanning the office walls which were adorned with framed film and TV memorabilia, neatly catalogued in a series of exquisite presentation frames.

"So you're Ferret the Nerd."

"The Geek Detective, actually."

"Good, because that's what I need — a know-it-all sleuthhound to get to the bottom of this ideas theft." Tim Tim turned away, looking out the window. "I have forty highly skilled, highly motivated employees working for me, all handpicked with impeccable references. I find it terribly hurtful to contemplate any one of them as a turncoat. The audacity! What persuades a man to undermine his employer like that?"

"I'm no expert on the dynamics of the master/slave relationship," said Ferret, blushing at his un-geek-like turn of phrase.

"It's the times we live in. The education system has been usurped, and there's simply no loyalty to the tie. It's all about the colour of your money and how much you have, rather than how you got it."

"I couldn't agree more."

"Good chap." The Old Boy turned on his heels, narrowing his gaze. His vulture-like eyes fixed on Ferret's neck. "I say, where's YOUR tie?"

"I'm undercover. It's in my bag," said the detective coyly. "Where's yours?"

Tim Tim patted his pocket. "Now, Ferret, I'm sure we've met before."

"If I recall, it was at your sister's engagement party."

"The less said about that particular event the better. You were with that specialist nose-candy chap." Tim Tim licked his lips. "You've really let yourself go. Those glasses make you look like a blessed computer gimp."

"That's the idea," said Ferret, removing the specs in order to get an in-focus glimpse of Tom Tom's brother.

Unlike his decanus, the Old Boy looked the pinnacle of achievement, standing confidently erect by the side of an ornately carved walnut desk, dressed in a bespoke light tweed suit and pink shirt combination, almost certainly from Savile Row. Ferret guessed Henry Poole. Cyrano would know for certain. The open collar and double cuffs, combined with two days' worth of shaving stubble presented a rather unorthodox look for an Old Boy, especially when complemented by an irresistibly sexy aftershave.

Ferret replaced the glasses, listening intently as Tim Tim explained how three of his people had had their brilliant ideas stolen from under their very noses. As the resident snoop, he was to interview the victims and work out which one was the guilty party. The Old Boy handed over a folded piece of paper containing three names written in flowing script, with instructions to mingle with the staff, chat with the trio, and report back.

The detecting consultant paced up and down, stroking his chin. Tim Tim's logic was sound enough: cover one's tracks by appearing as a wailing victim. It was a common enough movie plot and a definite possibility.

Smack!

Carelessly, Ferret tripped over his own feet and fell headlong into a cabinet.

"Ow."

"I draw the line at breaking in to steal my Philip Marlowe cigarette case," said the Old Boy, helping Ferret to his feet.

The consultant squinted hard.

"It came with the hat." Tim Tim puffed his chest up. "Sotherby's."

Ferret tried his hardest to focus on the assorted memorabilia in front of him. "Vulcan ears?"

"Elven, as worn by the dashing Legolas in *The Lord of the Rings*. If you like movies, you must take the Walk of Fame on the third. That's where I keep my most splendid items."

Contrary to Tim Tim's instructions and due in no small part to the revulsion caused by his unorthodox appearance, Ferret spent the best part of the morning in the Chillax Lounge, drinking espresso and observing the male staff from a safe distance. The detecting consultant knew the Old Boy network from his tenure in the City, where they favoured positions of extreme power, their offices located high up in exclusive banking towers, competitively decorated with fashionable works of art.

Tom Tom's client base, in fact.

Dressed in geek finery, DC Ferret found he stood out from the crowd in entirely the wrong way. Try as he might to converse, Old Boy after Old Boy turned up their nose at him, apparently detecting in his presence a bad smell of the thoroughly stinky variety.

Not that Ferret cared.

While they were busy pulling faces, he was busy testing his Ferret senses.

Two hours later, with a light lunch thrown in for good measure, the detecting consultant had a good idea what he was dealing with. As with all Old Boy strongholds, there was a veil of secrecy erected against outsiders. Behind the veil he sensed an underlying current of mischievous excitement. Try as he might, he was unable to put his finger on the cause. Briefly, he thought he was on to something when a pair of giggling Old Boys carrying a small wooden chest that was clearly precious blundered into the lounge. Flustered, they covered their cargo and ran away.

Shaking his head, Ferret unpacked the SniffPhreak, slung it over his shoulder and set off on his first undercover mission intent on acting as geeky as possible.

Fondling the Phreak's dials as though they were forged from pure dilithium crystal, Ferret made his way slowly around the lounge, then the rest of the fourth floor, detecting for listening devices, exactly as Marcus had shown him the previous evening.

Having verified that no GSM devices were operating in the prescribed frequency ranges, Ferret took the lift to the executive floor, where two of the suspects had their offices. Here, Ferret discovered an ornate coffee machine with highly polished copper pipes protruding from various points and looping back on themselves. Analogue dials indicated flow pressure and coffee density. From the rich roast smell emanating from its midriff, the machine contained not only the facility to grind beans, but also an advanced caffeine delivery mechanism.

Hyper-real shots, delivered fresh from a coffee-calculating engine, thought Ferret, stroking the machine.

On a hunch, he scanned the machine from top to bottom.

"Harry is definitely hot for one of us," said a chap in a sharp-cut dark-blue suit, accidentally barging Ferret out of the way.

"I do believe you're right." A chap in a sharp-cut petrol-blue suit accidentally dug him in the ribs from the other side. "She's the pinnacle of allure, old boy. One day my flag and I will scale those dizzying heights, and I shall plant her. Better make it a double."

"And when you've finished planting, you'll have her sacked," quipped Dark Blue.

Petrol Blue grinned from ear to ear.

Ferret stepped away from the coffee machine, removed the geek goggles and gave them a quick wipe. Glancing sideways, he spied a flash of shoulder-length blonde hair. The owner waved. He returned the gesture.

"Well, what do you know!" Petrol Blue strode purposefully into Ferret's personal space and gave his jacket lapel a good tug. "This isn't from the Row!"

"Excuse me!" said Ferret. "Hands off the Maison Burton."

"How dare you!" Dark Blue stood his ground, sizing up the situation. "A double double for me, old boy."

"He's not wearing a tie," jeered Petrol Blue.

"Slob," said Dark Blue mockingly.

"What IS it wearing on its feet?" Petrol Blue pointed down, chuckling.

"Clark's pasties," said Ferret defiantly.

"I say, Malory," said Petrol Blue, "do you think this thing has any taste whatsoever?"

"One doubts it, Clifford."

"This thing has a name," growled the detective, "and it's called Ferret."

"On a Grrr'sday one does not simply announce one's name." Clifford smiled sardonically.

"Grrr!" The detective raised his hands, offering up a set of claws. "I'm Ferret."

"Grrr!" replied Malory. "For your disgraceful behaviour, I pronounce you a naughty tiger."

"Before we punish you with the naughty tiger hat," said Clifford condescendingly, "what *are* you doing?"

"I work in computers." Ferret exhaled hard through his nose. "I'm checking whether your office is suitable for a wireless network."

"Then your firm better pull its polyester socks up," said Malory. "We already have one."

"Installed by my sapling of a brother. Are you questioning his integrity?"

"I'm sure it works perfectly well," said Ferret, "but I bet it's not as shiny as the new one."

"I'm not convinced I care for you," said Malory.

"Is it security-certified?" asked Ferret.

"We all know each other and each other's families," growled Clifford. "This firm is founded on personal trust."

"Ha!" said the detective. "Clearly you haven't heard of the cyberwarriors of doom, sworn thieves of data. They operate around these parts."

"Well," said Malory, "we have had some of our best ideas stolen recently."

Clifford screwed up his face. "You're not one of us, Ferret. Be off with you."

"That won't be happening," said Ferret. "I'm authorised to check out all the offices, find any potential hacker hot spots, and close them down. Starting with yours."

"You sad little man." Malory sneered contemptuously.

"Just so you understand," said Clifford, "we're both highly motivated, finely tuned tigers who don't have time for pond scum."

The two boys turned and marched off, coffees in hand. Ferret tagged along, half blind. As he passed the blonde girl's desk, out of the corner of the glasses he saw her flash him a wink, causing a stirring of the loins. Despite his appearance, evidently there were two games of tiger versus prey in town. The difference was if the tigress with the tresses caught him, he'd let her eat him in one bite, whereas if the boys tried any of that public-school nonsense, they'd get a damn good whopping.

After he'd scanned the executive suites for every type of surveillance device known to man, Ferret headed down to the admin floor and the Walk of Fame, discovering to his delight that Tim Tim specialised in collecting not only movie props but full costumes too.

He polished the glasses, reading a sign: *Raiders of the Lost Ark*.

"Who'd have guessed that Indy is so tall?" he mumbled to himself.

"Talking to oneself is the first sign of madness," said a voice from behind.

"And answering oneself is the second," replied Ferret, making claws. "Grrr!"

"Grrr!" The stranger smiled wryly, reading the detecting consultant's name badge. "Hello, Ferret. I'm Damien. You must be new."

"I'm doing a survey for a company-wide wireless network," said Ferret awkwardly.

"What did you do to earn the naughty tiger hat?"

"I upset a pair of clowns." The detective's hand moved instinctively towards the dunce's cap, embroidered with a motif of A.A. Milne's Tigger. "It's my reward for speaking out of turn."

"It's good you're participating. Many of our clients just don't get it."

Ferret blushed. "Actually, I think it's pretty cool. In a geeky sort of way."

Damien raised an eyebrow.

"What's your role here at Grrr!?" asked the detective.

"I'm the senior junior account executive for new media. Basically, anything to do with the Interweb."

Ferret felt butterflies in his stomach. He'd never really been one for disguises and pointless fibs. He reminded himself that Sherlock Holmes was an expert at both. His asked his suave new pal with tightly cropped black hair accentuated by extended black sideburns, a few questions about his job. All the while he was wishing it was he who was wearing the ultra-trendy black suit with a black shirt and black tie.

As the account exec jabbered away, Ferret saw his thumbs twitch. "You're a gamer," he blurted, flexing his own thumbs in a similar manner.

"Thank god!" Damien took a deep breath. "At last, someone who isn't a day-tripper. I'm a big fan of anything that involves killing Nazis, preferably first-person shoot-'em-ups with big weapons."

"For me it's zombies."

"Cool daddy."

Ferret was unable to stop himself from asking Damien the most pertinent question of the moment, the one on everyone's lips: "DeathWorld. What do you know?"

"Nothing much" The account exec moved in close. "Aw, what the hell. This is strictly hush-hush. We're running the communications campaign, in cahoots with *Boyztoyz* magazine."

Ferret rushed to ask the follow-up question: "Have you . . ."

"Does the Pope wear a salmon-pink corset?"

"Barbarous Monks Attack, the Vatican City Stakeout Pack," laughed Ferret. "That must be worth a high-five."

"Not on a Grrr'sday."

"Grrr!" they shouted together, clawing the space in between, falling about tittering.

Once the release of DW:A had been broached, Damien was unable to stop gushing.

"I've only had twenty minutes of play," he confided, "but in that time I found a chainsaw mounted on a codpiece. An escort tried to blow me, setting it off. I tell you, when the saw hit bone, my entire body shook. One of her eyeballs flew out and struck me on the cheek. It was wet. As in seriously gooey. This game has literally changed my life."

Ferret was so excited he tried to ask several questions at once. Instead of a coherent sentence, what came out was more of a strangled "werrrrg."

Damien looked guiltily at his watch. "I really must be going."

"It's been nice talking to you," said Ferret.

Damien nodded, half smiling, shards of sin spilling out from his soft brown eyes. Ferret sensed there was something else. Something exciting. Something he dare not tell, which involved a treasure chest of some kind. And then he was gone, whatever secret he was keeping fully intact.

"DC Ferret. The Case of the Missing Ideas. All suspects interviewed. If I had to place a bet, Damien wins hands down, although I so want Clifford and Malory to be guilty. Certainly, the senior junior knows something. However, I'm not convinced I've got all my ducks fully coconut-encased yet." Digging deep, Ferret came up with an old saying, reserved for just such a situation. "As they used to say at The Consultancy, if you're stuck, flirt."

Ever since their brief encounter earlier, Ferret knew he was destined to meet the executive Personal Assistant. While he hadn't yet seen her fully in focus, he knew instinctively from the wink and the way she rolled her Rs as he walked past that she was gorgeous. Although he liked the feel of a great-looking girl on his arm, for him, looks were not paramount in the same way they were for his French friend, who had far more patience than he when it came to high-maintenance women with eating disorders. Ferret preferred sporty girls with good teeth and something to grab hold of in the bottom department.

"So you're Ferret," said the executive PA, adjusting her shoulder-length hair enticingly. "Pleased to meet you. I'm Juliet. Tell me, what kind of a geek are you?"

"Actually," smiled the detecting consultant, removing his specs, "I'm not much of a geek at all."

The PA screwed up her nose. "If you're not much of a geek, you're wasting my time."

"Perhaps I'm a geek who can't tell the truth," said the detective, pitching to save the game.

Juliet pursed her lips. "I don't date frauds or liars. Heaven knows, it's not difficult to find either working here."

Ferret felt the situation slipping from his grasp. "If I tell you what kind of geek I am, you can't tell anyone else."

"Ah." The PA smiled. "You're a closet geek."

"You have to swear not to tell . . . on something really important."

Juliet produced a glossy magazine from her top drawer and put it face up on her desk, drawing attention to the feature article entitled 'Are Geeks the New Chic?'. "I swear on this month's *Glamour* not to reveal Ferret's inner geek."

There was something inherently sexy about Juliet that pressed Ferret's buttons. He leaned over to whisper in her ear, and as he did so, he caught her eye. He felt himself melt, slipping out of his body and into hers. He felt her hands, so tiny compared to his own; he felt her feet, as she jiggled them up and down beneath the desk. In shock, he jerked back, standing upright, his face screwed up into a tight ball.

"I knew it was too good to last." The PA glared at him. "You're a geek with special needs."

"I can assure you . . ." The detective stuttered to get the words out. In all his years, this had never happened before. He felt himself begin to melt out of his body again. "Jee . . . zuz!"

"You have Tourettes." Juliet shook her tresses. "I'm sorry, but last year's must-have fashion accessory isn't this year's."

"On my word." Ferret felt himself claw the air. "I do not have a medical condition."

"Are you sure?"

The detective whistled for breath, aware that as he pulled himself out of Juliet, a series of spasms visible to the outside world, racked his body. If he concentrated really hard, he was just about able to hold himself together. Feeling his composure return, he bent over the desk and whispered sweet words into Juliet's ear, surrendering the identity of his inner geek.

"Why," she said, "you sly old . . . Ferret."

Brring!

"Excuse me." The spell broken, Ferret withdrew his mobile phone. "*Bonjour, mon amie*. Uh huh. I'm really sorry to hear that. Yes, I'm holding to our bargain. Uh huh. Thank you very much. *Au revoir*."

The detecting consultant gazed longingly into Juliet's deep-green eyes, warmer than a forest pool. He felt himself teetering on the brink, ready to fall into her again, headfirst this time. "I was wondering, would you do me the honour of accompanying me to dinner tonight? There's a table for two come up at short notice at Hot Coco."

Juliet jumped up and kissed Ferret on the cheek. "You're a real luvvie! The waiting list for that place is three months long. Even Tim Tim can't get in. Sir Elton and David were there only last night. It's *the* place to be seen."

Ferret grinned.

Apparently, Lady Fortune was finally tipping him a nod.

Screw the geek finery.

Tonight he would wear his favourite black number, a slimming off-the-peg Armani suit that had long been his evening wear of choice.

Brring!

Marcus.

The detective's stomach turned a barrage of summersaults, emulating a Russian gymnast vying for a medal spot. He took the call.

"I'm really sorry," he said, hanging up, "but I have to leave early to meet a delivery man. I'll see you in the bar at Hot Coco at eight."

"Not so fast, geek boy." Juliet shook her head. "If you think for even one second that I'm going to the hottest place in town with you looking like *that*, you're sadly mistaken. You need a makeover. And that means a haircut, new togs, and some decent shoes. Plus, the glasses are disgusting."

"But I won't be able to see a thing," said Ferret.

Juliet clicked her fingers, summoning a girl with greasy hair and thick black glasses, from a nearby cupboard. "Intern, bring me the top-two magazines from the fashion rack."

The PA turned to Ferret. "If you want a date with me, all you have to do is bring together the look I choose in the next two hours. Intern: chop, chop. Hurry up, we don't have all day."

# Chapter Eight: Sparkles

Juliet was unsure what to make of her date for the night. Ferret looked like he should scrub up nicely, but it was impossible to tell with all that hair. What if he had a horrible-shaped head that looked like an orange? What if he was thinning on top and it was all an undercover comb-over? To begin with, she'd wondered if it was real; a quick feel when she'd given her geek boy that peck on the cheek confirmed that if it was a wig, it wasn't a cheap one.

What was she thinking, dating a geek?

Granted, he was different to the sort of gentlemen she usually went for, but was that a good thing?

What if he couldn't understand the menu, or had a grisly allergy?

If only she'd thought it through.

But Hot Coco was a dream date, far too good to turn down on a Grrr'sday night.

Against her basic instinct, she'd have to trust him. The problem was, trusting a geek wasn't something she'd tried before. What if he developed a crush there and then and tried to take her home and eat her? She'd read all about cannibal geeks. Malory had sent her a link earlier. She'd have to make sure he was full before they left the restaurant. She could do that. And she'd find out whether he collected freezers, because that was how European cannibal geeks stored their victims. According to Clifford, any-way.

Tattoos.

She hadn't asked her geek about tattoos. What if he was covered from head to toe in tribal art underneath those distasteful clothes? What if he had a crush on a pop star like Madonna? He might be covered in a Madge montage.

This was hopeless.

She pinched herself on the thigh.

He was a film geek with a nerdy habit for remembering movies, just like he'd whispered in her ear. He better not spend the entire night boring her with film facts that he considered interesting, which were really as dull as flat Champagne. If he did, she'd make it clear he was dumped, for now and eternity, in this life and the next.

He'd understand that. It would penetrate his possibly odd-shaped geek skull.

Thoughtfully, she'd had her intern print out an etiquette guide and hand it to him before he left for a haircut, just in case he didn't know the rules of behaviour for a restaurant. From what she'd read, geeks didn't really get out much and many of them had rare disorders that made them immensely clever but at the same time quite impossible to have a relationship with. Getting them out was the second step in the rehabilitation process, right after a good clip.

He was her new venture.

She would train him like a new dog.

A couple of her friends had tried dating geeks recently, but it had all gone horribly wrong. That was because they'd chosen runts rather than pedigrees. She'd checked Ferret's posture, his build, and his cheekbones. He certainly didn't look like the average geek; he had more of a rugby build. He certainly wasn't fat, but perhaps a little soft around the middle. Nice eyes, with a twist of hazel. Ideally, he'd need a nose job. It was just a little too long for her liking, with a bump where it had once been broken.

It was worrying that he'd had a spaz fit so near her desk. But he bravely worked through it and that showed training, just like stutter control. She'd simply be taking over where someone else left off and finishing the job.

"Perhaps we'll see you about later, Harry," said Hartley, heading for the door with Manleigh, his partner for the night chosen by draw earlier in the day.

"Goodbye, Harts. Mans." Harts looked great in his new tux, so she blew him a kiss. "And good luck. Both of you."

"Enjoy your date, Harry." Manleigh sniggered, throwing a small silver rugby ball, which she caught one-handed.

"Enjoy yours too."

Juliet looked at her gold-trim watch. Time to leave or she'd be later than her planned five minutes late. It occurred to her that she'd forgotten to tell her geek that there was a competition tonight, for a prize she was destined never to win. It was the one night of the month when all the boys went out in groups to get horrendously hammered on gak and alcohol and overturn as many celebrities as possible. She hated that word, gak. A lady would only ever consider calling it fairy dust or sparkles.

Grrr'sday night was all about capturing the most column space in the tabloids the next day. When all was said and done, she was a lady and tripping celebrities and pretending it wasn't her . . . well, that wasn't an act a real lady would ever be caught undertaking. She was more than just a lady, though. She was a prize filly, and that counted for something, no matter what the boys said. Her brothers both worked in insurance; they both ran their own firms. They'd been to the right schools. They had respect and a decent family name with entries in *Debrett's*. Everyone in the Home Counties knew the Harringtons. They'd lived there for six generations. Had she been a half filly, she'd have to marry anyone who would take her. As a prize filly, the choice was hers. Her family's approval wasn't guaranteed, but then she wasn't going to present them with a Half-Boy like Tim Tim's brother and fight them to marry for love. That *would* be silly.

In her opinion, the stigma of a Half-Boy brother was something that Tim Tim dealt with very well. Nobody mentioned it to his face, but they spread some nasty rumours about his mummy behind his back. What was she thinking, leaving her husband for someone who wasn't a Boy at all? His daddy was beyond reproach; nobody would ever dare say anything about him. In public, Tim Tim wore a brave face. He didn't ever say a bad word about his brother, who was the lowest kind of Half-Boy. In private, she'd heard him curse Tom Tom's name a thousand times. At least he had the decency to use his new daddy's surname, so no one from outside knew they were related.

Occasionally, Tim Tim cursed his sister too. She was from good stock and still young enough to change her ways and settle down, despite what happened at that awful engagement party. Juliet wasn't there, but she'd heard about it. It sounded like a public ordeal of the worst kind; horribly vile to watch.

Juliet reached into her micro-handbag, so sized because she had no intention of carrying anything other than minimal makeup, an emergency fifty-pound note, and a credit card. She withdrew a compact hand mirror and, fiddling with the silver rugby ball, forced it open to reveal a thumbnail-sized block of buttery white powder.

Sparkles, she thought. No point in not having a quick toot. They were heading to a fashionable restaurant to be seen, after all. It wasn't like they were going out to eat.

Juliet left the intern typing up notes and rushed to meet her taxi, knocking Junior Eric to the floor and almost spearing his head with her heel. Silly boy, always getting in the way. But then he was the litter runt, taken on as a favour to his older brother, Senior Eric, who Tim Tim once bunked with. Damien knew better than to get in her way. He anticipated where she was going, in that debonair way of his.

"Get up, boy."

Eric's bottom lip quivered. He refused to look her in the eye.

Damien and Junior Eric.

They were the nearest thing that Grrr! had to a pair of weirdos, but not as weird as the creep in the frock coat who appeared from time to time to see Tim Tim. He wasn't right. She was careful never to be alone with him, even if he was an Old Boy. There was something about the way he looked right through her that made her flesh crawl.

"Miss," said Damien, smiling to reveal a set of immaculate white teeth, framed by a set of devilish canines.

"Good evening, tiger."

"I hear you're on a hot geek date."

"And?"

Damien looked sheepishly away.

She left the pair talking about that silly DeathWorld game that every-one was so excited about. Even Ferret had asked her about it — until she cut him short and sent him on his way. It was a project. She made a point of staying away from projects, unless Tim Tim specifically told her otherwise.

Damien and Eric stood in the lobby watching her leave. She knew what they were really up to. They were going to share a special cigarette then sneak back into the office and get the Precious out while everyone else was busy playing the Grrr'sday Game. She felt their eyes fix firmly on her bum as she climbed into the waiting cab. Good. Her little red dress and Louboutin heels, set to stun, were supposed to turn heads. An audience was never a bad thing, even if it did consist of two weirdos and a cab driver.

Juliet directed the driver to the edge of Mayfair.

Quite how her geek had managed to get a table for two was a mystery to her. She'd been trying to get in for months. If the owners were Old Boys, there would be none of this nonsense. They'd be welcomed in like old friends and given the best table in the house.

The cab crawled out of Soho Square, heading south through bustling crowds who refused to stick to the pavements. Juliet put on her shades; immediately, people began to look at her.

Out in public, she was often mistaken for an A-list star, an identity mishap that had gained her entry into many a private party.

Sparkles.

Everything was covered in fairy dust. Her mouth felt dry. She needed a drink. Bubbles and sparkles. Was there any better feeling?

The PA's thoughts turned to Ferret. If he was a simple geek doing a simple geek job, she wouldn't be going out with him. Tim Tim had called her the other day demanding coffee, which was a job she usually delegated to her intern. That day, he was in a private meeting with his brother and she wanted to know what was being said. When she entered the office, they'd carried on plotting as if she didn't have an ounce of brains between her beautiful ears. Tom Tom promised to send a detective. She'd heard it loud and clear.

Which meant her geek was here to investigate the missing ideas.

The first idea went missing at roughly the same time as the Precious arrived. The Precious that they wouldn't let her see. The Precious that the creep in the frock coat demanded be veiled in the utmost secrecy. Everyone had stopped work and crowded around Tim Tim to get a good look. Apart from her and the intern. It was an Old Boy thing, subject to Old Boy Club rules, strictly no girls. She hadn't seen it, but she knew where they were hiding it. Officially, there were three victims, but she knew of more.

Clifford and Malory were going to get what was coming to them.

This much she swore, there and then on her rugby ball sparkles tin. It was months ago when it happened; she was sure they'd forgotten about it by now, even if she hadn't. It was the night of the BAFTAs. They'd asked her to look after an up-and-coming star. Give him the works, they'd said. Later, when she'd discovered he was a lost tourist, they'd laughed at her until she wanted the ground to open up and swallow her whole. It was like being a schoolgirl again, told off for getting glitter in her hair by old Miss Sourpuss.

The taxi pulled up outside of Hot Coco. Juliet climbed out, switching herself on like Norma Jean Baker. She paid the cabbie, leaving a smile and a nice tip. She'd have her vengeance on the two who'd humiliated her, in this life or the next.

Perhaps, thought Juliet, it was time to learn a new film quote.

# Chapter Nine: Hot Coco

Ferret felt a bit of a prat.

Under the rules of *castigatio*, enforced by his friend Marcus, his *dignitas* was subject to a series of compensation punishments. With the first one out of the way, he found himself in the hottest restaurant in town dressed in a baggy black-velvet lounge suit resurrected from 1975, its multitudinous moth holes patched with mismatched fabric. He'd half-expected the staff to refuse him entry to Hot Coco, but it transpired he was well within the confines of the establishment's dress code. He'd just arrived forty years too late to be considered fashionable. The detective shuffled his shoulders. The frilly shirt he was wearing was of equal age to the suit and it itched, while the bowtie he sported was the size of a very portly vampire bat.

"This is horrible," he said, trying without luck to summon a bartender. "Everyone thinks I'm contaminated."

"It's no fun for me either." Marcus, his appointed chaperone for the night, reached out and touched him on the arm.

Fortunately for Ferret, once the collection of proof was out of the way, his friend had agreed to stand down. Already, Marcus had taken a series of photos positioning Ferret against the distinctive red-papered walls, making sure to capture the red-and-green tartan furniture of the bar. Doing his best to ignore his embarrassment, the detective concentrated on the only good point of the evening: At least his French friend was unable to play any actual part in the campaign of humiliation.

Without warning, a commotion broke out outside.

Cameras flashed, lighting up the facade.

Someone in restaurant livery held open the door.

In strode Juliet, turning every head two hundred and seventy degrees, including the maître d', who dropped the spoon he was polishing. Her pores oozed class, her dress shouted style; her makeup was pitched perfectly, showing off her fresh skin; her perfume hit the high notes, begging for a senseless ravishing. The instant he gazed into her eyes, Ferret felt himself melt once more, just as he had done earlier, only this time he let go. Lightning crackled, arcing between them. The girl in the little red dress

smiled; her eyes sparkled mischief. She strode up to Ferret, put her arm around his neck and kissed him, full on the lips.

From that moment onwards, she owned the place.

With a look of awe, Marcus waved goodbye and vanished into the night. For all Ferret cared, his friend might as well have been abducted by demons. He was too busy trying to come to terms with the feelings racing through his body. It was as if he'd stuck his fingers in an electrical socket and chosen not to remove them again.

Two complimentary vodka martinis appeared. Ferret and Juliet toasted the evening. The detective found he knew what it was to be Juliet, knew all of her spicy little turn-ons. Every time she thought about what she liked and how she liked it, he felt the bar rock. A wave of intense pheromones bounced between them, which caused quite the commotion amongst the clientele. The restaurant's owner, a celebrity chef with a television show, popped out to see what was going on. He greeted Juliet with a kiss on the cheek and a warm French welcome, allowing Ferret to catch his breath.

"Wow," he said. "That was some kiss."

Juliet winked. "I had no idea geeks were so sexy."

Ferret wasn't sure whether the words had been spoken or simply thought. It didn't matter. His game-plan for the evening, which essentially involved saying sorry a lot for the dodgy attire and specs whilst promoting the fine haircut and shoes, was already in tatters. He felt emboldened — ready to ditch the geek mask and be himself — when something unexpected happened.

"How much of a film nerd are you?" asked the PA.

"Actually, I direct. Mostly detective films shot using guerrilla techniques."

"How exciting! I've always wanted to date a moviemaker."

Damn, thought Ferret, what a stupid lie. Whilst it was a great fib for one-night stands, it was hardly a good footing on which to build a relationship.

Dinner passed by in a blur. Ferret enjoyed each of the dishes in turn, which were cooked in the French style with a modern twist, served with wine to match. His palette performed summersaults at each taste sensation. Juliet drank the wine and played with her food, trying the odd item, all the while collecting compliments from a string of passing admirers.

The detective had dated a lot of girls from many different countries in his time, yet none of them were anything compared to the lovely Juliet. It was an old cliché, but he felt he'd known her for the whole of his life. As they laughed together, Ferret found that with a little practice he was able to regulate the feeling of melting into his date. He concluded it was rather like learning to drive a car — there were slow bits and fast bits, a few twists, the odd hairpin bend and once, an emergency stop.

How they giggled at each other's stories. Ferret embellished his tales of making movies at university, amending the locations to the streets of London. Juliet talked about how she disliked riding horses but loved participating in the hunt, obviously. Clifford and Malory took a pair on the chin for being generally obnoxious. Then there was the prize for the best night out — the one she was destined never to win for daring to be born the wrong sex. A plot began to form between them, unspoken but there nonetheless. The detective suggested cocktails; Juliet supplied the location: the bar at the Dorchester.

They took a short cab ride to the hotel. As Ferret was paying the driver, a Bentley shot past, squealed to a halt, and disgorged a lone passenger right in front of the waiting paparazzi.

"Is that . . ." Ferret felt the words slur.

Acting on impulse, the girl in the little red dress pushed him centre stage. He donned the bottle-ends and stumbled forward, reminded of muddy days on the playing field, vision obscured by dirt. Tottering, he regained his balance at the last, but not before he'd pushed James Bond to the floor, right in front of the cameras. A crazy barrage of flashes caught the act for posterity. Doubly blinded, Ferret held his hands in front of his face and apologised profusely, offering the fallen star his hand and a complimentary martini, shaken not stirred. James was having none of it until he saw Juliet, at which point he was suddenly having too much of it. Juliet tweaked Bond's bum, to a further round of camera action, blew him a kiss, then grabbed Ferret by the arm and thrust him into the car from which the film star had emerged.

"Soho Square, please." Juliet turned to face him. "Darling, there's something you must see."

By the time the car reached Grrr! it was well after midnight. Unable to contain himself any longer, Ferret's animal passion bubbled over in the foyer. Juliet ignored the alarm begging for attention until the last, when she pushed Ferret aside and confidently typed in the security code with seconds to spare.

On the third floor, they headed through a maze of open-plan walk-ways towards the Walk of Fame, where they passed a pair of costumes from the latest telling of *Robin Hood*, followed by a single hobbit suit, worn by an extra in the party scene at Bag End. At the gangster section, which contained costumes and gun props from *The Godfather*, they turned right and stopped, sharing a long kiss up against the cases, feeling up each other's assets and, hearts beating madly, carried through with an earlier dare to dress up in costume, selecting hero clothes from the movie *The Living Daylights*.

Inside, Ferret ached for some kind of release. The longer he'd stayed melted into Juliet, the stranger he'd felt, until he had to admit he was both giddy and stuck. To begin with, being part of his date was hot and horny, but now, hours later, he was exhausted, drunk, and truth be told, a little frightened.

"In here," said his date, dragging him into the boss's office. She pointed. "That's Moneypenny's desk."

"Really?"

"Let's do it justice."


Unable to separate his own feelings from those of his date, Ferret was overwhelmed with the love they made. He had no idea who he was any-more. His entire world sloshed from side to side; one moment, he was tumbling down a dune of hot sand, arm in arm, feet burning. The next, he was dancing through summer rain, hand in hand, soaked by a gentle downpour of lukewarm water. He closed his eyes. Earlier, he'd compared being inside Juliet to driving a car. Now it felt like he was in the driver's seat of an out-of-control truck, running away from a great ball of flame, careening wildly towards another truck, also chased by a fireball.

He felt nails dig into his shoulders, gently at first, then sharper than cat's claws.

Fireball.

No escape.

Head-on collision. Brace. Here it comes . . .


After they'd made Tim Tim's desk respectable again, giggling and caress-ing each other, Ferret found himself back in control of his senses. As long as he didn't gaze into Juliet's eyes with abandon, he was fine. That was the trigger, he was sure of it.

"Back to my place?" he suggested.

Juliet nodded and put her arm around him. He returned the gesture. He found he was overjoyed to finally be back in his own skin, even though the feeling of being within Juliet came with an intimate closeness he'd never encountered before.

As they closed the door to Tim Tim's office, tittering at their naughty exploits, Ferret caught sight of the small brass-bound wooden chest the Old Boys had been coveting earlier in the day. Now, thanks to the time spent in Juliet, he knew what it contained. The boys called it their Precious and somehow it was related to the Case of the Missing Ideas. He kicked himself. As Ferret the Geek, he'd scanned every office in Grrr! but one. First thing in the morning, he'd put that right.

# Chapter Ten: Bank of Lies

"DC Ferret. The Case of the Missing Ideas. Friday ten o'clock. My head feels like it's packed full of jackhammers. There's been a new development, best explained with an old consultancy saying that goes like this: For every truth told, one makes a small deposit at the Bank of Lies."

During his illustrious consultancy career, Ferret had made a habit of nearly always telling the truth in those difficult situations where a small fib was often more convenient. According to his ex-colleagues, he'd built up a veritable fortune in unspent untruths, the equivalent of a couple of free whoppers. The previous evening, he'd cashed a Bank of Lies cheque for a really small white one, thinking that was the end of it. Today, he hadn't yet stepped foot inside Grrr! and already he'd been accosted regarding his links to Hollywood.

Ferret spotted Damien and held the lift door open. The senior junior stepped in beside him, a grimace on his face, trying desperately to focus through bloodshot eyes.

"I hear you had quite an opening night last night, Mr. Movie Director."

Ferret stared back through equally tired eyes. "Rumour certainly travels fast in this company."

The senior junior rubbed his face. "I hear you tripped up 007. It's second spot in the morning gossip columns. They're all asking 'who's the girl in the little red dress?'"

"Really?"

Damien nodded. "From what I hear, you're in hot contention to win Prizeday. Harts had a great claim: he and Mans dropped a male Welsh singer — pockets stuffed with ladies underwear — outside a nightclub, but it didn't make the papers. A word of warning: Certain parties won't like your success. You better watch your back."

The lift stopped at the first floor and in stepped Tim Tim. The senior junior blinked hard and ducked out. The Old Boy pressed the button marked "6," then, looking Ferret up and down, ribbed him about the patched-up dinner suit and congratulated him on the new haircut. According to the Grrr!-vine, both were Harry's doing.

"I hear you tripped up Bond." Tim Tim tapped his nose. "And you make movies."

Ferret groaned.

The Old Boy explained how he'd always loved film trivia, launching enthusiastically into a discussion of Peter Jackson's interpretation of Tolkien's work. Ferret didn't have much to contribute on the usefulness of hobbits in an industrialised society or the value of elves in the education system, but did his best to humour the boss, who had an opinion on virtually everything, including the use of balrogs as part of the war on terror. Ferret knew a lot of movie facts. They were things his brain soaked up like a sponge. He did his best to pitch in, but was ultimately defeated by the Tim Tim's superior knowledge about the personal habits of Middle Earth's denizens.

The lift reached its destination.

"Follow me." The Old Boy led Ferret into his office and offered him a seat.

The detective obliged. Recalling unfinished business with the Precious, he opened his case and fondled the Phreak, eyes searching for the chest, unable to locate it.

"Your aftershave," said Tim Tim inquisitively. "Is it your normal brand? Peculiar, I know, but I swear I smelt it in my office first thing."

"I have no idea what I slapped on this morning," said Ferret, cashing a Bank of Lies cheque.

It was then that he spotted something he wished he hadn't. It was behind Tim Tim's desk, resting just above the eye line next to a string of shrunken human heads threaded together through the ears.

Tim Tim followed his gaze. "It's a tribal necklace from *Tarzan and His Mate*."

Ferret smiled inanely, dying on the inside. He vaguely remembered flinging Juliet's underwear in the air the previous evening. In their loved-up haze, they'd obviously failed to retrieve it, for there it was, hanging from the boss's bookcase.

The Old Boy shook his head. "I brought you here to tell you your investigation is complete. Damien is the guilty party. No buts. Go away, find some evidence, complete your report, and we'll sack him before the Prizeday presentation. After that, award ceremony and Champagne. I see no point in going into the weekend on a downer."

Before Ferret could say a word, he found himself ushered out of the door.

SLAM!

The detective set out for the Chillax Lounge via the executive floor, hoping to catch a glimpse of Juliet. He paused by the coffee calculating engine, where he summoned a moderately sized cup of demonically creamy Italian coffee from the bowels of the heaving contraption. He listened contentedly to the single piston clunking away while sweet-smelling steam hissed noisily from a frontal orifice, surrounding the cup with a balloon of cloying mist.

Pffftt!

Shaking his head, Ferret collected the coffee. He'd assumed when he took the case that he'd be doing real detective work rather than a consultancy-style fit-up. Not that it mattered. He'd already concluded that out of the three candidates, the senior junior was the most likely culprit, although the Precious still gnawed away in the background. He didn't have any concrete evidence — only a feeling gleaned from Juliet — that it was somehow involved. First, he had to find it.

Ferret eyed up the girl in the little red dress. One of the rules of Prizeday that she'd explained first thing was that for judging purposes, attire must match that of the photograph from the night before. Ferret found himself reliving the feel of her mouth against his as their tongues caressed. He remembered gazing deep into her eyes, becoming part of her.

"Well, if it isn't the nerd." Malory appeared from behind, spitting the words caustically into Ferret's ear, breaking the spell.

"The geek," said Clifford, approaching from the other side. "I hear he makes really terrible movies that no one bothers to watch, not even his family."

"Listen, child," said Malory. "We're here to threaten you."

Clifford smugly folded his arms. "We know something about you."

Malory took up a similar stance. "Vacate the premises by midday."

"Do not attend the Prizeday ceremony," said Clifford, "or there will be horrible consequences."

Ferret dismissed the threat and headed off to compile his report, thinking about Prizeday. The fact that he'd been menaced must mean he and Juliet were in a good place on the leaderboard. He wondered what the gruesome twosome might have on him.

They definitely didn't know he was affiliated with The Network or he'd be involved in a beating. The Old Boys didn't take kindly to rival organisations, especially the secret ones. And The Network was certainly secret. According to Tristan, who was the recognised authority on such matters, it was so secret it had never once been mentioned in print during its entire history.

Ferret put his hand in his pocket, his fingers coming to rest on a small rubber rectangle.

His father, he thought. They might know something about Wolfgang. Not that he wanted to go there.

All his father had left behind was a bunch of mouldy old files that didn't make any sense, a phial of liquid, and an obnoxious note that should have been an apology but wasn't. The old bugger was dead. Good riddance.

While growing up, he could live with the lack of a father figure. He'd enjoyed the space and sense of freedom. But when Wolfgang appeared unannounced at the weekends, those were the memories that lay waiting like deadly jellyfish, ready to sting. As everyone knows, the only way to deal with a jellyfish sting is for a fellow to urinate on it, and this pretty much summed up his relationship with his father: poisonous and full of piss.

In the last six months, he'd lost his job, his command of the decuria, and been the subject of an ongoing investigation by the Financial Standards lot.

Where was Wolfgang in all that time?

Ferret slapped himself.

Whenever he thought about his father, piss and poison was all that came of it.

He groaned.

This detecting lark was proving to be much more complicated than feeding proprietary knowledge in one end of his banking friend and watching bank notes come out the other. Not that this was an option. Until the investigation for insider trading was officially closed, he'd been warned to stay away from mergers and acquisitions.

Juliet appeared, and with a smile, took a seat beside him. "I've heard on the Grrr!-vine that more ideas have gone missing."

"You know about that?" said Ferret, caught off guard.

"Of course I do, silly."

This time the victim was Junior Eric, who the PA fingered as Damien's bestie. She supplied Ferret with directions, instructing him to be as discreet as possible. He agreed to follow the lead, tearing himself away from her contours with much reluctance. He moved to kiss her goodbye, only to receive a rebuke for being inappropriate in public.

Meow!

In the next few hours he had to complete a report proving Damien's guilt, dance around the implications of an unspecified character slur, win a prize, and, for the sake of his reputation, recover a pair of luscious scarlet panties and matching bra from Tim Tim's office wall before they were discovered.

DC Ferret headed to the desk of Junior Eric, who was busy tucking into a Soho Special hangover melt consisting of double bacon and Swiss cheese with triple analgesic. The detective salivated at the smell of cooked bacon, wishing it was he on the end of the baguette. He was about to introduce himself when he heard bustling from behind. Turning around, he found the boss inches from his face.

"Why aren't you following orders?" Tim Tim glared threateningly. "I didn't employ you to do your own thing."

Eric tried desperately to swallow a mouthful of melt, but not quickly enough for the boss, who cuffed him about the head for eating too slowly.

"I'm collecting evidence." Ferret lowered his voice. "Junior Eric and I should talk somewhere in private. May I borrow your office?"

"I don't do sharing. I'm an only child!" Tim Tim flicked his head back. "You're not sitting in Moneypenny's chair and that's that! Now, Mr. Movie Director, stop wasting my time and finish that report."

With which the CEO and owner of Grrr! stormed off, slamming doors behind him.

"Who . . . Who . . . Who are you?" stammered Junior Eric, swallowing a mouthful of food. "Last night I heard you make action movies, but it's hush-hush and I'm not to tell anyone — except then you were a geek, and now you make detective films and you don't look like the same geek anymore, and… and you might be going out with Juliet, except I've never seen your tie. I'm confused."

"Finish your breakfast," said Ferret, pulling up a seat.

Nervously, Junior Eric stuffed the baguette half into his mouth and began to chew, uncomfortably at first, all the while watching Ferret. He seemed to be expecting a slap for some ridiculous eating rule of which he'd previously been unaware. Finally, unable to stand it any longer, he savaged his breakfast like a hungry hyena. Tentatively, Ferret began to question him regarding the missing ideas, which he supposed were part of

a communications campaign. The junior let out a whimper and cowered in
the chair, covering his head with his arms.

"This is daft." Ferret backed off. "How can you know an idea you're
working on has been stolen if you can't show me where it's been used by
someone else?"

"It's the file I'm working on." The junior blushed. "It was there before. Now it's gone."

Finally, thought Ferret, they were getting somewhere.

"Could you have accidentally deleted it?"

"No. It was definitely there before . . ."

Ferret opened up his briefcase, pulled out the SniffPhreak, powered it
up, and checked the dials.

"Meet my lie detector," he said.

Junior Eric's eyes darted from side to side. Nervously, he twitched
his thumbs.

"You're a gamer," said Ferret.

The junior's head moved slowly up and down.

"Let's role-play a scenario. You were bored, you took five minutes
away from your desk for a secret session, leaving your computer unlocked.
When you returned, the files were gone."

"That's . . . about right."

"Then we must discover who was using your computer while you
were not."

"Damien does most of our support," said the junior, helpfully. "Unfortunately, he's in with a client. Why don't you call one of your nerd
friends? Nerds like you always have friends who know more about computers than they should."


"DC Ferret. The Case of the Missing Ideas. Soho Melt Bar."

Away from the cauldron of Grrr!, munching on a breakfast bap, the
detective mulled over the evidence.

Junior Eric's missing ideas were recorded in a computer file. Which
meant that in all likelihood, so were the other ideas. The junior hadn't expected the theft, which pointed to someone he trusted. He and Damien
were besties. It was impossible to be certain without the professional opinion of a techno-geek, but the working hypothesis was there: Damien, as
support guru, had a means of accessing all the Grrr! computers remotely.
The only thing missing was a motive. Banging away at the problem alone,
Ferret was reminded of an old consultancy saying that had served him

proudly for years: When the going gets tough, flood the project with more consultants.

Without a budget, this wasn't a serious option, which left only one clear course of action. He needed to interview as many account executives as possible to try and work out what Damien might want with all those brilliant ideas.

Back in the Chillax Lounge, Ferret set up stall.

"Thank you, Manleigh. Great performance," schmoozed the detecting consultant, waving goodbye to yet another account executive with stars in his eyes. "We'll be in touch. Tell Fearnley I'll be ready for him shortly."

Another half a dozen and he'd have all the non-suspect employees captured on his phone. It had taken a huge cheque from the Bank of Lies to make it so, but with so many fibs already in circulation, he figured one more would make little difference.

He felt tired. The hangover was shrieking away between his ears like a fire alarm, ruining his intuition. What he wanted was to lie down in a dark room, but instead, he'd been auditioning Old Boys, asking discreet questions only to discover that Damien was universally liked and considered a thoroughly dependable chap. The thing they were really interested in was Prizeday gossip. Ferret learned that Findley was out of the running. The tennis star he'd elbowed over was a look-alike. And Bentley's run-in with soccer royalty was also discounted, because he'd accidentally toppled the ex-popstar missus as well as the main man.

The detective was nearly done. Soon, he'd turn the screws on his gamer friend.

"Ferret!" growled a voice from behind. "My office. Now!"

The detective rolled his eyes and gathered up his bits and pieces. He followed the boss for another ritual telling off. The Old Boy's nostrils flared with the intensity of a donkey about to become a gelding. It certainly wasn't a look for the cover of *Vogue*. Cautiously, Ferret shut the door and sat down, choosing the seat nearest to Tim Tim's desk.

"What's this I hear about you making a movie?"

The art of lying is all about consistency, thought Ferret, liberally cashing another cheque. He explained that sleuthing was something he'd started doing alongside his moviemaking career, which was based around the crime-thriller genre. While he was finding the evidence he needed, he'd hit on the idea of a movie set in a communications company. It seemed reasonable, therefore, to run a series of casting auditions to find out how many of Tim Tim's valued employees displayed thespian tendencies.

"You're audacious beyond belief!" Tim Tim strode over to the window and turned away.

Taunted by the underwear in front of his eyes, the detective leant forward and snatched at the bra and briefs, which annoyingly remained just out of reach.

"I'm waiting . . ."

"Tim Tim." Ferret inched the chair forward as far as he dared and, sequestering a starry-tipped wand from its mount on the desk, tried really hard to retrieve the smalls. "May I conduct an audition on your premises?"

"I'm still waiting . . ."

It was then that the penny dropped. "You want to be in the movie. Absolutely. No audition required. In fact, I've already written you a part. I was saving it as a surprise."

"Really?" Tim Tim turned around, catching Ferret in the act.

"By the power of Hogwarts, I declare it so," said the detective, improvising with a wave of the wand.

"I've always dreamed of being on the big screen," said Tim Tim, a mist drifting across his eyes.

Ferret returned the stick to its mount. "Do you think I might continue the auditions in here?"

Tim Tim took a deep breath, snorted impressively, and bellowed: "Out! And don't shut the door behind you. That's my privilege."

SLAM!

The detecting consultant looked at the cheap plastic watch adorning his wrist. Midday. Perhaps he might interest his new girlfriend in a spot of lunch. Given that she knew all of the account executives, interviewing her might just enable him to complete the report without resorting to outright fabrication.

"Mr. Movie Director." Juliet wound a lock of hair around her finger as he approached her desk. "What a pleasant surprise."

"Ah, Ferret," said Malory, sidling out of the shadows, voice brimming with smug self-satisfaction. "It's time to spill your secret."

"As the game of accusation and denial is so terribly passé," said Clifford, approaching from behind, "we've prepared a jingle."

"There's a nerd who's not a nerd," sung Malory in an impressive baritone.

"An accursed trouser ferret," sung his partner.

"Who directs most awful films."

"Which have no saving merit."

"This noxious lying vagabond."

"All of Grrr! did fool."

"He wears no tie, he has no house."

"He didn't go to public school!"

"We found your social media page and asked around," said Malory. "No one remembers you."

"Not even with a nose like that," added Clifford.

"Is this true?" asked the girl in the little red dress, her lips quivering.

Ferret blushed, lost for words.

"There's more," said Malory, clearing his throat. "A British icon he did trip."

"A most unsavoury action," sung Clifford.

"He insults our queen and realm."

"With his lack of traction."

"You're no longer funny," said Malory in a high, pathetic voice.

"You're a scared little bunny," improvised Clifford.

"Be a gentleman tiger."

"Admit you're a fraud and a liar."

Ferret felt a chasm open up in front of him. He teetered on the brink, remembering how it felt to be a part of the girl in the little red dress. "I . . ."

"I thought I knew you," sobbed Juliet. Taking her micro-handbag, she headed for the ladies' bathroom. "Just stay away from me. In this life and the next."

Not wanting to let go, Ferret gave chase, only to have the door to the ladies' slammed in his face. He felt his head whirl and his legs turn to rubber.

"As you've chosen not to leave," said Malory, barging past the detective, "you simply must attend the awards ceremony."

Clifford pushed past on the other side. "It's going to be quite the show."

As the pair departed, chuckling, Ferret felt the breakfast bap start to shift. The loss of his new love so soon was too much to take in. His stomach began that familiar reel, reminiscent of an old wooden big dipper without the benefit of modern hydraulics.

Bringing his many years of hangover experience to bear, Ferret composed himself and headed for the gents' room, determined not to let a minor setback ruin his day.

The detective stood hesitantly outside Tim Tim's door.

Once again, he'd been summoned to see the headmaster for what felt like an alleged impropriety behind the bicycle sheds. Perhaps he should simply leg it and make his apologies from a distance.

What might the great Sherlock Holmes do?

He wouldn't be in this predicament, thought Ferret. He'd have solved the case the previous day, within ten minutes of walking through the door. Some detective he was shaping up to be. A humble consultant with a hangover dressed as a geek, pretending to be an undercover movie director, with a very hot ex-girlfriend. Damn the Bank of Lies for its flexible monetary policy!

On the plus side, he concluded, at least it couldn't get any worse.

Ferret knocked, and upon hearing Tim Tim's voice, entered.

"Ah, the man of the hour." Tim Tim turned to gaze out of the window, looking down on Soho Square.

Nervously, DC Ferret positioned himself as close to the frillies as possible, realising for the first time that what he was looking at was Tim Tim's "Barbarian Wall," which included a pair of Achilles's sandals from *Troy*, a polished silver facemask from *Gladiator,* and a cutlass from *Sinbad and the Eye of the Tiger.*

"I have recently spoken with my younger brother," said Tim Tim, turning around. "We'll come to that shortly. Have you finished your report?"

"It's as polished as possible, given the time constraints."

"Excellent news. Since we last spoke, I've had a revelation. Damien is innocent. The real perpetrator has been running rings around us all this whole time, and they almost got away with it." Tim Tim thrust a slip of folded paper into the detective's hand. "A last-minute rewrite, please."

In an instant, Ferret found himself ejected, the door slamming behind him, the Old Boy's orders ringing in his ears.

He had an hour and a half to rework the evidence to fit the new culprit. Then, thanks to blabbermouth Tom Tom, he had to showcase his consultancy talents and dismiss the thief permanently from the Old Boy fold.

The detective chewed his lip.

With the hangover finally abating, his intuition was back. He hadn't opened the slip of paper; he didn't need to. It was written all over Tim Tim's face. Given this development, he was now certain that Damien and the newly fingered thief were stooges. Whatever the Precious was, it was key to solving the case. He had to find it, and fast. Otherwise he'd lose the girl, lose Prizeday, and have his detecting credentials permanently blackened.

# Chapter Eleven: The Precious

Damien tapped slender fingers on the underside of the desk, picking out the tune to *Night on Bald Mountain* to remind himself he was still alive. He'd had to endure two hours of pointless planning with Brundt, an Old Stamfordian with aspirations, who couldn't tell his posterior from his synovial hinge joint, while Bramley, the senior account executive, droned on and on about rubbish that didn't exist outside of his own imagination. When they were done, his orders were to turn the senior's fantasies into a believable interweb ad campaign. For now, he wanted nothing more than to get out of here and fondle the Precious. He loosened his tie. Even thinking that word made him feel libidinous inside. He'd swapped his allotted timeslot with Pratley first thing, who had in turn swapped with Cholmondeley.

Come twelve forty-five, it was his. If only for a while.

Assuming, he thought, no one had made off with it. Such a situation was possible, just highly unlikely. The Precious must remain on the premises at all times. Everyone knew that, even the City Old Boys, whose visits were becoming ever more frequent. Sadly, due to a lack of title, none of the Grrr! Old Boys had the gravitas to quell the intrusions. Not even Tim Tim, despite his shouting and pouting, and attempts to turn the whole company prematurely deaf.

The boys had done a fine job keeping the Precious away from Ferret and his box of tricks, shifting it around in its carrying chest so it was always where he wasn't. In many ways, Damien considered this a great shame, as the moviemaker was no day-tripper. One mention of DW:A and he was off, a mechanical lurcher with the scent of quantum hare in his nostrils, desperate to dig up treasure. He had that look in his eyes, born from hours questing and killing for glory or damnation.

If the boys remained true to form, today he'd find damnation. The senior junior shook his head. They'd have him removed before the ceremony on a ridiculous, trumped-up charge. As to Miss Harrington's commanding lead in the competition, they'd make up a rule with which to disqualify her.

Damien thought about the pale chap with the black pointed thumbnails who dressed in a raggedy frock coat the colour of dusty coal. He'd brought the Precious to Grrr! and given it to Tim Tim as a gift. With special provisos attached. If the pale chap discovered there was an outsider on the premises with technical listening gear, the repercussions were unthinkable. None of them knew precisely what he was capable of, but he certainly hissed a good threat. With a click of his fingers, he'd killed Hartley's smartphone dead, turning it into an expensive brick. The boys wouldn't take any risks. They'd ensure the moviemaker was ejected before he accidentally stumbled over what was really going on.

What Damien wanted to do the moment the meeting finished was skip and jump all the way to the Precious. Unfortunately, he had to remain calm and show Brundt the door while Bramley paid a quick visit to the boss to take the credit for everything they'd just agreed on. Cordially, he showed the Old Stamfordian to the lifts, accompanying him to the ground floor and exchanging small talk. All the while he was bursting inside like a ripe cherry tomato. They shook hands and agreed to a lunch update the following week.

He waved goodbye. Brundt thought he was so important, so worldly, but behind his back the executives laughed at his backwater tie and called him a clueless jerk.

The senior junior's anticipation reached a crescendo. He smiled. Officially, he might be limited to just two fixes a week while the seniors gorged themselves stupid, but he knew a few tricks that the seniors didn't.

"You'll never guess what," said Junior Eric, appearing at the bottom of the stairs, cigarette in hand. "Cliff-face and Malcontent lost the vote."

"Really?"

The junior nodded. "I heard it was Ports who called in a favour from a Lord. It's been ruled that Miss Harrington was within her rights to appoint a champion to act on her behalf. Cliff-face says he has proof that Ferret isn't even a Half-Boy, but the judge wasn't interested."

"Wow."

"I'm off to smoke this now," said Eric, waving the ciggie. "You might want to drop in on the Chillax Lounge on your way to the you-know-what. There's an audition. Oh, and I had another idea stolen."

"Later," said Damien, pressing for the lift.

The senior junior exited on the fourth floor, where he found a host of unusual activity taking place. Eric was right. How exciting! Miss Croft, the intern, certainly thought so too — until he walked over to talk to her. Blushing, she scooted away, clutching a pile of untidy papers.

"Damien," said Ferret, ushering Granleigh out of the lounge. "What a pleasant surprise."

"Afternoon," replied the senior junior. The geek looked much better than he had earlier. "I'm surprised you're still here. What are you doing?"

"It's a casting call for my next movie. Do you want a part?"

Did Damien want a part? Of course he wanted a part! The only thing he'd ever wanted to do was tread the boards. That was before his father had a word with him and murdered the idea. He didn't just shoot it, oh no. He skinned it, roasted it, ate it for dinner, bones and all, and once he'd shat it out, he belted what remained with a shovel to show his son just how much he truly disapproved of the acting profession as a whole.

"Not really," said Damien half-heartedly.

"You don't look like a man who isn't interested."

"Can we do this later?"

"It's now or never."

The senior junior made his choice. He memorised the lines Ferret gave him, then performed to the best of his abilities to rapturous applause from a crowd of assembled juniors, shuddering at the thought of his father finding out. It was only a few scenes. He could always turn down the role later.

Once they'd finished the take, Ferret explained to all present how he'd started out as a moviemaker, only to end up as a detective. It was in this capacity that Tim Tim had secretly employed him to investigate some missing ideas. Damien tried to stifle a smirk. The whole of Grrr! knew about the missing ideas. It was one of those annoying things they'd all learned to put up with. Ferret confessed he was in a predicament. Just as he was putting the finishing touches on his report and naming the guilty party, Tim Tim had closed the investigation and revealed the culprit.

Here it comes, thought Damien. Junior Eric. The ritual sacrifice. If only he'd kept his mouth shut.


"Miss Harrington?" Damien felt his jaw drop open like a theatre trap door, while the juniors voiced their discontent. "But that makes no sense."

Except it made perfect sense. Cliff-face and his buddy had tried everything to stop her from winning Prizeday, and they'd failed. This was their last throw of the dice.

"I've been dumped on too," said Ferret. "A certain pair of gents wrote a rather splendid jingle which they then performed in front of Juliet. We're no longer an item."

Damien sighed. "I did warn you to watch out."

"And I thought it was just a silly competition. I didn't think they'd deliberately split Miss Harrington and I up, then order me to sack her."

"They're a pair of bastards." Damien gulped. "Speaking as the senior junior, we'd love to help you out. But if we do, they'll string our guts up around Soho Gardens. I'm sorry."

"We can't just let them sack Harry," said one of the juniors. "They'll replace her with a dragon and it'll be ten times worse."

"Yeah," said another. "It's time to get our own back."

Damien put his palm to his forehead. "Meet me in the backup conference room in twenty minutes. We'll talk there."

In a tizzy, the senior junior proceeded as fast as he dared to the rendezvous point. If he made himself wait any longer, he'd surely damage an organ.

Early on, just after the Precious had arrived, a major argument had broken out when a meeting overran and the next in line was late for his turn. Enraged, Trumpleigh demanded his time back, threatening fisticuffs. The seniors took a vote. All meeting overruns were declared an act of God. Those on the rota, whose time was impacted? Tough cheese. The incumbent was henceforth granted licence to continue until stopped by the next in line.

As a consequence, the seniors on rota now took a junior to every meeting, enabling them to leave on time. When the City Old Boys heard about the Precious and began exercising their privilege at random times, any senior who lost their turn was granted the right to swap their session with a junior.

It was all highly unfair.

Damien found Cholmondeley hiding away in the graveyard for empty boxes that was the backup conference room. The lights were dimmed, and the door was locked. The speakers, however, were blaring heavy music of a genre to which an Old Boy would never admit to listening, even under torture. Damien knocked the knock. He heard movement from within. A quick shuffle and the wailing stopped. Presently, Cholmondeley answered the door, holding it slightly ajar.

"Agent Tiverton reporting for duty."

"The password?"

"Sméagol."

"Proceed. And good luck."

Damien dived in. He was already fifteen minutes late, thanks to that damnable Ferret. No point in messing about. Straight down to business. He relaxed, took hold of the Precious with both hands, felt its golden glow, welcomed its wash.

It was a miracle.

No one knew how the device did what it did, but that was hardly a concern. What mattered was how it felt. He grasped the Precious tightly, feeling a tingle all the way to his toes.

This was it.

Close your eyes.

Think being born.

Knock! Knock!

Damien jumped out of his skin, ruining the experience of birth. The door handle moved down; the door opened. Ferret poked his head through the gap.

The senior junior froze. Horrified, he realised that in his haste to get a fix he'd failed to follow basic security protocols.

"Come in," he hissed, "and lock the door. No one's supposed to see DeathWorld: Apocalypse before its release, but what the hell. Meet the Precious. It's a next-generation gaming interface. One of a kind. Watch and learn."

Ferret sat in Tim Tim's office, occupying a grand old oak chair located to one side of Moneypenny's desk, facing the room. He twiddled his thumbs, awaiting an incoming crowd of hostile Old Boys. The last hour had proved to be one of the bleakest of his professional career, tougher than the time McGyver spent a morning taunting him for having hair the colour of chewed bubblegum. The long walk of shame later in the day to clear his desk was a real ego bruiser. He felt as though he was shaping up to take a similar walk, this time on his hands, whilst drinking bleach through a funnel.

He fiddled with a rubbery object in his pocket.

Focus on the things that will go right, he reminded himself.

Firstly though, there was a minor complication to overcome. Thanks to a funding update from the Bank of Lies, the performance he was about to give was not an authentic rendition of the run-through he and Tim Tim had undertaken ten minutes earlier. The detecting consultant looked pensively at the large, centrally located semi-portable video screen and speakers, and crossed his fingers. If his act suddenly sprouted breasts, there was little room for manoeuvre. He had to grab the situation by the throat from the outset and shake, pretending to be Marianne.

Trust your instincts. Those were her words.

Play to your strengths.

And pray one's allies stay true.

"Valued employees," said Tim Tim, playing the role of Shakespearean overlord, ushering in the last of his highly motivated, extremely hungover account executives. "Welcome to Prizeday. You all know Ferret the Geek by now, and it's an open secret that he makes detective movies. What you don't know is that he's also a professional sleuth who I tasked with looking into the disappearances that have been plaguing us all of late."

Ferret stood up, smiled broadly and gestured to the crowd of executives and juniors with open arms. The claps he'd anticipated didn't come. Fortunately, neither did the boos. Carefully, he removed the nerd glasses and placed them methodically in his jacket pocket, mindful not to inadvertently gaze at Juliet.

"I do believe we're two men down. While we await their arrival, do you all agree that every idea that ever was had on these premises — no matter how great or small — is inspired by Tim Tim, your leader and friend?"

"Ow!" said Bentley, looking around to see who poked him.

"Ouch!" said Bramley, searching for the culprit who stamped on his foot.

"We have two takers. Hands up, everyone who agrees with them. There's no need to be shy. It's not as if a part in my new movie is at stake."

The juniors raised their hands enthusiastically, followed by the seniors.

"Your point?" said Tim Tim, arms folded, chin jutting forth.

"The loss of brilliant ideas is really much greater than you've been led to believe."

"Whatever do you mean?" The boss shuffled from side to side.

"Everyone whose hand is up has lost an idea."

"Curley?" said Tim Tim. "Is this true?"

Hesitantly, Curley nodded.

"Manleigh?"

A further nod.

"You'll find that everyone here has lost at least one brilliant idea. Some have lost three or four. There are two notable exceptions: Harry and your good self."

"I knew it!" Tim Tim banged his fist on the table. "This confirms her guilt beyond any shadow of a doubt. The ideas thief is finally revealed."

A series of gasps ruffled through the audience. One by one, all of the Old Boys turned to face the executive PA, who burst into a flood of tears.

"I would never do that!" she squeaked defiantly.

"Ferret!" Boomed the boss. "As we rehearsed."

All eyes turned to Ferret. Behind the assembled crowd, the office door opened a tad and two latecomers crept in. The detective nodded like a parcel shelf dog.

"Clifford and Malory!" Ferret enunciated the two names. "Are you looking for something, perchance?"

"Absolutely not!" spluttered Clifford.

Malory shook his head.

Ferret took hold of a piece of black cloth atop Tim Tim's desk and pulled it away to reveal a small, brass-bound chest. Where the lid and bottom met, an eerie band of yellow light spilt forth. The detective flipped the lid open, bathing the room in gold and causing a fundamentalist murmur to transit the room. All present stood transfixed, their eyes held fast by the hypnotic golden glow.

Cautiously, the detective lifted the Precious from its case. Shaped like a fat new moon, with the points rounded out, the contours felt perfectly smooth to his touch. A brushed bronze material formed the central core, with the rounded points fashioned from a clear material through which the eerie golden glow leaked into our universe from the depths of another plane. In the very centre of the bronzed area lay an embossed circle, lit up like an off-world jewel, mined and fashioned by a smith with elven hands.

Ferret felt a power course through his veins, multiplying his confidence. He was the man; this was his hour. It was time to unmask the true villain of the piece.

Clifford's mouth dropped open. Malory turned white.

"My Precious!" Tim Tim's jaw clenched tight. "How dare you! Hand it over this instant."

The boss strode forward, barging into Ferret, who stood his ground and held on firmly with both hands, forcing Tim Tim to face him and stretch in order to curl his fingers around the glowing golden points. The boss let out a whimper. Myriad emotions crossed his face. One second his mouth was pointed down at the edges, the next his cheeks were lit up like landing lights. Ferret felt the Precious, a spinning majestic whirlpool enrapturing his senses.

Not one of the forty assembled employees spoke or moved.

Lips quivering, Tim Tim tried to let go of the device.

"Close your eyes," said Ferret, stroking the Precious's embossed circle and releasing it from his grip. "Then imagine you're being born."

Wavering, Tim Tim closed an eye.

On the big screen, a message popped up: "DeathWorld: Apocalypse: Connection Spooling"

"No!" shouted Clifford and Malory, surging forward together.

While the seniors were busy gawking at the screen, the juniors gathered in front of the gruesome twosome, interlocking arms. Junior Eric dropped down on all fours, shuffling behind Clifford. One of the juniors pushed the account executive in the chest, causing him to tumble over the boy. Eric shuffled along on his hands and knees, taking up position behind Malory, who was toppled in a similar manner.

One of the juniors yelled: "Scrum!'" and jumped on the pair.

The response was immediate and overwhelming. Years of Old Boy training kicked in, causing an automated Pavlovian response from the assembled Old School mass, who in a state of trance found themselves acting exactly as instructed. Firstly, the seniors piled in, pinning the duo to the ground, followed by the rest of the juniors who led with their elbows and knees. Gradually, the pile of bodies on top of Clifford and Malory reached critical mass, with fists, legs, and ties flying everywhere. Ferret exhaled loudly. It had taken all of his people skills to persuade the juniors to fight back. Now it was his turn.

Hands encased in the ethereal glow of a thousand sunsets, Tim Tim succumbed to the temptations of the Precious and closed his other eye. Ferret recalled the feeling of being surrounded by ebbing sticky fluid, unable to breathe.

"Go with the contractions," he said.

On screen, a character dressed only in boxer shorts was ejaculated from a hole in space, a gigantic galactic yoni and deposited onto a cold, hard concrete walkway. The yoni flapped noisily shut. Ferret remembered feeling grit between his toes, his knees knocking together, his hands shaking.

Tim Tim's character climbed to his feet, breath visible, teeth chattering and pulled on a pair of pants and a shirt, orienting himself in the great concrete jungle that extended in every direction. To the left, an onscreen health indicator flashed into view, along with an inventory list; to the right, mapping functions made themselves available, indicating the cardinal compass points.

"Welcome to the City of Gold," said a soft, soothing feminine voice.

Ferret strode over to Moneypenny's desk, all the while glancing back at the golden glow. From behind it he produced the SniffPhreak and, adjusting its crystalline dials, focused the collection grid on the Precious.

Beep!

"This geek toy shows what's going on in the world of wireless communications," he said, his audience amounting to Juliet, Damien, and Junior Eric.

Tim Tim's character moved woodenly about the screen while the boss learnt the rudimentary controls, eyes closed, face tight in concentration. Ferret had had fun mastering the basic movements. To borrow a phrase from Damien, it was like learning to ride a giramel: a cross between a giraffe and a camel.

The detective explained how the SniffPhreak was analysing everything that was happening. He pointed to dials and counters showing connections in real time, then turned to a laptop on Tim Tim's desk and highlighted a window showing a list of files.

Ferret's hand moved to his mouth. The list was static.

Earlier on, while showing off his DW:A gaming skills, Damien had theorised that the Precious was responsible for borrowing the missing ideas, which was why he'd left his mobile phone outside the room. Out of curiosity, Ferret had checked his own phone, only to discover that all of the audition videos he'd taken were missing, thus adding weight to the theory.

The detective felt his palms moisten, as his brain moved rapidly into overdrive. What if the Precious didn't steal every file? What if it only took things it deemed to be of interest? Thinking on his feet, he withdrew a memory stick from his pocket and inserted it assertively into the laptop.

Beep!

A new tracking screen opened on the Phreak, displaying a stream of data that was being transmitted on a recently initiated, previously unused, encrypted channel.

Ferret put his hand on his heart. "As you can see, amongst its many functions, the Precious is configured to harvest brilliant new ideas."

"What?" Tim Tim opened his eyes, only for his attention to be captured by the big screen. "If I didn't know better, I'd say I was in that game."

"You are," said Ferret.

Tim Tim moved a leg without moving a leg. "Extraordinary."

"It's so remarkable that your employees have been enjoying the experience in secret."

Tim Tim tore himself away from the screen and tried to put the Precious down. "How many of my employees?"

"All of them bar two. Harry and her intern."

"Then she's innocent."

"Correct. Everyone else, however, is guilty of using the Precious without permission. If you look at the transmission dial on the geek toy and compare it to the list of new ideas on the laptop, you can see the ideas list is shrinking. I submit this as conclusive proof. If you want your ideas back, see the supplier of the Precious."

"That won't be necessary," said Tim Tim quickly. "It appears I owe Harry an apology. And a prize. If only I could let go of this thing."

"Let me help," said the detecting consultant.

"Don't you dare."

Ferret smiled.

As much as he wanted to tussle with Tim Tim, he didn't need the grief. And besides which, he'd just solved his first case. It felt as though he had sunshine pouring out of every pore. He looked over to Juliet and raised an eyebrow. She winked in return. What an actress she'd turned out to be! The best of the bunch by far.

The detective heard a tiny voice, like that of a small mammal.

He craned his neck, listening.

"*Sohn.*"

It was coming from the Precious.

He seized the little rubber rectangle as fast as he was able, but not quickly enough. By the time he'd removed the finger-stick from the laptop, the file count, originally in the thousands, numbered just six.

Ferret sat in the Chillax Lounge as white as a funeral sheet, turning the memory stick over and over in his hand, unable to comprehend his own stupidity.

Juliet planted a huge smacker firmly on his lips.

"We won Prizeday," she gushed. "For the next month, I'm Queen of Grrr! I've waited so long for this moment. I thought it would never come. There's special dessert for you tonight."

Ferret took out an imaginary cat o' nine tails and flagellated himself. "They're irreplaceable."

"And so are you, my wonderful geeky movie director. I'm so glad we met."

"It's true," said Ferret, breaking the cycle of self-harm. "Without a doubt you're the best thing that's ever happened to me."

"I'm so glad you turned out to be a man of truth and integrity."

Ferret shrugged his shoulders meekly.

"It was lovely to see those two take a beating. Let's go out and celebrate."

"Yes, let's," replied Ferret glumly.

His father's files.

Gone.

When he had them, they were just a bunch of mouldy old ones and zeroes, despite his father's claim that they were priceless beyond compare. Now that they'd been stolen, he felt violated. What was he to do? If he told Tim Tim they had worth, the Old Boy would demand a big fat finder's fee. If he pretended they were worthless, the Old Boy had no incentive to retrieve them. Ferret closed his eyes, screwed up his face, and pushed his thumbs into his tear ducts until his vision filled with chequered patterns, something he hadn't done since he was a child.

"Have a sip of Champagne."

"Thank you." Ferret felt his mood lighten. It was impossible not to be cheered by bubbles.

"To us," said Juliet, leaning over to kiss him.

Finally, despite the rumpus, he'd got the girl.

He patted his jacket pocket.

In the confusion, while Tim Tim sorted out the scrum, he'd even managed to retrieve the scarlet panties and bra. But how on earth was he ever going to get his files back?

# Chapter Thirteen: Hacked

Unlike the rest of his decuria, who were obsessed with the trappings of wealth, Marcus had a love for the simple things in life. The travels by London bus had originated in his childhood on long days out with his mother. The older-style buses he considered an iconic design, instantly recognisable, the top deck being the scene of many of his more memorable encounters. They came to an abrupt halt shortly after London Transport installed CCTV.

Marcus stuck out his bottom lip.

While he was able to get from his home to the rendezvous point in twenty minutes by taxi, he found the ride from the Embankment to Baker Street by bus soothing on the senses. He placed his hands behind his head, leant back and smiled, gazing out of the window at the people milling around below. He mused on how rarely anyone bothers to look up these days, fawning instead over their personalised mobile devices.

The intelligence man pretended to turn up the volume on his personal stereo, whilst tuning his ears into an interesting debate taking place across the aisle between a self-proclaimed financial whizz kid and two of his pals. Trailing blabbermouths was not officially a part of his job. He had people to do that for him.

Old habits die hard, he thought.

Brring!

Number withheld, noted Marcus. "Hello?"

"The water lily is in bloom," said a gravelly voice on the other end of the line.

Marcus hung up.

Good.

His people were now recording the group's economic conspiracy talk remotely via their smartphones, to be passed to an analyst, catalogued, and then added to the already-vast database his department had spent the last ten years collecting. The bashers of big government complained in the press that Big Brother was on the way and Britain was soon destined to be a police state. Not that the population cared. They were too busy feeding a love triangle consisting of self, online presence, and smart device. If they were to wake up from their self-obsessed narcissistic comas for ten seconds, they'd realise *1984* was here.

It began with the ring of steel around the City of London, installed after a disenfranchised Irish faction blew up the Baltic Exchange. There was no argument; it had to be done. Even the libertarians rolled over. So successful was that endeavour that the various security agencies combined forces to help Parliament push for the installation of CCTV on every street corner, allowing individuals to be tracked across most of the country. The main difficulty his department faced these days was too much data. That, and losing the footage that the establishment didn't want the public to see. One day soon, they'd have automated body-recognition software in place that selectively deleted his people from incoming video feeds in real time, allowing them to move under the radar once again and function like men in black are meant to.

Marcus chanced a wink at a solitary youth in his early twenties. Encapsulated by headphones, the boy didn't even notice him. How did the youth of today ever have random encounters? There were clubs that catered for those preferences, of course, but pretending a paid pick-up was a chance romance didn't really cut the mustard. He'd only tried the club scene once and had inadvertently gone home with a Russian honeypot. Marcus felt his chest tighten. Once he'd realised his error and confessed all, the stink of fish had lingered around the department for days, like a choice kipper placed strategically behind a warm radiator.

His stop.

Unobserved, Marcus dropped a card in the youth's man bag and continued on his way. Saturday morning was the nearest he came to this thing they called downtime. That, and Sunday lunch once a month. In the defence of the Realm, one had to be eternally vigilant, forever on one's guard, especially now that Europe was being flooded with waves of enhanced student super-spies.

The intelligence man stood in front of the Iron Barista, located just behind Baker Street station, its awning raised, wide glass frontage open, tables spilling onto the pavement. He scanned the faces, nodding at Douglas, a regular, and waving at Samuel, who he knew to be a copy editor from a brief conversation they'd once had when he was badly stuck on a crossword clue.

"Good morning," said Ferret in a tremulous voice from inside the establishment, raising an espresso cup to his friend.

"Such a fabulous day," replied Marcus, showing his top row of teeth. "You even got the giggle spot!"

"I'm never one to disappoint when it comes to finding the G-spot."

Marcus deposited his jacket on a hook and fussed over the table, cleaning away crumbs. Verity Jane came tottering over on a pair of unfeasibly high heels, which she was wearing for charity. The intelligence man dropped some coins in her collection tin, confirming he'd like the usual. The *adiutor* sat next to the legionnaire, positioning himself in such a way as to hear all his friend had to say in his best ear, whilst retaining a panoramic view of the outside world and easy visual access to any mincing fashion disasters sullenly making their way home from the night before.

"How's business?" asked Ferret, fidgeting with his thumbs.

"I had a case come across my desk yesterday that is right up your street."

"Do tell."

Marcus recounted the strange tale of the ice man who was observed breaking into a secret base, the location of which must remain exactly that. The guards had reported the incident because it didn't fit the profile of the normal protests. The most intriguing aspect was that neither the burglar nor the bike he escaped on gave off any detectable heat signature.

The intelligence man tapped his nose. "I have it on good authority they sealed off half of Wiltshire looking for him."

Ferret stroked his chin. "Could it have been a ghost?"

"You know I don't believe in that nonsense."

"As Holmes himself might say . . ."

"Our best guess is he was wearing some sort of cold suit. Mighty odd though, finding him near an experimental bunker that hasn't been in use for thirty years."

"What did they do there?" asked Ferret.

"I'm not at liberty to say."

"You mean you don't know." Ferret winked, chuckling to himself.

Verity Jane made her way over, precariously balancing a tray containing a latte and croissant, which was stuffed with melted cheese and ham. Marcus took delivery of the savoury breakfast and tucked in, while Ferret recounted the remainder of his adventures at Grrr!, beginning with the toppling of James Bond. All the while, the man from City Intelligence kept his keenest gossip ear open, aimed roundly at the consultant.

"There's something you're not telling," he said, scooping the chocolate coating from the froth on top of the coffee.

"I'm saving the best and worst until last."

"No, you're not. You're winding me up." Marcus dug his friend in the ribs.

Ferret sighed. Marcus stirred what remained of the chocolate into the coffee while his consulting friend explained how the missing ideas were really missing computer files, which had mysteriously vanished from random computers across the company. In the process of solving the crime, he'd done something really silly and lost nearly all of his father's files.

"Excuse me?" said Marcus, dropping the stirring spoon onto the floor. Seeing the accident, Verity Jane clicked her high heels and teetered over to deliver a fresh one.

"I was rather hoping you might be able to recover them for me."

"Do you have the memory stick?"

"Here," said Ferret, placing a rubberised rectangle onto the tabletop.

Marcus picked it up, gingerly examining the case, noting a slight indent. He hadn't paid it any attention the other day; it was only a memory stick, after all. Except this was no longer true. To be absolutely sure, the intelligence man donned a pair of gold-rimmed spectacles and squinted again at the thumb-sized notch on top of the device.

"Do you know what this is?" he asked.

"Deep joy from my father."

"It's a government-issue encrypted memory stick with fingerprint control." Marcus furrowed his brow.

"I must have activated it when I put it into the computer."

"That's not the point. Any file present on the encrypted partition cannot be deleted without administrator authorisation."

"So my father made me an admin."

"Only the spook squad have such authorisation." Marcus looked his friend in the eye. "It's part of the government's joined-up security system, to aid the protection and tracking of information across environments. If what you say is true, this is a serious breach. How did it happen?"

"That," said Ferret excitedly, "is the good news, the bit you're never going to believe. I've played DeathWorld: Apocalypse using the new controller."

"You've done WHAT?!?" spluttered Marcus, ejaculating a cone of froth across the table.

Ferret told the story in such a whirlwind fashion, without once pausing for breath, that Marcus had to stop him and make him start again. By the third time of telling, the man from City Intelligence had all the facts lined up. They just didn't make sense when replayed with a bullshit filter in place. Given where they were in the technology sizing cycle, the device his friend described couldn't exist, not as a box of tricks only notionally larger than his breakfast. If it did, and the British had invented it, he'd know about it. If it was an American invention, then the Israelis would have it and he'd still know about it. Every obvious question he asked, Ferret had an answer for.

Marcus summarised the likely design details in his head: the gaming machine and joystick are one and the same; no power cord, it draws charge from the ether; it has the ability to interface to any device, so possesses next-generation communication capabilities; no display cable, it uses wireless output. But most important of all, it steals interesting ideas from unsuspecting punters.

"You're remarkably quiet," said Ferret.

Marcus put both hands on Ferret's hand. "This is really important: Who have you told about this?"

"Only my best gaming buddy."

"Swear to me, legionnaire to *adiutor* that you won't utter a word of this to anyone else."

Ferret tucked in his chin. "You have my word."

"Now, my friend, we must hurry back to your place. I wish to examine the stick in private."

Once they were locked securely in Ferret's den, Marcus had a jolly good rummage through the memory stick's partitions. Rapidly, he came to the same conclusion as his friend: There were only half a dozen files left. If, as the evidence suggested, the hardware delete function had been activated, then the missing files were gone for good. He opened one of the stragglers and read the contents out loud.

"'Fifty-nine millilitres being the axis point of gold and silver.' Are they all this nonsensical?"

"There are a lot of numbers," said Ferret. "As I'm not a math geek, I switched to killing zombies instead."

Marcus nodded and moved on to the Phreak, examining its data cache. Detailed log analysis was not his strong point. He'd need to borrow a department know-it-all for such a task. For now, a cursory glance told him all he needed to know.

Keeping the keys to this great island kingdom safe from foreign interference had always been a remarkably tricky business. The recent explosion in wireless technology made it more difficult than ever to tell the good from the bad and the bad from the downright ugly. High-resolution cameras were plentiful and cheap, and low-orbit satellites were available to rent by the hour to any tin-pot dictator with an international credit agreement. He dealt with all of these things on a daily basis. Assuming Ferret wasn't delusional, the evidence he'd presented suggested that the Precious belonged in a special category reserved for game-changers of an epic proportion. Based on his experience, it posed the greatest penetration threat he'd ever encountered to the realm's security systems.

Allegedly, it was due to go on sale any day now.

"Were you able to look into my father's accident?" asked Ferret from the kitchenette, fixing a pair of cheeky martinis.

"Well . . ." Marcus chewed the edge of a fingernail, a habit he thought he'd conquered long ago. "There are a few details about his death that don't add up. Officially, he fell from a cruise ship and drowned. However, when the body was recovered, the head had been severed clean off. His chest cavity was ripped open, and all the intestines were missing."

"That's gross."

"The autopsy claimed his injuries were consistent with propeller damage. However, he was also an ex-weapons inspector and that means I have to be sure. It appears his laptop was missing from his belongings when we searched his cabin, and that should have set alarm bells ringing. Except it didn't."

"Is that normal?"

Marcus shook his head.

"In that case," said Ferret, "I intend to make it my number one priority to get those files back."

"You'll need my help. Starting Monday, I'll have our friend Rajesh assigned to the case."

"Thanks," said Ferret, walking through to the lounge. "Hugs."

"Hugs." Marcus found himself thinking very hard about a brick wall he knew only too well. Whoever had ordered the hit on Wolfgang — because that's what it smelt like — they were busy covering their tracks.

The intelligence man squeezed Ferret tight.

A missing laptop was just about acceptable. But the forced closure of Wolfgang's case on the same day his files were stolen was stretching the bounds of credulity a step too far.

# Chapter Fourteen: The Ginger Terror

"Jupiter's perineum!" Flamen winced in pain.

Hobbling along Regent Street on a pair of borrowed crutches, he tried his damnedest to keep weight off the right ankle, which was swollen to the size of a grapefruit and strapped-up to oblivion.

He gritted his teeth.

In all likelihood, it was broken.

If he dared hospital treatment and his description plus injury were crosschecked, the security services alert board would flash bright red. After that, it was only a matter of time before the authorities collected him from the streets. The mission was far more important than a foot. The future of The Brotherhood was at stake. He had to unmask the turncoat, bring the full weight of justice crashing down, and with luck, recover that which was stolen.

In order to fool the military and put intelligence off their stroke, the priest had driven east at high speed, then southwest, roaring through the English countryside in an open-topped sports car, roof down, lights out, refusing to stop until he'd put fifty miles on the clock. Only then, when the adrenaline kick subsided and the dull ache of reality set in, did he dare pull over and assess the damage which, in his opinion, was more than a scratch but less than life-threatening.

Over the next few days, he'd worked his way back east along the south coast, one car at a time, staying off the main roads until he'd reached Brighton. Once there, he'd sent out for a change of clothes and taken an inspiring soak in a borrowed bath. Using various ointments and lotions, bandages, and splints, he'd patched up the throbbing, violet ankle. The hot knives in his calf whenever he banged his foot, he found rather cathartic but, in an effort to limit the damage further, he'd mounted a length of rubber off-cut to his right heel. Revitalised, he'd boarded a train to London, determined to make a pre-scheduled meeting on time.

Flamen leant against a wall, panting.

Initially, he'd intended to fly solo. However, given the recent turn of events, an accomplice was now a necessity. In the forthcoming fight, he'd need his old circle of contacts to act as his eyes and ears. Of paramount importance right now was the reactivation of his old friend, the ebullient

Sir Edward, who, despite his outlandish appearance, was the only person in the whole of London whom Flamen dared trust.

Turning along Margaret Street, the priest slowed, approaching Cavendish Square with caution, searching for anyone casually observing the flight of steps that led to the carefully prepared bolt hole.

His hackles rose.

Out in the open, he felt very exposed.

Plonking his bum in a seat at a nearby pavement café, he procured a stool for the leg and ordered a cup of tea and a sandwich. While the tea cooled, he cocked his head to one side, relaxed, and spread out like a human pancake, testing the crevices, filling the cracks with batter. Sensing nothing untoward, the priest pulled himself together.

It was so difficult to be sure.

He picked up a newspaper printed that morning and thumbed through it, scanning random articles without reading the content. This was the part of his old job he disliked the most: the waiting for nothing to happen. All those years sitting around drinking tea had equipped him with a bladder the size of a dirigible and yet today, every time he sat down, he wanted to pee.

"Jupiter's catheter!" exclaimed the priest, scrambling to his feet. With assistance from the waiter, he made his way to the bathroom.

As he relieved himself, Flamen cursed the lack of access to his old department's mainframe. From that, it was possible to plot the old team's recent movements. The lack of diligence on his part had cost him dearly. If only he'd taken more precautions while he'd had the opportunity.

All was not entirely lost.

Sir Edward's arrival was imminent.

Much to the annoyance of the staff, Flamen sat outside all afternoon, observing the steps near the Square. He smirked at their dilemma. They wished he'd leave, but they couldn't possibly throw out a cripple who was never without a cuppa.

Five o'clock came.

The priest bolted upright and, folding the newspaper, waved to a fellow across the road. "Sir Edward!"

The chap, who was dressed casually in slacks and a long-sleeved check shirt complemented by a tasselled hunting jacket, stopped in his tracks, ginger whiskers and bushy sideburns protruding above the collar fleeing his face in every direction.

"Over here." The priest waved again.

The ginger chap walked over; Flamen climbed to his feet, offering his hand. "You made it."

"Do I know you?"

The priest nodded. "I will help you remember. Assist me to my office where all will become clear."

The moment he'd arrived from overseas, the priest had checked out the various hideaways he'd put in place while still resident in his homeland. The Piccadilly address, from where he'd planned to base his operations, was long ago compromised. For some unabashed reason known only to monarchy, the Crown Estate chaps had chosen to redevelop an entire city block without first seeking his permission.

How dare they!

He'd found a similar situation in Southwark, where the council had let development plans run amok, encasing the backup hideout in a thousand tons of concrete.

This left just a single option on the table.

Slowly the pair descended into a well-lit parking area, the priest grimacing at every jolt.

"Are you sure I know you?" said the ginger chap, furrowing his brow.

"In here." Flamen pointed to a battleship-grey metal door marked "Danger! Keep Out."

"I don't understand."

The priest fiddled with a set of keys. "You've been undercover for a very long time. You've forgotten who you are."

Flamen ushered the man with the whiskers inside, slammed the door shut, and flicked a light switch to reveal a power distribution centre, roughly ten feet by twenty, its sole occupants a pair of well-worn rectangular work benches. One end of the room was taken up by a run of floor-to-ceiling storage lockers.

The priest's nostrils twitched at the combination of diesel oil and ozone; the man with the whiskers twiddled his beard.

Making his way over to the middle set of lockers, Flamen pushed. Nothing. He tried again. The ginger, who stood a good two inches taller, drew up level and put his shoulder to work. With a loud click, the central section moved backwards on a set of well-oiled runners, coming to rest in line with the wall, revealing a short passageway terminating in a door. A further pair of doors lay left and right.

"Welcome to Listening Post Zelda," said Flamen, heading towards the door opposite. "Come, Sir Edward. Time is of the essence."

The ginger chap hesitated. "My name is Gerald."

"It matters not who we are now. What is important is who we once were. Before your memory was hidden from you, you were known by another name."

The priest opened the door and switched on the lights. Behind him, the secret panel swung shut. Inside, the room resembled a Victorian study. Across from the door, a sturdy desk held court and a high-backed leather-bound chair presided over proceedings. To the left, a custom-made teak bookcase enveloped the entire wall, bursting with hardback volumes. On the wall to the right hung a series of medical charts with a crash trolley beneath, prepared for use.

Flamen ordered the chap to undress and lie down.

The ginger squinted at the priest. "I've been here before."

"Indeed you have." Flamen ushered the patient onto the makeshift bed and, resting on the right crutch, clicked his fingers. The ginger chap slumped back, eyes closed. "Once upon a time, my friend, you were involved in a clandestine operation based in Porton Down. There were things you did for which amends must be made. That is your purpose. One of the old team is a turncoat, responsible for stealing what remains of SK-13. Our task is to get it back. Rest, relax, and hold out your hand. When you awaken, you will be born anew."

For the next few hours, Flamen busied himself checking Zelda's catalogue. Thanks to ministry overkill, the bolthole was equipped with rations and water for a staff of three for the best part of a year. However, the field packs in question were twenty years out of date and tasted like fermented cardboard. Before setting out for the bunker, he'd stocked up on cheese, crackers, cow juice, and most important of all: English tea.

The priest flipped through a novella by Robert Louis Stevenson, an early tale of split personality disorder. Every ten minutes or so he checked on the ginger's progress. It was strange how they always slept like grinning babes after the liquid took effect. He'd seen the transformation many times, but it still amazed him how they went from terrified to sublime in such a short space of time. Back in the day they'd called the condition *Verpuppung*, as a mark of respect to the original research team.

The ginger chap sat up and rubbed his eyes. "Well, I'm dashed. No, that sounds wrong. One is dashed. One needs one's hat, jacket, and smoking pipe. And tea."

The priest pointed to the back of the door and a bulge in a plastic sheet.

"One has picked a splendid day to awaken from a decades-long slumber." The ginger swung himself to the side and onto his feet. "Has one assembled a field kit?"

"For this mission, we rely on our wits. No technology. No credit cards. And certainly no mobile phones."

The ginger chap paced around the floor, testing his legs. The priest marvelled at his hirsute body, red hair spilling from every pit and fold.

Oh, to look so young and virile.

The ginger pulled the plastic cover from the door and, finding a deerstalker, tried it on for size. "One mentioned the team earlier. What of our friend the chemist?"

"Dead," coughed Flamen.

"And his son?"

"Compromised." The priest felt his shoulders sag.

The ginger chap tugged his beard. "One needs a battle trim."

Unable to contain himself any longer, Flamen hugged the hairy orangutan. "Welcome home, Sir Edward."

The ginger chap nodded, picking up a golden snow globe from the desk. "Sir Edward. One remembers."

While Edward dressed, the priest told him how The Brotherhood had changed and how the values they once held dear had gone down the pan.

"Then we must adapt." Sir Edward slapped the table. "The boy will be met. We will make him an offer."

"It is unlikely that the turncoat acted alone. If he or his accomplices even suspect what the youth is capable of . . ."

Sir Edward let out a great belly laugh. "One will put the fear of god into them all! They will be so preoccupied with the ginger terror, they will have no time for him."

"You follow a perilous notion."

"Danger is one's middle name, Thomas. Now, where is he to be found?"

Flamen opened the top drawer of the desk and withdrew a dossier marked "Secret," which he handed on.

"Outstanding," said Edward.

"You'll find details of each of the old team and their immediate relatives," said the priest. "The standout from the crowd is our chum the brain doctor, who's embraced pop psychology and published a book to great acclaim, expounding on his outlandish theories. His audience is quite fervent, hanging on his every word. I say we save him until last."

# Chapter Fifteen: Love "B"

While Maria, Ferret's hired hand, made herself busy in the guest lodge, tenaciously attacking the kitchenette and living room with dusters and a vacuum cleaner, the detective passed time studying his global collection of alcohol, deciding which bottles to expatriate. He'd spent Sunday afternoon moving a selection of books and magazines from the den, which represented the film geek he wanted to be, along with basic foodstuffs, beverages, and condiments. Now, halfway through Monday, with the Champagne chilling, the dilemma was over which vodka to take.

The detecting consultant pawed each bottle in turn, reliving fond memories. He was reminded of an old consultancy saying: Never leave your wingman behind. At least that's what they told the juniors. The truth was, wingmen got burned all the time. It was only the bagman who was guaranteed a search and rescue party.

Shuffling containers, Ferret tutted to himself.

There was a good reason why he'd left his account at the Bank of Lies untouched, despite being massively in the black. It wasn't the initial lie that caused the trouble. It was the massive cast of supporting lies that trotted behind, like a stable of fine racing horses awaiting hoof inspection. The slightest cough might startle them and cause a stampede in random directions, upending apple carts.

His thoughts turned to Juliet.

On Prizeday evening, they'd wandered into Soho, supped a round of power cocktails, and then crashed home early, intent on enjoying each other. After a mutual shower, they'd lain around naked, telling war stories about getting caught in the act. He'd soon discovered his new girl had sensitive toes, and the addition of bubbly turned her giggles to gasps. He'd gazed into her eyes, letting go. Before he knew it, he was melting into her again, tumbling through summer meadows.

She'd left later on, citing an appointment with friends first thing, which made going to bed easy. He'd simply locked up the guest lodge, which he'd figured was an appropriate abode for a geek moviemaker, and moved back to his preferred sleeping quarters. Now, with the prospect of Juliet staying over on an open-ended invitation, the lubrication of the lie was becoming vastly more complicated. Once a fib is up to speed, he reminded himself, it requires an inordinate amount of resource to assure its momentum.

Brring!

"M," said Ferret, fingering his phone. "What a pleasant surprise."

"It's Marianne now," said Marianne. "How the devil are you?"

"All things considered, I'm feeling rather good." Holding the phone under his chin, Ferret tried, with the aid of a mirror, to dampen down the annoying curl on the side of his head.

"I gather you want access to my publishing contacts. Why?"

Ferret explained in a cursory fashion how he'd lost a set of confidential files and the only lead he had so far was a magazine called *Boyztoyz*. With the aid of a search engine, he'd discovered they were owned by Banoffee Publishing but was unable to find a physical address, only a p.o. box number, which had set alarm bells tinkling.

"I still lunch with the literary crowd," said Marianne, her voice wavering. "I'll ask around."

"Thanks. In the interests of expediency, I've employed myself to track those files down. It would be most embarrassing if I failed."

"Your first case." Marianne let out a whoop. "Congratulations!"

"Why, thank you." Ferret decided not to argue the toss. In his estimation, the Case of the Stolen Files was actually case number three, the Devil Dog of West London being number one. "I'm rather pleased to win the business, actually. The competition was quite stiff."

Marianne laughed. "I trust you remember The Consultancy guidelines for dangerous work: Always keep a junior handy in case things turn sacrificial."

"I shall heed that advice." Ferret grinned. "When are you next in town?"

"Friday." On the other end of the line, Ferret heard an anxious whisper. "Apologies for cutting you off, but I must dash. There's an altercation in progress between two of my rival managers. I thought the armed forces were the armed forces, but it appears the ex-Navy chaps won't share a kettle with the ex-Army chaps and vice versa. The only thing they can agree on is that they both detest the flyboys more than each other."

"Dinner Saturday?" asked Ferret.

"Done. Text me the details." With which Marianne hung up.

Damn, thought Ferret, feeling his intuition waver. A few seconds more and he'd have known details of the company merger she was involved with. His banking friend was not going to be happy. On the other hand, with the insider-trading investigation still ongoing, any delay was a good thing. The only unknown was the means by which they'd exploit the information, assuming Marianne wanted a cut. They'd hammer that out over drinks, as always.

Ferret picked up a controller and resumed the game he was playing, jabbing a lolloping zombie clean through the eye with a pair of gardening shears, filling the screen with spatters of blood. No matter how many undead he made undeader, this wasn't a patch on DW:A.

He felt a hole where the Precious belonged, hankering for it in the same way he hankered for a cigar two days after the last one. In a couple of weeks, god willing, he'd have a Precious of his own, once the annoying file-stealing bug was ironed out. For some reason, the press had started calling the next generation interface "Nigel," which all things considered was an insult. If he had to name the Precious, he was a she and her name was Scheherazade.

A minute past midnight the day they went on sale, he'd have one.

He administered a lawnmower to the back of a zombie's head, lopping the top of the skull clean off, spraying one of his virtual friends with brains.

Now that he'd stopped thinking about it, the answer to the vodka dilemma was obvious: Purchase duplicate bottles.


Ferret sat in the guest lodge, thumbs twitching.

It was only two hours since the last zombie fix and already he had that parched feeling in his throat. Against his better judgement, he'd left the gaming apparatus configured in the den and was now desperate to waste heads, yet was unable to satiate the lust. He examined the bra and panties he'd rescued from Grrr! He'd tried on both items in order to feel closer to Juliet. Although the bra was extremely tight, the knickers fit him just fine around the waist, the elastic pinching the tops of his legs. It was strange how Juliet hadn't missed them.

Ding Dong!

Ferret checked his smile in the mirror, made sure the damnable curl was neutralised, hid the underwear in his sock drawer, and strode down the stairs towards the front door, ready to greet his new girlfriend. Observing Juliet's contours through the frosted glass, it wasn't possible to see her curves in all their glory, only that she was dressed in thrilling black. He felt a stirring in his loins. He opened the door, eyes half closed, anticipating a lingering kiss.

"What a frightful choice of shirt," coughed Cyrano, blowing smoke in his face. "Have you been chopping down trees?"

Ferret's mouth hung open.

His French friend looked like a million dollars, dressed in an elegant black suit, trimmed with capped buttons, complemented by a crisp white shirt and polished black evening shoes.

"Well, invite me in." The Frenchman stubbed out the cigarette against the wall.

"What in the blue blazes are you doing here?"

"And I'm happy to see you too. I rang your doorbell for a good ten minutes before I thought to come around the back. Perhaps he's in the garage, playing with the Maserati, I thought." Cyrano barged past, thrusting a box which was neatly bound with grey ribbon at him. "Come on. Where is she?"

"Who's 'she'?" said Ferret. "And what's this?"

"I found it on the doorstep," said the Frenchman, peeking through the lounge door. "Don't play me for a fool. The whole decuria knows about your new girlfriend."

"You have to go." The words hissed from the detective's tongue like air escaping from an inopportune puncture. "Now."

"As you can imagine," said Cyrano, grinning, "I've been asking myself what you're doing in the spartan guest lodge, when you've got the full spread available."

"You can't be here."

"Existentially speaking, I feel compelled to correct you."

Ding Dong!

Ferret felt a fiery pit open up around him,

"Take a seat and behave yourself," he said, putting down the box and pointing towards the lounge. "Prepare to meet the gorgeous Miss Harrington."

"Good evening, Mr. Movie Director." Juliet wrapped her leg around Ferret's, leaning up to embrace him with a kiss. She kicked off a shoe. "We have an hour to ourselves before dinner."

"Then let's make the most of it," replied Ferret, loudly. "My friend is just leaving."

Cyrano appeared in the doorway. "*Enchanté, mademoiselle.*"

"*Monsieur,*" said Juliet, holding out her hand, which Cyrano took in his and delicately kissed.

Standing between his friend and girlfriend, who wore a short, figure-hugging champagne dress finished with mother of pearl, Ferret felt quite out of place.

"This is Cyrano," he stuttered.

"Actually," smiled the Frenchman, "we were about to partake of the finest flake this side of Caracas. You're more than welcome to join us."

"You have sparkles?"

"For you, I have diamonds."

Juliet giggled. "How charming."

Ferret glared at his friend. "What are you doing?" he mouthed.

Cyrano ignored him. Returning to the seat, he withdrew an antique cigarette case embossed with his initials and flipped the lid to reveal a nest of implements, along with a compressed block of cream-coloured powder the size of his little finger.

"See how she flakes like snow," said the Frenchman, teasing a layer of powder from the block with a scalpel blade. "This particular Cru is reserved for royalty, to whom *mademoiselle* is no doubt related."

Juliet ran her tongue across her top lip. "What line of business are you in?"

"I produce films," said the Frenchman, offering a dozen snowflakes to Juliet on a piece of silvered glass. "Mostly French Art House."

Behind Juliet, Ferret glared at his friend and drew his index finger across his throat.

"And how do you know Ferret?" Juliet took the flakes, along with a short silver straw.

"He directs for me now and then." Cyrano winked at his friend. "As it happens, I'm also his landlord."

Juliet took a toot and handed the mirror to Ferret. She turned to Cyrano. "You own this house?"

"This is the guest quarters of my London residence." Cyrano pointed through French windows at the three-storey property visible across a short length of garden, the outside lights illuminating the glass and chrome atrium, throwing shadows across exposed brickwork. "I let my friend stay here for a nominal donation to charity."

Ferret blushed bright red, his cheeks warm enough to fry an egg. "And you were just leaving." He took a toot and handed the empty mirror back to the Frenchman.

"Indeed I was." Cyrano cut himself a deep pile of snow, snorted it up, shook his head and packed the paraphernalia back into the carrying case.

"I'm delighted to make your acquaintance, J. I trust we'll meet again soon."

Juliet stood along with Cyrano, encouraging him to kiss her on each cheek, which he did willingly.

"*Au revoir*," said the Frenchman, handing Juliet his card. He turned and headed for the French windows, patting his pockets. "I appear to have misplaced my keys. Ferret, may I borrow yours?"

"They're in the fruit bowl, handsome." Juliet pointed to a cut-crystal container on top of a sideboard.

Ferret pursed his lips.

Cyrano picked up the keys and, turning to Ferret, said: "Tristan demands an audience. Be there tomorrow, eleven o'clock sharp. Not a second late."

He sauntered down the garden, whistling *La Marseillaise*.

"What a lovely man." Juliet let out a sigh. "How many more good-looking friends do you have up your sleeve, I wonder?"

"He's no friend of mine." Ferret felt his nose go numb.

"What's in the hat box?"

"I have no idea."

"I have a thing for gentlemen in hats." Juliet winked.

Ferret undid the ribbon and read the accompanying card, which simply said: "All my love, B." Opening the box, he took out the most gorgeous grey-felt fedora he'd ever seen in his life.

"Philip Treacy," said Juliet. "How fabulous."

Ferret donned the hat, adjusting its horizontal tilt in the mirror. It wasn't an item of clothing he'd choose for himself, but the moulding of the lines was magical. Once he lost the lumberjack shirt and stepped into one of his suits, no one would doubt he was a detecting consultant.

"Do you happen to have a video camera to hand, Mr. Moviemaker?" Juliet placed her hand on his bum.

"I do."

"Since you shook things up, Tim Tim no longer trusts the boys." Juliet took Ferret by the hand and led him up the stairs, her eyes glistening like a pair of svelte emeralds. "I've been promoted, and guess what? I'm going to New York."

"That's great news." Ferret kicked off his slippers. "But I'll miss you."

"When we return, I'm to take charge of the launch party for that silly game everyone's so excited about."

Ferret swallowed hard. "Will you be bringing the Precious home with you?"

"It's locked up in Tim Tim's safe." Juliet unzipped her dress and let it fall to the ground.

Ferret stood transfixed, unable to prise his eyes away from her underwear, or rather the assets her underwear barely covered. The only thing he wanted right now was her. He ached to be with her, to gaze into her eyes, to fall into her.

She wanted the same.

He felt it, breaking across the room in waves.

He pushed Juliet onto the bed and unfastened her bra before gently tugging at her briefs with his teeth.

She let out a soft moan.

Ferret glanced towards the sock drawer, then at the curtains, which were wide open, affording an unobstructed view of the main residence. Cyrano was probably watching.

Let him.

He ran his tongue up his girlfriend's tight belly, finishing on her lips in a soft kiss. Juliet wrapped her legs around him and removed his shirt. Ferret moved to take off the hat, in order to lose his T-shirt, but Juliet stopped him.

She made a snipping motion with her middle and index fingers.

"Bedside drawer."

Juliet cut the tee from his body, flinging the rag that remained to the floor. She ran her fingers across an old battle scar, a twin set of lightning strikes etched into the skin near his collarbone, accrued on the field of play in an historic altercation. Then she set on the trousers, reducing his attire to something one might find on a shipwrecked sailor.

"Moneypenny's desk," he whispered.

"That was so exciting." Juliet wiggled her hips, tearing his trousers off. With a saucy grin, she applied the final chop.

Their eyes met. Waves of lust struck him, a lifeboat on turbulent seas. He felt himself melt, his feelings flowing into her. She fell backwards, trembling, her back arched, eyes closed, hair cascading across the pillows.

He cocked the hat and smiled.

Glancing over his shoulder in the direction of the main house, he willed his French friend towards the rear windows.

Heart beating faster, he uncocked the hat.

In silhouette, his French friend was busy talking with a man in a deer-stalker, who looked to be a cardboard cut-out of the great detective himself. Shaking his head, Ferret dismissed the image and re-cocked his fedora. It was going to take more than a stranger in Victorian garb to put him off this stroke.

# Chapter Sixteen: Banking Towers

Ferret watched storm clouds gather ominously above the steel and chrome panoply that occupies the eastern side of middle London, seeing angry grey tendrils reflected in tempered glass. Early on in his consultancy career, he'd paced the perimeter of the Square Mile, marvelling at the remains of the London Wall and the effigies of dragons protecting all the major entrances. Out of curiosity, he'd visited each of the City's many churches, lunching in their gardens. In the area occupied by finance an architectural renaissance was underway, spearheaded by the iconic Gherkin, built on the site of the old Baltic Exchange. In Ferret's opinion it was a great tick of a building, mandibles sunk deep into the earth, sucking away at the blood of Britain's financial system.

Briefly, the sun poked out, anointing the landmark with a crown of jewels, transforming it into a beacon of light, a great advertising hoarding linking past, present, and future with a single inviolable aim: the provision of velocity to the vast resources of wealth gathered within the City gates.

Ferret gazed at the king of buildings and panted.

The closer the cab's proximity to Threadneedle Street, the more excitable he'd become, fiddling first with his thumbs, then his cufflinks, and finally playing with the fedora, poising it this way and that, trying to decide which angle best fit his face. The City of London, with its frenetic pace of life always had this effect on him. In his opinion, for pure adrenaline rush, there was nothing to rival the Square Mile anywhere else in Europe.

This was his first visit since the split with The Consultancy. Intuitively, he soaked up the atmosphere. It felt as though he had a digital abacus inside his chest with the entire system of finance coursing through it. He was a new breed of superman, able to feel the ebb and flow of financial transactions in real time.

Damn, it had never felt this good before.

The detecting consultant cocked his fedora to one side.

His hat was a film star.

He hadn't thought to ask Juliet what she was going to do with the tape they'd made; she'd left in a hurry first thing to catch a plane. Hopefully, they'd watch it together. He felt a tightness in his trousers, followed by the pain of his nails digging into his palms.

If Cyrano tried to muscle in with this one, he predicted blood.

The cab passed the Bank of England.

Ferret signalled to the driver to pull over, intending to partake of coffee in one of the many City rat runs, his haunt of choice being the sister establishment to the Iron Barista. He ruminated on the wonderful aroma of a well-crafted artisan espresso. Sadly, time was against him. He dare not be late for his appointment with Tristan the Centurion.

"Carry on," he said. "99 Bishopsgate."

The cab crawled the remaining distance, sandwiched between a pair of double-decker buses. Ferret paid the driver, wished him a great day, and strode into the lobby of First National Global. Smartly dressed businessmen and women criss-crossed the atrium, brandishing laptops and folders, some alone, some in pairs, a veritable stream of corporate ants. He let the excitement wash over him, feeling multimillion-pound deals winging through the ether, permeating every pore of his being, soaking him in delicious zeroes.

Here in the City, the Old Boys ruled with an iron hand and, according to his banking friend, had done so since the fifteenth century. He'd dealt with them on many occasions, usually through middlemen, as they preferred to remain anonymous and aloof. Post-Grrr!, he now knew what to look for and the tells were obvious, in little gestures and mannerisms, haircuts, and shoes.

He shook his head.

In comparison to the major deals that the Old Boys oversaw daily, the deal for which McGyver had tried to crucify him was merely a teardrop in an Olympic-sized swimming pool. That was finance for you. If you weren't to the manor born, the best one could hope for was scraps from the top table — or in his case, a rather tasty pie crust soaked in gravy.

Tristan's office was located on the eighteenth floor amongst a suite of offices allocated to the investment bank's senior deal makers. Ferret collected an ID badge and climbed into the first available lift along with a gaggle of young pretenders, who he identified as Old Boys based on their Windsor knots.

"Have you?" asked one of the lift occupants, to the rest of the group, a smirk upon his face.

"Have you?" answered one of his fellows.

"Last night," winked the first Old Boy.

"I heard they'd opened up a second front."

"Not in front of the unwashed."

Inquisitively, Ferret used his intuition to discover whether the Old Boy was involved in something exploitable. He raised an eyebrow. If he didn't know better, what he was sensing was the same extreme excitement he'd encountered at Grrr!

The lift stopped at Tristan's floor.

Ferret stepped out, stroking his chin, and left the Old Boys to journey on up to the rarefied heights in which they made their homes. He preferred the buzz of the trading floor, with its ducking and diving, to the serene upper levels where money was made with a nod and a wink.

"Good morning." Ferret tipped his hat to Catherine, Tristan's assistant, who looked stunning in a dark-blue silk suit and cream blouse, her hair tied up in a chignon.

"He's expecting you." Catherine crinkled her eyes.

"Are you free for dinner on Friday?"

"You already know the answer." Catherine chuckled to herself. "You're such a naughty little Ferret. What would your new girlfriend say?"

Ferret tipped his hat and nodded. "Ma'am."

The detective sat back in one of his banking friend's plush leather recliners, while the man of the moment ran around the perimeter of his office whooping.

"My god, our French friend has some impressive contacts." Wide-eyed, Tristan flicked his head back and inhaled deeply, trying to surprise any powder residue clinging to the insides of his nostrils. "I haven't felt this profound since, oh . . . last night."

Ferret felt an ear-to-ear grin install itself across his face. "I wish to fly for Britain!"

"You know where the window is."

"I've changed my mind. I wish to swim for our hallowed isle instead, for I am Aquaman, the lord of the seven seas."

"Jolly good." Tristan dibbed his snout back into the trough. "Another hit, my optio?"

Ferret nodded nervously, his stomach in knots.

"Hurry then, or I'll have the lot."

Snort!

Snort!

"Whee . . .hew!" Tristan whinnied like a stallion on Mating Sunday, blonde mane trailing behind. He glanced one way, then the other, trying to decide which hot mare to mount first.

Ferret spread his arms, allowing liquid to drip down the back of his throat, numbing his neck on its way down. "How does the world of Banking Towers find itself this fine day?"

"Harlot!" Tristan picked up a cricket ball from the trophy shelf and pitched it at a reversed picture on the edge of his highly polished teak desk, smashing it to smithereens. "She intends to have my wad and after my wad, my job. The temptress is a whore, I say!"

Ferret felt his stomach churn.

"Do not utter her name," said Tristan wagging a finger, "for I do not wish to hear it spoken. Henceforth she is known as 'Babylon,' for she hath thirteen heads, and each head doth have thirteen mouths, and yea each mouth doth contain a spurting phallus. And about her body she has thirteen times thirteen gaping holes, and verily each is plugged by a pair of panting, pox-ridden demons."

Ferret had to concede his friend was dealing with a pretty serious whore.

"Do you think Cyrano would like a go?" Tristan tried to reinstall the picture, but the collapsed frame gave out instantly. "I hear he'll stick it anywhere."

Ferret chewed his lip. "Right now, he's intent on having a go on my new girlfriend."

"Indeed," said Tristan. "He was here yesterday, moaning about the insult to his *dignitas* caused by your failure to be a failure. I told him to go ahead — it's not like you're engaged."

"I'd rather you'd ordered him to back off."

"Where's the fun in that, my furry friend?"

"I really like this one. She has a figure to die for." Ferret paced nervously around the office, chewing his jaw.

"When all's said and done, it's only a bit of jiggy-jiggy. It's not as if money's involved, unlike my Babylon." Tristan stamped on what remained of the photo frame. "Whore!"

Ferret buzzed around the spacious office, lifting each of Tristan's belongings in turn to check for dust, never settling for more than a few seconds on any one item. His hand hovered above the centurion's ceremonial dagger, or pugio, which he decided it was impertinent to touch. "I've only ever slept with one of Cyrano's ex-girlfriends, whereas he's tried it on with every one of mine."

"I always knew there was something deeply sinister about that man," said Tristan, following in Ferret's footsteps, straightening ornaments. "Explains why I like him so. That, and his fine taste in New World ordinance. By the way, I dig the new hat. Very down and groove groovy. It makes you look like a sleuthy sleuth, you crazy, old-style cat. Meow."

"Excuse me?"

"They call it street jive. I heard the youth of today using such language only yesterday, which makes them the youth of yesterday, I suppose. Innit? They say that too, you know."

"Never!"

"One must always strive to keep up with modern parlance. Otherwise, a morning will come when one wakes up unable to speak one's own language." Tristan slumped into a high-backed chair behind the desk. "Not that I want one, but just in case I decide to throw a detective party, where did you get the trilby?"

"It's a fedora," said Ferret. "It's a gift from a secret admirer."

"I'm sure I don't need to remind you, but it's quite impolite to wear a hat indoors. Why don't you see if you can throw it onto my coat stand?"

"I'd rather not."

"My expensive designer coat stand."

Ferret shook his head.

Tristan raised his arms to the ceiling. "As your centurion, I *command* it."

"Very well." Ferret removed his hat, and taking careful aim, flung it at the stand, landing it on an outstretched arm."

"Good shotity shot." Greedily, Tristan ran his finger along the oily residue left on the table and licked it clean. "Sit."

Reluctantly, Ferret obeyed, a ball of nervous tics and lightning streaks.

"I called you here today to talk about your earnings, which have been zero for the last three months and well below standard for the last six. You will not continue to let the decuria down like this."

Ferret felt himself blush. "I have a hot tip in the works."

"In the works is useless to me. I need it in the system."

"By the weekend, I promise."

Tristan spun his seat three hundred and sixty degrees and pressed a button on the intercom. "Assistant, we require iced Andorran mineral water and artisan rice cakes. Hold back on the artichoke ones. I have an important meeting later in the day."

Ferret and the centurion sat across from each other, immersed in a pair of soft leather sofas. Nibbly nibbles were laid out on the table. Despite the troubles with his whore, Tristan remained upbeat, alluding to a deal he'd sniffed out that had the potential to net the decuria a tidy profit.

The banker flicked his nostrils. "There's a new game about town called Planet Death, which the Old Boys are spurting in each other's pants over, which means I must know about it too. Henceforth, I command you to be my eyes and ears into the sordid world of video games."

"That rather contradicts Tom Tom's orders," said Ferret. "He told me I must leave them alone."

Tristan cuffed Ferret about the head. "I don't care what that imbecile says. This is an order from me, which overrides all other orders in existence, forever. Eyes and ears, I'm placing you under the personal protection of Tristan the Impervious, as afforded by the terms of *munerum indictio*. From now on, you report directly to me on all matters concerning Planet Death."

"DeathWorld: Apocalypse," corrected Ferret.

Tristan cuffed him again. "Should anyone dare to question your mission, refer them to me. Now, about these ridiculous stories concerning you becoming a paranormal investigator."

"Detecting consultant." Ferret drew his jacket about him. "It's my latest hobby."

"You're not wasting your time on such spurious nonsense." The banker handed Ferret a letter.

"What's this?"

"A declaration. You are hereby banned from carrying out all forms of paranormal detective work, ad infinitum, until the end of time. I'll not have my fellow centurions laughing at me. Sign."

"I'd like to run it past our *adiutor* first."

"Not necessary." Tristan passed Ferret a pen. "He's already signed off on it, as has your decanus."

Reluctantly, Ferret did as he was told.

"Good." Tristan stood, raising himself to his full height of 5 feet 8 inches, and pulled his shoulders back, assuming his favoured ordering-people-about pose. "If I hear you've broken your contract, legionnaire, I'll damn well have your balls. Understood?"

Ferret nodded. He felt the pits of Hades open up inside, tossing up a blast of flames from the depths.

Tristan reached out to take a rice cake, then changed his mind. "I'm having your trouser press as compensation for the detective work you carried out for our decanus."

"That's outrageous!" Ferret folded his arms. "I was following orders."

"Irrelevant."

"By my reckoning, you've fined me twenty-two trouser presses over the last year." Ferret rubbed his nose. "Why do you need another?"

"Have it delivered here by tomorrow."

Ferret sighed. "There's one last thing. Cyrano has moved into my house, and I want him out."

Tristan waved his hand dismissively and turned to face the window. "Your audience has reached its conclusion. Please close the door on your way out. While I'm commanding, I command you to leave that bag of marching powder behind as an offering to your superior officer. I need something substantial to see me through the pain of sacking Babylon. After I've screwed her first. Up against that wall, I imagine. That's where she likes it best. Whore!"

# Chapter Seventeen: True Blue

The rain beat down mercilessly on the streets of Soho, ricocheting off the pavement, soaking even those lucky enough to have an umbrella. Despatch riders hurried about their business, searching for their stops in a desperate attempt to find shelter. Along Dean Street, passersby huddled in shop doorways, summer clothes stuck fast to their pimpled skins. Those with a little time on their hands found solace in one of the many bars.

Holding a newspaper defiantly over his head, Cyrano hurried along Meard Street until he located a nondescript door protected by a gate made from gloss-black iron railings. Without knocking, he slipped inside, brushed the water from his light summer suit, dropped yesterday's paper on bare floorboards, and followed the rickety stairs to the first floor.

There was a time, he thought, when this area of Westminster was a seedy, run-down dive, full of wall-to-wall sex shops and clip joints, offering every service known to man in their curtained-off back rooms. Law enforcement did their best to ignore the criminal activity taking place under their noses. Unless a protection payment was missed. Then the entire police force would descend en masse.

In this culture of filth and sleaze, private clubs prospered, counting the artists and poets of the day among their clientele. The Emerald Room, tucked away down a small side street, towered head and shoulders above them all.

The Frenchman's nose was assaulted with the tang of damp mould, which built in intensity with each step until even the great dollop of eau de parfum he'd applied that morning no longer blocked out the odour. He chuckled to himself, nostrils arching like Tudor roof beams. He hadn't been in this nest of unwashed tramps for nearly a year, although in that time little had changed.

Taking a seat by the bar, he flipped a coin.

Heads.

Leaning forward, Cyrano pointed at a bottle, rudely interrupting a conversation in progress. Mimi, the owner, ruffled her skirt, flashing many layers of petticoat; she then adjusted her pendulous breasts and looked him up and down with a twinkle in her eye.

"Go fuck yourself." She returned to her other customer, who Cyrano recognised as a rock guitarist.

The Frenchman responded with a roar of laughter. Where else in central London was it possible to receive such an outstanding level of service?

Seconds later, a shot of *la fée verte* appeared, along with a tumbler of water, a slotted spoon, and a cube of sugar. He gave Mimi the thumbs up and tossed her a wrap, which she caught and stuffed in her bra.

He laughed again, pulling up a stool. Where else in London was it possible to pay one's tab with a line of sweet cocaine?

His eye strayed to the peeling wallpaper above the bar. He counted the length of a clump of roof fungus in emerald-green squares. It was definitely still growing and had been since he'd first discovered the club, the year he and Ferret had moved to London. Having abandoned the treasury post his father had pulled strings to secure, he'd toyed with the film industry, flitting between a handful of small companies, quickly becoming disillusioned with the work-reward ratio. His plans to become a producer suffered a further setback when Ferret surrendered all notions of directing, a desire he'd harboured for years, joining The Consultancy instead.

The Frenchman's top lip curled in ire.

What a damnable fool his friend was.

Still, but for that change of direction he wouldn't have found his way to Peru and met José, a fellow legionnaire with a spanking new coca plantation who was in need of a distribution deal.

Cyrano returned to the preparation of his drink, fussing over the addition of water to absinthe, ensuring the cube dissolved fully to create a louche that met his exacting standards. Once he was satisfied, he removed the spoon and took a gentle sip, the first of the day.

"1975." He swivelled in the seat and scanned the club for takers. "Who remembers that year?"

"No one here remembers a thing," said Mimi. "That's our *raison d'etre.*"

Cyrano stared at the sullen clientele congregated on a trio of worn sofas, their structural integrity compromised years ago. "A bag of candy for the best story regarding that summer."

"That was the year I screwed your mum," said the rock star, slamming a glass down on the bar.

The Frenchman shook his head. "Papa?"

"With lips like that, you're one of Mick's." The guitarist kissed the hostess on each cheek, turned sharply on a pair of Cuban heels and departed.

Cyrano took another sip of bitter aniseed liqueur and leaned towards Mimi. "Care to tell me about True Blue?"

"Shush!" Mimi raised a finger to her lips.

She dipped her head slightly to one side, a movement Cyrano judged imperceptible from a distance and mouthed two words that he interpreted as "over there."

The Frenchman nodded just a little, finished his drink, and pointed at the bottle of Fairy. While Mimi refilled the apparatus, he spun on his seat and focused on the sofa group who were playing a card game involving the continuous consumption of sipping whisky, interspersed with lines of powder and the occasional scream of joy. In the dark corner, which had been unlit for as long as Cyrano could remember, he caught a flash of silver.

Outside, the rain continued to lash against the windows, tinkling out a tune of abuse on the long-suffering panes.

Woody would be here soon.

Three o'clock.

By the time Woody the dealer finally rolled up, the lacrimal clouds were busy patching up their sob-fest. The aging hippy nodded at Cyrano and leant against the bar, dreadlocks tumbling past the patched denim waistcoat he favoured and pulled out a six-inch bifter from an inner pocket. Mimi provided a firestick.

"All tha way from Kingston," he said, blowing a wavering smoke ring that climbed intact to the ceiling.

"Nice." Cyrano focused on the fungus, which pulsated rhythmically, following the melody line of the conversation. He felt goosebumps speckle his arms. Spontaneously, the mushroom opened an eye and winked.

"Crap day." Mimi wrestled the joint from her client with both hands and took a long drag. "About to get better."

The joint came Cyrano's way. He inhaled, held the smoke into his mouth for a few seconds, then let it go. As much as he enjoyed getting high, it was a pastime he reserved for blazing hot days on the beach, when there was nothing to do but roast and giggle.

He looked Woody in the eye. "Would you do me the honour of accompanying me onto the roof?"

"Cost you a beer, man."

Cyrano nodded and tossed another wrap to Mimi. There was no point in hurrying Woody. He lived life on his own clock.

According to Emerald Room hearsay, the hippy had begun selling weed back in the day when it was still exotic and difficult to obtain. Legend had it he'd bumbled his way into a sound check and with a combination of charm, cheek, and a bag of very good marijuana, secured himself a job working for Led Zeppelin as their new dealer. Their old one having been busted with a K of Morocco's finest down his pants the night before.

That was Woody's story, and he was sticking to it.

Once he'd finished the beer, he burped the first line of "Jamaica, Land We Love" to a round of applause from the sofa gang. Cyrano borrowed a key from Mimi, tossed her another wrap and made his way outside, past the shadow corner where a weasel of a chap in a dark overcoat was doing his best to hide his features beneath a wide-brimmed hat. The Frenchman felt his pulse quicken. He stepped to the side and let Woody go first, glancing back to make sure they weren't being followed. With the door unlocked, the hippy held out his hand, declared the rain had eased off sufficiently, and stepped out onto the terrace, where puddles of water gathered around a pile of fight-smashed furniture.

"What's up, man?"

"Tell me again about True Blue."

Woody looked nervously from side to side, indicating in signs that he wanted paper and a pen.

"Can't you whisper?"

"Satellites," said Woody.

Cyrano felt his patience wearing thin. Using a combination of fingers and makeshift visual images, he put together a deal that suited them both. He'd whisper the question, the hippy would write the answer, then, once he'd read it, Cyrano would eat the paper. To the best of Woody's knowledge, the Feds hadn't yet invented a poopscope that could decrypt soggy, half-digested calligraphy.

The Frenchman withdrew a few slips of lined paper from his wallet and handed them to Woody, along with a pen.

"Let's start with the summer of '75."

Cyrano left the Emerald Room feeling full of words. They careered around inside him, banging into each other, forever shortening themselves, or worse, ganging up and making new words that had no right to exist. He hailed a cab and set out for Regent's Park, burping verbs and pronouns. Had he locked the door to the roof? He was sure he had. He'd even checked it on the way out.

He'd call Mimi in a moment, to be sure.

The Frenchman turned his attention to his new home. He wasn't sure if their banking friend had formally ordered him to move in, but he certainly hadn't ordered him not to. The centurion had spun a persuasive tale about it being payment due for his consultant friend daring to score a beauty when he was supposed to be the centre of ridicule. Yesterday, with a brain full of flake, it was an excellent idea. How they'd laughed at his friend's expense.

Cyrano bit his thumb.

The centurion had suggested he invite over some street scum and trash the place, but in all honesty, he couldn't bear to destroy such a lovely house. Besides, what might Juliet think? Once his friend tired of the blonde, she'd need a shoulder to cry on. Then, once the dirty deed was done, he'd move back to the Savoy.

The Frenchman rubbed his chin.

There was always the slim possibility that once he hooked up with her, Juliet was a keeper. If that happened, his lie was going to fall apart in double quick time. He needed a backup plan, which was where their friend the firebug came in.

Ferret wouldn't see that one coming.

Cyrano settled into the ride, considering Woody's story, the narrative battering away at his colon. He'd first heard of True Blue when still an impressionable youth. And it made a cracking tale; truly the stuff of urban legend. Later on, he'd heard it again. By the tenth time of telling, the scope was so profound, it was no longer possible to separate truth from braggadocio.


There once was a soap research chemist who accidentally produced a batch of blue liquid with incredible properties. Knowing his employers would make his discovery their own, he destroyed all the evidence, quit his job, and installed a home lab, creating a bathtub full of the stuff. Somewhere along the line he met a frontman called Ginger, who was a one-man party machine. And party they did, from dusk until dawn, every day of that incredible summer. Ginger introduced Pink Floyd to True Blue and later, through Woody, the Zep. The circle of users, tight-knit to begin with, grew steadily larger until half of Soho was getting off on the stuff. True Blue was the drug of the moment, set to become a massive global phenomenon when, without warning, Ginger announced it was all over. It was New Year's Eve. Ginger vanished. No one ever saw him again. One theory stated he was working for the military and the Soho scene was a cover to test combat drugs on an unsuspecting public. Another theory suggested that the soap scientist was arrested by the security services, who stole his formula and locked him up in solitary confinement, which is where he languishes to this very day.

The Frenchman had always taken Woody's story with a pinch of salt on the grounds that there is a proven relationship between belief in outlandish conspiracy theories and the consumption of marijuana.

Yesterday, this all changed.

A stranger with untameable red hair, partially quelled beneath a deerstalker, came knocking at the Regent's Park house. Having mistaken Cyrano for Ferret, the stranger inquired whether his father had left him anything in his will. A small bottle of blue liquid, perhaps?

Initially, he'd dismissed the man who introduced himself as Sir Edward as a coffin chaser, hoping to procure something of value for a few weasel words. The more he thought about it, the more curious he'd become until he was sure he'd explode with the suspense of not knowing. Was this man a relative of the mysterious Ginger? Was Ferret's father the chemist?

He simply had to hear the story again.

Cyrano instructed the cab driver to pull up opposite the Georgian terrace where Ferret's townhouse was located and climbed out, eyeing the high columns, topped by a Grecian frieze, reminding him of The Network's secret logo. Today, the columns bulged in the middle, resonating in time with his breathing. The Frenchman crossed the road to watch the pulsing and squirming from the park, wary of myriad quacking ducks that were much larger than they ought to be. As he turned around and looked up, one of the three muses atop the roof took a twirl.

A second cab pulled up; its passenger walked hurriedly away, a spring to his step. For a second, the Frenchman thought it was the chap from the Emerald Room, until he examined the attire. The fellow wasn't wearing a hat for starters. Or a coat. Only a backpack.

And yet . . .

It could easily be him.

He gave himself a metaphorical slap.

It was impossible to trust one's faculties when wormwood was involved.

Cyrano clicked his tongue against the roof of his mouth.

He hadn't intended to pass himself off as Ferret — until the prospect of a tidy profit reared its head. When Plutus puts an opportunity one's way, he reminded himself, one has no option but to grab it with both hands. He'd met some outstanding chemists over the years. With a sample of True Blue, any one of them was able to analyse and synthesise. As the sole owner of True Blue Inc., the value of his business empire might easily run into the tens of millions. With his banking friend's financial clout and The Network as a distribution chain, the true value escalated into the billions.

The only point on which he lacked clarity was the drug's effects. Woody's words bubbled around in his stomach: "It's like ecstasy, man, but a hundred times better. It lets you inside someone's soul. The more you take it, the better it gets. They call it getting shelled."

If shelled was what they called it, that's what Cyrano intended to get.

The Frenchman returned to the problem at hand. Sir Edward had told him where to meet the following day if he had a change of heart and wished to talk further. To fully engage as Ferret, he needed access to the files his friend had collected from the family solicitor. Given the current state of his relationship with the consultant, how on earth was he going to persuade his friend to part with them?

The Frenchman found a free bench and sat down, watching the muses waltz. From here, his friend's den, which was built above the original roof level between two stacks of chimneys, was really rather ugly. Perhaps he'd have it torn down.

He swallowed hard and raised his eyes to the sky, the anger building inside.

Without his influence, his consultant friend would be nothing. But for him, he'd be a ludicrously inept paranormal investigator trapped in a small provincial town. He'd rescued his friend from that fate and dragged him off to university. It was he who had introduced Ferret to The Network; it was he who had suggested forwarding the mergers and acquisitions information leaks to their banking friend, which had, in turn, funded the house.

All he had to do was rifle his way through a few drawers, read a few mouldy old files, and convince a stranger that he was Wolfgang's son.

Granted, he had some unsavoury habits, practised in private, but the one character trait he'd long prided himself on was his ability to keep an oath. His friend was a fellow legionnaire, one of a select group he'd promised not to lie, cheat, or steal from.

Break a solemn oath, or pass up on a billion-pound opportunity?

What was he to do?

# Chapter Eighteen: Revenge

A welcome breeze swept through tight streets, rustling the leaves in Soho Square Gardens, causing the statue of old King Charles to stir from its slumber, flexing stiffened limbs. Damien sat on his favourite bench, a tribute to the singer Kirsty MacColl, with a cigarette between his lips, listening to the sounds of a gruff street cleaner hard at work scrubbing away the remains of last night's party from a soiled shop front. Frantically, the senior junior searched for a lighter. Finding one in the last of his pockets, he sparked up, kick-starting his lungs, emitting a geyser of blue-tinged smoke far into the sky.

If you're going to poison yourself, he thought, looking at the statistics on the packet of golds, at least have the temerity to do it properly.

Presently, Junior Eric hobbled into view, accompanied by a pair of grande coffees. Damien sucked on the thin, white pleasure stick, watching the junior painfully traverse the Square. He rubbed his hand along his jaw, testing the length of his stubble.

Eric took a seat. He looked pallid and drained.

"Cigarette?" said Damien.

"I'll have one of mine."

The senior junior sipped milky coffee. He reached inside his jacket pocket. "Painkillers?"

Gratefully, Eric accepted a pair of pills and knocked them back with a swig of latte. "Now, about our revenge."

Monday morning was when it all went to hell on a hang glider. Tim Tim called a meeting first thing to announce how unhappy he was with the seniors' leadership skills. While this was ostensibly true, Damien knew it was the manner of the cover-up, or rather lack of, that had curried the boss's goat. An outsider uncovering a conspiracy to lie to the boss by omission was bad enough. To then have the same outsider run rings around them all, well, that was a stain on the seniors' reputations.

As punishment for their collective sins, Tim Tim locked the Precious away in his safe.

When the first of the City Old Boys arrived demanding access by right of sovereignty, Tim Tim stood guard with folded arms, refusing to divulge the combination. Wave after wave of City Old Boys arrived, only to be ushered away. Behind the scenes, someone must have muttered something in someone's ear, because it wasn't long before the pale chap in the raggedy frock coat pitched up like a storm front to batter the boss's shutters senseless with blustery threats and squall. He even tried pressing in Tim Tim's eyes with his thumbs, causing the boss to leave in a huff. Later, Tim Tim had phoned in, booking the rest of the week off, citing urgent business in New York. He'd flown the coop, taking Miss Harrington with him.

Clifford and Malory, now nominally in charge, were livid. They expected a queue of City Old Boys to form around the block, to beat the combination out of them. When no queue was forthcoming, they become angrier still.

The senior junior felt a dull ache in his ribs.

Tentatively, he touched the spot where the head of a prop Victorian walking cane had caught him. He'd expected a tongue lashing for his part in the Precious debacle, but not actual physical abuse. The duo had questioned him relentlessly about Ferret. Was that his real name? Where did he live? They'd kept all the juniors back against their will until after Miss Harrington's plane had landed at JFK, then made him call her. Politely, she'd refused the invitation to discuss her new paramour.

Damien rubbed his lower legs.

That had cost him a cane from *Tom Brown's Schooldays* across the calves.

Eric was in much worse shape.

They'd really gone to town on him, punching him in the kidneys and smacking the soles of his feet until he was hardly able to stand. And for what? It hadn't got them the Precious back.

"What do you think they'll do next?" asked Eric, his eyes glazing over.

Damien sniffed the air. "Is that cigarette loaded?"

"Sorry," said Eric, handing it on.

The senior junior took a toke and wished he hadn't. "Soap bar."

"I bought it on impulse from a street urchin." Eric smiled apologetically. "Please don't hit me for making a bad joint."

Damien laughed. "Your paperwork is excellent, as usual."

"Do you think we need some exercise books to put down our trousers?" asked the junior.

"I think we're probably safe."

"If there's one thing I've learnt about being a junior, it's to always be prepared to take a beating."

Damien sighed. "Your brother's a someone, so they're bashing you into shape as a favour to him."

"I'm supposed to be grateful?"

"That's the idea." Damien scratched his head. "One day you'll have juniors of your own. That's when you get to feel better about the system."

"Only if you're a narcissist with sadistic tendencies."

Damien shook his head. "Where did you learn language like that?"

The junior explained how his mummy had sent him to counselling to try and wean him off the comics and video games before his daddy found out. The adjustments were likely to take years, beginning with the quest to find out why he hated daddy so much. The first practical exercise was to go shooting until he was able to kill a stag without crying.

The senior junior sighed.

Every once in a while the Old Boy system produced a throwback who simply wasn't cut out for a life of ruthless conquest. In the olden days, they used to prescribe the priesthood and, if that didn't work out, a riding accident or a fall from the battlements. These days it was all about automobile accidents and drug overdoses. Damien was sure this was what his own father planned for him if he ever tried to follow his dream of treading the boards.

Away in the direction of Soho, a bell chimed, indicating a quarter hour. Damien looked at his watch. Nearly 6:00 a.m. The Square would soon be chock-full of cyclists.

"Are you going to Bogart that jay all day?"

"Sorry." Damien offered the dog-end to his pal.

Eric sucked out all remaining life from the joint and hurriedly sparked another.

Damien twitched his thumbs. What he really wanted was a good, hard toke on the Precious. Failing that, a rooftop snipe of Nazi generals who looked like Cliff-face and Malcontent. He took the second funny fag from Eric, drew hard on it and, holding down the smoke, passed it back.

Fortunately, the only job on the board for today was a press release for DW:A, which was already prepared and signed off.

Eric sat back on the bench, puffing away. "This is the life," he said in his most sarcastic tone.

Damien took a swig of lukewarm coffee and spat it back into the cup. "If only we didn't have jobs."

Later in the day, once he'd taken a shower, had a shave in the company amenities and sent out for clean underwear and a new shirt, Damien reflected on where they were with the launch of DeathWorld. According to the schedule to which he was working, the hardcore beta testing was now complete. He'd reported the loss of computer files, as verified by Ferret, only to have the pale chap in the frock coat dismiss such trivia as irrelevant. With a wave of his bony hand, he'd declared the product was certified bug-free.

Given the lack of City Old Boys queuing for a go, thought Damien, the second stage of the plan had obviously been brought forward.

Brring!

"Damien Tiverton speaking. How may I help?"

"Andrew Fletcher, gaming correspondent, *Evening Standard*."

The senior junior launched into a well-rehearsed speech, confirming that the launch of DW:A was proceeding as scheduled. Full details to be confirmed in a separate press release, due on Monday. And no, he was not in a position to exchange event tickets for alcohol.

This was how it had been all day, ever since the deliberately bungled press release which featured his personal contact details instead of those for the DW:A hotline.

Brring!

Damien let his phone ring, intending not to answer it, only to have a change of heart at the last. When he heard the voice on the other end of the line, he nearly fell from his chair.

"Go away," he hissed, hanging up.

But not quickly enough. In a flap, he collected Eric from the kitchenette, where he'd been seconded to the task of washing up dirty crockery, a job that required him to stand. The junior hadn't had the opportunity yet to wash or shave and was, as Fearnley had so eloquently put it, "pleasantly piquant with the makings of a couch grass goatee."

Outside, Soho Square teemed with tourists busily trying to figure out how to navigate around without missing any of its key features. An Italian lady stopped them, asking for directions to Paul McCartney's production company. Hobbling badly, Eric crossed the road and pointed to the right, sending her in the wrong direction.

Damien huffed. Scanning the garden's benches for a dishevelled tramp with bottle-end glasses, he didn't recognise the smartly dressed dude in the trilby.

"Afternoon." The moviemaker tipped his hat.

"Afternoon," said Damien tersely.

"Oh," said Eric sourly, rolling up his sleeves. "What's *he* doing here?"

What Ferret wanted was a name. Not any old name, but the name of the company responsible for the manufacture of the Precious.

Damien folded his arms. "Walk with me."

Eric took up a position on the other side of the moviemaker, wincing with every step. "We should kick your backside all the way to Battersea for the trouble you've caused us."

"You and whose army?" Ferret smiled and tipped his hat at the junior.

Eric aimed a kick at the moviemaker's ankle. Shifting his weight onto one leg, he let rip. Ferret grimaced in pain. The junior toppled over in agony.

"That wasn't very nice." Ferret held out his hand. Eric accepted, then tried to pull him over.

"Stop it, both of you!" yelled Damien.

"Why? It's his fault your ribs hurt and I can't walk."

Ferret nodded. "I feel your pain. What they've done to you isn't fair. Thanks to the same people, I lost something very dear to me and I need to get it back. The only way to do that is to track the Precious to its source."

Damien proposed a deal. One piece of confidential information for another. Surprisingly, the moviemaker politely declined the offer, refusing to confirm whether Ferret was his real name.

They parted company as amicably as possible, both sides agreeing to consider the situation and review their respective positions by the end of the week.

"He's hiding something." Eric located a free bench and took a seat.

"I reckon the claim that he's a detective is true," said Damien. "And he's definitely a geek. I've hung out with media types all my life and I'm pretty certain he's not directly involved in the business, so possibly a freelance short maker with aspirations. Do you remember the way he ran the Prizeday meeting? He could easily be a trained management consultant."

Eric produced a state-of-the-art mobile phone and typed Ferret's name into an internet search engine along with the words "consultant" and "detective." "Bingo." He handed the phone to Damien.

"Ferret: London's Premier Detecting Consultant," read Damien. "That makes him a detectant. Eric, you're a genius."

"We better tell the seniors."

"Let's get a good night's sleep first." Damien yawned. "We can talk about it tomorrow."

"Let's not." Eric perched his chin on his fists. "All my life I've tried to be nice to people, and look where it's got me. Comics taught me that you know who the bad guys are because they wear evil costumes. But real life isn't like that. No one dresses up, and everyone is horrible to everyone else. Except for me. That's why I've been sent to see a shrink, to correct my behaviour. I want to be horrible for a change. I want to know what it feels like."

"Please don't." Damien grabbed Eric's arm. "I know what they've got planned. They're going to set Tidley-Jones on him."

"The bone-crushing legend?" Eric let out a long whistle. "No one's heard from him in twenty years. He used to be built like an armoured personnel carrier. I'll bet he looks like a main battle tank by now."

"I'm serious," said Damien, tightening his grip. "He'll pulverise the moviemaker."

"The trouser ferret lied to us, and that's a crime. If I tell Cliff-face and Malcontent where to find him, they'll like me for finally being horrible to someone properly. I might even get a promotion out of it. Then my brother will be happy, which will make daddy happy. If I'm evil enough, for long enough, who knows — I might even get my inheritance back."

# Chapter Nineteen: Suits

Ferret hurried along Savile Row, past Henry Huntsman, tailor to generations of Old Boys, pausing to adjust his fedora. He felt the crackle of foil beneath the crown. A stranger bearing a placard declaring "The End is Nigh" had approached him earlier in Trafalgar Square, assailing him with a series of persuasive arguments regarding government monitoring. After much haggling, the chap with the wild ginger hair had installed a custom-made anti-electronic harassment device, thanked him for the business, and invited him to a meeting of likeminded individuals later that evening, which, despite his warm overtures, Ferret graciously declined.

He remained doubtful the spies in the sky were targeting him, but as his father's files had been stolen by off-the-grid technology, he was taking no chances.

In a final display of histrionics, the charismatic wild man pointed to a leather-clad girl hunched over a motorcycle and named her as a probable agent of the state.

Which state, he didn't say.

Outside Three Savile Row, the detective bumped into a pair of tourists arguing over a guidebook. He pointed to the roof they were looking for, explaining how the profile had changed since the Beatles played their final concert there forty years ago.

A posed photo and he was on his way.

Walking quickly past Gieves & Hawkes' flagship store, he glanced behind him. Being so close to the largest enclave of Old Boy wealth in Europe always made him nervous, even though Mayfair itself was now populated mainly by foreign interests. Legionnaires, as he knew only too well, were prohibited from frequenting the row by a Standing Order. According to his banking friend, there was a clothing-based incident some years ago, which culminated in the outing of two Citizens of Rome. The Old Boys beat them with canes, turning them over to the Bullie Club, who shaved their heads, applied strong glue and feathers, then handcuffed them naked to a lamppost outside the Ritz. In retaliation, every shop in the Row had its windows smashed.

Ferret turned left, then right. Halfway down Sackville Street, he stopped, looked furtively from side to side, then ducked into a shop doorway where he sounded the buzzer.

"I have a three o'clock appointment to see Raffles de Souza."

He headed to the back of the boutique, away from prying eyes, where he was joined by a short, wiry chap of similar age, fine blonde hair neatly cropped in a parting to the left. Raffles the tailor wore a three-piece suit with four pockets, cut in a light-brown check. The lapels were a good centimetre thinner than those of Ferret's own suit.

"A good day." Raffles held out his hand.

Ferret smiled and embraced his friend, causing him to blush. "It's been a long time, partner."

"Sir."

The detective eyed up the tailor, unsure what to say next. He settled for: "How's business?"

"Hectic. The Old Boys are hosting a gala event later in the month and the row can't keep up."

"I thought you were independent of all that malarkey."

"We all muck in when the going gets tough."

Ferret removed his jacket and placed it on a free peg. "I'm all yours."

"Very good." Raffles produced a tape measure from his pocket. "Stand still and don't move."

Ferret twisted around and found himself face-to-face with a pen-and-ink drawing of a ferret decked out in rugby kit and a portrait of a handsome, suited ferret in a hat.

"You still have them . . ." he said, reaching toward the pictures.

The tailor slapped Ferret's wrist with his hand. "No touching. Now, do as you're told or next time it's your soft bits."

Raffles sped around Ferret's top half, jotting down measurements. As he worked, he entertained with stories concerning the comfort and detail offered by bespoke, a facet of clothing fully understood by the Old Boys. In comparison, the label generation, addicted to their off-the-peg Gucci and Armani, with a smattering of Dior for those who dress on the other side, were clueless when it came to what it felt like to feel comfortable and in charge. In Raffles's opinion, the difference between the City Old Boys and the new wave of finance wannabes was all down to their first and last visit to a tailor.

"The Old Boys shop here from bespoke christening gown to bespoke burial shroud." Raffles checked the size of Ferret's chest. "In comparison, a wannabe's first visit is likely to be the day after an unwarranted bonus, when they've already purchased everything else they can think of. Afterwards, they'll never be seen again."

The detective laughed.

His old partner from his teenage ghost-hunting days, who he'd first bumped into in the nursery school dressing-up box wearing a frock and a floppy hat, was now quite the clothing philosopher.

"I hope you don't think I'm a wannabe."

The edges of Raffles's mouth twitched. "The thought has yet to cross my mind."

Ferret reminisced with his old friend about how they used to love nothing better than beating an Old Boy team, his hand straying to the old battle scar close to his collarbone. On the day it happened, he'd been accused of ungentlemanly conduct on the field of play by the Old Boys' captain, who claimed he'd sneaked into their changing rooms and stolen their game plans. The subsequent war of words escalated into a full-on scrap involving thirty pairs of crazy fists and ended in absolute uproar when it became apparent that one of the Old Boys was wearing an embossed gold ring bearing his initials, the source of the trophy mark. The Old Boys beat a bloody retreat, thanked Ferret's team from a distance, and then set about thrashing their fellow, intent on teaching him a lesson for bringing the game into disrepute.

"Sir appears to have taken on additional luggage since we last met." Raffles pulled up a stool and sat down, intent on taking an inside leg measurement. "What car does sir drive these days?"

"Well," said Ferret, feeling hot inside, "I own a Maserati that I don't use as much as I'd like."

"Colour?"

"Yellow."

"And does sir still see the Frenchman?"

Ferret breathed in a great lungful of air and snorted derisively. "I was recently forced to employ a pair of bouncers to throw him out of my own home. As it happens, he doubled their salaries and turned them against me."

"Then sir's relationship is as it ever was." The tailor brandished his tape measure, confirming the length of Ferret's inside leg at thirty-one inches. "Has sir met the right lady yet?"

"I've certainly found *a* lady." Ferret felt himself blush. "Why do you ask?"

Raffles licked his lips. "A gentleman should always be prepared, suit-wise, for the day he proposes."

The muscles in Ferret's neck stood taut. "Whether this lady is the right lady remains to be seen, but in the meantime, I must look smarter than Cyrano. To this end, I require two fabulous suits."

The detective had planned on spending an hour at most with his old friend, until the books of luxury fabric were revealed and he became captivated by the various patterns and weights, diving into the library of Scottish dyed wools without restraint. Some of the designs he recognised instantly, such as dark blue with a white pinstripe and light grey with a pink pinstripe, both old banking favourites. One by one, he identified the patterns worn by his friends, both in finance and consultancy. The tomes of softer, single-colour fabrics with an embossed design repeated throughout the weave were new, although their feel was not lost to his touch.

"This, I like." Ferret stroked a swatch of black dogtooth, comprised of new wool and cashmere. "None of my friends has such a suit."

"Sir has impeccable taste." Raffles picked up a booklet of linings and laid it by the fabric.

Ferret flipped through the pages and pointed to a shiny lime green.

"If I may." Raffles found a dark burgundy. "We can match the buttons to this colour."

The detective nodded in agreement.

Raffles folded up the tape measure. "The black suit will look elegant as a two-piece with a three button jacket. If I may be so bold, taking sir's past endeavours into account, something a little racier for his second choice."

"You mean submit myself to extreme dandification?"

"Liberal dandification." Raffles tried to hide the smirk upon his lips. "I have a vermilion check, just in from Italy, that will suit sir's requirements. I suggest a three-piece, three-button jacket, with an additional side pocket. Sir will need to add a pocket watch for maximum effect."

"That sounds splendid. My only requirement is that whatever you decide, it must go with the hat."

"As sir has yet to take it off, this much we'd already assumed."

"There's one more thing. The ferret portrait on the left. I'd very much like a copy, if I may, to use on my new business cards."

Later that evening, following a brief exchange of saucy texts with Juliet, Ferret settled in for a session of zombie violence, determined to trash his own high score in fragmented heads before Marcus arrived around eight. Embarrassingly, despite his best efforts, he was still occupying the guest lodge, having lost control of the main house. As *adiutor*, Marcus would soon sort out the truculent Frenchman. In the meantime, thanks to a timely bribe to the bouncers, he'd rescued the games console and several other favoured items from the den, which he'd relocked afterwards.

Ferret's thoughts turned to the Precious; his heart beat a little faster.

Unless he had one soon, he'd surely explode.

He took a glug of white wine, sloshed it around inside his mouth, the crisp gooseberry notes of sauvignon blanc setting his senses alight. All that was missing was a dab of flake, which was not a habit he indulged around Marcus.

The detective made his way from easy chair to wine chiller and administered a top-up. Glass in hand, he assessed the artwork which he'd moved from the main house earlier in the day. It was Tom Tom's idea to purchase old Hammer movie posters from the 1950s as an investment. He'd even provided advice on the frames, which was a level of commitment that Ferret couldn't be bothered with.

How strange, he thought.

The pictures on the walls had been shuffled around and were now in alphabetical order.

*The Curse of Frankenstein*; *Dracula*; *The Hound of the Baskervilles*; *The Mummy*; *The Quatermass Xperiment*. He'd seen them all, many times over. *Village of the Damned*, which hung in the bathroom of the main house, being neither Hammer nor from the 1950s, was a particular favourite. As a boy, it resonated with his unusual intuition. The detective settled on that thought. He'd been able to accurately predict the feelings of others for as long as he cared to remember, apart from that dreadful period just gone.

Knowing how others were feeling gave him a certain edge. He'd exploited his intuition to become fly-half, captaining a winning Millfield team. And later, after he'd joined the legion, his intuition enabled him to secure the role of decanus three years running.

Brring!

Number withheld.

Jovially, Ferret answered the phone, anticipating the voice on the other end.

"A good evening to you too," said Marcus, his usual friendly tone tinged with seriousness.

Ferret took a sip of wine. "Will you be late?"

"Sadly, I shan't be there at all."

Ferret kicked a skirting board and set to deriding his friend for a lack of commitment, only to discover that the opposite was true. Marcus was detained on the work front, busy defending the realm, possibly for the next few days.

On an unrelated note, he provided an update on the analysis of the SniffPhreak's logs. Rajesh had discovered a file fragment relating to something called D-XIII and an experiment to test its sheer thickening qualities.

Ferret shrugged his shoulders.

"Imagine a swimming pool full of custard," said his friend. "Now think about walking on it."

"You can do that?"

"Certain liquids, when put under pressure, behave as solids," said his friend. "As you can imagine, there is both a commercial and a military application for the right liquid with the right properties."

Ferret cracked a joke about his father weaponising custard, only for it to fall flat. His friend remained serious, stating that he had no clear idea what Wolfgang had been up to, other than he'd officially retired from post on his sixtieth birthday and was later retained as a freelance consultant.

"One last thing," said Ferret. "The letter you signed for our banking friend."

There was a long pause on the other end of the line. "Excuse me?"

"The one he had me add my signature to, that stipulates he can fine me in toys if I persist with my detective fantasies."

"How many times must I tell you," said Marcus. "Never sign anything where that friend is concerned."

Ferret slapped his forehead.

"I must go. Take care, my friend."

"You too."

Marcus hung up before Ferret was able to relate his encounter with Damien. He'd used his intuition to try and ascertain the manufacturer of the Precious.

Two words had resonated on the senior junior's tongue.

RockSlut Research.

Ferret stroked his chin. RockSlut Software were the creators of DW:A, so the information wasn't that surprising, except for a rumour he'd heard back in his mergers and acquisitions days. Allegedly, the RockSlut board had unceremoniously jettisoned their entire research division on the quiet for one pound. He'd spent weeks trying to discover the identity of the mystery buyer, convinced it was the investment opportunity of a lifetime. He ultimately drew a blank. There was perhaps a column inch in the business press and a few pages in the gaming magazines. And then nothing.

Until now.

With the aid of an internet search engine, he had an address. First thing tomorrow, he'd pay them a visit. After all, finding his missing files hardly involved the paranormal. He patted himself on the back. And his banking friend *had* ordered him to investigate DW:A.

As for the rest of the evening, it was now his own. Earlier on, he'd received a text from filthy Cristina, inviting herself over for a glass of fizz. He'd ignored the temptation due to his appointment with Marcus.

Just seeing her couldn't do any harm, surely?

He'd tell her he had a girlfriend and they'd part friends.

Quickly, he bashed out a reply and hit send before he changed his mind. Then he headed towards the drawer in which he kept the flake and removed a hollowed-out paperweight. As he did so, something caught his eye. Or rather the lack of something. He tipped the contents of the drawer onto the floor and spread them out, an ominous swirling feeling forming in the pit of his stomach.

The manila envelope containing the letter from his father, along with the glass phial — they were no longer there.

Blam!

"Holy sweetbreads of Jupiter!" Flamen ducked behind a bush, urging Edward to do the same.

Since the power cut ten minutes earlier, much of Soho had been plunged into darkness, making it difficult to see without assistance. Pressing a pair of night-vision glasses tightly to his face, Sir Edward peered into the darkness, counting shapes and giving a rolling update. There were four men armed with rifles on various rooftops around Soho Square providing cover and three plainclothes on the ground. A further two were now inside the target building, escorting the man they'd spent the day following. An unmarked van remained in position around the corner, controlling the operation.

The acrid stench of spent gunpowder wafted across the priest's nostrils, causing him to gag.

Projectile weapons so lowered the tone of an engagement, he thought.

He gritted his teeth, adjusting his leg. "Who are they shooting at?"

Edward pointed and handed him the glasses. "Fourth-floor balcony."

The priest picked out a heat signature, glimpsing smooth contours around the figure's outline. He located one of the men on the roof, for comparison. The chap was wearing full combat gear, with a Kevlar cuirass. Lithely, the first figure performed a backflip, her torso flinching mid-flight.

"Bull's-eye," said the priest.

With a spin, the figure caught the railing of the balcony below.

Blum!

Flamen recalibrated the binoculars. One of the plainclothes was flapping his arms in a panic, trying desperately to brush something off. Perhaps he was surrounded by a swarm of stinging insects too small to register individual heat signatures.

Blum!

The priest flipped back to the gymnast. Following an outstretched arm, he located one of the men on the roof behaving in precisely the same fashion as the fellow on the ground. He returned to the gymnast once more, in time to catch a weapon being sheathed in a leg holster.

Efficiently, a padded elbow jerked backwards.

Crash!

Tinkle!

The gymnast pulled a window open and slithered nimbly inside.

"Jupiter's colossal teats!" The priest handed the glasses back to Edward. "The uninvited guest is a girl."

"Well, one is damned." Edward pushed a tuft of stray hair under his hat and returned to the vigil.


Flamen sighed.

The ginger terror had turned the Cold War listening post into a full-scale war room in record time, dusting down an old tea urn and assigning it the field rank of corporal. He'd installed a map of Greater London, decorating it with red, green, and blue pins connected with matching coloured cotton to a series of handwritten notes, scrawled in illegible script, pinned at the edges of the map. A further set of notes remained unconnected. Photographs of the twelve members of Project XIII plus Lewis were added, framed in blue. Wolfgang's photo, along with Lewis and four others were crossed out. Two additional cards, coloured red, were connected to pins near Regent's Park and Chelsea Embankment.

They'd split the living members of the team straight down the middle, taking three each. Flamen began with the flyboy, nesting near Hampstead Heath. Since retiring, he'd taken to researching his family tree. Flamen phoned him to discuss a long-lost relative residing in New Zealand. The ex-pilot was an obsessive detail junkie, capable of talking inane nonsense for hours. With his recent promotion to proud grandparent, the priest judged Orville Pratt an unlikely saboteur of the realm. He paid an ethereal visit to be certain, then put a cross through the photo. Edward took the submariner, only to discover that ironically he'd been involved in a parachute accident the previous year, skydiving for charity.

Another cross.

Many years ago when Flamen had prepared the hideaway, he'd deposited a bundle of cash and two hundred gold sovereigns in a concealed floor safe. The notes were no longer legal tender and required cashing in at a bank, a task which delighted Sir Edward, much to the chagrin of the priest. The ginger terror exchanged the currency with relish, never more than fifty pounds at a time, inventing stories on the fly as to how the money had come into his possession.

"Your ebullience will get you noticed," Flamen chastised his accomplice.

"In order to out the thief, it is advantageous if word of one's re-emergence reaches his ears."

The priest found it difficult to argue with this, although the possibilities for unpleasantness were far greater than his own plan, which involved following each of the team in turn, clandestinely administering knockout drops, and with the assistance of some thick cord and a few exotic methods of pain administration, extracting the facts they needed.

Edward objected.

Obtaining access to Compound-13, he argued, had required a chain of bribes all the way to the prime minister. Furthermore, the programme of work was clearly at an advanced stage, which meant there was the expense of keeping it hidden from the security forces. Anyone prepared to go to such extremes would not think twice about employing professional bully boys for the purposes of reciprocal torture.

Flamen considered this a little paranoid, but given his friend's peculiar relationship with the universe, he let it go. For the time being, they would sniff out their targets with Edward as bait, collecting information and eschewing direct engagement.

With their finances in order, Edward paid an early-morning visit to Waterloo Bridge, intent on locating his old ring of informants. Grimes, a long-time resident of cardboard city until its demolition, soiled himself when he saw Edward's hirsute face, leering at him from the shadows.

"You're dead," he said, rubbing his eyes.

The street gent had very little information to give, and what he did have wasn't free. A half bottle of whisky bought his attention and the revelation that there was a new paymaster in town. A further half bottle, dangled at a distance, secured a name.

"We call him Sneak." Grimes coughed into a dirty hanky, lustily eyeing the liquor just beyond his reach. "You don't see him coming or going, and he never shows his face."

Edward handed over the drink, promising more if Grimes persuaded the rest of the old ring to re-join him. Grimes swore his lifelong devotion, there and then, on bended knee. Carrier bag clanking, Edward set off on his rounds, Grimes in tow, offering a gallon of scotch to those prepared to pledge their allegiance.

Uptake was universal.

There was one old friend on whom Edward wished to call more than any other, who had assisted him in the past, taking flak when things became too hot to handle. In Flamen's opinion, this action was fraught with risk and he forbade actual physical contact. Depending on which path the fellow had taken, they might easily end up as prisoners of the state — or worse, surrounded by the Praetorian Guard. Earlier in the day they'd tracked him from a distance, observing as he casually cased out Soho Square for a likely operation later that night.

"One must know what's happening inside," said Sir Edward, determined to get involved. Using the night-vision glasses, he checked the location of each of the armed men in preparation for a dash.

"Let me use my remote viewing skills." The priest closed his eyes and settled into his happy place from where he peeked out, scrutinising the brickwork of the building, searching for their man.

Flamen concentrated on constructing a three-dimensional wire model in his mind, his imagination filling in the building's infrastructure. Water and waste pipes, electricity cables and wiring looms, telephony and networking cables; all became briefly visible before blending into walls or vanishing beneath floors. On the fifth floor, he located the man they were following hunkered down behind a desk, flanked by a pair of bodyguards.

In his mind's eye, Flamen searched for the gymnast. The pictures he made were not of a girl composed of skin and bone, but a ball of silver energy, fluid in motion. The more he tried to lock on to her, the slipperier she became. By Jupiter's love truncheon! It was worse than trying to grapple with a wriggling piglet covered from snout to tail in basting oil.

Finally, he locked on to her. She was in the front stairwell between the fourth and fifth floors. He felt the three men in black exit the building's central stairwell on to the fifth floor. They donned darkened glasses and placed their hands firmly over their ears. The priest opened his eyes. Inside the building a flashbang detonated, illuminating the windows.

Flamen blinked to clear his retinas. From behind him, he heard the dull clang of wooden implements beating against sheet metal. The din echoed around the Square. Edward raised his head to discern what was happening, only to find his line of sight obscured. He crawled away, keeping low to the ground.

The priest concentrated his entire being on the top two floors, attempting to see and feel everything but the girl; using this methodology, he constructed a negative image of her. As the details flooded in, he let out a gasp.

"By the seminal vesicles of Jupiter! There are civilians inside."

"One senses trouble," said Edward, returning from his foray. "Grimes and his vagrants have broken their promise. Instead of partying in the gardens, they hold a line near the van."

Flamen scrunched up his face. The gymnast had that same otherworldly feel as the girl on the motorbike they'd observed *observing them* in Trafalgar Square.

Inside the building, Flamen located the men in black once more; he felt them make their way cautiously towards the front stairwell and the only set of stairs to the top floor, where three of the civvies crouched around a safe, examining something of great interest that emitted waves of energy that lashed out like a dozen golden whips. Two more civvies cowered in a kitchen a few yards away.

He bit his lip.

That pattern — he knew it of old. Unless he was mistaken, it was one of Albright's battlefield globes.

Confused, the priest took a metaphysical step backwards.

Despite Edward's bluster, there was a real possibility the man they were following had gone rogue, dismissing the directive to protect the realm. Equally, it was possible that the gymnast was working for the security services, safeguarding crown assets.

In an instant, the girl was upon the group of three. Using a combination of fists, knees, feet, and elbows, she dealt with each of them in rapid succession. Picking through the bodies, she retrieved the globe.

While she was distracted with her precious prize, their man entered the room. Both bodyguards opened fire, hitting her two, three, four times. Flamen felt her curl up into a foetal position, her body heating up with each successive shot until she exploded, uncoiling like a vengeful cobra. Gracefully she flew through the air, striking one of the men in the face with her heel. Backwards she tumbled, twisting and turning, cracking the other bodyguard about the head.

BANG!

The Square and gardens lit up a deep cherry red, basking in the glow of an angry, pulsing flare. Taking this as their cue, the line of vagrants rushed the van and began to beat it with clubs. A smaller group spun off and rushed the plainclothes on the pavement.

Assisted by Edward, the priest struggled to his feet. "Damn Grimes! We must go."

He looked around. One side of the van was rapidly engulfed by men with outstretched arms. A plainclothes officer went down, swarmed over by the other group, disappearing under the weight of bodies. The one remaining plainclothes turned and fled, pursued by individual gang members, brandishing a combination of chair legs, planks, and cudgels.

Crash!

Flamen winced at the sound of metal smashing against concrete, reminding him of his injured ankle. The group of men let out a whoop of satisfaction and beat their weapons against the prone vehicle, chanting for blood. His arm around Edward, the priest staggered to the corner of Greek Street, keeping to the shadows cast by the canopy of leaves. He looked up. The rooftop observers were too busy dealing with the spontaneous riot to notice them.

The flare was on its last legs.

Any second now.

BOOM!

Across the Square, the toppled van exploded in a ball of orange flames that leapt forever upwards, licking at the cool night sky. The gang let out a roar of approval, waving their weapons above their heads.

"Jupiter's glans!" Flamen staggered backwards, knocking Edward over and skinning his knuckles against a wall.

A searing pain flashed up his leg.

He blacked out, suspended between worlds, thinking of the youth who'd identified himself as Wolfgang's son. Edward had insisted they played the level three True Blue "name my decuria" game, leading to the conclusion that the youth was a gecko, having none of the characteristics of the turtle in its shell. Their friend the chemist was a cautious, clever man. It was possible his son, who purportedly smelt like a Frenchman, had no notion what had been done to him. The terror had made his excuses and left Regent's Park, agreeing to a second date in a few days' time. The boy was disappointed but accepted the revised terms, a deep-seated greed flickering in his eyes.

The priest felt something slap his cheek.

He opened his eyes to Edward's pinched face.

With the surrounding area in total darkness, the flames from the van cast an eerie glow around the Square, throwing up a monster under every bush, a potential gremlin lurking in every doorway. He smiled. Let the creatures of the night try to take them.

In the gardens, spontaneous smaller fires broke out.

With assistance, the priest limped away.

The gang of vagrants bunched together, waving burning wooden sticks and singing a song of victory. They moved as one, occupying the turf in front of the southernmost office block, cheering and drinking. On the eastern side of the Square, a siren sounded, accompanied by a pair of flashing blue lights.

Hurriedly, the pair ducked deeper into the shadows.

They crept along the darkened street, hugging the brickwork. Across the narrow road, an emergency escape door flew open, illuminated by a torch from within. Panting for breath, a smartly dressed man whose face was hidden by a balaclava crashed out onto the pavement, a look of bewilderment in his eyes.

"Bromeliad . . ." Edward's face cracked open in a wide smile. "Is it really you?"

"You're dead!" exclaimed the man they'd spent all day tracking. He peddled backwards, coat tails flapping.

"Old friend." Edward held out his arms.

"Stay . . . away . . ." With which their target turned and fled, vanishing into the deep, dark labyrinth of Soho.

The wild man rubbed his chin.

The emergency door flew open a second time, revealing a well-proportioned girl dressed from head to toe in a tight black catsuit. She flicked a streak of dark hair from the mask covering her eyes and pointed a weapon at Edward. "Which way?"

"Whose side are you on?" stuttered Flamen. Behind him, the blaring siren count was increasing by the second.

A vagrant ran past.

Then another.

Sensing hesitancy, Edward barged into the girl. Instead of giving way, she held firm and with a huff, misplaced Edward's centre of gravity, toppling him onto his back. Narrowing her eyes, she put a boot to his throat and levelled a gun at his head.

"That way," pointed Flamen.

The girl nodded, patting her pocket.

"Come, my friends, oh come, my friends, come oh my friends to me."

Flamen felt the words flow through him like a silvered torrent of Jupiter's piss after a night on the tiles of Capitoline Hill with Dionysus; Edward lay there staring at the sky, transfixed. She'd sung the words so clearly, so note perfect, it beguiled the senses.

Then she was off, hot on Bromeliad's heels.

"My god!" said Edward, tottering to his feet.

A ragtag bunch of vagrants brushed past, chasing after the girl; the last one turned around and tossed a hubcap with frightening ferocity, catching the priest in the head. The rebound struck Edward in the chest.

"Jupiter's prostate!" Flamen wiped blood from his forehead.

"The moment is ruined!" gasped Edward. "I wished to be with her for the rest of my life."

The priest helped Edward upright and hurried along. Given that their chosen disguise for the night consisted of ragged clothes, it was long past scarper time. Behind them, the police tried valiantly to seize control of the situation. More law enforcement officers were arriving by the second. Without warning, the group of vagrants gave a blood-curdling roar and scattered in every conceivable direction. Those who were too slow found themselves cuffed, loaded into the backs of vans.

Flamen gazed forlornly over his shoulder.

Tonight, they'd stayed in the shadows while Bromeliad stirred things up. In the process, he'd posed more questions than answers. Going forward, they would need more coloured cards, more photographs, and a bigger map.

Possibly a larger war room too.

# Chapter Twenty-One: Agendas

For the second morning in a row, Juliet found herself alone at a table for four in a vast, buzzing Beaux-Arts restaurant, populated with snappy dressers engaged in the business of breakfast. According to her body clock, it was mid-afternoon, and she really didn't feel like eating. Removing her jacket, cut by Stella McCartney, she hung it carefully on the back of the chair to her right. A familiar aroma wafted her way; she glanced over at the table opposite, where the waiter was busy delivering a modest mound of glistening scrambled egg topped with ribbons of smoked salmon. In the background, Shirley Bassey blew her a kiss of death, purring out the words to *Goldfinger*.

Juliet smiled.

She settled for coffee, toast, and a style magazine, which she thumbed through, voraciously taking in her daily fix of what to wear and where to be seen. She flicked her tresses and attracting the waiter, who fussed politely, tidying up crumbs with a miniature dustpan and brush. She complimented him on his manners and ordered another coffee. With a flamboyant twirl, James declared her to be "the finest of English flowers." He minced to the kitchens, humming a tune. He returned with a tray containing a cup of coffee and a red rose for the lady.

Juliet blushed.

She held the rose to her nose, inhaling the soft fragrance. Politely, she acknowledged James for his exceptional service.

Her phone beeped. She didn't recognise the number but read the message anyway, which purported to be from a concerned friend. Something had gone awry at the London office; the police were busy assessing the damage.

Surely, thought Juliet, tossing the phone into her handbag, this was Tim Tim's domain.

Later, they had tables booked at Eleven Madison Park, which, according to her friends, was the only place to be seen in New York. She pinched herself. This afternoon, she'd shop in preparation.

Handbag and heels.

Miss Harrington covered her mouth to stifle a yawn.

Yesterday afternoon they'd been out with business associates in the Grand Central Oyster Bar when something exploded. According to the news channels, there was a massive crater emitting a cloud of steam higher than the Chrysler building. Everyone assumed it was terrorists, and quite a panic had broken out. Concerned that the city was under attack, they'd gone to try and help. Tim Tim had assisted by directing traffic. In response, the New York cab drivers were very rude. Officer O'Malley of the NYPD had taken them under his wing and offered a guided tour of the danger zone. They'd been spotted by a news crew and asked for an interview. As a concerned tourist, Tim Tim had obliged, saying kind words about the professionalism of the emergency services.

After the excitement, the boss and his associates had excused themselves, leaving her to amuse herself for the night. She'd met one of her old girlfriends for bubbles and they'd put the world of fashion to rights. If only Stella would consider leather for the riding set; if only Lagerfeld would change his embalming fluid; what WAS Donatella doing with her brother's fashion label? Juliet had told her friend all about her interesting new lover, skipping around the less savoury details of his wardrobe. Once she'd finished, Ferret would look like his producer friend who, with his broad shoulders and pinched-in waist, was a classy style icon. She'd wondered about hooking Cyrano up with her friend and dismissed the notion. The Richmond set was better suited to his international lifestyle. A man who was constantly a dash required a filly with trust. Or, if he turned out to be a player, a girlfriend of equally untrustworthy character.

The Richers had the lot.

They'd get to the bottom of who he was. And if he turned out to be genuine, she might even have a go herself. At the thought of this, Juliet parted her thighs just slightly and wiggled her bum, grinding it into the chair.

Ever since he'd introduced himself, she'd toyed with Cyrano's business card, wondering how she might see him again without making her interest obvious. It wasn't that she didn't fancy her moviemaker, it was just that the Frenchman with his fine taste in suits looked far more elegant on her arm. She felt herself flush. Until Tim Tim had made her an offer she'd be certifiably insane to turn down, she'd intended to persuade her geek to bring the Frenchman along on a blind date to meet the girls.

Her hand hovered over her handbag.

Should she?

*Hello C, this is J. How are you?*

There. It was done.

Juliet drummed her fingers. 9:34 a.m. What was Tim Tim doing? If he took much longer, they'd be late for their ten o'clock appointment. Then they'd miss the Empire State Building at two, unless they skipped being seen out for lunch.

Beep.

*Bonjour mademoiselle, I am well. How may I be of assistance? C*

Before Juliet was able to tap a reply, Tim Tim tumbled down the stairs with the top four buttons of his shirt undone and the tails hanging over his trousers. He remained upright by virtue of birthright alone.

"Coffee," he stammered.

Juliet blushed, trying to hide behind the magazine. Tim Tim spotted her, waved, and waddled over, head downcast, a hand pressed to his forehead. She noticed, to her horror, that he wasn't wearing shoes or socks.

"Robbed blind."

She felt herself redden, wishing to be anywhere but here.

The boss took a seat. "Last night's Thai bride was a man. His accomplice threatened me with compromising photographs if I didn't stump up."

"You poor thing." Juliet frantically tapped the keys on her mobile. "Shall I cancel the meeting?"

"It goes ahead." Tim Tim took a seat. "No one must know, especially the police."

"Where did this happen?"

"A motel somewhere. I was so distraught, I got horribly drunk with Alfred."

Juliet glanced up. "Who's Alfred?"

"I thought he was my drinking buddy until he fleeced me at knifepoint down a dark alley. The cad stole my footwear and my phone!" Tim Tim rubbed his eyes, cuffs flapping. "Until I purchase a new one, you're in charge. I've had the hotel fax the office to let them know."

"I'll move the ten o'clock to ten fifteen and bring tomorrow's midday conference call forward to today."

The boss nodded. "Invite Clifford, Malory, Hartley, and Manleigh."

*My girlfriends need a man for Saturday night. Are you equipped for the challenge?*

Juliet hit send.

She signalled to James, smiling sweetly on his arrival. "A café corretto for the boss, please."

James raised an eyebrow.

"You're right," she said. "Make that a double in every respect. Also, we have a meeting shortly and a shave is required."

"I'll call the barber right away."

"Thank you." Juliet's phone beeped once more.

*Will you be there?*

She pushed a cup of strong black coffee towards Tim Tim, whose need was greater than hers. He accepted it gratefully, knocking it back in one swallow. Her thumbs moved rapidly from side to side.

*I'm in NY. Back Sunday. J x*

Factual and polite.

Tim Tim stared at his bare wrist. "Vandals at the gates of Rome! They've had my watch as well."

Juliet and James played tag, first encouraging and then cajoling Tim Tim into assembling his act. Once he'd been forcibly shaved, dressed, and gently perfumed, he looked and smelt like the boss she knew. As they left the hotel, he mumbled something incoherent and followed the revolving door through two cycles, searching for the faces of the guilty in the crowd. Finding no one he recognised, he moved on. By the time they'd completed a short taxi ride along Madison Avenue, the previous evening had happened to someone else. He even shared a joke with the driver regarding the bad luck of his friend.

Their first appointment was with Campbell Campbell, an Old Boy advertising executive who'd swapped London for New York some years previously. His offices were located high up in the Time-Life building, affording a splendid view. Juliet's job was to look fabulous and help secure favourable terms for the U.S. advertising contract for that silly game. She took rough notes and drew a series of sketches illustrating the city below, all the while exchanging texts with Cyrano and her friends. By the time the meeting broke for coffee, Saturday's venue was fixed.

It sounded dreamy, she thought. Such a shame to miss it.

Miss Harrington considered the day back on track. She was about to reward herself with free sparkles from the Campbell Campbell Advertising sprinkler, when she received a further message from her mysterious benefactor in London. Apparently, reality was being spun in order to concoct a burglary. Juliet huffed and continued with her quest.

She wrinkled her nose, hiding a line of powder up each nostril plus several more in her purse for later. Instantaneously, her head was full of spangly labels, plucked from the garb of the ad agency staff, a veritable crowd of hardcore fashionistas.

She wound her hair around her finger, obsessing about the message.

Break-ins happened, she thought. So why text?

Either the boys weren't in control, or it wasn't a normal break-in.

The PA found herself grinding her teeth.

Time to talk.

She complimented one of the Campbell Campbell account execs on the cut of his suit, tantalisingly revealing her inner tiger. Within seconds, she'd drawn quite a crowd. They loved her accent. They loved Stella McCartney and Christian Louboutin. Was she free that evening? Or the next? There were people she simply must meet. She took a selection of business cards from the men, settling on the most attractive and the most powerful for special consideration, promising to date them both in the next forty-eight hours.

What a fine life they live, she thought, here in the city that never sleeps.

Once the meeting was over, Juliet and Tim Tim made their excuses and hurried back to the Carlton for the midday call, arranged in the boss's suite. Harts, bless him, was all alone, left to engage in small talk until the rest of the boys arrived.

What were they up to, she wondered? Tardiness was not a Grrr! trait.

Nipping outside, she called her intern's desk, only to discover from one of her boys that Miss Croft had sloped off home mid-afternoon on a sickie. Her suspicions deepened. The moment she heard that Clifford and Malory had been sucked into a Category A client meeting and were unable to attend, she knew for certain that something wasn't right.

"We're sorry to hear about your phone," said Mans, huffing and puffing.

"Down a storm drain," added Harts. "So unfortunate."

Tim Tim thumped the table. "Obviously, we'll overcome this minor inconvenience."

"Of course," said Mans.

Juliet twiddled her thumbs while the boss caught up on what was happening with the press releases for that silly game. She supposed she should pay it more attention, but it was all so boring.

The boss nodded, ready to close the call. "Anything from you, Harry?"

"How's Tim Tim's safe?" she asked.

There was a long pause.

"Locked, of course," said Mans, his voice cracking.

"I declare this call closed." Tim Tim's voice boomed around the room. "Same time tomorrow."

Miss Harrington glanced at her mobile, reading the last message from her mystery friend for the umpteenth time. Mans had told a fib, of this she was certain. In fact, the whole thing reeked of week-old monkfish. Which meant they were lying to an agenda. She read the message one last time:

*Tell the moviemaker to watch his back.*

She hit "dial," crossed her fingers, and prayed she wasn't too late.

# Chapter Twenty-Two: Battered

Ferret propped himself up in a corner, snatching quick breaths. He ran the back of a hand across his lip expecting to see blood, but found none. Relieved, he slumped.

His calves ached.

The small of his back throbbed.

His bum felt like a piñata party pack.

The only thing for it was not to move, but even that hurt.

The girl leading the beating tagged her partner, who rubbed a pair of gnarly hands together and pulled him by the ankle from the safe space into which he'd crawled. She loosened her shoulders, showing off a toned midriff between sports bra and shorts, then using her ample rear as a jackhammer, pounded his sternum with a series of well-aimed thumps.

He rolled onto his stomach, gasping for air. "About that date . . ."

Jackhammer girl tagged her equally endowed colleague, who sat on him from above, pummelling the centre of his back with her pile-driver bum, knocking what wind remained clean from his lungs.

"Oh, god." Ferret felt his ribs creak.

It was over a year since his body had taken such a thorough battering. He hadn't realised how unfit he'd become after such a short rugby retirement. The bruises, when they ripened, were going to be entertaining for days.

"He'll do," said pile-driver girl.

It was the first time either of the pair had spoken since his arrival at the police station some hours ago. He crawled upright, hugging his knees, careful to leave a gap between thighs and ribcage. He'd once paid for a team massage in an East End parlour that had ended something like this, except for the expense and the grand finale.

"I don't suppose . . ." The detecting consultant left the sentence hanging.

"Tidy yourself up." Jackhammer picked a pair of judo robes from a hook and flung one to her partner.

Slowly, Ferret tucked his shirt into his trousers and straightened his tie, fingers pulsing where they'd been bent backwards as soon as the door closed. They'd thrown him about like a pig in a sack after that, buffeting him between them, using the padded walls as a third man. It was only when he'd tried to fight back that they'd punished him with an impressively large wooden spoon slapped against his thighs.

"Follow us." Pile-driver tossed him a pair of shoes with the laces removed.

Ferret winced.

His feet felt much wider than normal, as though they belonged to a clown.

Exhausted, he found a wry smile. He'd endured two hours of abuse with not a single question asked. Such a shame it was all over. Pain was one of those great levellers; once one immersed oneself in the mechanics, there was no other experience quite so thrilling. Ideally, he liked to dish it out too.

But not today.

On the plus side, at least he hadn't had to cash any more Bank of Lies cheques.

Pile-driver and Jackhammer led him to an interview room, pushing him roughly through the door and flinging his laces at the table. He took a seat, cursing when the tops of his thighs brushed the table's edge. Presently, two plainclothes officers entered, taking up position opposite. A short chap with an alien-shaped skull full of teeth, which looked like they'd been used for gnawing blubber, introduced himself as DC Growler. A well-built Afro-Caribbean lady with Amazonian tendencies who stood a good foot taller gave her name as Detective Constable B'Con.

After the girls, who Ferret had to admit he'd taken quite a shine to, this was reality with a bump.

"Do you have any idea of the trouble you're in?" said DC B'Con, leaning on her knuckles.

"In truth," said Ferret, massaging his ribs, "I have no idea why I'm here."

DC Growler glared intently from the other side of the desk. "You sure about that?"

Ferret nodded. He'd returned from a jog to discover a black car with tinted windows waiting in the road outside his residence. Initially he'd wondered which of his neighbours had upset the Russian mafia. It was only when he approached the front door that a pair of plainclothes officers announced themselves and invited him to join them at Savile Row police station.

His thoughts turned to the most recent bout of naughtiness he could recall, involving a certain fedora and its movie debut. He felt a tightening in his trousers. Surely Juliet hadn't been so bold as to upload their intimate soiree for download already? "It's all the rage," she'd insisted. "This season's must-have fashion accessory."

Growler raised a hand and inserted a finger into his ear, moving it rapidly from side to side, creating a grotesque noise.

Ferret felt his toes turn red.

The law already had a name for their indiscretion: the squidgy-slurp tapes.

B'Con wrinkled her nose. "Did you learn that disgusting trick working for the vice squad?"

Growler's face glowed the colour of an indoor heat lamp.

The detective smiled sweetly. They couldn't possibly know it was him. Apart from his credentials, obviously. As a professional, he wasn't about to submit to a credential identity parade, not without a top-class lawyer present.

The two DCs continued to bicker.

Ferret learned that Growler had been reassigned from a firearms unit after taking aim at a terror suspect and missing a headshot seven times in a row, while B'Con was on temporary secondment from Bridgetown, Barbados, to learn about city policing. This was their first week together and despite the obvious fit, neither one wanted to play the role of bad cop. In fact, they didn't even want to be partners. Both were convinced their assignment papers had been chewed by dogs, their transfers fudged.

Ferret coughed loudly into a clenched hand.

"What do you want?" said both DCs simultaneously.

"To be involved in my own interview."

"Just tell us where you were last night," said B'Con.

"Surely, we're here to talk about Monday night?" Ferret twisted his lips, sucking on an ethereal lemon.

"Last night!" barked Growler.

"At home with a lady," said Ferret, recoiling. "Not the same lady as Monday. I'm confused. Why am I here?"

"Were you anywhere within the vicinity of Soho Square at two thirty this morning?" asked B'Con.

Ferret raised an eyebrow, knowing exactly where he was. He hadn't intended to get it on again with filthy Cristina, but once he'd gazed into her come-to-bed eyes and discovered what she had in mind, temptation took over.

Knock!

In strode the desk sergeant. "You're free to go."

"That can't be, sir! He's as guilty as sin, sir." B'Con wandered around the desk. "We were just getting to the bit where we threaten him and he confesses and admits he broke into Grrr! and pocketed the smalls."

"Smalls . . ." Ferret felt his throat tighten as his brain performed a summersault.

Surely, he thought, they belonged to his girlfriend. He'd hardly stolen them.

"We should at least search his house, sir," said Growler. "Look in his sock drawer."

"Whatever for?" asked the desk sergeant.

"It's called psychological profiling, sir." Growler folded his arms. "Villains always store anything worth hiding in their odd socks. It's a well-known fact of criminal life."

"In his case, stolen smalls." B'Con glared at him, causing him to shrink away. "See."

Ferret hobbled from the interview room, contemplating the remarkable accuracy of DC B'Con's snout. Growler brought up the rear, muttering to himself.

"Bloody friends in bloody high places."

The detecting consultant signed for his belongings in a crabby hand and slowly sat down to lace his shoes. He couldn't help but notice that all of the police officers parading in and out of the station were female, of a certain age, and had distinctive bottoms forged from hours in the saddle.

Ferret donned the fedora and doffed it at the desk sergeant.

As he exited the cop shop, a commotion broke out from the direction of the cells. A chap with tumbleweed sideburns, who looked remarkably like the gent who'd sold him the tinfoil insert, was embroiled in an altercation with two female constables, demanding they keep their hands to themselves. Ferret rubbed his coccyx. It couldn't be the same man. The seller wore a fine tweed suit and a deerstalker, whereas this chap was dressed in rags, soiled with grease, and spotted with dried blood.

The chap's eyes twinkled with mischief, then recognition. Ferret tried to smile, but what came out was a grizzle. He turned on his heels and left as quickly as he was able. Associating with mad men was one thing, entertaining the homeless quite another.

The chap called to him, fortunately not by name. By the time the words had echoed around the lobby, the detective was out of the door and heading away from Mayfair. Within fifty metres, he realised he was in pain. Under the circumstances, there was only one reasonable course of action: alcohol, marching powder to numb the aches, traditional opiate-based painkillers to complete the job, and a good night's sleep. Before that, he owed Tom Tom a debt of gratitude for his quick release. Given that the art dealer's gallery was just off Regent Street, that was where he headed. With a tip of his hat, he easily persuaded one of the arty juniors it was wine o'clock and was halfway through glass number two, articulating his appreciation for Keith Haring, when the boss appeared.

Tom Tom voiced his surprise that the police had let him go at all. He'd pulled all the strings he knew to little effect and, unable to reach the *adiutor*, he panicked and called their banking friend.

Ferret shook his head. The last thing he needed was to owe Tristan.

"Our friend has ordered me to order you to meet him at the green place, wherever that is, at six o'clock sharp." Tom Tom scrunched his lips together, dabbing at his forehead with a handkerchief.

"Are you sure? I find it hard to believe our banking friend would frequent such a dive."

The art dealer took a large glass of wine and gulped half of it down. "Ask him yourself."

"Fine." Ferret bashed the keys on his mobile and hit send.

Tom Tom tutted. "You know he hates texts. His fat little monkey fingers can't find the keys."

Ferret laughed. "I expect to hear from Catherine shortly."

"Congratulations, by the way, on solving your first, last, and only case."

Ferret felt his heart sink.

"Tristan took great delight in bragging about how easy you are to manipulate."

Outside, two female police officers walked past the window. One of them patted her rear and waved. Ferret felt his calves stiffen. Curious as to what was occurring, Tom Tom looked over his shoulder, just in time to see the officer blow a kiss.

"Friends of yours?"

"In a manner of speaking." Ferret thought about returning the gesture, then abandoned the idea. "How much do you know about Old Boy bullies?"

"Not enough to answer any questions," said the art dealer.

"That's a shame. Someone left me a threatening voicemail earlier, warning me to watch out for tiddly Jones, the legendary Old Boy bone-crusher."

A look of outright fear crossed Tom Tom's face. "If I was you, I'd pack my bags and leave town."

"He's real, then?"

"Oh, yes. My father used to tell me tales about how he tore off little boys' winkles in their sleep. It was horrid. I still leave the light on at night, even now."

Ferret finished the glass of wine, thanked the junior for her kind attention, gave Tom Tom a quick hug, and departed for Soho, stopping briefly at a pavement café for more wine.

Clearly, he thought, the Old Boys had it in for him. They'd staged a break-in, fingered him as a thief for taking his girlfriend's underwear, then had him taken in for a good old-fashioned softening up. With the introduction of the bone-crusher, they were trying intimidation too.

Under the circumstances, there was only one thing for it: return the underwear as quickly as possible. But first, he had a call to make.

Brring!

"You have reached the voicemail for 51R 3D. Please leave a message after the tone."

"Marcus. Good afternoon. As you may have heard, our banking friend had to extricate my sorry derriere from the Row. Since my release, I've been followed by several pairs of female bobbies, who are taking far too much interest in my business. Please do your thing and make them stop."

Ferret finished the glass of wine, paid the waiter, and hailed a rickshaw, destination Wardour Street. Upon arrival, a pair of highly polished silver doors cut in the Art Deco style greeted him. He bit his lip and checked the list of companies, only to find RockSlut Research was permanently closed, with no forwarding address.

He sighed in despair.

Beep!

Ferret checked his watch.

Five fifty-two.

He prophesised a couple of drinks accompanied by a telling off for a random, non-existent transgression. Then he'd head home.

The detective shuffled slowly up the fusty, threadbare stairs, cursing the lack of fitness on his part. The stink of puke and piss, which had always been a staple of the corner at the bottom, caught his nose. Above, The Ramones belted out the opening bars of "Too Tough to Die." The corners of Ferret's eyes crinkled. As always, the club knew exactly which song to greet him with.

Brring!

He answered the phone to his girlfriend, immediately professing how much he missed her, hearing the same back. Before long, the stench of stale urine attacked his sensibilities, prompting him to climb higher.

"Would you believe I was questioned by the law about some missing underwear stolen from your offices last night?"

"The briefs of the warrior princess? Tim Tim was looking all over for them."

"Ah . . ." Ferret took a deep breath, finally realising his mistake. "Apparently I'm now known as the knicker nicker of Soho."

Juliet laughed. "I'm sure we'll get it all sorted out. In the meantime, take care."

"You too. Kisses."

Ferret felt a fuggy cloud of despair hanging over the Emerald Room long before he reached the top of the stairs. With every step he buffeted against it, a giant, translucent, inflatable cumulonimbus that was desperate to keep him out.

Much to his surprise, the clientele were too busy mooching about, imbibing on unhappy tales, to pay him any attention. Usually, one might count a dozen guests at most, but today there were three times that number. He cast an eye about the place, noting the thick layer of dust on the old tiled mantelpiece, the hearth full of dog-ends. Above the fireplace hung a pen-and-ink drawing of the owner, signed by Francis Bacon. Eventually, his eyes locked onto the Frenchman, manning the bar.

The club's resident rock star stood next to him, pulling a pint of beer.

"Well, well. Look what the cat dragged in." Cyrano spat the words like a lump of chewed-up old gum, striking him straight between the eyes.

Ferret narrowed his gaze. "Good to see you too, my friend."

"As I recall," said the Frenchman, "friends don't change their locks on each other."

"Neither do they steal personal letters and effects."

"I would never read a fellow's private mail. Withdraw that slur this instant."

"Oi, you." The guitarist eyed him like a little black-combed cockerel. "We're having a sombre moment here. Either order a drink and join us, or fuck off."

"Double vodka," said Ferret. "Out of the chiller. One for me, one for the Frenchman. And one for your good self."

"Excellent choice." The rock star handed the pulled pint to one of the regulars, a bleeding-heart poet known for his bearish temper tantrums, and headed to the back of the bar.

"Our banking friend has been waylaid," said Cyrano. "He orders you to remain here until he arrives."

"This is quite some party." Ferret cocked his fedora. "Where's the sarcastic owner with the stupendous cleavage?"

The Frenchman screwed up his face in disdain. "You don't even remember her name."

The guitarist returned with three frosty shot glasses, each containing far more than a double. The liquid was thick and clear with the consistency of syrup. In the background the tune changed to Iggy and The Stooges.

*I wanna be your dog . . .*

The rock star grinned, handing out the liquor.

"To Mimi." Cyrano raised his voice and his glass at the clientele, who turned on command and raised theirs too.

The detective and the rock star synchronised with the Frenchman, downing their vodkas.

"That'll be £300." The guitarist smiled.

"The prices in here have certainly kept pace with inflation." Ferret fumbled in his wallet, coming up £50 short.

"That'll do." The rock star stuffed the wad of notes into a jar.

"And where is Mimi?" asked Ferret.

"She's a little off-colour." The guitarist turned to serve another customer.

"Hospital." Cyrano shook his head, eyes full of fear. "She had the *merde* beaten out of her last night."

Ferret felt a horrible twisting in the pit of his stomach, a nest of vipers uncoiling.

The Frenchman continued: "They made everyone leave first. Except for Woody."

"Rasta Woody?" Ferret hadn't really paid much attention to Cyrano's friendships struck up in the Emerald Room, but he certainly remembered Woody.

"They made him watch. Well, we think they made him watch. It's a bit difficult to ask a man with no tongue."

"Say what?!"

The Frenchman inhaled deeply and drew a cross across his chest. "The police found him on the roof, tied to a chair, his tongue nailed to his foot."

"That's awful." Ferret signalled for another round of vodka.

Cyrano looked his friend squarely in the eye, lips trembling. "I believe whoever did it was sending a message."

"How so?" Ferret took a step backwards.

"The last time I saw Woody, we had an interesting conversation regarding his past dealings. There was a stranger who paid too much interest. He followed me back to Regent's Park."

"You led him to my house?"

"Our house, dear director." The Frenchman winked and handed Ferret a set of keys. "It's all yours, despite what our banking friend says. Funnily enough, I've gone right off living by the park."

# Chapter Twenty-Three: The Old Man

"Be a love and order a cab for eleven fifteen." Marianne removed her glasses and rubbed her eyes, well-manicured nails brushing the bridge of her nose.

"Yes, ma'am." The junior wavered. "Where to?"

"You booked the hotel. Come on, chop chop!"

Quivering, the junior scuttled off.

Marianne gave a sigh of relief. Thankfully, this one didn't burst into tears whenever she raised her voice.

None of the children liked to be alone in her company, especially late at night. And that suited her just fine. They were merging two companies together; it wasn't meant to be fun and frolics amongst the daisies. She'd told each of the juniors in turn when she'd taken them on that the hours were long, the pay demeaning, and she didn't suffer social media. Yet as soon as it reached eight o'clock, the excuses began in earnest. At the end of the first month they expected a little extra for the hours they'd put in; the disappointment was palpable.

She gave them their wage slips personally, insisting they open them there and then. It was part and parcel of being a good boss. If they had any complaints, the opportunity was there to say something.

So far, none of them had.

Hamish, one of the senior consultants popped his head around the door. "Do you have five minutes?"

Marianne smiled. "For you, always. Scotch?"

The senior closed the door and pulled the blinds, following protocol.

From her bottom drawer Marianne produced a bottle of Islay whisky and two tumblers. "Water?"

Hamish winked. "You know better than to ruin decent single malt."

Marianne poured, three fingers each. "What troubles you?"

The senior consultant loosened his tie and took a swig of scotch, explaining that legal still hadn't heard from the old man or his lawyers. The rumour on the grapevine alluded to him taking some sort of preventative action which, coupled with a forthcoming office move, was causing the planners — to cite an old consultancy phrase — to birth litters of hairy kittens.

Marianne sat up straight, adjusting her shoulders. Her backers had prepared for just such a scenario. "What if we refuse to play the game by his rules and up the stakes?"

Hamish squinted. "I'm not sure I'm comfortable with actual physical violence."

"And neither am I, which is why we have specialists for that sort of thing. All you have to do is look the other way."

Hamish took a gulp of spirit and cocked his head to one side, words forming on his lips. Nothing came out.

"You're wondering how I'm going to deal with the latest outbreak," interpreted Marianne. "Suspension, pending the outcome of a psychological assessment."

"Good call." Hamish finished the glass of scotch and moved to open the blinds on his way out.

Marianne shook her head. "I need five minutes alone."

The boss topped up her glass with a finger of scotch, adding a further two fingers of mineral water. She pushed a pair of rimless reading glasses to the top of her pert nose and returned to a folder of paper marked "Confidential. Company Eyes Only."

The old man really was a stubborn bugger. She'd had to drag him kicking and screaming this far and still he refused to accept he'd lost his company. Technically gifted he may be, but when it came to business, he and his cronies were pretty damn naïve.

For her initial approach, she'd chosen a pair of crimson high heels with matching bag, complemented by a stylish mid-grey suit with a jacket that accentuated her boobs and a skirt that rode several inches above the knee. Tentatively, she'd valued the old man's company at twice what it was worth, then lent forward, just a tad, flashing her cleavage. Instead of jumping at the offer, he exploded, invading her personal space in an abrasive tirade.

Every time she backed off, he moved forward, threatening to cosh her with his stag's head walking stick.

"Be off with ye, hag face!" he'd shouted, breath sour with crab apples.

Marianne shuddered at the thought of the ungrateful highlander, bulbous red nose overflowing with unkempt nasal hair, reminiscent of a pair of excited red setters. He'd chased her from the office as though she'd come bearing a copy of *The Watchtower*. In all her years in consultancy, she'd never once run into a character quite as gnarly as MacGregor Cocks.

The truth she reflected was that she'd finally found an incorruptible straight man impervious to her charms.

Over the ensuing weeks, her aides had approached each of the major shareholders in turn. Initially, the reaction was the same, albeit not as curt.

Marianne stretched her arms.

The Consultancy always stressed to its young hopefuls never to go into business with their own family.

And with good reason.

The united face a family firm presents to the world is a distraction. Somewhere in the sibling closet, buried from public view, is the skeleton of a nasty, unresolved feud. A few choice coins distributed to one of the minor shareholders had unearthed a pile of bones which, once rattled, spurted forth a fountain of pus. A few further coins, wrapped in promises, fired the whispers of discontent, cleaving the family clean down the middle. Brothers and cousins, once steadfast in their resolve, were no longer certain who their real fathers were and with this revelation came a truckload of unaired grievances.

Once the battle lines were drawn, the inflexible grumpus with the iron cane, who ran his company with grunts of withering sarcasm, was isolated.

After that, it was simply a case of mopping up the stragglers.

The file on her desk had been appropriated by the disillusioned son while the tyrant was busy verbally assaulting his daughter-in-law. Marianne re-read the executive summary. Apparently, the old man was once involved in a series of highly classified battlefield experiments which, much to his chagrin, bore no fruit. Based on the accumulated test data, he was able to assemble a series of untested product designs, which, although unpatented, were owned by his consultancy.

Marianne chuckled to herself.

Should have kept them in your own name.

Her nose for business told her that the contents of the file, along with the two in her briefcase, were what her backers really wanted. Everything else was window dressing, part of the great charade soon to be played out in court and then across the pages of the financial press. The old man knew it too. He couldn't say a word, though, because the moment he opened his mouth, she'd know she was right.

Marianne put the folder down.

She'd read the specification half a dozen times, but without pictures, it made no sense at all. Even with an online dictionary on hand, following the narrative was like herding cats uphill with a rake. Whoever penned this was good. If one of her reports had written this as a contractual deliverable, she'd have them handsomely rewarded in public.

She sighed.

The scientific terms and acronyms such as D-XIII were obviously there to scare off the uninitiated. What was needed was a friendly boffin with a military background, capable of translating geek-speak into plain English.

Knock!

"Come in."

"Ma'am," said the junior, trying to hide quick-bitten fingers, "your taxi will be here in ten minutes."

"Thank you." Marianne paused, allowing the silence to run until the junior squirmed. "Tara. You may go home now."

The junior's shoulders sagged as she closed the door. Marianne wandered over to the shutters and peeked through. Although she wanted to celebrate, the junior held on to her emotions, clearly knowing better than to dance within sight.

Marianne smiled.

This one, she thought, might actually go the distance.

Finishing the glass of scotch, Marianne placed the folder in her briefcase and locked it, secreting the key into a hidden compartment in her handbag. Her backers had many fingers in many pies, and whilst the deal she'd struck was good for both parties, the old man's product specifications were her insurance just in case they decided to renege at the last. Without a doubt, they had dirt on her too, for exactly the same reasons. Hopefully, with time and success, their understanding of each other would render such precautions unnecessary.

The boss picked up her suitcase, matching briefcase, and suit hanger, turned off the lights to her office and carefully locked the door. A taxi to London was an extravagance she denied her staff; taking one herself made it absolutely clear who was in charge.

As she headed for the lift, one of the spotty bean counters intercepted her.

"Ma'am," he said nervously, thrusting a clear plastic wallet under her nose, "here are the reports you asked for. It's as you suspected. There are some anomalous asset transfers hidden in with the operating costs."

"Thank you," said Marianne, a wry smile crossing her face. "Light reading for the journey."

"Very clever," continued the accountant, round glasses riding down his nose on a thin veneer of sweat. "I nearly missed them. Had to go back two years. When you add them to the consultancy payments . . ."

"Well done," interrupted Marianne, reaching out and touching him on the shoulder. "Does anyone else know?"

"Just you, ma'am."

"Excellent. Make sure it stays that way. And you may take tomorrow off."

"It's Saturday. Oh. Thank you, ma'am."

This was the breakthrough she needed.

When Hamish Cocks decided to take Judas's silver, she'd demanded a little more to prove his fealty. What she got was a name, which meant nothing at all.

To begin with.

She smiled.

When in doubt, follow the money.

Marianne stepped into the lift, stroking her chin. The canny old fox was a man with a Forces background, Army through and through, trained in the military mind-set. Any doubts she had concerning the funding of off-the-books black projects were history.

For now, the discovery was staying close to her chest; no one else must know. In her opinion, having pitted her wits against the old man for several months, it was highly likely that whatever the grizzled old bugger had designed all those years ago, he had a prototype built in secret.

The next step was to find a trustworthy scientist to decrypt the product sheets.

Then she'd be cooking with gas.

# Chapter Twenty-Four: Spiked

Ferret groaned and rolled over, groping for the alarm clock. 4:27 a.m. His head felt like an inverted roasted marshmallow: full of gooey goodness on the outside, toasted to a crisp on the inside. He put his hand to his mouth to ensure he still had his tongue, accidentally brushing his cheekbone below his left eye.

"Ow."

RockSlut Research bubbled to the surface.

Offices closed.

He moaned and buried his head under the pillow, realising the bed was not his own. As he remembered it, Cyrano had fled the property just before their relationship had degenerated into a brawl. So why was he still in the guest lodge?

Memories solidified.

According to his French friend, the main house was no longer safe.

Despite his injuries, he'd pogoed to The Ramones. For half the night. There were lights. Blurred sweat. And a desperate thirst. Sweet water. Cyrano's contorted features filled his brain; the Frenchman's aquiline nose pecking away like a curlew, unearthing hidden gems, swallowing them like juicy sand worms. Was it true his father began his career in soap?

Ferret pulled the pillow over his head, the chorus line to "Somebody Put Something in My Drink" racing around his skull.

Goddammit.

Spiked by a Rolling Stone.

The Frenchman hadn't fared any better. He was running around, cuffs flapping, punching the air. More members arrived to pay their respects, including a well-known comedian who'd been barred for life. Twice. He gave a flowery speech full of superfluous adjectives for which he received a standing ovation. The drink flowed liberally. PC Plod popped by, keeping out an eye for the ruffians who'd accosted the owner.

Life-size cardboard cutouts of Mimi and Woody appeared to raucous cheers.

The vodka ran out; they had to send for more.

Eight grand. That was the final tab. To be donated to Mimi's get-well fund. Cyrano paid four. Half in cash, half in cocaine.

They'd finished up around six thirty in the morning. He remembered watching the sun rise from the roof, his arm around his French friend.

No centurion.

Tristan the Impervious had stood him up.

Ferret pulled the pillow tighter over his head and tried to sleep. Instead, he found himself doing the opposite. The sheath of codeine, which had insulated him from the world, was fraying around the edges. He remembered looking at himself in the mirror on the way to bed. Despite the stiffness, there was not a bruise in sight. The tag team who'd done him over were nothing if not expert at disguising their handiwork.

Knickers.

Warrior princess.

Word of his arrest had reached the Frenchman's ear. Delicately, his friend's beak prized his skull open like a ripe oyster, demanding a pearl. For what reason had he been taken in for questioning? Ferret felt so happy he'd gushed answers, all the while hugging his friend. Out it came, a stream of unconscious ectoplasm, soaking through them both.

Ferret bolted upright.

With the party winding down, Cyrano had had a panic attack and invited himself back to the guest lodge, convinced he was being stalked by a weasel in disguise. His untrustworthy friend had asked to see the bra and briefs, then pocketed them, promising he'd deliver them to Tom Tom, who'd return them to his brother. At the time it all made sense. With the underwear returned, the Old Boys would order titchy Jones, the midget bone-crusher, to stand down.

Ferret's stomach grumbled. He lay back down, wishing the bed to swallow him whole. An hour like 4:30 a.m. was far too early to eat.

Slowly, Ferret opened an eye and looked again at the clock.

Saturday.

The empty box of pills by the bed confirmed it. He'd lost a day.

His stomach turned.

He picked up his phone. Two missed calls from Tristan, a missed call from Tom Tom. A text from Catherine confirming breakfast, another from Marianne, and one from his girlfriend enquiring about a detecting consultant for hire.

He groaned.

Evidently, she'd seen the website.

From Marcus, nothing. Despite the drunken calls he and Cyrano had made at one in the morning.

Ferret resorted once more to the pillow, burying his head, letting out a low, guttural moan. Holmes wouldn't let it end like this. He was certain that someone must have put something in the great detective's drink during his long career and it never did him any harm.

Curious, he opened the text from Marianne. She'd come up trumps, finding an address for Banoffee Publishing.

Ferret rubbed his eyes.

The old Hammer building. Wardour Street.

The offices next door to RockSlut Research.

There was an itsy-bitsy chance his files were still in Soho. No matter how minute that chance, he had to follow it up regardless of the centurion's opinion on the matter.

Holmes would settle for nothing less.

# Chapter Twenty-Five: Orchis

As was his wont following a less than satisfactory mission, Marcus had spent the previous day inserting as many superfluous swear words as possible into every internal memo he wrote. He had a favoured stock phrase to summarise his feelings, repeated often throughout his scribblings:

*She gives me the willies.*

Every time he wrote those words, he erupted in a fit of giggles.

Truth be told, humour was the only thing keeping him sane. His department had dedicated a great deal of brainpower and processing cycles into calculating every possible permutation, every potential scenario surrounding the raid on Grrr! Communications. And yet the moment they acted, the whole escapade had collapsed, leaving a dozen agents in the hospital and a pair in comas, with no real clue as to how they'd been incapacitated. For now, both men were in a secure unit on life support, with specialists working around the clock to revive them.

The intelligence man removed his glasses and rubbed his eyes. Since the bungling of a simple clandestine robbery, the enemy had a face. Previously, he wasn't even sure the realm had an enemy, not outside of the usual suspects. All that was needed to complete the picture was a name.

"Sir."

Marcus looked up from the desk. "Yes, Rajesh."

"The car will be along shortly to take us to the next secure location." The junior clutched a wad of folders to his chest.

Marcus smiled, flashing his top row of teeth. "We can discuss the reports en route."

Raj continued to linger.

Not wishing to miss an opportunity, Marcus put down his glasses. "What will you take from this job?"

"Regroup, move on, and make sure past mistakes don't happen again."

"Very good."

Those words, which his old boss had instilled in him during their most creative period together still held sway. Rajesh was smart and efficient; a good pupil. One day, if he continued to make the right decisions, he might be the one giving orders. He certainly hoped so.

"I've been thinking, sir."

Marcus knew the look on Rajesh's face. With a quick twist of his legs, he adjusted his trousers. "Pull up a chair."

Rajesh obliged, dumping the paperwork on the desk. "The voicemail message our friend with the hat left you suggests that the insurgent device was created by RockSlut Research, which makes sense. If it really does function as described, they'd want to keep the development in-house."

"I reasoned the same." Marcus looked deep into Rajesh's soft brown eyes, focusing on their liquid-caramel centres. "So what have you found?"

Rajesh explained how he'd spent the last day trawling through the security service's Commerce Monitoring Database, accumulating information. Marcus listened intently, losing himself in the junior's delicious eyelashes, which gave him the appearance of a roe deer. His voice was so yummy, Marcus had to pinch himself hard to wake from his daydreams.

Just in time, he learned that RockSlut Research had spent five years working on a next-generation gaming device, which was declared a failure in a series of captured internal documents, carelessly emailed as attachments shortly before the company was sold.

Marcus smiled, suppressing a wink at the last.

"I was able to retrieve and decrypt a confidential document from CMD, which shows there is an exclusive agreement in place between RockSlut Research and RockSlut Software, granting first refusal should the device be successfully completed."

"Very good." Marcus leant forward, touching Rajesh softly on the hand. "Go on."

The junior let his boss's hand linger for slightly longer than necessary before withdrawing. "I haven't yet completed a full analysis, but I have a good idea who the mystery buyer of RSR is."

Rajesh spread the plotter output from CMD across the desk, showing a mesh of interlinked boxes. Marcus marvelled at the cool toys the security service's youth had at their disposal, wishing it had been so easy in his day. Then again, he mused, the complexity of modern fraud is directly proportional to the tools available to the law for penetrating the camouflage of deceit.

"There's a series of shell companies that track out to the Caymans and from there to the Virgin Islands." Raj pointed, guiding his mentor through the web of lines.

As Marcus well knew, the Caribbean financial scene was a hotbed of outright piracy and hidden loot. Ever since the Spanish started shipping stolen Aztec gold via that route in the sixteenth century, monetary shenanigans had run riot throughout the region. A combination of intentionally lax policy and the need for discreet squirrel holes for the uber-rich made it no different today.

"At this point, there's only a smattering of tier two link emails plugging the gaps." Rajesh ran a hand through thick black hair, preparing to deliver the final point.

Would it be too forward to give his protégé a nickname?

There was certainly a precedent within the department for that sort of thing, although it was all so *laissez-faire* these days. Secrecy was half the fun of it, not knowing whether one might get caught and outed, not being certain whether one's beau really was one's beau or simply an object on a pedestal.

Orchis.

That was what he'd call him.

"I'm ninety percent certain that this is the owner of RockSlut Research," said the junior, dropping a printed page on the map and pointing to a box outlined in red.

Marcus adjusted his glasses and read the text. "Are you absolutely certain?"

"Formally, it's going to take a pile of writs as thick as an elephant's trunk to prove it. Assuming we have a year to spare."

Marcus rested his chin on his palm. "Have you any idea who the Carlsgrove Group is?"

"Only vaguely. When I tried to pull up their secret history, CMD squealed that I don't have the necessary clearance."

Marcus felt his heart jump.

For all his brilliance, the junior had made a schoolboy error. He chewed his lip. Hopefully, the failed access request wouldn't be flagged up the food chain for further investigation.

"Did I do something wrong?" asked the junior.

"That depends on who's watching the watchers." Marcus sighed.

It was time for his young protégé to learn some of the more unsavoury aspects of the job, beginning with the private equity investment group known as Carlsgrove, who, from his experience, had a tentacle in every succulent pie the government had ever baked. Their impressive list of associates included ministers, captains of industry, ex-prime ministers and presidents. Able to trace their roots back to the old East India Company, they were widely regarded as the last of the traditional Old Boy firms. Since the Thatcher era, they'd become involved in the privatisation of sensitive government assets in the UK and abroad, which was great business if one happened to be on the inside. For the department, however, they were a real nightmare due in no small part to an unethical business model that was wont to attract prying journalists.

"Our job," said Marcus, in conclusion, "along with the Metropolitan Police Force, is to shield Carlsgrove from all that nonsense."

Raj undid his top button and loosened his tie. "What do we do next?"

"We tread very carefully. If the people involved get even an inkling of what you've uncovered, there's a good chance we'll both be retired for good."

"What of our friend in the hat?"

Marcus loosened his own tie and smiled.

"I see," said Raj. "He doesn't work for us, so there's nothing to connect him back."

"Good boy." Under the desk, Marcus fiddled with a small, black, rubberised rectangle. "We let him stick his nose in their business, and with fortune on our side, pick him up after the event. He asked for a detective adventure. Let's give him one."

Ferret covered his eyes, temporarily blinded by ripples of cascading light bouncing off the confluence of the Grand Union and Regent's canals. He removed a pair of shades from a jacket pocket and slipped them into place.

All around the prominent café in which he sat, adjacent to Paddington Basin, people bustled about their business. Below, a series of resident houseboats nestled in tight, defensive columns. The clamour of cooking utensils interspersed with the sizzle of sausages caught his ear. A kettle whistled its approval. The aroma of bacon flirted with his senses, carried high on the slight breeze.

Delicately, he sipped a cup of ginger tea that zinged across his taste buds.

How he loved the distractions of Little Venice on a Saturday morning.

Back in the real world, Tom Tom was irate with him, Tristan was irate with him; he was irate with Cyrano.

All in all, a normal day.

Given the string of expletives left on his voicemail, bookended by a pair of veiled threats, the centurion's deliberations concerned him the most. The fact that he was forbidden from dating his friend's PA made their weekly debrief that much more exciting. And besides, coffee was coffee, not a date, even though he planned on ordering breakfast of eggs Benedict and many rounds of wholemeal toast.

Catherine arrived precisely on time. She wore a floral-patterned summer dress, which showed off her dusky tan, complemented with flat brown suede sandals and a matching bag. Each removed their glasses. Nodding in appreciation, they kissed, French style. Ferret complimented her on the exquisite look she'd fashioned. He'd fancied her for a long time, but circumstances had always colluded against him, usually in the form of a new girlfriend. One day, he mused, he'd bear witness to her hair tumbling across the pillows, engulfing them both in a dark sea of uncontrollable passion, tossing them this way and that in a storm of sensual depravity, all resistance surrendered to the kiss of tempestuous foam.

Despite the temptation, he held firm against the inclination to gaze into her eyes. There was something pure about her spirit, which was remarkably incorrupt, despite years of servitude to the City. In comparison, he was like a storm drain, polluted with twigs, filthy water, and the occasional dead rat. His French friend still took the prize as a sewage pipe, pumping out effluent twenty-four hours a day.

He smiled, watching the PA seductively insert a long, slender cigarette between plump lips.

"And you're sure Tristan isn't angry with me?" he said, offering a light.

"No more angry than he is with the rest of the world." Catherine held up a menu and beckoned him in close. "HR was not happy with his conduct during a recent dismissal. They've demanded he consent to a drug test."

Ferret chuckled to himself.

Inserting a spoon in the coffee froth, the PA scooped up foamy chocolate and provocatively popped it into her mouth. "Cyrano paid a visit yesterday. Apparently, detective, you're intent on locating some missing files."

Ferret's mouth turned down at the edges. He took a cigarette from Catherine's packet and sparked up, sucking hard, holding the smoke down until he felt wobbly.

"As I've been tasked with completing the paperwork, I must warn you that Tristan intends to fine you your Maserati should you persist."

"That's preposterous!" growled Ferret.

Two summers ago, he and the Frenchman had driven from Bilbao to Milan in the GS, top down, along dusty Spanish highways, navigating across the Pyrenees, following roaring French freeways, and finally threading their way through high snaking passes peppered with quiet alpine villages, picking up a bevy of hitchhiking girls along the way. As soon as they'd crossed into Italy, the Maserati was treated like a rock star, applauded wherever it went, thronged with onlookers clamouring for photos, deliriously caressing the horny dash and dials.

Grumbling, he flicked ash on the floor. Thanks to an Old Boy judge who'd stuck his nose where it didn't belong and issued him with a lengthy ban for driving whilst under the influence, he hadn't been behind the wheel for quite some time. As his licence was due to be returned any day, the proposed fine of his favourite toy really stung.

Once breakfast was done, the detective and the PA took a leisurely stroll around Rembrandt Gardens, laughing and giggling. Finally, Ferret walked

Catherine the short distance home to her apartment. He composed himself. If ever there was a time to invite himself in, this was it.

Catherine smiled, revealing a series of cute laughter lines at the corners of her mouth. "Every week you think this is the week, and it never is. On the day you walk away from the City for good, I'll reconsider."

He reached out and touched her hand. "What if I said one last job?"

The PA pulled her hand away. "That's what they all say."

Moodily, Ferret stood on Blomfield Road, arm outstretched, as yet another cab cruised on by. He felt the scar on his collarbone throb. Glancing towards a nearby tube station, the urge to enter became overwhelming.

How peculiar, he mused. If he didn't know better, he'd swear he was being directed towards London's Underground by an external force. He shook his head, remembering the rumble of the GranSport's V8. Change of plan. He'd travel by tube to Oxford Circus and from there on foot to Soho, where he predicted he'd find the offices of RockSlut Research and Banoffee Publishing closed, thereby putting an end to the quest for good.

"Does one know one?"

Ferret snapped from his daydream, which had been induced by the lullaby motion of the tube train. The chap in the rabbit costume, who'd appeared from nowhere, seemed familiar, with a voice as sweet as mead and eyes that crackled mischief. The detective looked into the stranger's eyes, trying to place him, when unexpectedly he found himself melting into the fellow's insides.

The gent sat upright.

Ferret recoiled in shock, shards of cobalt lightning trailing from his fingertips. He hadn't intended to try and melt into the bunny chap. Not that it mattered; the fellow was surrounded by an impenetrable barrier of superheated electricity. Thrown backwards, the detective found himself bathed in warm sunlight, holding the gent in a comforting embrace. They were lying in sticky Grecian sands, naked legs and arms intertwined, clear blue sea lapping at their toes. He felt his loins stir.

"Stop that!"

The chap winked. "One must learn restraint."

Ferret touched the fedora, feeling the sharp crackle of tinfoil beneath the crown. With his wild hair contained beneath the pink bonnet of the bunny suit, the chap was no longer a fashion disaster, merely an oddity. Only his bright red whiskers gave him away.

"One has been in the wars."

Ferret squinted across the tube carriage.

In response, the chap pinched his nose and held out his right hand, the little finger and index fingers pointing outwards, middle fingers tucked against the palm, thumb horizontal and innermost.

The detective pinched his own nose and reached out, matching the fellow's hand pattern; simultaneously, each rotated the sigil through 180 degrees, bringing the two Vs together in mid-air, culminating in the joining of thumbs. "To friends."

The chap pointed tactfully. "We are being observed."

Ferret's eyes darted to the side, following the finger. Farther down the carriage he spotted a man in a raincoat, head bent, shoulders hunched, backside occupying two seats, dark glasses covering his eyes. Between his legs, resting against immaculately polished shoes, lay a white stick.

Through the dull ache of bruised ribs, Ferret felt his chest tighten.

"Our follower is an agent of the state, with whom one will deal shortly. Firstly, we play a game. Name the decuria to which one belongs."

The detective pushed his hat back and scratched his temple. "How?"

"Watch and learn."

Ferret heard the words clearly, although he swore the chap's lips remained static. He felt a searing meteor land behind him, throwing up a wall of flame. In his mind space, four reels of numbers sprung into existence, spinning and tumbling, part of a great copper-and-brass gaming machine. One by one, the reels thudded to a halt.

"One one three thirteen," said the bunny chap.

"That information is confidential," said Ferret, his face reddening. "Who are you, friend?"

The chap smiled, his eyes jutting forth like a pair of ping-pong balls. He clenched his fists tight, closed his eyes, and hugged his knees. "As a citizen of The Brotherhood of Light and Reason, one must learn to follow a fellow's lead."

Screech!

Thunk!

In the beginning, there was light.

Then there was dark, shot through with fire and spark.

Finally, all went black.

In the confusion, Ferret struggled to recover his composure. Lying in a crumpled heap on the dirty metal floor, amidst a collection of grimy newspapers and discarded transport ephemera, he clutched his fedora for comfort. His scuffed knees screamed out for attention, his ribs ached uncontrollably. Gradually his eyes and ears adjusted to the dark, bringing the shouting and wailing of displaced human cargo sharply into focus.

"Daddy, is it terrorists?"

". . . bloody antiquated transport system."

"We've simply got to get out."

Slowly, he picked himself up, the pain cauterised by a much-appreciated burst of adrenaline. In the low light, punctured by the occasional cigarette lighter, he felt his way over to the seat where his new friend had been sitting prior to the impact; it was as empty as a junior's pocket at two in the morning.

"Friend!" shouted Ferret, his cry lost amongst the myriad voices busy working the hysteria towards a good old-fashioned panic.

The escape by torchlight through a darkened, rat-infested passageway was led by a fearless, quick-thinking driver, concerned only for the safety of the passengers. Moving in single file, one hand placed upon the shoulder of the fellow in front, Ferret felt certain that the *Evening Standard* wouldn't report the facts, preferring to sex up the truth with innuendo and speculation, insinuating, if necessary, that the train driver was drugged out of his mind on a strange concoction of jungle herbs and spices.

A pile of shattered wood supplemented by four legs and a nest of twisted wire interspersed with hammers and keys didn't require a forensic scientist equipped with a doctorate to speculate on what it was prior to impact. He reached inside his jacket pocket, running a finger down a length of ivory that was over a hundred years old. It wasn't a question of what the tube train hit, but rather of what a grand piano was doing on the track in the first place.

Ferret walked from Oxford Circus to Wardour Street in a daze, feeling reassured by the acrid taste of exhaust fumes. Several times he glanced over his shoulder, searching for the huge spook. Finally, he stopped outside a pair of burnished Art Deco doors, sunlight glinting off the chrome. As he searched for the buzzer, a courier exited the premises. Holding himself erect, Ferret slipped inside. Ominously, the door squealed on its hinges, thumping shut.

"Hello?" Ferret's words echoed around the reception area.

The only answer was provided by a fly with a white head buzzing noisily around the ceiling, careering off the ancient light fittings.

He checked the directory, ordered by floor, and learned from the sign that the offices were once inhabited solely by Hammer Films.

His hackles rose.

Warily, he headed for a heavy oak staircase that was flanked by a pair of sarcophagi. Taking the steps sideways, he brushed through a screen of spider web hanging limply from the corners of the roof, fully convinced that if he turned his back on the desk, a dark-haired vamp would jump up, sinking demonic fangs deep into his neck.

Creak!

A shiver shot up his spine.

Damn floorboards.


The premises he sought were located on the third floor, hidden amongst a collection of media companies at the far end of a dark corridor. One or two of the offices had their lights on; the occasional tap of a keyboard reverberated through the warm, still air. As he neared the destination, Ferret's ticker thumped hard against the inside of his rib cage, desperately trying to escape.

His hand hovered near the door to Banoffee Publishing. He recalled the smell of new black leather. Taking a series of long, slow breaths, he wrestled control of his nerves and knocked twice on the glass, causing it to judder in its mountings.

"My god!" Behind the door, there was a brief sound of scuffling, followed by a smash.

Ferret poked his head inside, followed by his body.

"You scared the living bejesus out of me." The voice, which belonged to a thin, shrew-faced woman in her late thirties rasped across his eardrums.

"Sorry."

Shrew-face, who was dressed in grey jogging bottoms and a tight white T-shirt that revealed her slight bosom, bent to pick up a broken plant pot, its contents spewed across the carpet and forming a ridge of roots and dirt. "What the hell are you doing here?"

"The front door was open . . ."

"I don't think so." Shrew-face peered fixedly through thick, black-rimmed spectacles that made her eyes look like tiny black peas. "We're closed. So quickly, what do you want?"

"I'm here to collect my father's files." Ferret heard the words blurt forth at the same time he was composing his apology.

Shrew-face squinted, folding her arms.

Ferret relaxed, finding his patter. "He was the victim of a horrendous accident. They say he tripped on loose decking and ended up enjoying the spectacular scenery of the fjords, from the fjords. While he was bobbing up and down awaiting rescue, he was cut to pieces by the propellers of a Spanish shrimp smack illegally fishing in foreign waters. Possibly you read an account of the accident in the papers, although it wasn't widely reported outside of the broadsheets. You know how it is with scientists."

"I'm sorry for your loss." Shrew-face's top lip curled at the edge. She moved into the detective's personal space. "Now, off with you."

Ferret's eyes widened as a warm spark of comfort transited his spine, arcing through his skeleton. "They're behind that door."

Shrew-face pushed, ushering him out.

"My files." He had no idea how he was going to liberate a set of ones and zeroes, but he had to do something. Acting on impulse, he stepped to the side and rushed forward.

Shrew-face moved quickly, sticking her leg behind his and attempting a throw down. Ferret countered instinctively, tossing the skinny woman to one side. She landed on her bum with a thud.

"Stammy!" she shouted. "There's a mad crackers bastard in here, gone bonkers!"

The adjoining door burst open and in barged a brute of a man packing a finely chiselled jaw. A distinctive birthmark shyly poked forth from the beefcake's hairline near the right temple. Ferret scanned the brute from head to toe, concluding that his exquisitely cut suit was Italian in origin, although he was unable to name the fashion house.

The detective backed off, considering his options.

"Well, well," said the beefcake in a public school accent, stroking his chin. "What do we have here?"

Shrew-face sneered from her position on the carpet. "He assaulted me."

The brute waved his hand, a ring on one of his fingers throwing off a sparkle of light. "Maddie, lock the door."

Ferret stepped backwards, putting himself between Shrew-face and the exit. He felt behind him for the door handle. There was something familiar about his opponent. He'd seen that birthmark before.

"I'm sure I know you . . ."

The brute of a man's face cracked in a half smile, exposing a gold-capped incisor.

Ferret's hand drifted towards his collarbone. "Well, if it isn't Stamford Strauss. My, how you've grown."

"Damn me, it's the trouser ferret." Stamford tapped the gold incisor. "I chipped this tooth the day you cheated to win the cup. Kicked in the head by my own team."

"It was certainly one heck of a final." Ferret found the handle. "Is that the ring that cut me?"

"Oh, you beauty." Stamford cracked his knuckles.

The detective felt a cold wind of hostility blow in hard from the north, bringing with it a ship full of hairy, unwashed Vikings, axes sharpened for combat, intent on furiously venting their blood lust on an unsuspecting populace.

Shrew-face jumped to her feet, brushed past Strauss, and headed to the inner door.

In a prime state of health, with the element of surprise, Ferret was confident of toppling the big man. But not today. He raised his hands, palms facing the smartly dressed juggernaut and reached out, consciousness arcing skywards arrow sharp, through office after office, depositing behind globules of steaming cobalt syrup. He found a towering mast throwing radio waves in every direction, a stream of bits with which to synchronise his feelings. Down the cables he crashed, riding a log flume, buffeted from side to side.

Stamford ground his foot against the carpet, testing for grip. Satisfied with the results he lowered his head, bellowed, and charged.

In a blaze of euphoria, Ferret made contact with his files. Less than a second later, the taurine behemoth crashed into him, leading with a shoulder. The detective timed his twisting jump so that when they made contact Strauss struck him in the stomach instead of the ribs. A quick punch to the kidneys and he was over the top.

The pair slammed into the door together, Ferret's backside striking the glass partition, pushing it from its mounts. The frame juddered and splintered.

Crunch!

Bull crazy, high on a neck full of spears, Strauss backed up and thrust forward again, his momentum causing the remains of the portal to give way and fly off its hinges.

Crack!

Ferret took a deep breath and waited for the impact, bringing his knee up at the last into Stamford's jaw, pushing and rolling to avoid the falling weight. He hit the deck hard, followed by the big man, the wind knocked from both. Strauss lay face down, moaning. The Old Boy's size might have changed in the last fifteen years, but his tactics were still as dumb as ever. Groggily, the detective stirred, his rear end on fire, trousers cut to ribbons.

A good old fashioned jolt of battle juice pumped through his veins.

Invigorated, he pushed Strauss to one side and clambered to his feet, retrieving the fedora just in time to take a plant pot to the side of the head.

Smash!

A second and a third plant pot flew through the air. Ferret pushed them away with his arms. Out of ammunition, Shrew-face unsheathed an undead wail and charged, nails drawn. He tried to keep her at bay, but she simply stepped up the intensity, attacking him in a flurry of claws, elbows, and knees, each sharper than the last. Behind him, he heard a crunch of broken glass; he glanced over to see Strauss roll upright. Shrew-face wriggled closer, raking her nails down his face and biting his hand, drawing blood.

A red mist descended.

Smack!

Ferret's fist made contact with the side of the shrew's head; she crumpled to the ground, glasses smashed.

He felt blood drain from his face.

Full of remorse, he bent forward to pick her up and apologise.

"Son of a bitch!" Strauss clambered to his feet and lurched forward, groping the air.

Ferret turned and ran, passing a pair of confused onlookers who'd poked their heads out to see what all the commotion was about. Ignoring his injuries, he bounded down the stairs, two steps at a time.

A part of him wanted to go back.

He kept on telling himself that Shrew-face was no lady, confident that on this point his French friend would agree. Crashing out onto Wardour Street, he upended a smart chap with a movie camera who shouted after him.

He kept going.

He'd send flowers as an apology.

After all, he was a gentleman, not a thug.

"Tristan sends his regards."

The cameraman's words echoed through Ferret's brain.

The detective cursed. He should have used the tradesman's entrance. Or gone in disguise. Anything other than what he did. He was a great consultant, without a doubt. As a detective — to borrow a phrase from his old employers — he was all lemons and no meringue.

When he'd made contact, over half the files were gone, torn bit from byte. He'd found the remainder hiding away in a darkened recess, scared for their very existence. He reached out to embrace them, but they retreated, finding crevice after crevice in which to hide.

Whatever was going on in the adjoining room, owned by RockSlut Research, it wasn't pleasant. In his mind's eye, Ferret imagined a combine harvester, gathering up ones and zeroes, sucking the goodness out, packaging it up, binding it tightly in string, the remaining husks discarded.

His files were not alone in their nightmare.

Others were being processed too. Thousands and thousands of them, torn into component particles.

Ferret thought hard, letting his feelings take form.

Just before the big man had crashed into him, he'd felt something malevolent, a foreboding presence. It wasn't a piece of technology; it was a someone, dark as night with the wings of a crow, the canopy of feathers wrapped tightly around a golden glow, allowing only a chink of light to shine through.

Ferret gulped.

As hard as Strauss was, he was only the monkey. The someone: he or she was the organ grinder, the master of the Precious. While he was busy running away, they were processing whatever fibre was contained in his father's files. Rushing down the stairs, he'd heard their death screams, felt their naked terror, seen them sliced in two by a swinging pendulum.

It was Hammer Horror at its most theatrical.

The detective took a deep breath.

The files really were gone.

Forever.

He closed his eyes and let out a muffled sob.

That knowledge had cost him his dignity and a bright-yellow, thrill-packed, traffic-stopping GranSport Spyder. If the centurion had his way, undoubtedly he'd demand another trouser press too.

# Chapter Twenty-Seven: Down Periscope

Cyrano paced frantically up and down the length of his suite, feet falling in the same spot with each passing. He hardly noticed the tasteful beige décor accentuated with pale-yellow soft furnishings, or the prominent candelabra sparkling with cut glass. During each circumambulation of the room he tested the lock on the front door, its brass chain, the outside windows, and the patio doors leading to the roof terrace.

Given that his stalker liked to change faces regularly, he thought, one cannot be too careful.

He ran his tongue along his top lip. But for True Blue, he'd be lying on a yacht, basking in the sun. Some things, he reminded himself, were worth taking a risk for.

Such as a billion dollars . . . and lifelong notoriety.

He cussed.

The business plan he'd put together relied on him obtaining a sample of True Blue — something he'd so far failed to do. Upon examination, the phial he'd borrowed from the Regent's Park house was empty and the envelope, undoubtedly from Ferret's papa, contained only ashes. In desperation, he'd once again pretended to be Ferret and he'd met up with Sir Edward in the Turbine Hall of the Tate Modern. Unfortunately, Ginger didn't have the merchandise with him, necessitating a third meeting later tonight, which Sir Edward had promised to attend without asking the venue.

Out in public without the twenty-four-hour party posse as cannon fodder, Cyrano had soon realised he felt conspicuous and vulnerable. In response, he'd reduced his footprint and downed periscope. Once he had True Blue, the Côte d'Azur beckoned. The scoundrel who'd maimed Woody would never find him there.

The Frenchman strode over to the coffee table, where a pair of greasy parallel smears begged for attention. He ran a finger the length of both, licking it clean.

He felt his cheeks.

Three days' worth of itchy, black stubble greeted his fingers.

Unheard of.

Not since the jungles of South America, nearly a decade ago, had he
let himself go like this.

Picking up a mobile phone, he hit redial.

Brring!

"You have reached the voicemail for 51R 3D. Please leave a message
after the tone."

Beep!

"My friend, you're a deadweight."

The Frenchman hung up. There was no point in calling their decanus
again. He was an even deader deadweight. He took a deep breath . . .

Knock!

. . . and jumped out of his skin.

Nervously, he strode over to the door and peered through the spy
hole. A someone — dressed in black, with a white shirt, a splodge of black
around the collar, and shades — stared back.

"Is that Jake or Elwood?"

"Elwood."

The Frenchman opened the door a tad, careful to leave the safety
chain on. Once he'd confirmed the chap's identity, in as much as Elwood
was the name he'd given to the taller of the two security bruisers he'd stolen from Ferret, he shut the door, released the chain, and let him in.

"There's a geezer to see you."

"Who?" Cyrano flicked his nose. Please let it be Edward.

"Says he's called Tristan. Looks like a ponce."

"Thank you for your opinion." The Frenchman snorted in disappointment. "The next time you give a critique of one of my friends, I
expect a smile."

"Smiling is extra." Elwood grinned. "Five quid."

"Itemise it and add it to the tab."

"And the latent homosexual?"

"Tell Jake to send him up."


"Royston Smythe?" Tristan raised an eyebrow. "Of all the names in the
world you might have chosen, you had to pick one that doesn't suit you in
the slightest."

Cyrano paced up and down, chewing his lip.

The nature of his chosen profession demanded he often travel under
an assumed name. Jean-Paul was his favourite. After that, Patrice. Having

his choice of pseudonym openly criticised was not something that had happened before.

"It's necessary," he said, scowling.

"Yes, Roy. Of course, Roy." The banker shuffled his backside, digging deeper into the sofa.

"I wish to remain anonymous."

"Why is that, Roy? And why aren't we in your usual suite at the Savoy, Roy?"

"It's being redecorated."

"Oh, this is horrible. I command you to not be a Roy Smith anymore."

Cyrano strode over to the patio doors and checked them. "You don't have to call me Roy. In fact, I beg you not to."

"If you're going to beg, do it properly." The centurion offered his foot.

Cyrano gazed longingly out of the double doors across the London skyline. "I have your monk's urine."

"Really?" Tristan let out a whoop of joy. "May I see?"

"It's in the fridge."

The banker jumped to his feet and began opening every likely-looking unit. At the third attempt, he jiggled his feet, withdrawing a bottle of pale-yellow liquid. Holding it up to the light, he rotated the container, gazing joyfully at the contents. After a few seconds, he popped the cork and took a sniff.

"It's glacial melt water, passed by Buddhist monks from the Paro Taktsang in Bhutan," said Cyrano. "Guaranteed free of additives."

"How disappointing. For a grand, I expect gold flake."

The Frenchman laughed, strongly advising his friend against such an addition. Unusually, his banking friend agreed. Under the circumstances, he announced loudly, the last thing he needed was to be placed under investigation for smuggling precious metals out of the company vaults in his bladder.

Tristan's attention soon turned to the ladies. "Which agency did you say they're from?"

Cyrano sighed, checking the patio doors again. Five minutes into the biggest night in living memory and already he was having serious doubts about his choice of partner for the evening. If Catherine hadn't inadvertently let it slip, he'd be flying alone.

Six into one was a much better ratio than three into two.

"They're friends of Juliet," he said.

"And how is the furry one?"

"Sore. He's convinced he was spiked with ecstasy by a rock star."

"Ha!" The banker cackled mischievously. "As promised, you'll be amply rewarded for picking his brain."

Cyrano listened to the banker castigate his consultant friend for behaving like a jerk and allowing video evidence to be gathered, placing him inside the very offices he was forbidden from visiting. To top it all, their friend the art dealer had a taped confession, in which Ferret admitted the files weren't even there.

The Frenchman waggled a window handle.

Hopefully, his friend had now come to his senses and this was the last of it.

"For the record, our consultant friend is meeting in secret tonight with an old flame, to discover more about a company merger," he said, thinking aloud. "Whatever you do, you're not to mention this to the ladies."

Tristan mulled the suggestion over while he returned the bottle to the fridge. "Do you want a sports car?"

Cyrano shook his head. "Do I look like a chap who enjoys driving a giant wasp?"

"If our friend fails to deliver the information he promised, I shall take it to the races and have it pranged. In front of him, I imagine." The banker smiled and flexed his fingers. "Why am I not flying off my tits?"

"Top drawer."

"Oh, goody good good. Do you fancy a trouser press?"

"Certainly." The Frenchman turned around and headed to the bedroom. "I'll store it at Ferret's place."

With a fellow legionnaire present, Cyrano finally felt able to relax, albeit just a smidgeon. Leaving the banker to the bag of goodies, he announced he was taking a shower and promptly retired to the bedroom.

Unbuttoning his shirt, he tossed it into the dirty laundry pile.

Whatever happened tonight, it was going straight back to Juliet. He hadn't met the Richmond set, but he knew groups of girls. Any juicy preference whispered in a stripper's ear was a secret shared by all. The set was there to gauge him and check out his portfolio, whilst digging to uncover any stray facts about his ferrety friend.

Cyrano hung up his trousers, pulled on a bathrobe and headed to the bathroom. His consultant friend changed girlfriends on a regular basis. Always had. Give it a week and he'd move on. Until that point, their combined reputations had to remain spotless. Quite how he was going to achieve this with the centurion shadowing him, he didn't know.

Perhaps his banking friend had a set of hitherto undiscovered manners, reserved for special occasions.

The sounds of snorting mixed with the dull moans of ladies being pleasured drifted in from the TV in the living room.

A cork popped.

"Jolly Bolly!"

Entering the shower, Cyrano concluded he was more likely to discover that hell had a skating rink, a downhill slalom, and an ice cream stall.

The Frenchman finished his ablutions in his own time, running the water extra hot to soften the stubble, leisurely razoring it away. He fixed his moustache, playing with the wax, then applied a splash of aftershave to his face, followed by a river of eau de parfum to his torso.

By the time he returned to the lounge, suited and booted, his banking friend had transferred half of the stash to the insides of his hooter. The centurion's pupils were a pair of black holes, sucking in all surrounding matter.

"I saved you a portion." Tristan pointed at the table, pressing rewind on the TV controller. "How can a girl do that? It's not natural."

"Cocaine and a lot of practice." The Frenchman adjusted his cuffs.

"I hear you're going into business with our friend the fire starter."

"It turns out his rich and desperate parents have stupendous media connections."

The centurion grinned, pointing at the screen. "Do you see that black chap who's hung like a donkey? Just once, I want to see a huge negro with a minute penis who suffers from premature ejaculation. Humiliation porn, I call it. In fact, I command you and Blair to make such a movie."

The Frenchman shook his head. "Is there any Champagne left?"

"Fridge." The banker waved his hand dismissively. "Next to the monk's piss."

Cyrano topped up the centurion, pouring himself a half glass, which he downed in one to take the edge off the gnawing cocaine rodents in his belly. He pulled on his jacket and headed for the door to go downstairs and finalise details with the hotel's restaurant prior to the ladies' arrival at seven thirty.

"I'm coming too." Tristan glugged half the Champagne and threw the glass against the wall, plastering shards and fizz everywhere. "Tonight I'm a rock star, and this is the room I shall trash."

Cyrano did his utmost to remain calm.

"Later," he said, voice cracking.

"I like your thinking, legionnaire." Tristan slapped him across the back. "The girls will not be impressed if we invite them back to a pigsty. However, if we trash the room while they're here . . ."

The Frenchman huffed, swallowing his anger. He checked the windows one more time, locked the patio doors that his banker friend had opened, and shut up shop, heading towards the lift with the centurion in hot pursuit, flexing his upper body as if he was a boxer warming up for a fight.

Elwood nodded, his face a mask. Then he remembered their deal and cracked a smile.

This is going to cost me a small fortune, thought Cyrano.

He pressed the down button. Looking behind, he stopped the banker, just as he was liberating a painting from the wall.

"It's not an original," he hissed.

"Good call," said the banker, pushing his way into the lift first. "That maintenance man was very odd."

The Frenchman's eyes narrowed, arrow slits in an otherwise impervious castle wall.

"Arrived while you were in the shower. Said there was a problem with the cable, although the porn channel seemed perfectly OK to me."

Cyrano clenched his fists around Tristan's lapels, pulling him close. *"You let him in?"*

"Steady on." The banker's face flushed pink. "Remember whom you address."

Cyrano tightened his grip. "What did you tell him?"

"If you must know, I told him to fuck off. I'm not having a random oik question my viewing preferences."

The Frenchman let his friend go.

*Merde!*

Ever since he'd glimpsed the weasel chap at Mimi's get-well party, he'd been ultra-careful going about his business. He'd flashed false names at every opportunity, employed random drivers, left establishments by the back door and entered others the same way, always fibbing about his next destination.

Despite the false trails and layers of misinformation, the nutbag who'd disfigured Woody had somehow managed to track him down.

The Frenchman slapped his forehead.

Filthy Cristina.

After he'd wheedled her details from his consultant friend, he'd smooth-talked her into coming over for supper.

Damn.

Somehow, they must have followed her.

Was there no one in the whole of London he could trust?

# Chapter Twenty-Eight: Seven Seven

Ferret cast a longing eye over his dinner date, remembering the best of times and how, in their fury, they'd taken on the world and beaten it into submission with hammers and Stolichnaya. In his early twenties, he had a preference for experienced women, mid to late thirties. As he aged, he'd expected his preference to shift upwards accordingly.

Except it hadn't.

On the run up to thirty, he dated Marcie, a junior straight out of university, followed by her hot best friend. Shortly afterwards, his French friend introduced the pair to his drugs cabinet, permanently addling their minds. Later, in a show of beasting, McGyver ordered both sacked.

"I'm so glad you owe me dinner in London." Marianne reached out and touched his hands. "Cheltenham is a glorious place to work but the absolute pits for restaurants of note."

Ferret ran bruised fingers through his hair, feeling for the bump that Shrew-face had inflicted. "My pleasure." The words came as a soft purr.

Marianne flashed her eyelashes.

Surrounded by diners decked out in formal attire in a Network-endorsed restaurant-cum-hotel, Ferret felt protected from the weary world outside. He relaxed, allowing the ambience to wash over him, voicing his appreciation for the décor which was comprised of soft toned ivory and dark chocolate. He glanced over at a nearby coat stand where a grey felt fedora nestled sweetly between a pair of light summer jackets. It was less than a week since a secret admirer had made him a gift of it, yet he now felt naked without it.

He'd get used to it.

Later tonight, he'd have a ceremonial burning, just as he'd done with the website earlier in the day. With his files desecrated, the detective dream had curled up at the edges. And thanks to a centurion and decanus double act, it was disembowelled, lying gutted on the mortician's slab.

The consultant held his breath until he saw Marianne's chest begin to fall; he synchronised his breathing with hers, taking care not to gaze too deeply into her eyes. Intuitively, he imagined they were lying together, half naked, beneath the goalposts at Twickenham on match day, covered in patches of slippery brown mud, wet stuff oozing between their toes.

The crowd roared them on.

Marianne closed her eyes and dug her nails into his hand.

His face itched to be scratched. He stopped himself. The makeup artist's instructions were very specific: Leave it alone and you're good for three hours.

"Sir." The sommelier's words broke the spell. "My name is Pierre. This is my recommendation for your first course."

Marianne loosened her grip and stuck her chin forward, grinning like a naughty schoolgirl.

Pierre cut the lead foil with a small pocket knife and extracted the cork, sniffing it lengthways. He looked to Ferret. With a flick of the wrist, the consultant pointed to his accomplice.

"This wine comes from one of the greatest of the Grand Cru chateaux, which number but seven." Pierre poured. "The slopes of the vineyard are orientated towards the southwest, which results in this extraordinarily complex wine."

Marianne picked up the glass, sloshed the contents around, brought it to her nose and inhaled, declaring the scent reminiscent of broken biscuits; she took a sip. "A racy little number."

The sommelier filled two glasses to the halfway point, inserted the bottle of Chablis in a bucket of ice with a white-gloved hand, sloshed the slush, and left the pair to their private party.

Ferret raised a glass. "To secrets."

Inside, he felt like a barrel of frogs in the spring. If ever he needed his friend in intelligence to appear, now was the time. Earlier on, hoping for a last-minute reprieve, he'd visited Marcus's embankment home, only to find the blinds down and no one home.

Marianne clinked glasses and dropped a plastic rectangle on the table.

Ferret picked it up, noting the logo. "Dickson Associates. For such a well-known defence contractor there can only be a limited pool of worthy contenders."

"Our partner is based in Bath."

Ferret felt his smile dissipate, as the edges of his mouth developed a complex system of pulleys and weights.

"Touché!" Marianne giggled. "I once spent eighteen months trying to send you there and you wrote an encyclopaedia of hitherto unheard excuses avoiding the place. Why was that?"

"It's a long story." Ferret focused on his phone and furiously tapped the keys. "Cocks Associates."

"Very good."

"That would make you Dickson Cocks."

"Quite a mouthful, huh?"

Ferret felt himself blush. "You're rebranding."

"And you're wearing makeup. One story for another."

The consultant described what had happened earlier in the day when he'd visited the address Marianne had supplied, and how he came within inches of having his eyes scratched out and his brains dashed in by the gerbera airborne division all over some misappropriated files that were, ultimately, of no value. As he told the story, he pointed to each of the scuffs and scrapes, proudly counting them out as badges of honour.

Marianne leaned forward, flashing her cleavage. "If you like, I'll pay them a visit, see if I can gain traction."

"There's nothing left to recover." Ferret bent over the table and met Marianne's lips. He felt tears well in his eyes. "My foray into the world of detection is over. As of now, I'm recommitting my future to high finance."

Behind him in the bar area, its walls adorned with erotic artwork, the consultant heard a commotion break out.

"Leave it, lover boy." Underneath the table, Marianne put her hand on Ferret's knee and gave a quick squeeze.

The crash of breaking glass cut the air; shrapnel spilt across the marble floor, tinkling to rest. The restaurant fell silent, with the exception of the piano player, who carried on for three notes. All heads, including Ferret's, turned towards the source of the disturbance.

"Whoops," said a short gent in a black dinner suit, surrounded by three equally well-presented fellows, who in turn surrounded a member of the hotel staff. "Go back to your dinners, diners. I command it."

The piano player resumed a groove.

"Tristan . . ." The word had barely left Ferret's lips before it was buffeted by another: "Cyrano . . ."

"You know them?" said Marianne, surprised.

"Excuse me a moment, but I must find out what in the blue blazes they're doing here."


"Furry one." Tristan bowed. "Apologies for the short notice, but we intend to smash this place up."

Cyrano hissed a command through gritted teeth, motioning to a pair of well-built bruisers to escort the centurion away.

The banker squirmed free and quickly headed towards Marianne. "I shall amuse myself with your dinner date, while you assist our French friend. He thinks he's being shadowed by ninjas. Discuss."

Ferret felt his heart sink.

"Jake!" barked the Frenchman. "Find that maintenance man."

The squatter of the two bruisers forced a smile and headed off.

"Explain yourself," said the consultant, keeping a keen eye on the banker.

"Our friend is ramped up on Colombian bath salts."

"I mean your presence here at Seven Seven. You live at the Savoy and you only ever eat at Simpson's."

Cyrano lowered his voice. "Despite taking the utmost care, my stalker has found me. By implication, they've found you too."

"Whatever sleaze you're embroiled in," snapped Ferret, "I want no part of it."

The Frenchman stared back through sharp, unblinking blue eyes, spinning a story that was — on the face of it — quite incredible. "Your father," he concluded, "was involved in the creation of industrial quantities of love drugs. The one who maimed Woody is convinced I have the formula, thanks to my accidental association with a certifiable crazy."

"You created the mess, you sort it."

"My boy . . ."

Fuming, Ferret departed, leaving his friend ordering another round of bodyguards whilst also grovelling profusely to management for the banker's excessive enthusiasm with an antique glass vase, promising on his word no more breakages.

His intuition told him that Cyrano believed his father was a drug baron, but that didn't make it true. It was possible, just highly unlikely. Ferret felt his mind sharpen, shifting up a gear. What if his father *was* involved in a drugs program? A *military* drugs program. Ferret recalled his father's abhorrence of drugs, even the legal steroids he'd taken in his youth to improve his physique on the field of play. It didn't make sense, yet the queer blue liquid he'd dosed himself with had definitely had an effect.

Ferret stopped in his tracks. He remembered the argument with his father clearly for the first time. The allegations of financial impropriety, the stinging rebuke over his proposed purchase of the Regent's Park house. High on cocaine and brandy, he'd told his father he was a bitter old curmudgeon. Wolfgang pulled a gun out of a desk drawer and apologised. It was for the best, he said. Abuse of a gift was sacrilege.

Ferret shook his head.

Water off a duck's back under a bridge.

His father was dead.

The files were gone.

That was the end of it.

"The ferrety one returns from battle unscathed." Tristan rose and bowed. "Your trousers are in need of a press."

Marianne knocked back the remains of her wine. "Your friend is quite the business mogul. You're so lucky to have such a clever gent in charge of your finances."

"He's more of an advisor," said Ferret guardedly.

"No, I definitely manage them. Has Cyrano told you he's bought a television production company with Blair? Good solid business cards." Tristan tapped his nose.

Ferret grimaced. "I hadn't heard."

"Enough about me, the girls have arrived. I bid you both *bon soir.*" Tristan eyes shot furtively from side to side. "Innit. The youth of the French ghettos simply have no respect for the language of love."

Ferret took a seat, eyeing his banking friend with suspicion, watching him waltz an imaginary partner through the bar, narrowly avoiding a waiter on his hands and knees hard at work with a hand brush. Six girls, dressed in a combination of long, flowing evening wear entered in single file, each lovelier than the last. Cyrano greeted them in turn, with a kiss to each cheek. Tristan followed suit, standing on tiptoes to reach the most willowy of the gaggle.

The first course arrived: a platter of Irish oysters.

"They have a private dining area." Under the table, Marianne touched the top of Ferret's shoe with a stocking-covered foot. "You didn't offer me such luxury."

Ferret stared at the procession of ladies. Stunners, all of them, and not one over thirty. Not that he would ever guess a lady's age as anything greater than twenty-nine. A gentleman would never dare stray into such soggy marshland.

Marianne kicked him in the ankle. "I realise you're taking one for the team, lover boy — your finance friend's words, not mine. Your attention. Now!"

"Sorry." Ferret turned around. "I was just wondering where Cyrano met such a fine bunch of English fillies. He usually dates Russian girls called 'Svetlana'."

"According to Tristan, they're friends of Juliet."

Ferret felt his face fire up.

Marianne giggled and put a finger to her lips. "Don't worry, I won't say a word to your girlfriend. Just as you won't spill the beans to my man, who by the way, you're never going to meet. After all, we both know what The Consultancy has to say about such things."

"What happens on the road stays on the road."

"Actually," Marianne ran her toe up Ferret's shin, "I was thinking of the other one: Careless talk costs wives."

After dinner, Ferret retired to Cyrano's terrace for Japanese whisky, port, and men-only cigar conversation, while Marianne dealt with an urgent phone call related to her merger. His misgivings were great, but an order from the centurion was an order. Being elusive was one thing; direct disobedience quite another. The consultant touched his fedora, a habit he'd grown accustomed to of late, only to find it wasn't there.

The three friends leant out over the balustrade, pointing to various London landmarks and boasting of their achievements, puffing away on unfeasibly large cigars, the centurion's clocking in at a good ten centimetres longer than the other two. Surrounded by the legion, Ferret let his shoulders go, the tension ebbing away. Although they were in St. James on the edge of Mayfair, close to the heart of Old Boy territory, it was unlikely they'd send tiny Jones to do the dirty over dinner. Just to be sure, Ferret had made excuses throughout the evening, checking under all the tables.

"What a wonderful life we have," said Cyrano, puffing up like a male pigeon with its beak stuck in a bucket of popcorn. "Here we are, frequenting one of London's more fashionable hotels, its restaurant renowned the world over with a waiting list as long as your arm, eligible bachelors each of us. Ferret in his Armani dinner suit, infinitely datable. I, in my finest Zegna, a picture of exquisite refinement. Tristan wearing whatever bespoke it is he wears these days."

"Who cares!" The banker downed a shot of Yamazaki whisky and threw the empty glass at the road below. "Tristan demands Charles. Order one of your goons to cut it."

The Frenchman shook his head. "They don't know how you like it."

Whooping in agreement, the banker bounded indoors, face alight with mischief.

"Is that wise?" asked Ferret.

"Relax," said his friend. "I hid the Colombian and replaced it with mellow flake."

Against the odds, it transpired that Tristan was actually in with a chance with one of the ladies. As long as they kept him calm for the next two hours, nature would take its course and the hotel, along with their reputations, would escape unscathed.

Ferret squared up to his friend, prodding him in the chest. "What are you playing at, dating my girlfriend's friends?"

Cyrano's mouth pinched tight at the edges. "Gorgeous, aren't they?"

"That's not the point."

"Oh, it's very much the point. Juliet and her friends are way out of your league. Which is why I'm assisting you, by bolstering your portfolio. Every fact I whisper will wing its way home."

"And you expect me to trust you?"

"Relax, my boy. I admit I badgered your girlfriend for a date with one of her friends, which was really rather crass. But I was envious. She offered to send six to choose from. What was I supposed to do?"

"Say no."

"With our banking friend on the case? This evening is his doing, I swear."

The consultant looked his friend in the eye, feelings slurred with alcohol. He was unable to tell where he ended and the Frenchman began. "Just stay away from Juliet."

"Sweet is served!" came the cry from within. "Hurry, my trusty legionnaires."

"Humour him," whispered Cyrano, recovering his composure. "Very shortly he'll be giggling like a girl."

Two lines later and Ferret felt all of his muscles relax as the flake did its work. For the first time in days, his troubles ebbed away. Jokingly, he poked Cyrano, who raised an eyebrow. The banker sat cross-legged on the floor, chopping up more lines of powder. It was only when he handed on the mirror for the third round that Ferret realised there were two bags on the table.

"Tristan finds the insanity soap very much to his liking," chortled the banker, his pupils glistening like obsidian marbles. "So much so, he pocketed several servings earlier for his personal consumption. Now, furry one, Tristan orders you to undress him! Frenchman, hum a striptease tune!"

Reluctantly, the consultant did as he was told, beginning at the bow tie and ending with the trousers, the banker's shoes being declared a no-go zone.

"Tristan has to wonder," said the centurion in a smug tone, posing in front of a mirror in red-silk boxer shorts, "why does Ferret shake a leg with grandma when he has access to a private room packed to the rafters with supermodels?"

"I'm following your orders," snapped Ferret, recoiling, but not quickly enough to avoid having his ears slapped.

With the banker stripped of clothing, both friends had to admit they were impressed by his lean physique; they'd always assumed he was an indolent consumer of fine cuisine in his spare time, flabby to the core. Ignoring their appreciation of his six-pack, Tristan ordered a piggyback ride and climbed on Ferret, commanding him to race three laps around the patio, using his ears as accelerators.

"Tristan declares that Ferret is a dum-dum detective whose movies require pelting with rotten tomatoes," laughed the banker, tweaking the consultant's ear. "Vroom! Vroom! We demand more cocaine!"

While Cyrano did the honours, Tristan sped around the suite tilting pictures, allowing Ferret to catch his breath. He rubbed his ears, wondering what was happening with his date.

The banker, full of crackling, nervous energy, rifled through Cyrano's sock drawer. "What do we have here?"

Surprised to discover he was holding the bra and briefs of the warrior princess, Ferret protested. They were a valuable TV prop, the property of Tim Tim, their decanus's brother. Tristan admitted to being a huge fan of the warrior princess TV show and, in his altered state, commanded the underwear to impart superpowers to the wearer. Tossing his boxers aside, he donned the bra, pulled on the smalls and ran around the terrace whooping, throwing plates.

"Ai ai ai aiiii!"

Ferret turned his back to mouth his discontent, only to see a look of horror cross his French friend's visage. By the time he looked back, the banker was gone. He peered over the balcony, watching Tristan's sure-footed descent. He felt numb, all the way to his toes, yet his heart pumped liquid fire. It was like being a snowball with lava at its core.

Cyrano surveyed the scene of devastation that was his suite. "What are we to do?" he wailed.

"Thank our good fortune that our friend has stubby little fingers that prevent him from scaling anything serious." Ferret sighed, eyeing his timepiece. "I really must go. My date awaits."

"My god!" The colour drained from the Frenchman's face. "*Les belles filles.*"

"If our friend feels half as horny as I do, that's where he's headed."

Cyrano slapped himself across the cheek. "We must stop him."

"Good luck with that," laughed Ferret, picking up his jacket. "To-night I'm on a mission that ends with me making a small fortune. Just like the good old days."

"My boy," said Cyrano, straightening his bow tie, "let me apprise you of your predicament: There's a soap-powered lunatic on the loose, with a motormouth and little sense of decorum. What do you think will happen if he reaches the girls before us and, in an act of foolish bravado, spills the beans on your make-believe film career?"

Ferret's jaw dropped.

"That's right. Unless we intercept him, you can wave goodbye to your relationship. Juliet, like all the others before her, will be consigned to the pages of history."

Summoning the last of his ebbing strength, Flamen Dialis of The Brotherhood of Light and Reason pulled himself upright and, taking a flask of water from beside the bed, poured it over his head, flushing away stale sweat. His teeth chattered. Creaking joints he was used to; regular yoga was his panacea. The fire in his ankle, the hot needles above the knee. The dull ache all over . . .

He took a deep breath.

This was no longer a condition to hobble off.

Beneath the bed sheet, the priest moved his leg a fraction; stabbing pains shot through his insides. "Jupiter's smarting buttocks!"

He gritted his teeth, cursing the laws of physics. The gods allowed a certain leeway, a turn of the cheek. But even with the power at his disposal, he was still only able to manipulate, not break, the chance alignments that bound reality together. Without the insight of a healer, this body was done for.

His thoughts turned to the girl in the cat suit. She did not give up her pursuit easily. But then she was young, an athlete, her life ahead of her. He was a spent old man.

Damn Edward's hot head.

If only he hadn't insisted on chasing Bromeliad, their planned escape route wouldn't have been blocked by police reinforcements.

Even in his youth, Flamen despised the sewers. Now, in his condition, they were life-threatening. Edward had taken the rap while he'd slipped away, losing his footing on a greasy rung, banging his leg, and passing out in agony.

After his release, the ginger terror rode a whirlwind, rounding up Grimes and the other vagrants who'd spontaneously joined the girl's army of the night. In a controlled rage, he dropped his trousers and assaulted the tramp, threatening him with a damn good rogering. Grimes shook his head, claiming he was unable to recall the episode in detail.

Edward attacked one tramp after another, always hearing the same story: They'd come to the Square as requested and were milling around drinking when they heard the most enchanting of voices singing the most beautiful of songs. When the girl stopped, they did whatever she asked, on the promise she'd sing again.

While Edward assailed the homeless across the breadth of London's tube system, Flamen used his remote viewing skills to investigate the two remaining suspects on his list. Moon the orderly proved difficult to track down, and with good reason. According to his doctor's notes, an over indulgence of conspiracy theory and non-prescription drugs had addled his brain, forcing him off the grid. Eventually, through a neighbour of Moon's sister, he found an address.

The man was a paranoid, broken wreck, armed to the teeth with medieval weaponry and a box of high explosives. Could Moon the Loon really be calling the operations tune from a dank cave in Wales?

With a shake of his head, the priest put a cross through the photograph and moved on.

According to a dossier he'd viewed remotely, MacGregor Cocks had spent the last twenty-five years living in the West Country, consulting in the field of mechanised death. He was an obsessive collector of war memorabilia, preoccupied with perfecting durable combat chariots. Apparently, he preferred the company of tanks to people and found it nearly impossible to make new organic friends.

Flamen smiled.

He'd always held a deep, unspoken respect for the Army man's simplicity. There were no lipstick-painted pigs or cats disguised as dogs with him. The priest paid him an ethereal visit to catch up and was stunned at what he found. The officer was barricaded in an office, tables upturned, sleeping in a tent, surviving on field rations and whisky, a potted plant and a pail playing vital roles in the regime.

This wasn't right.

And what's more, he'd developed a silver tinge.

Flamen considered how he might contact the ginger terror, who he'd sent off in pursuit of Barry Albright the psychologist, now a minor celebrity thanks to a ridiculous self-help book that claimed all objects contain an embedded history of pictures and sounds. According to the offshore bank accounts Flamen had viewed, Albright had developed a penchant for embezzlement, growing wealthy at the expense of his country.

Defender of the realm indeed!

The priest's only regret was that he was unable to chase this lead down himself.

Albright was a smug, self-centred bastard. Always had been. In the final days of Project XIII, he'd mounted a personal crusade, determined to prove he could create a battalion of fearless warriors using his battlefield globe. His work was doomed to failure, of course. How one of the globes had found its way to Soho remained a mystery. It was best explained by the man himself, whose comeuppance was long overdue.

With his eyes shut tight, the priest located Edward. He wasn't where he was supposed to be.

"Jupiter's elephantine oboe!"

Rather than following orders and bringing in the turncoat for extended questioning, he'd headed off to torment Walter Troutman instead, visiting the bean counter's apartments in St. James Square. It was said of Troutman that he snuck into the mortuary at night and replaced the brass handles on Lewis's coffin with painted plastic. He'd ordered the sandbags that counted for the bodyweight to be filled from the practice range. For these heinous acts, Edward had named him Toad, and much to Walter's disappointment, the name had stuck.

On the morning they'd recovered Lewis's body from the immersion tank, Toad fled the bunker, his knees quaking and threw up his breakfast on the grass outside. Edward penned an ode to his weak constitution, while the rest of the team played rummy on Lewis's corpse as a mark of respect.

Poor Lewis.

They'd taken his body to pieces with scalpels and a saw. Toad insisted that Porton Down pick up the autopsy costs; they weren't coming from his budget. Backed by the team, Edward called him a ministry miser lacking in compassion. After that, Toad kept a very close eye on the ginger troublemaker, their relationship marred by a series of ugly spats, each one messier than the last.

Unfortunately for Toad, mused Flamen, it was difficult to put a price on the spoils of war when they didn't have any recognised commercial value. All that SK-13 with a book value of zero. How infuriated Toad had become when Wolfgang and the Army man finally threw in the towel. Zero value when he started, zero value at the end.

The priest's eyes spread wide, the size of flying saucers.

Zero value.

With a storage cost attached.

That made it a yearly net loss on the books.

"Jupiter's crinkled cavities!"

For all of his cleverness with red tape, there *was* a loophole. That was how they'd justified disposing of the remains of the stockpile, sneaking it out from under the noses of the ministry. That sort of devious, exploitative thinking had pond slime smeared all over it. It wasn't the work of a cavalry officer or a psychologist.

"Jupiter's hirsute anus!"

He'd underestimated the most annoying member of the team.

Walter was a cautious man, who believed all risks must be mitigated. Which meant if he was the culprit he'd have a plan in place for each and every possibility.

"Jupiter's velvet conkers!"

Edward was walking into a trap.

Flamen wiped the sweat from his forehead and, grasping a lock of ginger hair, closed his eyes.

He had no time at all to lose.

# Chapter Thirty: Verpuppung

Sir Edward stroked what remained of the great ginger sideburns that had, for years, been the cornerstone of his trademark look. The cavalier beard had undergone an overhaul, along with the mop of curly red hair that marked him out as a true Celt. According to the chart on the wall of the ex-forces barber he'd employed, he now sported a style known as a Nimitz.

All for his Bromeliad.

Peering out from the shared doorway in which he was hiding, he twiddled his moustache. Damn priest. He'd get to the brain boffin soon enough. First though, he intended to partake in a spot of good old-fashioned Toad baiting.

His target walked arm in arm with a lady, chatting blithering nonsense, in a clipped public school accent.

Somehow, the repulsive amphibian had a dinner date.

With someone half his age.

Together, they made a rather odd couple. He with his weak double chins and expansive waistline, badly disguised by a black cummerbund; her a church mouse, dressed in a dark-blue ladies' two-piece suit, padding along in flat shoes.

Edward shook his head. Toad's date was obviously hired for the night. Clearly, the sly old amphibian had finally relented, joined the club and become a fully paid up sex pervert.

Content that his quarry was oblivious to his stalking, he put away the magnifying glass he was using to study the list of residents. He'd stalked his target for most of the afternoon, following him about his business, wheedling his way into the Mayfair apartment block where the amphibian resided, sidling all the way to his front door. He'd rung the bell, intent on charging Toad down with a walking cane and punching him in the paratoid gland for crimes past, when a peculiar notion overtook him, causing him to run away. It was a most odd reaction, one which he thought he'd given up for good the day he finally graduated to long trousers and holstered the catapult.

The terror moistened his lips. Since his return a week ago, it had been work, work, work. Oh, for the good old days, when it was all a bloody good laugh, playing chess with the Russians, each side baiting the other's ministers with underage jezebels, exchanging negatives for favours — and on occasion, other negatives.

Edward tailed the unusual pair along the edge of Mayfair. Past the glitzy façade of the Ritz they strode, passing through a wide arcade of glass-fronted shops, never once stopping to admire the wares on display. They doubled back, down a street of shoes, crossing St. James's, waved on by a series of Union flags fluttering in the tepid breeze. They came at last to a wide gate, the clubhouse of the Over-Seas League, flanked by an exclusive safe-haven hotel on one side, a modern office block on the other. Edward remembered Park Place well, although it was many years since he'd been here.

As the terror increased his pace, ready to charge down Toad from behind, a voice in his ear begged restraint.

Very well, he thought, clenching his fists tight and closing his eyes.

Smash!

A plate broke on the ground behind the happy couple, shattering into a dozen fragments.

Smash!

Smash!

The girl spun around and, dropping to the ground, drew a handgun from a holster concealed under her arm. Impulsively, Edward raised his hands. The girl looked up, tracing the crockery to its point of origin, on top of the hotel. With a shake of her head, she sheathed the weapon.

Toad looked straight at him. "Sir, I do apologise."

Edward lowered his hands, the element of surprise gone. The road upon which he was walking was a dead-end. If he approached any closer, he'd be recognised and the game was up.

"May I buy you a drink as compensation?"

The terror shook his head, closed his eyes tight, and clenched his fists once more.

"Ai ai ai aiiii!"

One of the Over-Seas League's staff, who'd been attracted by the plates, pointed to the roofline where a fellow hung upside down by the knees, wearing nothing but ladies underwear. Two gents beckoned from above. Tarzan whooped defiantly, flipped upright, clambered sideways, and, swinging by the arms, sailed through the air, catching a balcony rail.

"Call security," shouted a footman emerging from the hotel. "Tell them we have a live one."

With Toad and his date distracted, Edward dived into a nearby stairwell and pressed himself hard against the wall, breathing rapidly. Truth be told, he felt rather queer.

"Jupiter's grizzled walnuts!"

In fact, he hardly felt himself at all.

Dismissing the voices, Edward peered out from the hiding spot. The chap in the crimson bra and panties had made it safely to the ground and was now in the grip of a black-tie thug, gyrating madly. Despite the gravity of the situation, the wild man found himself quite aroused.

"I shall have your balls on a plate," squealed the cross-dresser.

"Sunshine, you're barred."

The chap continued to wriggle. "I command you to summon my friend Cyrano and the fabulous furry Ferret."

"Four-seven," said the thug into a concealed mic. "Assistance required."

At the mention of Wolfgang's son, Edward felt himself beam. As always, he'd found his man without even trying.

Unable to contain himself, Edward stepped out from his hiding spot, rear-ending Toad, who turned around and looked him straight in the eye, the colour draining from his pallid face.

The terror elbowed the amphibian in the ribs. The girl slipped her hand inside her jacket; swiftly, Edward brought his walking cane down on her knuckles. Pulling the weapon back, he aimed a blow at the side of her head. She ducked to one side, causing Toad to take a silver bull's head to the man boob.

The girl grimaced, positioning her hands in front of her.

Edward took up a similar position, cane at the ready. He too had studied karate. The two circled, sizing each other up.

"Old man," taunted the girl.

"Dyke," nodded Edward.

"Sir Edward." Toad's jowls wobbled as he spoke. "Why could one not let things be?"

"A member of one's team was brutally slaughtered in a staged accident and one expects no consequences?"

"It was not my doing, this much I swear."

"Why then the bodyguard?"

Toad writhed in discomfort, beetles crawling under his flesh.

Two flustered chaps in dinner jackets emerged from the hotel accompanied by a second thug. Edward recognised one of them as the chap who'd introduced himself as Wolfgang's son, the other as the chap from the tube train earlier. Distracted, he lunged at the girl and missed.

She delivered a scissor-kick to the side of his head, spun, and administered a punch to his stomach. Edward dropped to one knee, ribs rising and falling rapidly.

Ah, he thought, the agility of youth.

The girl paused, awaiting instruction; Toad nodded.

Sir Edward closed his eyes tight and, clenching his fists, uttered a short prayer.

The two thugs each put a hand to an ear, screeching in pain as their communications earpieces emitted a frightful squeal. The girl clutched her ear likewise and moved her head forwards, then backwards. Taking a step, she swayed, lost her balance, and toppled over.

Sensing his luck had changed, the cross-dresser bit the thug on the arm and squirmed free, kicking the chap behind the knee.

"Ladies, I'm coming!" he yelled, running into the hotel, pursued by the two dinner-jacket chaps.

Considering his options, the ginger terror decided to accept the party invite and rushed towards the wide stone steps, bounding up them two at a time. By the front door, he ran into the chap who'd previously identified himself as Wolfgang's son.

"Follow me," said the chap.

Beaming widely, for once Edward did as he was told.

From his vantage point beside a pale-cream sofa bedecked with yellow cushions, Sir Edward scanned the coving, searching for hidden cameras. Content there were none, he produced an imaginary handheld scanner and, vocalising operational tones, checked each direction in turn while the young man whose suite they occupied paced nervously up and down.

"A moment." Edward headed over to a junction box by the TV and struck it with his cane.

The young man dabbed his brow. "Does one have the merchandise?"

Edward nodded.

"How do I know it's the real deal?"

"One must sample it," said Edward, producing a small cobalt phial from his waistcoat pocket.

A bead of sweat ran down the young man's face as he took the container and held it up to the light. Hands shaking, he pulled out the stopper and put the bottle to his lips.

"Stop!" The terror waved his hand. "One behaves like a gecko."

The young man wiped his forehead and, under instruction, handed back the phial.

"Strip!" commanded the terror.

For the third time since their arrival, the young man checked the doors and windows to ensure they were locked, drawing the curtains during his transit across the room. Content that the apartment was secure, he opened the door an inch and whispered to the thug on the other side, instructing him to prevent entry to all and sundry.

"You can't see me," came the reply from outside, "but that was a smile."

The young man removed his clothing, one item at a time, methodically hanging up each garment, stripping down to underwear, socks and suspenders. Edward cast his eye over the youth, noting the authentic tribal tattoos that adorned his shoulders and hip.

Not really his type.

He preferred them younger and tighter.

"One must be naked."

The terror licked his lips.

Back in the halcyon days of the seventies, whatever was taboo was a rule to be broken.

That was the creed by which he and his hedonistic compatriots lived.

Edward looked the naked young man up and down, noting the neatly manicured pubic region, the bare chest and hairless bottom, concluding that the usual dose would suffice. He removed the stopper from the phial once more. "Hold out one's hand."

The young man did as requested.

Deftly, Edward took the youth by the wrist and expelled the contents of the bottle onto the top of his outstretched hand. He stepped back, bowing theatrically.

The globule of liquid spread out, lapping around each finger. Out of curiosity, the youth rubbed the spot of cobalt with the index finger of his other hand. Where contact was made, a second spot formed, rapidly engulfing the finger. The original spot continued its advances, flowing up to the elbow.

Edward chuckled to himself.

This was the point when they panicked.

Any second now.

"How fascinating." The youth observed his refection in a full-length mirror. "Presumably, it will engulf my entire body."

"One's father named the process *Verpuppung*."

"It tickles." The boy moved to scratch himself, resisting at the last. "I understand now why they call it 'getting shelled'. The gecko becomes a turtle."

The liquid surged, an azure tide that flowed around the youth's shoulder on one side, his hand on the other. Edward closed his eyes and hummed a tune. By the time he reopened them, the youth's torso was enveloped, the major splodge joining up with the minor, running as a collection of iridescent tendrils flecked with points of gold. The youth's manhood was swallowed right up, his legs eagerly devoured, until only his neck and head remained untouched.

"My heart is racing." The young man held his chest.

Edward remained silent while the *Spezial Kobalt* completed its job. In a final mad-dash flurry, the boy's head turned lapis blue. The liquid rushed into each of his facial orifices, cascading around his ears, forcing its way into his mouth, colouring lips and tongue. Finally, his eyes flashed over.

He staggered in a mad pirouette, reaching out for a solid surface.

"How does one feel without one's sight?" Edward coughed. "Frenchman."

Those were the last words the imposter heard before his hearing ceased to work. Cut off from the world, cocooned in his own little bubble of Pharaonic blueness, he had only the shells of the astral for company. Very soon, his heart would slow to a virtual stop.

On cue, the youth collapsed to the floor, facial muscles tightening around the bottom of his cheeks.

"Once upon a time, one made mock of me at a graduation ceremony." Edward spat on the unmoving body. "Now, faux Ferret, one mocks you back. Think long and hard over the coming hours and days about one's devotion to Plutus."

The terror rummaged through the Frenchman's belongings, locating the empty cobalt phial which the youth had used as provenance. So typical of the uninitiated, he thought; prepared to go to any lengths for a dose of True Blue.

Before they'd perfected the technique, there had been many fatalities.

Rats.

Chimps.

Lewis.

Edward recalled, in vivid colour, the evening he and the impetuous Welshman sneaked back into camp. It was a Friday night, the longest day of the year, a full six months before they fully understood what they were dealing with. They'd tossed a coin; depending on one's perspective, he'd lost. With Lewis suspended naked on a moveable platform, an inch above the vat of liquid, the chain mechanism jammed. In a fit of petulance, the terror bashed a set of submerged wheels with a crowbar, splashing liquid all over his protective clothing. It was only later — when he eventually aligned his beliefs, discovered his spirit guide, and broke free of purgatory —that he realised that in his exuberance he'd ripped the bio-suit.

Under the influence, he'd been out there exploring the astral realms for what he imagined to be a fortnight, only to discover less than forty-eight hours had passed.

By then, it was too late for Lewis.

His friend Wolfgang filled the void. Locked away in secret, the scientist worked through Project XIII's classified research notes, retranslating them, pinpointing where they'd erred. Based on the monomolecular sheath theory devised by the Germans, he'd calculated an average safe dose.

Edward smiled to himself.

He'd shared the secret with half of Soho and yet, to this day, the team didn't know.

The string of eligible young men reached around the block. It was their eagerness that made them so pliable. Talked through the experience by a learned turtle, they came back altered. Once that rock-and-roll guitarist chap joined the party, bringing along a sprinkling of theatrical Victorian parlour magick, full swing was attained. Between them, they'd unleashed a beast that neither was able to control.

Hiding his habit had been easy to begin with. He'd simply borrowed a portion of the Army allocation and blamed the cavalry officer's sloppy handling techniques for the shortfall. The system worked just fine until the day Toad demanded a recount. Shortly thereafter, the recriminations began in earnest; and with the team at each other's throats, the amphibian rallied his superiors to shut down Project XIII.

They'd resigned before he got his way.

Walter's unwillingness to look the other way for his country still stung, even now.

The voice of the priest bubbled through his brain.

Albright was innocent.

Toad was the one.

This discovery stung like . . . Edward pictured a jar of urine in a tornado.

In all likelihood, the slimy one was responsible for the death of his friend the chemist, the world's only expert on SK-13.

Edward took a cigar from a box on the sideboard and, sparking his thumb, lit it, filling the room with the sweet smell of Cuban tobacco.

The girl was out there, somewhere.

Watching.

Opening the doors to the terrace, he stepped outside, allowing his feelings to drift, orientating himself with the picture in his mind's eye. Invisible against the skyline, she crouched low on a neighbouring balcony, encased in a glowing silver aura.

Escape by foot was out of the question.

Possibly he might be able to clamber between buildings, but she was faster. There was another way, provided by the universe. Not an impossible way, merely an unlikely way.

What it was, he didn't know.

This was what made wishing for gifts so ultimately rewarding.

The terror waved his arms above his head. "Yoo-hoo!"

Without warning, a series of high notes accompanied by a wave of silver light smashed through his body, bowling his senses over. He flopped into a chair and lay there transfixed, watching the cigar burn down.

By Jupiter, she had him with her outrageous promises. How was he supposed to resist the feel of supple leather, the restriction of buckles, and a parade of brown boys dressed in loincloths, worshipping him at the altar of truth?

Bang!

"I command you to open the door."

The terror lay there entranced, remembering his crimes.

"By Jupiter's hoary bastards, she will not take us!"

Snapping from the malaise, Edward clenched his fists tight, closed his eyes, and wished very, very hard.

A dark shape floated through the evening sky, carried on a gentle breeze. As it passed overhead, the ants in the street below pointed, watching as it blotted out everything above.

The banging on the door increased in velocity.

A fire extinguisher crashed through the wood, followed by an arm. Edward waited until the last possible second, then climbed aboard.

"Goodbye, Frenchman," he waved. "Edward will return, to talk one home. In the meantime, consider one's choice of god and ask whether he is able to perform miracles equal to mine."

# Chapter Thirty-One: Chasing Shadows

Ferret crouched low over the tank of a vintage Ducati he'd borrowed from the parking lot of the Over-Seas League and sped down the Mall towards Trafalgar Square, all the while keeping an eye on the sky.

The motorbike weaved in and out of traffic at speed, narrowly avoiding a collision with an oncoming cab, which was forced to swerve onto the pavement. Ferret opened up the throttle, speeding past Nelson's column, determined to catch up with the ginger troublemaker who'd sold him the tinfoil insert for his hat near to this very spot. Hunkering down, he switched gears. It made no sense that the hot air balloon he was following was moving faster than he was, but then hardly anything had made sense since the moment the banker had slipped over the side of the terrace.

Ferret ground his teeth.

Just when it looked like Tristan was contained, he'd escaped and locked himself in the restaurant's private dining area, professing his undying love to the girls, who had difficulty keeping a collective straight face. Try as he might to get in, Ferret was unable to open the door. In a panic, he'd turned to Cyrano, only to discover his friend was missing in action. A couple of security chaps had appeared, taken a good, hard look through the window, and chortling at the banker's attire, decided he wasn't going anywhere.

The consultant requested their assistance. Receiving nothing but a disparaging glare, he'd barged at the door with his shoulder, once, twice. Before it was off its hinges, a silver wash had swept through the hotel, hitting him like a tidal wave. In the private dining area, the girls stopped laughing at his friend. He listened intently to a solo female voice singing a siren song. Respectfully, the piano was quiet. All conversation had ceased.

At that moment he realised the dinner guests had been transformed from executives and partners into an army of mesmerised slaves, eyes as lifeless as lychee compote. Intuitively, he'd tried to discover what the nearest guest was feeling, only to find the chap's mind a blank. The door to the private area flew open; Tristan staggered past mumbling threats of retribution and headed up the stairs. From the bar and restaurant, the staff joined his friend, including the doorman who took on the menacing tones of an undertaker in his stiff black top hat. On impulse, Ferret palmed a steak knife, ready to behead diners should events take a turn towards the carnivorous. Then he'd played dumb, carried along by the zombie throng, who were all heading in the same direction. Towards his French friend's suite.

Ferret gunned the bike's engine, hurtling down the Strand and onto Fleet Street, jumping set after set of traffic lights in an adrenaline-fuelled fit of folly, trying to keep pace with the balloon. He heard the roar of burning gas, caught a glimpse of red and white. St. Paul's cathedral whizzed past; the buildings grew in height on each side. He wasn't sure, but he thought he saw a flash of flesh, accompanied by a scream. Still he pressed on. Level with the Monument, he looked up, realising he was chasing shadows.

He pulled up by the side of the road, scratching his head. Had the balloon veered off north or south? Either way, the centurion was a damn fool.

What had possessed him to leap from the edge of Cyrano's balcony, catching hold of one of the balloon's trailing ropes? In his exuberance, the banker had almost capsized the basket. Ferret recalled the heat on his face as the ginger troublemaker opened up the burners in a desperate attempt to dislodge his escape vehicle from an errant flagpole.

A better question to ask, thought Ferret, was how on earth had the winds carried a vacant inflatable across the rooftops of London, only for it to arrive on his French friend's terrace at precisely the right moment? Holmes's solution to such an intractable problem no doubt involved the application of advanced mathematics along with a Venn diagram of probable accomplices.

Ferret removed an ivory piano key from his pocket and felt the smooth surface.

It was as if the ginger chap had the ability to make objects appear at will.

He was in two minds as to whether the zombies were the ginger troublemaker's doing too. Possibly they were rushing to protect him, but from within the throng of diners, it had felt more like a pack of dogs on the hunt.

He recalled the pandemonium on the roof terrace. Once the balloon was free, its basket swinging wildly powered by a cussing half-naked ape pendulum, the ginger madman had shouted something very specific. Words for his ears only, projected not spoken, which reverberated around the inside of his skull like a metal ball racking up pinball points.

"One knew one's father."

Unlike his French friend, he'd never really taken the oaths he'd sworn that seriously, except for one: A legionnaire in distress is never alone. Having scribbled a note to inform the hotel concierge that Cyrano was passed out on the floor of his suite, he was honour-bound to locate the centurion. Ferret fired up the engine once more and took a right turn, heading for the river and open skies. With luck on his side, he'd not only find the banker but the ginger madman too.

# Chapter Thirty-Two: Old Billingsgate

Standing on the rusty lip of a decrepit river barge with the old fish market to his back, Ferret caught an unpleasant whiff of the harvest of the sea. It was twenty-five years since Old Billingsgate had closed its doors, yet the hum of halibut and herring, monkfish and mackerel, and whiting and whale still stunk up the present, the past projecting a salty stench far and wide across the barriers of time.

Nostrils flaring, the consultant prodded the carcass of a half-deflated hot air balloon with a boathook.

He felt the still-warm burner.

Shaking his head, he dropped down into the hull of the barge, pulse racing.

"Urrgh!"

A noise from underneath the deflated canopy caught his attention. Cautiously, he lifted the canvas, expecting to see Sir Edward. Instead, amongst upturned barrels of virgin olive oil, he found the scantily clad body of his banker friend huddled in a ball.

For better or worse, the centurion was alive.

"Stay there."

Holding his nose, the consultant made his way around the market back to the parked bike. He unrolled a canvas overcoat tied to the rear of the machine and returned, tossing it to his friend.

"I had such an awful dream." The centurion sniffed the air, rubbing his forehead. "One of those flying nightmares that ends with a plummet. Where am I?"

"By the river."

"It's coming back to me now. The girls?"

"Gone home, I imagine."

"You were on a mission." The centurion closed his eyes.

Ferret nodded. "It's a merger."

"Good. We like those a lot. What's the payoff?"

"There are a number of niche products yet to come to market."

Ferret wasn't proud of the way he'd wrestled the information from behind Marianne's lips; it was a dirty thing to do. Glibly, he explained the complication: Both companies were privately owned.

The centurion staggered to his feet and drew his arm back. "Assume the position."

The consultant lowered his head and waited. Just as he thought the centurion had changed his mind, along came the customary cuffing.

Smack!

"I can't place a twenty-million-dollar bet in the biggest gambling casino in the world on a private merger! Now go back and persuade your contact to go public. Consider this your final warning."

Ferret looked his friend in the eye, careful not to melt into him. Dressed in an open mac, the scarlet bra and briefs of the warrior princess on display, it was a little hard to take the centurion seriously.

"What do you say?"

The consultant broke eye contact, suppressing a snigger. "My apologies. It won't happen again."

"You're fined a trouser press." The banker rubbed his nose, slumping to his knees. "Now, I don't suppose you've any of those bath salts to hand? It's been a long night; I'm exhausted, and my nose is bloody famished."

Following a brief one-way discussion composed of non-negotiable orders, Ferret hailed a cab and bundled his superior officer into the rear, instructing the driver to take him home. He handed the driver a large note for his troubles and at the last, divided his personal stash in half, giving a portion to the banker.

"What will you do now, my optio?"

"I'm going to sit awhile by the river and compose myself. After that, I'll get right on it. The deal will be finalised and in the system before you wake."

"It's good to have you back in the family, legionnaire." The banker nodded. "If this is what you and the Frenchman get up to every Saturday night, you'll be seeing a lot more of me."

"We'll enjoy that, sir."

"Good. I don't know who the crazy balloon pilot was, but he certainly knew you." Tristan jabbed Ferret in the chest with his finger. "You're not to try and find him, is that clear?"

"Perfectly."

"If you renege this time, it will cost you more than a damn car." With which, the banker slammed shut the cab door and vanished into the night.

Ferret gathered a handful of stones and took a seat on the quayside, his eye catching a chunk of floating debris. Guiltily, he thought of his French friend passed out on the floor of his suite. Taking aim, he threw a pebble as hard as he was able, targeting the lump of wood.

Splosh!

Problem solved. Cyrano's mess was his own making. A night in the hospital with a stomach pump might just do him some good.

Beep!

Ferret withdrew his phone to read the message:

*How could you two-time me with granny? You're dumped. In this life and the next.*

He shook his head.

Just when he thought it couldn't get any worse.

Technically, because he was now no longer dating Juliet, the Marianne dilemma had been solved. He'd do the dirty, nail the deal, and sweet talk his ex around when she returned from New York. Just like the bad old days. He aimed once more at the target.

Splosh!

Perhaps not, he thought.

Only one stone left. What of the ginger chap? Assuming he wanted to be found, there were three obvious places to go: the Tower of London to the left, Tower Bridge in the middle, and *HMS Belfast* across the river.

His intuition told him to try the bridge. Narrowing his eyes, he took aim, loosing his best shot.

Thunk.

Nodding, he returned to the bike. From one of the panniers, he withdrew a fine felt hat, uncrumpled the crown, and adjusted it for fit. Pulling up a pair of goggles from around his neck, he climbed onto the motorcycle and revved the engine, revelling in the throb of hot metal between his legs.

His mind was set.

"Stay your ground, friend," he said. "I'm coming!"

As far as any potential fine was concerned, there was a third way.

Hopefully, it wouldn't come to that.

# Chapter Thirty-Three: Agent TJ

Rising high above the Thames on twin piers pumped rigid with concrete, clad in Cornish granite, the painted steel and stone bridge cut an impassive silhouette against the cold night sky. Warm exterior lights bounced off tiers of Portland stone, playing tricks on the eyes, creating frightening, deformed creatures concealed in crevices of shadow, ready to prey on the unwary, ripping flesh from limb, stripping bone bare.

Ferret tipped his hat in the direction of the pale-blue-and-white marvel, sure in his mind that this was the ginger chap's intended destination. He parked the Ducati tight against a wall away from the road and skirted around the tower, hurrying along the wharf past Traitor's Gate and Wakefield Tower.

This was a place he'd done his best to avoid, ever since his mother was shipped home to France. Too many painful memories, he reminded himself. In the olden days, a diagnosis of melancholia was likely. In the modern era, a string of psychologists had each argued the case for their favoured mental disorder, their only common ground being plenty of rest. That was nearly twenty years ago. He wondered whether she'd been at his father's funeral, unsure whether he'd even recognise her after so long.

The detecting consultant skipped through Dead Man's Hole, where plump, bloated bodies were once fished from the Thames, and bounded up a flight of well-worn steps, checking his timepiece. Four o'clock. It truly was an ungodly hour of the morning, traditionally reserved for men of the post and men of the milk.

And the slaying of zombies.

Ferret exhaled loudly; what came out was more of a whinny than a snort.

A pair of youths danced past, dressed in matching sky-blue hooded tops, braided with fluorescent banding.

"Dave, Dave! I'm givin' it some in the middla Londy Bridge!"

"Awright babe, nice one. We betta getta vid. Easy, give it large, your most mungus moves. Sweet . . .as squizza shit . . ."

Ferret shook his head in disdain.

The day his banking friend had predicted was finally dawning. With sunup, he would no longer understand his own language.

Ignoring the four-legged party machine, the detective leant against the pale-blue lattice railing, facing the seductively lit Lord Mayor's Pineapple, gazing longingly into the murky bosom of the Thames-Isis. He imagined how sweet it must have smelt two thousand years ago, when compatriots from a different, more brutal legion first set foot upon the marshlands surrounding old Londinium. According to Tristan, it was from the old Roman code of conduct that the current Network rules were derived, even though such rules received scant mention in any official history book. Then as now, a legionnaire surrenders his old family the moment he swears the Oath of Eternal Allegiance to Rome.

Was it even possible to leave? The detective winced. If push came to shove, it was worthy of consideration. The forfeiture of his most coveted possessions to the legion was one heck of a price to pay for a detecting adventure involving a family that gave up on him long before he reluctantly did the same.

Ferret's legs ached and his ribs throbbed, dragging him down and dampening the day. What he really needed was to let off some steam. He reached into his pocket and withdrew a portable snifter, thrusting it up his nose.

*I see one found the motorbike.*

Ferret looked around, bemused.

*As a citizen of Rome, one should know that The Brotherhood of Light and Reason built this bridge, along with many of London's other fine monuments. That was before we did something indescribably rash and fell out with the Masons.*

The detective looked right, then left. "Where are you, friend?"

*Before one reveals oneself, one must first dispose of the spook.*

Ferret felt the powder kick him up the bum, casting a glorious golden shadow across all his aches and pains. Mouth and brain disconnected from his spinal column; greedily, Ferret took another jolt, feeling the *lorica segmentata* of cocaine armour slot positively into place. Leerily, he set a brisk pace towards a giant of a man dressed in a long tan raincoat, who leant solidly against the stonework, white stick propped by his side. Nonchalantly, he scanned yesterday's newspaper.

"Dave, Dave! Your go, Starbabe. Wear my bra for the hits . . ."

Ferret strode confidently up to the huge spook, who stood a good forty centimetres taller than he, and defiantly snatched the giant's shades. The big man moved his head to the side, his cloudy right pupil glistening in the half light.

"You assault the partially sighted?"

Ferret felt the fires of provocation burn inside of him. He grabbed the agent's stick and vigorously prodded him with it. "To what end do you follow my friend?"

"Stealing my tools will not improve your life, but it will degrade mine. Return both, please."

Ferret shimmied around, wielding the stick like a fencing foil. He opened the giant's tent of a coat with the end of the stick, revealing a black wool and mohair pullover, complemented with dark-green corduroy trousers. The big man's shoe-canoes, a pair of black brogues, were polished to perfection.

"I was under the impression that spooks are supposed to blend into the crowd."

The giant carefully folded his paper. "Why do you attack me?"

"Tell me who you work for and I'll stop."

Ferret saw silver foam lapping at his feet, soaking his ankles. He snapped to attention, searching for signs of the zombie army.

The big man raised an eyebrow.

Ferret threw the cane to the floor, grabbed the agent by the lapels and pulled his face close. "Their name."

"Mate!" came a cry from some ten metres away, "there's a geyser 'ere in a porky, slappin' a stumbler."

"Gettin' it all on vid."

Ferret glanced over his shoulder. The two youths had multiplied into a dozen washed out human wrecks, a mixed bunch of giggling girls and lanky lads, moving in lockstep to an imaginary tune.

"Fight!" The demand was issued in unison.

"We need to get out of here," hissed the giant, as a second wave of silver splashed across the pavement.

The detective shook his head. He was sick of all the shilly-shallying.

"Fight! Fight!"

Now! Screamed Ferret's fists. Throw the first punch!

A look of horror crossed the agent's face.

Ferret hesitated.

Intuitively, he ducked, rolling to one side, narrowly avoiding one of the hoodies who came flying through the air, his kick aimed squarely at the space where the detective wasn't. The clubber struck the big man in the midriff, a matchstick bouncing off the trunk of a gnarly old oak tree. Deftly, the giant grabbed the assailant's ankle, twisting and lifting.

"Twatpussy!" exclaimed the hoodie, shoulder striking the ground. "My leg man, it's busted. You is so sued!"

"Mikey!" yelled one of the female protagonists, her voice splintered with anger. "You poor fing. Do 'em lads!"

Ferret jumped to his feet, facing the agent. A knowing look passed between the pair.

"My glasses."

Ferret handed the shades back to their owner.

Four of the lads circled, two against each of the allies searching for an opening, while the girls dragged Mikey away. The minx with the camera instructed her minions to scour the area for bottles, cans, and stones to create hail from hell, all the while commentating on events.

The detective and the giant took up position, back to back.

One of the hoodies threw a punch; Ferret dodged to one side.

Slap!

"Happy slappy!"

Brring!

Momentarily, Ferret was distracted by his phone.

Slap!

"Reverse sucka slap!"

Ferret lunged wildly, blood boiling.

"Keep your cool," said the giant, his voice a whisper.

With great difficulty Ferret obliged, feeling his anger shift into his fists. He flexed his shoulders, ready to spar.

Two of the lads leapt onto the big man, determined to take him down. A third youth took a run-up and launched himself at the agent, who stiffened his frame, rooting his feet to the spot; the harsh sound of tearing fabric filled Ferret's ears. He heard the thud of fists smacking into flailing cloth. A deluge of obscenities crowded the air; the detective glanced backwards to see one of the attackers lifted clear off the ground. Limbs flailing, the agent pitched him into the group of girls who were baying for blood.

Brring!

Distracted, Ferret took another slap to the side of the head, followed by a numbing knee to the bum.

Another two lads moved in, exchanging a volley of half-punches and slaps with the detective, leaving his face feeling swollen yet numb. He relaxed. When the next punch came, he anticipated the predictable slap-through, grabbing and twisting, bringing the lad's arm behind him. Whooping, he lifted, eliciting a howl of pain. The screaming boy was bundled hard to the ground. Ferret stepped on the small of his back, pulling the arm sideways until he heard the shoulder joint click. Only then did he let go, spinning on his heels, fists at the ready.

The big man lunged at one of his assailants, pulled him off his feet and threw him aside like a human ragdoll, knocking another attacker off balance. The remaining hoodies backed off. One snatched the white stick from the ground.

"Stay away, man!" he shouted, waving the cane wildly. "I'll stab yer eyes out an eat yer heart. Don't fink I won't."

"Boo!" the agent leapt forward, causing the startled lad to drop the stick and break into a run. One by one the broken gang picked themselves up and skulked off, shouting sullen insults as they left.

"We is coming back."

"Tooled up."

"Wiv massive fuckin' planks."

Brring!

"Excuse me," laughed Ferret, "I really must take this call."

"Ferret," said a voice on the end of the line. "I had a bad premonition. You must stay away from Edward."

"Marcus, who's Edward?" The detective felt the silver wash cascade through him once more, tickling his synapses. He shook the phone, examining the display. No signal.

*If one wishes to survive, one must move towards the middle of the bridge.*

The words tumbled around inside Ferret's head. He walked quickly, as instructed, beckoning the giant to follow. A lone skater shot past, head down.

Ferret chewed his bottom lip. "It's about time we introduced ourselves."

"Agent TJ at your service," smiled the giant, sticking out a huge hand. "Your friend Marcus ordered me to ensure you come to no harm."

"Tell him I'm forever in his debt," said Ferret, shaking hands.

Out of the corner of his eye the detective caught sight of a pair of cyclists, peddling as fast as they were able. The slower of the two glanced behind, increasing his effort.

Agent TJ nudged Ferret, pointing his stick towards the bridge's north gate, where a group of youths were assembling, swarming from all directions, arms laden with makeshift weaponry. The detective spotted chair legs, several estate agents' signs, metal railings, and bicycle chains. From the south gate, a terrible clamour arose. Metal objects clanged against each other, making passionate, unabating love, the racket growing louder with each passing second. The echo of implements of destruction baying to be put to use was backfilled with murderous chanting. Indecipherable screams oscillated back and forth, taking the form of words in a menacing tone:

"Death to Edward!"

Ferret shook his head.

They were in this one balls-deep. No backing out now.

A lithe figure tumbled gymnastically across the road, some fifty metres to the south. The girl stopped by the inner edge of the tower, took out a grappling hook and, swinging it about her, released the device into the air towards a balcony set midway up the tower. She tugged on the rope, once, twice; confident in her purchase, she climbed.

*Have you worked out one's decuria?*

"Now is hardly the time," mumbled the detective, replying to the voice in his head.

*By great Jupiter's flaming balls, now certainly is the time! One's decuria is the very reason you're here at this juncture and not tucked up in bed.*

"Death to Edward!"

The two gangs marched forward to the edges of the bridge's dual arches, closing the gates to traffic behind them. Ferret estimated there were a hundred per side, including the hoodies who had attacked earlier.

He felt his heart thump wildly.

Above, the girl reached the end of the rope and hauled herself onto a balcony. Stone by stone she climbed, forever upwards, aiming for the bridge's high-level walkways.

*Yoo-hoo!*

Ferret spotted the balloon pilot, waving from the top of the eastern walkway. He tried really hard to ignore the baritone grunts and throb of weaponry. Truth be told, he felt ever more fearful of the consequences of doing nothing. He could deal with a room full of angry PowerPoint addicts demanding video and sound, but this was way outside his bailiwick.

"There are too many," he said, turning to Agent TJ. "I can see only one way out."

"Very well." The agent folded his stick, then his glasses. "I must warn you I am not agile in water."

A shiver ran down the detective's spine. "It's not exactly my preferred environment for doing business."

The beating of clubbed weapons against makeshift shields stopped. The two gangs let out a single, combined roar and charged.

Ferret and Agent TJ ran for it. They crashed against the first road barrier, bundling over in one then sprinted across Tarmac and over a second barrier, reaching the guard rail in double-quick time. Ferret looked down, tottering, suddenly aware of the distance to the water. He froze.

Surely they wouldn't really kill him? he thought. A medium beating, perhaps, for the beating they'd given the youths.

Whites of eyes came into sharp focus, and as they did, the detective's intuition screamed a message, loud and clear: These people are not playing games!

In a blur, Ferret was on top of the rail, helping the agent. He bundled the spook over the side, looked backwards, hesitated, closed his eyes, and leapt.

Grasping hands purloined him by the dinner jacket, arresting his fall. He felt a horrible, heart-wrenching tear beneath the armpits as his arms folded backwards. Despite the stress, his clothing held, suspending him above the Thames.

Ferret wriggled, kicking his legs, but the grip on his arms was firm. In desperation, he flexed his hips from side to side, contorting his shoulders, swaying and kicking.

Rip!

Seams surrendered to gravity.

Tear!

He fell.

Fingers crossed, he prayed really hard.

Deep water had never been his thing.

Not that he cared to admit it.

In swimwear, he stood a chance.

Fully clothed, he'd sink like a stone, choking all the way to the bottom of the Thames. His pulse quickened. Already, he imagined the piss of Isis filling his lungs, stifling his screams, ready to send him to Traitor's Gate.

Close-up and personal, thought Damien, the silver tide was more like an argent tsunami. When it first struck, it turned him over and over, inside to outside, until he no longer knew left from up or right from down. He stared at the morning sky, lit brightly along the Eastern edge illuminating Canary Wharf and squinted, shielding his eyes. The sun ducked under a bank of dark, ill-tempered clouds, sending it vermillion with crazed anger painting the Thames with blood.

Ahead of him, Junior Eric beat a section of metal downpipe with a slat torn from a pub bench, yelling for retribution at the top of his voice. The youngster had certainly gone to town since his decision to express his darker side; the wispy blonde goatee was never going to intimidate Doctor Doom, but it certainly gave him an air of purpose.

"Death to Edward!"

The senior junior didn't have a downpipe of his own and Eric was far too quarrelsome to share, so he made do with a metal post torn from the lawns of the Tower of London, topped with a sign that proclaimed "Dogs Must NOT Poop Here," which he banged hard against tarmacadam.

The silver wash carried with it instructions delivered in a clear, Shakespearean voice. He was determined to carry out the orders with passion. If he deviated, he might not hear the girl sing again, and that voice — such clarity; such sweetness! Not even in heaven, where the angels eat the manna of the Lord, is such perfect pitch to be found.

Eric called him obsessed.

Perhaps the junior was right.

Ever since the night the Precious was stolen, he hadn't been able to get the girl out of his head. Not that Eric fared any better. Looking at him now, screaming for resolution, he'd bought deeply into the tide too.

"Death to Edward!"

Damien smiled wryly. Not knowing who Edward was made it that much easier.

The mob surged forward; gates clanged. A slim figure clad in tight leather appeared, athletically flip-flopping through the crowd. A roar passed from one end of the bridge to the other. She climbed high above the road and took a bow, basking in the applause.

"Come, my friends."

Notes sparkled, suggesting an order.

Charge!

He didn't recognise the giant, but he knew the dress code, down to the very English shoes. The accursed trouser ferret certainly had a strange array of companions. Eric was desperate to beat the pair senseless, the frustration on his face was palpable, but he was squeezed tightly amongst a bunch of hoodies, arms pinned down.

The giant jumped.

Thump!

Ferret struggled.

Thump!

All that was left were two arms of a dinner jacket, quickly torn to pieces by the lusty mob. A figure dressed in tweed leapt from the bridge's high-level walkway, arms outstretched; it whooshed past, headed for the water.

Thump!

The pack squeezed forward. Damien craned his neck from three rows back, banging the sign up and down, whooping and stomping. Beneath his feet, he heard the horrible screech of metal tearing against concrete, saw bundles of red and white cloth come slowly into view. Caught in the momentum of the tide, a rusty barge pulled away from the bridge, bearing a strange, half-inflated cargo.

He glimpsed a large letter "W."

Withdrawing a packet of golds from his pocket, he turned it upside down. A sponsored balloon. That made sense, in a broken sort of a way.

He chortled to himself. "Who says smoking is bad for you?"

A push from behind.

The clubbers they'd seen sitting around the tower earlier heaved a collection of missiles, saturating the space between the bridge and the boat with bricks, bottles, and stones.

Splosh!

Not a chance.


Damien felt a rope strike his shoulder. The crowd parted. He looked up to see the girl who'd stolen his heart abseiling down from above. He took a deep breath and tried to introduce himself. The words lodged in his throat, translating into a mousey squeak.

The girl nodded, pale-brown eyes aglow. She handed him a catapult and a bag of steel balls. He so wanted to run his fingers through her deep-brown hair, tied at the back in a tight ponytail; to touch her fat lips with his; to kiss the little pock mark on her temple and to sponge her light-mocha skin with milk under a full moon.

Junior Eric barged past, elbowing his daydreams in the nuts, desperately snatching for one of the distance weapons along with a bag of ammunition. He caught sight of a katana strapped to Eric's back.

What on earth?

He'd promised to leave it in the car.

Seeing the blade, the girl narrowed her eyes, nodded, and handed out a double ration.

Eric started the bombardment.

Click the steel ball to activate; load, aim, and fire.

Boom!

Following the junior's lead, a dozen of the mob took aim, peppering the barge, trying to hit the trio of figures. All around, spray flew in plumes. Those who knew what they were doing soon found their distance. Shot after shot hit the target, blowing pieces of shrapnel all over.

Boom!

After each direct hit, a cheer erupted from the bridge, encouraging the marksmen. It looked mightily impressive, but Damien doubted they were causing any real damage. They certainly weren't going to sink the boat, which was the ultimate objective. The girl picked out the top three marksmen, and from a rucksack she handed each of them a bright-red string bag of ammunition.

Unlike Eric, Damien simply wasn't accurate enough.

The junior's first shot hit the canvas of the balloon, which was flapping gently in the wind. An expansive ball of flame erupted, vomiting fiery liquid in every direction. More shots followed, finding their mark, igniting everything in view. Within seconds, the entire barge was a funeral pyre.

What, thought Damien, had this Edward done?


From their hiding place in the top-floor kitchen, he and Eric had seen and heard everything the night the Precious was stolen. Cliff-face and Malcontent, unable to live without their fix, had employed the skills of Slickhands de Souza, a well-known amateur cracksmith from the Row, in what they termed "Operation Click Click." In violation of Old Boy protocol, they'd succeeded in liberating the Precious, only to have it taken from them. The girl had held it for perhaps five seconds before a man in black emptied a magazine in her direction. In the ensuing fight, she beat up two of the spooks and gave Cliff-face and his sidekick a professional hiding when they tried to run away.

That was the moment when Damien knew he was in love.

Eric was much more coy.

Later that day, the senior junior caught his pal drawing pictures of the girl. His illustrations were remarkably accurate, if perhaps a little breasty. Miss Harrington's intern had reacted with a mixture of embarrassment and horror, calling him a disgusting little pervert.

The security services dropped by later in the day and questioned them both extensively, taking away the illustrations and ordering them not to tell anyone what they'd seen, for the good of their country.

Grrr! throbbed with rumour regarding the break-in. The spook squad's retainers had worked tirelessly throughout the night, making proper any damage. For insurance purposes, the police were called. Fortunately, the only thing stolen was a film prop. Eric stuck his hand up. He knew who the culprit was; he'd seen him eyeing up the smalls a few days beforehand.

Later, a different set of spooks dropped by to ask yet more questions. By now, Manleigh and Harts, under instruction from the chap in the frock coat were frantically trying to downplay the whole dang mess. The cracksmith, who'd taken a nasty blow to the head during the brouhaha, claimed he was an innocent bystander, taking measurements for a new pair of suits. With a nod and a wink, the spook squad sent him on his way.

It was Miss Harrington who Damien felt sorry for. Her newfound authority was being deliberately undermined. Using an unassigned mobile phone from the company store, he'd dropped a massive hint and warned her to tell her boyfriend that trouble was coming.

That evening, tired and strung out, he'd discussed the girl at length with Eric, fantasising about her mission. He was firmly of the opinion that she was a cat burglar working for a rival games company, out to steal the Precious, only to be thwarted by the spooks for reasons as yet unknown. They had the Precious, and it was only a matter of time before it was returned.

Junior Eric remained unconvinced.

"She's working for Frocky," he said. "You saw her posture, how she held herself. She's one of ours, a filly. And what's more, I heard her take the Precious from Cliff-face."

They argued until exhaustion set in, seeking revival in a pair of triple espressos and a joint of finest caramello. After that, the only thing they were able to agree on was their mutual desire to see the girl again, preferably as soon as possible.

The question was how?


Carried by the current, the blazing boat drifted out of range. Shots were falling metres short now. Damien saw a lone figure running from side to side, extinguishing flames with buckets of water. With the balloon incinerated, it was unlikely they were going to pull off another miraculous airborne escape. Perhaps a submersible was in order.

The chap next to Damien shook his head, dropped a chair leg, and wandered off.

Others followed, leaving a core group of around thirty.

The girl put down the field binoculars she was using to track the boat, removed her backpack, knelt on one knee, and opened it. What Damien saw emerge caused the colour to drain from his face.

"That's an M72," he stammered.

"Nice," said Eric, pocketing the catapult and a handful of leftover ball bearings.

Until now, Damien had always assumed that the things he learned playing computer games were irrelevant in the real world.

Clear the rear. Extend the tube to cock the weapon. Align the sights. Safety catch off. He'd done this so many times with a joystick, he knew the routine with his eyes closed. Apparently, the girl did too.

Cursing his knowledge of confrontational hardware, the account executive dived to one side, insisting Eric follow. The junior was having none of it.

"Miss the biggest explosion I'm ever likely to see?" he said, withdrawing the sword from its sheath and waving it in the air. "You're bonkers."

Damien covered his ears and waited nervously.

He heard a contained explosion that sounded like an engine being revved. Turning his head to the side, the sharp whiff of ordinance in his nostrils, he counted to five.

**BOOM!**

Eric stood rooted to the spot, mouth wide open.

A second later, the shockwave hit, warming their faces.

"Wow."

The mob, dispersed the length of the bridge, turned to see what was happening.

"Death to Edward!"

Calmly, the girl packed away what remained of the rocket launcher, slung the rucksack over her shoulder, and walked away, heading towards the tower.

Damien and Eric followed at a safe distance, one eye each on the Thames.

Mangled metal and shards of wood continued to fall on the water long after the remains of the barge had sunk beneath the waves. Traces of red-and-white fabric littered the surface, along with a slick of shiny oil.

"I told you she was dangerous," Eric whispered, careful not to draw attention.

Damien looked up and pointed. "A flying . . ."

No.

It was just a hat.

"I feel really horny," said Eric. "Where can we get girls and a drink?"

"I know a club in St. Katharine."

"Let's go."

Damien tried really hard to intellectualise what he'd just been through. Apart from his feelings for the girl, which he knew to be real, none of it made the slightest bit of sense. He reached inside his breast pocket for a joint.

No, Eric was right.

The occasion demanded a stiff drink.

How else was he going to summon the courage to tell Miss Harrington that her boyfriend was toasted fish food?

Not that he and Eric saw anything.

Their presence here raised too many awkward questions.

The two juniors slowed their pace until they were a good fifty metres behind the girl.

Damien chided himself.

He hadn't intended to become a stalker.

Yet here he was, and it was all thanks to Eric's hunch.

The junior had argued that the trouble with the Precious began the day the moviemaker detectant arrived at Grrr! Follow him and eventually he'll lead us straight to her. Using Ferret's website registration details, they'd worked out where he lived. After that, it was a simple case of wait and follow until things got out of hand at the restaurant. They'd watched the girl take delivery of a motorbike and a change of clothes. When the balloon arrived, Ferret had filched an old Ducati and given chase with the girl in hot pursuit. They, in turn, followed her in Eric's car, which he'd collected from Soho Square and parked around the corner from Park Place.

"Hold this." Eric handed him the sword.

Damien protested, but not quickly enough.

The junior opened his shirt, showing off a hollow Perspex cylinder, approximately six centimetres in length, attached to a cord around his neck.

"It looks like a bullet cartridge," said Damien, scratching his head. "Where did you get it?"

"I found two of them on the pavement the other night."

"Nice." Damien pointed at the smoking debris with the sword, marvelling at how comfortable it felt in his palm. "Edward, the trouser ferret, and a giant of an Old Boy, all dead. How will they explain that away?"

"You think too much." The junior shook his head. "Where's this club?"

"Down there." Damien indicated towards the next set of steps on the right.

"Did you get a look at the big man?" Eric paused, a twinkle in his eye. "I'm certain I recognise him from my brother's old rugby mags. It was before our time, but you know the story: Rising Blackheath star injured in car crash."

"Holy crap!" squawked Damien.

Eric smiled. "Karma sure is a bitch."

# Chapter Thirty-Five: Cease and Desist

Morning dew hung like bejewelled limpets on slender stalks of grass, sparkling in the glow of a new sun, caressing the river bank with rainbow cascades. Marcus stood in contemplation, dressed in a silk gown and leather slippers, drawing hard on a menthol cigarette, his finger wrapped tightly around the filter.

He felt shambolic.

Unwashed.

His degradation completed by the oldest of his filthy habits.

Behind him, a ramshackle old mill house sagged on its haunches, decaying brickwork scarified by absent mortar. The water wheel, once an integral part of the building, was long gone, leaving only nubs of timber protruding from a rectangular splash pool. An inert mallard pulled its beak from under an oily wing and gave him the eye of duck.

Quack!

The intelligence man rubbed his eyes, red and puffy from lack of sleep.

He dropped the cigarette butt onto damp gravel, extinguishing it with his heel.

Back to work.


The portable security service's newsfeed, hastily thrown together in the lounge, had been active all night spewing out spontaneous snippets of data from across the capital. In the last few minutes another handful of random alerts had appeared.

How, thought Marcus, do we order this jumble to form a coherent story?

Rajesh stumbled through from the kitchen, tripping over a harsh stone step. Displaying the adroitness of a juggler, he rescued the tray he was carrying from certain disaster. A pair of cups tinkled against saucers, hot buttered toast shifted position; a full cafetiere sploshed coffee from side to side, depositing granules against the contoured lip. The junior bustled frantically, bronze dressing gown cord swinging like a pendulum as he created a space amongst the nest of electronics that occupied a large oak table pushed up against a wall.

He deposited the quivering payload, brushed a thick mop of black hair away from his face, and smiled. "Breakfast is served."

Marcus looked up, keeping an eye on the newsfeed. "There are reports coming in of a significant explosion near St. Katharine docks."

Rajesh took a bite of toast. "Whatever it was, it'll be reported as a batch of improperly stored chemicals."

"You learn quickly." Marcus stood and kissed the junior on the cheek, feeling stubble brush against his lips.

Raj blushed. "I was taught by the best."

The intelligence man pressed the plunger on the coffee jug and poured two cups, his own last. He allowed the brew to cool slightly, revelling in the warm aroma of roasted nuts while he nibbled on a corner of toast. His laptop beeped away, merrily pulling data from a secure satellite link.

Rajesh took up position at a workstation opposite.

Beneath the table, a pale golden glow cut through the darkness in a narrow horizontal band, hugging the carpet, pulsing at regular ten-second intervals. The black cloth under which the light originated was there to hide the Faraday cage in which the contents were trapped.

"We know more or less what it can't do." Marcus yawned. "Sooner or later we're going to have to find out what it *can* do."

"And risk discovery?" Rajesh tutted. "We only just escaped from the last safe house."

Marcus took a swig of coffee. The only way to investigate the golden croissant properly, he mused, was via the use of a government lab. Such luxury, however, was currently denied them thanks to a tactical error on his part the previous afternoon. They'd had the device cornered in an isolation tank with its outer shell removed and the nodule of golden jelly at the core exposed, proprietary hardware in place to analyse its use of communications protocols when, without warning, it initiated a link to a mobile phone.

Stunned by the croissant's pugnacity, he'd wavered for a few vital seconds, allowing the pesky device to steal a set of private photographs, leaving no doubt as to its fabled capabilities.

Rajesh had moved first, sealing the naughty croissant in a lead-lined box, circuits hanging loose, and ticked it off with a wagging finger. When the junior had threatened to spank the errant device, Marcus lost himself in the innuendo, turning pink with embarrassment at the thought of a firm bat to the buttocks. Fortunately, he'd had the *nous* to follow standard procedures for a security breach, pulling the batteries from both their phones and vacating the premises. They were turning out of Marylebone Mews at the same time that the girl, clad in tight-fitting black leather, pitched up on a motorcycle.

Marcus berated himself.

He felt bad slinking away from the fight, but what other option did they have?

Marcus added marmalade to a round of toast, re-reading the email he'd received from Tom Tom the night before, sent shortly after Hades opened its gates in St. James. While the entire picture was not yet clear, one thing stood out from the chaos: His friend with the hat had been set up. The selection process regarding who to send on the detective mission to Grrr! was far from random: Tim Tim had specifically asked for "the one with the hooter." The rest was simply a case of steering Ferret in the right direction, from behind the scenes, until the appropriate opportunity arose.

The data fragment he'd retrieved from the Phreek confirmed his suspicions. There was something in Wolfgang's work that was of specific interest to the owners of the croissant, and sheer thickening — or, as his friend in the hat had put it — the "weaponisation of custard" was a key ingredient.

Marcus found himself thinking back to first principles.

Who exactly *was* Ferret's father?

What *had* he been up to?

A delve through the security service's data banks confirmed Wolfgang's records were purged from all government systems on the day he retired. Data backups were deleted, paper copies of his activities redacted. Beyond the fact that he was a weapons inspector, there were no clues as to what he'd been working on for the last forty years or, indeed, who he'd been working for.

All traces erased.

Marcus put his hand into his pocket and turned a lucky charm over and over, hoping his friend with the hat was well, but secretly fearing for his life. According to their large man in the field, who was tasked with apprehending the ginger terror, Ferret had set off in pursuit of the hot-air balloon that Edward was piloting. He'd dialled his friend dozens of times in a twenty-minute period, trying to warn him to be careful, only to be shunted to voicemail.

When he finally got through, the call was cut.

He huffed.

So this was what it felt like to be on the receiving end.

"Be a good Orchis and have another look at this." Marcus tossed the rubberised rectangle to his protégé.

"Shall I cut it open?"

"Please, no. It has sentimental value."

On screen, Marcus flipped to his security services email inbox and to an urgent message received late last night from the secretary of defence that he had not yet dared open.

Dear Mr. Harwood

His heart fluttered, a gigantic moth battering at a paper lantern. He placed his feelings in a box and tied it tightly with pink ribbon, determined to give nothing away to the junior. Check the CC list: other department heads, a handful of disinterested ministers, and a member of the upper house to show they meant it.

With a lump in his throat, Marcus began reading.

Blah, blah.

No evidence.

Blah.

Implied demotion.

Blah.

Furthermore, we have received in writing an official apology from RockSlut Hardware for the accidental release of an untested copy of beta code into the field.

Blah.

In order to conclude this matter to the department's satisfaction, it is to be returned forthwith.

Blah.

There it was: coded language for cease and desist.

Marcus felt his throat go dry.

He took another sip of coffee and swallowed noisily.

Whilst the message appeared to lack menace, it was really a veiled threat, looming large like a disfigured spectre in an opera house of fears.

Not only was the enemy good, he thought, they were connected. All the way to the top. The whiff was pure Carlsgrove.

The incoming newsfeed flashed red.

"That incident on the river: It was a barge going *boooof*," said Raj, ever alert. "Eyewitnesses report there were people on board. All are missing, believed dead."

"What does the surveillance footage show?"

"That's strange." Raj shuffled his feet. "The data has been reclassified."

Marcus jumped from the chair. "We're being cut out."

"Oh . . . my." The junior inhaled deeply.

"What is it, my Orchis?"

"I have the tracking information for our friend in the hat's phone. Last confirmed location . . . middle of the river, east of Tower Bridge."

Marcus dropped his coffee cup, spilling thick brown liquid all over his slippers and splashing the front of his dressing gown. Sympathetically, the junior steered him towards a dark-maroon leather sofa, sitting him down and fussing over the stain with a sponge.

"I'll pour another coffee."

"Add brandy." The words came as a croak.

Marcus felt queer.

Beyond lightheaded.

The room spun around his very soul.

From his seat, he slumped forward, clenched his buttocks and hugged his knees, hanging on to himself for dear life. His fingernails dug into soft flesh, drawing blood in eight crescent moons. He closed his eyes tight, tears welling at the edges.

"Please, great Jupiter, not Ferret."

The premonition didn't have to come true.

It wasn't fixed in stone.

The intelligence man stuffed his box of feelings down deeper inside, imagining them buried under a mountain of Earth. He dare not listen to his heart right now. He had to follow his superiors' orders, hand the precious back to Carlsgrove. Forget about his friend.

The alternative was a ruined career at best.

Concrete flippers at worst.

Such was the price of servitude to the realm.

# Chapter Thirty-Six: Engaged

"Hey, Miss Harrington," purred a mellow voice from the other side of the bathroom door, "you English roses sure know how to keep a guy waiting."

Juliet checked her crimson negligee in the mirror, smoothing out an annoying crease. She messed her hair up and practised the sultry stare one more time. Then she took her phone from the accessories cabinet and pressed the speed-dial key assigned to Ferret.

Engaged.

She stamped her tiny feet up and down.

Nolan was a smarty-pants jerk. All he wanted to talk about was how much he was earning and where he liked to eat. They must go to the Hamptons for the weekend. Take his boat out. What kind of a slut-cessory did he take her for? Didn't he know a weekend away was date number four? She made her excuses and left him standing there, alone. For about five seconds. He produced a platinum credit card and waved it in the air. Before she'd even reached the door, he was surrounded by professional dating girls who savaged him like piranhas on a ham shank.

So much for her grand exit.

She called Grant.

He'd spent time in England, a year out at Oxford.

He knew the ropes.

He was also a charmer with dancing blue-grey eyes, a clever tongue, and a suit cut by Brioni. What a contrast to her moviemaker, who didn't have a clue about cloth. She'd slept with him on their first date too, but that was different. They'd sparked. Being with him made her feel like a magical princess. She inhaled a deep breath. He looked a shambles in that dreadful dinner suit, but that's what one gets when one dates a geek.

Except he was busy two-timing her with a dinosaur from *Jurassic Park*. And he was wearing an Armani two-piece.

So said her friends.

Prat!

Possibly there was a good explanation, except Thursday and Friday are the nights when one acquires a date for Saturday evening — the night when the dirty deed is done.

He must have dumped a pong when her friends walked in with the Frenchman.

Now *he* was a darling.

She pressed the speed-dial key assigned to "C."

No answer.

"Miss Harrington?"

"Coming."

Technically, she was no longer dating the moviemaker, which meant she couldn't be two-timing him. He, however, had a lot of explaining to do. Detecting consultant for hire. An Old Boy would never consider such a profession. What if Clifford and Malory were right about him not even being a Half-Boy?

Then there was the older woman.

She redialled one more time.

Engaged.

Juliet removed her pearl bracelet and ran it through slender fingers, feeling each of the coveted spheres in turn. She had to get a hold of herself. Stop being so silly.

BBC World News said there was a chemical explosion on the Thames. The chances of him being involved were so slight.

Miniscule.

Not worth bothering about.

She closed her eyes and thought about how intimate it had felt when he'd gazed into her eyes. She gasped for air.

He had no business being on a barge laden with gas canisters at four thirty in the morning. He was busy with HER. Three bodies, they said. Three out of fifteen million.

What, seriously, were the odds?

Redial.

Engaged.

She stamped her dinky feet one more time. Messed her hair one more time. Took a sip of bubbles. Played with her breasts in the mirror.

"Miss Harrington."

She purred seductively.

And pouted.

The dump text was a dumb idea, sent in fury. She hadn't meant it. They were still an item. Until Monday, at least. Otherwise, what was the point of revenge screwing Grant? To do it while single was no kind of revenge, and no kind of thrill at all.

Ferret tumbled through the air in an uncoordinated arc, arms flailing, hugging the trajectory of the ginger madman who, in turn, followed a spinning sheet of tempered steel, its blackened edges trailing thick fingers of smoke.

Crash!

The plate-glass picture window blocking their path shattered into ten thousand fragments, coating the landing area in sweet sugar frosting.

Thump!

"Urgh." The detective rolled onto his back, clawing for air, battered knees popping.

"One really must work on one's landing technique," said Edward, standing to adjust his bow-tie.

Lying splattered across a king-sized bed, all Ferret could hear was the rush of wind, so he made up the words. Gingerly, he initiated a limb check.

"Agent TJ?" It was like shouting into a blizzard.

"At the bottom of the river." Or something similar. "Now, be a good chap and name Edward's decuria."

The ginger troublemaker slapped himself.

"By Jupiter's grizzled nipples! Get a hold!"

Ferret caught sight of a sooty-faced riverbank vagrant in the mirrored ceiling, dressed in tattered rags. He gasped. The annoying curl popped out, confirming his worst fears. He licked a blackened finger and dampened it down. Somehow, Edward had escaped virtually unscathed, his tweed suit sporting just a single ember burn near the front pocket. Unlike his own, it was entirely serviceable and unlikely to attract the wrong sort of attention in a crowd.

Edward rubbed his eyebrows, which were reduced to withered curls of amber. "Bromeliad, I come to thee."

The detective staggered to his feet, crunching glass underfoot and clicking his jaw from side to side. He surveyed the scene of devastation that was once a lavish penthouse bedroom, hoping that the owner was well insured against airborne metal sheets the size of a small cow, backed by a tempestuous storm of extra virgin olive oil. He shuddered at the thought of all the associated paperwork, especially the box marked "description of accident."

Wasting no time, the ginger troublemaker headed for the front door. Ferret followed hot on his heels, the white noise gradually subsiding. From beneath the smoking fragment of the ship's hull, lodged tightly against a set of oak-frame fitted wardrobes with bird's-eye maple panels, he heard pained groaning. He wasn't certain, and he had no intention of hanging around to find out, but it sounded like whoever was trapped beneath the debris was giving voice to a series of obscenities regarding a badly mangled trouser press.

For a chap who had recently broken the sound barrier, Edward was certainly in good shape, vigorously thrusting his frame along the corridor and down the stairs, two at a time. Ferret gave chase, using what remained of a shirt cuff to wipe the dirt from his face, mindful of the block's residents, many of whom had been sleeping soundly, until rudely awakened by a terrifying explosion.

A half-naked man stumbled out of a doorway, blocking their passage, irately demanding an explanation with his arms. Edward bundled the chap roughly to the ground, whipped away the initialled towel covering his lower half and pointed, laughing out loud. While the startled gent covered up out of embarrassment, Edward wiped his hands and face clean, tossed the mucky rag to one side, and with a cry of "Onward!", doubled up the pace, bounding resolutely towards the lobby.

The detective shrugged his shoulders. He thought about apologising. Reaching up to doff his hat, he realised he'd lost it. He winked instead, growing increasingly uncomfortable with his surroundings, which were materialising into something far too familiar.

The ginger chap flounced out of the communal entrance to what was once a riverfront warehouse. The dark-brick façade soaked up the glowing rays of the morning sun, which danced between Prussian blue downpipes, jogging towards the dock where a dozen high-masted yachts were berthed along with many smaller river craft, merrily bobbing up and down. Ferret followed the troublemaker across a road bridge constructed from girders tossed haphazardly together.

"Bromeliad!"

Edward vaulted a thin metal fence and dropped down onto a narrow wooden jetty, hurriedly dancing the boards.

By the bridge, a shape crawled out of the dark waters of the dock and pulled itself up a ladder, whereupon it slumped in a heap coughing up filthy water. Warily, the detective approached the cetaceous blob, prodding it with his shoe.

"Ferret," it said, coughing up water. "You're alive."

The detective put his arm around the giant and helped him shed what remained of his sodden coat. Free of the garment, Agent TJ rolled onto his back, gazing at the last vestiges of the summer star field with his good eye, pullover ragged and torn.

"Edward?" he asked.

Ferret glimpsed a flash of check across the marina by the medieval hall. He pointed.

Agent TJ doubled over, spewing up half a river, a ball of fur, and a used condom. Once he finished gagging, Ferret helped him upright and fumbled in the coat pocket for a white telescopic stick, stashed there earlier. It was smashed beyond repair.

"Damn!" cussed the giant. "Comms are down."

"Fortunately, you have me."

As they stood there, the agent sopped water upon the planks of the bridge, a puddle gathering around his well-polished shoes. Hastily, the pair agreed on an exit strategy involving the acquisition of transport.

The detective grumbled, heaving Agent TJ through the arched gateway from St. Katharine Docks. The twin elephants atop the gateposts eyed them with outright suspicion. He bundled the giant across the road, painfully aware of their proximity to the bridge. He reasoned they could make their escape on the Ducati, the agent riding pillion, ankles scraping along the ground. The only complication was the enemy, who stood between them and the bike's hiding place.

Already they'd encountered a few stragglers wandering around lost, expressions vacant, arms stretched out in front. Like slow-moving mannequins on roller skates, they bounced off any walls blocking their path.

Ferret sucked his teeth. "Change of plan."


Many moons past, in a different life that felt like a million years ago, Ferret was once seconded to a financial-services company based in the old Royal Mint complex, which stands diagonally opposite the Tower of London. Remembering how he used to abuse the system and leave his bright-yellow sports car parked there overnight, that was where he headed.

"Stealing cars is not really my forte," he said, eyeing a sleek black Audi TT.

"It really is no different to purloining a motorcycle."

"I'm fairly new to that scene too."

The big man shivered. "Choose one that looks like the owner doesn't care."

Finding the door to the first sports car locked, the detective tried a Mercedes Kompressor, followed by a crisp white BMW rocket. Of the eight cars on display, any one might do for a quick getaway, except the mud-encrusted diesel estate with plastic hubcaps and a smashed bumper.

Finding it unlocked, Ferret grinned at Lady Fortune. "Bingo," he said, removing a key fob from behind the driver's sun visor.

Agent TJ fumbled with a pair of cracked shades. "What are you waiting for?"

"It's a Skoda." The detective snorted derisively. "You'll have to drive."

"You think so?"

"I can't possibly take the wheel."

"And I'm qualified how?"

Reluctantly, Ferret cleared the passenger-side footwell of junk food wrappers and helped the agent into the car, taking up position in the driver's seat, conscious of the smell of stale smoke. He remembered the judge's orders: Consider your relationship with alcohol and cocaine. His response had been equally unambiguous: We get on perfectly fine, m'lud; no divorce required. That act of bravado had cost him an extra year of waiting for a return to the wheel. And now, tantalisingly close to the anniversary, rather than driving a souped-up engine with a wheel at each corner, his first escapade in two years was at the helm of an underpowered tractor, fit only for the farm.

"Given all that's happened," said the big man, "your home can no longer be considered safe. My last instruction was to head out of town to one of our safe houses. The Old Mill near Chorleywood."

Ferret fired up the car, the fuel gauge registering a smidgen below full. Curiously, he opened the glove compartment and discovered a half pack of reds. Moistening his lips, he turned to face Agent TJ, whose angular, smoke-stained jaw was peppered with a thin coating of stubble. Knees digging deep into the dash, the agent pulled on a lever and pushed the passenger seat fully backwards.

Ferret laughed. "It's a shame we're not a hundred and six miles from Chicago."

"Hit it," growled the giant, squelching Thames water into a pile of empty crisp packets.

The detective considered a squealie, then thought better of it. The tang of low-profile Pirellis was one thing, the acrid stench of cheap rubber quite another. Cautiously, he reversed the deep-green automobile in a wide arc, playing with the electric mirrors and windows. Finding his stride, he directed the car towards a pair of tall, skinny gates and pulled on a seatbelt, strapping himself in.

"Well?"

Ferret sighed. It had been a long night. He felt tired and washed out, in need of a jolt. "Cigarette."

"Must you?"

"Judging by the state of the ashtray, it's compulsory." The detective cracked open the reds and inserted one into the corner of his mouth. He tipped up the packet, shook out a firestick, and sparked up.

The giant drummed fat fingers on the dashboard, tapping out a rudimentary tune.

Ferret exhaled, following through with a little cough. "I've been wondering about your name. What does 'TJ' stand for?"

"There's something I have to tell you . . ." The agent stopped mid-sentence, ears attracted to a muffled bang. It was followed by a yelp, then another bang, this time louder.

Beyond the gates, Edward danced into a yellow hatched box, which was part of the arrangement of a complicated road junction. A metallic projectile sped between his legs, exploding on contact with the road.

Boom!

A car skidded to a messy halt, narrowly avoiding the ginger madman; metal and glass contorted, screaming in pain as the auto was broadsided by a London cab. The cabbie climbed out and shook his fists, mouthing Cockney profanities at the first driver who, in turn, remonstrated with Edward.

Agent TJ strapped himself in. "Collect your friend and get out of here."

The detective slipped the car into gear and shot forward, halting a few metres from the gate. All around, a stumbling mob was steadily reanimating. He stabbed at the accelerator, aiming for a gap in the groggy zombie horde.

He rubbed his eyes. "I know that boy."

On the periphery stood Junior Eric, catapult cocked, searching for an opening. To his side was Damien, trying his best to dissuade the junior from taking the shot. Some distance away, he spotted a girl dressed in leather, slowly adjusting to her change of fortune. Crossing his fingers, Ferret pointed the car at Edward.

In a daze, the chequered rapscallion fell across the bonnet, onlookers tugging at his clothes.

"By Jupiter's gnarly gherkin!" The fear in Edward's eyes spread to his brow line. "One is here in the nick of time!"

Ferret inched the car forward, gradually separating his friend from the many pairs of grasping hands.

"Get in," hissed Agent TJ through a partially open window.

The car's rear door flew open.

"Legionnaire!" The words thundered through the cabin. "What part of 'leave the madman the fuck alone' do you not understand?"

The detective let rip; the car shot forward a good twenty metres, leaving the centurion flailing, his face a deep shade of crimson.

"Bromeliad!" Edward staggered to his feet, heading for the rear passenger-side door.

A clear, melodic female voice sang the opening line to a song. The vocals were accompanied by a wave of silver cannon shots, which smacked Ferret about the torso, shredding mast and splintering rigging, knocking the breath clean out of him. The big man slumped back in his seat, the deeply etched lines in his forehead gently smoothing to a blackened paste.

"My name is Tidley-Jones," said the giant, calmly.

The cogs in Ferret's brain whirred away in overdrive. So much for the theory that the Old Boys had despatched a midget assassin armed with a stiletto to do him over..

"I presume you intend to bash my head in."

"Twenty years ago," said the agent, "I was a man who crushed bones for a living. I'm over that now. Your friend Marcus trusts me, which is why you can trust me too."

Without ado, the zombie horde built a steeple of discord, raising it to the skies.

"Death to Edward!"

To the detective's astonishment, the agent mouthed the words too. The rear door opened; Ferret felt a pair of metal prongs press into his neck.

"Unless you desire ten million volts of stun gun for breakfast, my optio, your flight stops now." Tristan turned to the baying crowd: "I have them, my people. And this time there's no escape."

# Chapter Thirty-Eight: Clockwork

Flying high, Cyrano felt empowered. The mighty clockwork wings which he imagined held him aloft beat in time with his heart, while below, the cool, calm streets of inner London splayed out like asphalt veins. The Frenchman heard the rush of cobalt-fortified blood firing through atrium and ventricle. He concentrated on the rise and fall of his chest; the perspective shifted, allowing him to watch *le muscle de l'amour* expand and contract from the viewpoint of a steely-blue erythrocyte, massive liquid-packed chambers echoing to an orchestral barrage of thick-skinned bass drums.

All was one, orderly and constrained.

True Blue dug its nails into his soul.

Beads of time slipped between greasy fingers.

From his vantage point, he watched Edward's balloon careen haphazardly across rooftops, smashing slate and chimney pot. It skirted Nelson's column, pushed ever faster by an arcane whirl of wind. Near St. Paul's, the supernatural gust exhausted itself. The balloon's burner burped thick black smoke. Devoid of hot air, the inflatable crashed through a line of trees where it was eagerly devoured by the river.

To the east, a thin, ethereal cloud raced about its business, edges scorched by a great globe of golden fire inching its way above the horizon. Cyrano saw beyond the outer orange shell, glimpsed the glowing grey matter that lay behind, and saw humanity's cortex. The people-sardines going about their business beneath him were universal neurons interconnected by a complex system of synapses responding with verve to electrical instructions pumped forth from the cosmos. Unknowingly, they dashed towards their destinies, oblivious to the demands of the divine.

An amber blip. Then another.

He knew without knowing that he was seeing freewill in motion, a determined stand against a predetermined outcome. Like a great factory ship, he felt the universe adjust imperceptibly to each insignificant aberration, a degree here, a degree there, its progress unstoppable, the bounty of the human ocean its harvest.

The man-sardines were simply cogs within cogs, components of a great perpetual engine moving in synchronous accord.

The old City lay beneath him, glowing the colour of the greenback, its entrances marked by rearing dragons. Links of shining emerald stretched into the distance across the oceans to Amsterdam and Frankfurt, New York, Hong Kong, and Tokyo.

The stylised lizards shared their memories, showing how the secret societies of old had dedicated a square mile of turf to the great god of capital. They had erected magnificent edifices in his name that reached to the skies with their spires, grounding his presence and making manifest his reign on Earth. The world at large remained oblivious to this interconnected financial empire, whose looted jewels included all the world's banking centres. He learned from the universe how, within the last decade, the three legions had wrestled global control from the Old Boys, surrounding and ousting them from their colonial towers until only London remained under their tenuous control.

The Frenchman smiled.

Plutus was an honourable god. Ruthless to the core, yet fair to those who whispered his name and carried out his rituals, committing blood sacrifice.

Curiously, he examined the glowing links that bound the great system together, noticing how they resembled the double helix of life, composed of intertwined pictures, sounds, and feelings. Insightfully, he dived into his own DNA, picking it apart strand by strand, trying to determine if he was one of François Mitterrand's bastards, as his mama once claimed.

So much history, he thought, feeling generation upon generation line up behind him.

So much conflict; so many secrets.

All to produce him, the pinnacle of his family's ambition. French to the core, yet according to the memories held within his cells, hardly French at all.


On the river, a rippling blast of amber fire begged for attention. Multiple blobs of orange spread out from a liquid core, disrupting the calm.

Dissidents, refusing their destiny.

Unlike the previous amber blips, this set refused to die, burning ever brighter, creating ripple upon ripple. The Frenchman forced his wings to stop beating and, with great effort, slipped back into normal time, setting a glide path for the globs of napalm that now glowed an eerie shade of aquamarine. As he closed in, a sphere of silver light exploded in a series of rhythmic pulses, tearing through him, scorching his flying apparatus, leaving only a pale-blue latticework of ribs.

He plummeted straight into the glowing body of his old best friend, upon whom he'd heaped scorn and derision for feeling like he felt now.

Devil dogs and leprechauns.

He saw both.

And glimpsed an undeniable truth.

Enclosed within the skin of his friend, Cyrano felt waves of silvered light slice through Ferret's dumbfounded pores, causing his thoughts to billow forth like ticker tape. Any second now, Edward would pull open the rear door of the Skoda and smash the banker about the head with a random object plucked from the ether.

Perhaps a vase from the Ming dynasty.

Or an antique thunderbox replete with mummified load.

Cyrano felt his friend's head turn; two metal prongs pressed firmly against his neck.

Outside the vehicle, a jubilant crowd jostled, pushing hard against the thin metal shell, their chant reverberating through him like a deathly wind laced with fine-ice particulate.

"Death to Edward!"

The crowd formed a circle around Sir Edward, two deep, buffeting him roughly and administering a series of free fire slaps.

"Jupiter's teeth!"

Out of the corner of his eye, a flash of diamonds.

New arrivals dressed in formal evening attire.

Men in suits and bow ties, ladies in evening gowns.

A waiter.

Jake and Elwood.

Juliet's girlfriends.

All the while, the mistress of the silver wash surveyed the scene from a safe distance. Cyrano felt satisfaction splash around his feet, forming a pool, deep and wide. The newbies packed the outer circle tight, while the oldies jumped from side to side. Bored with the display, the girl in charge folded her arms.

The circle closed tight; fists and open palms rained down mercilessly, legs pumped frantically. Someone pushed forward with a broom; opposite, an estate agent's sign entered the affray.

Briefly, the crowd parted. A booted foot kicked Edward to the ground.

"Oh, goody." The voice of the banker boomed forth. "I do so love it when someone brings a knife to a fisticuffs party."

It was unclear from where the sword came, only what must be done.

A twinkle of silver bounced from the blade reflecting in the door mirror, throwing myriad glittery thoughts this way and that. In a single stroke, the etched katana cut down through morning mist, which was rising gently from the surface of the road. The sword clattered to the ground, coming to rest on its side.

A manhole. Cyrano heard Ferret's thoughts clearly. Edward had escaped into the sewers.

One of the crowd reached down and gathered up a football, glistening with sticky sauce.

The broom became a standard, the bearer of a grisly trophy raised high. The crowd whooped and stomped, its voice building to a crescendo.

"Death to Edward!"

Cyrano felt his friend's palm press the car's horn, adding to the musical cacophony. Like a great clockwork toy, the crowd turned away from their sweet victory, stepping out in unison to form a wide circle around the vehicle.

The seat belt loosened; Ferret climbed out, shouting and waving. Edward was a survivor, thought his friend. So full of life, so determined. The last living link to his father.

The Frenchman snorted. Finally, Ferret's detective dream had ended. Their friendship was secure. Ferret tried to deny it was real, tried to turn his head away. He made him look. Forced his eyes open. One lid at a time.

Edward's body twitched in a pool of blood, his clothing ripped. Liquid spurted from the neck. A battered head lay several metres away with a pole protruding from its base. The human machine whirred once more, each cog turning mechanically through 180-degrees.

Cyrano felt his friend's stomach pitch one way then the other.

Miles away across the city, the Frenchman heard a ringtone. That old Roy Orbison hit "Pretty Woman."

Finally, he thought, she deigned to call.

In an instant, he was back in his hotel room, trying desperately to answer the call. Displaying great temerity, the phone refused to be solid.

How dare it!

The Frenchman realised he was not alone. A funny little man in maintenance overalls was busy instructing a pair of scruffy youths dressed in ill-fitting suits on how best to shove a naked cadaver into a body bag.

He caught sight of a snake's head tattoo on the left hip, inked by aboriginal hand and saw the tip of an eagle's wing on the left shoulder blade. In an explosion of fingers, he poked one of the youths in the eye, raising his voice in anger when his finger passed straight through the chap's head.

He hung in the air cursing in time with Roy, who stopped abruptly, replaced by the metallic clack of a zip fastener. Barked instructions summoned a folding stretcher.

"Careful!" he screamed.

In blatant disregard, the morons in suits thumped his head on the floor.

The Frenchman drifted aimlessly, hearing Edward's parting words over and over again: *Recant one's love of Plutus or remain forever trapped.*

Absurd.

Cyrano huffed as the stretcher was wheeled away. There was no doubt that True Blue was the most powerful psychotropic substance he'd ever taken. It kicked the *merde* out of ayahuasca, imparting a clear understanding of the universe, its structures, its hierarchies, and most important of all, his place in it.

Edward was an ambassador sent to recruit him to the ranks of *Bleu Vrai*. At the head of an all-conquering army he'd marched, ginger, gifted, and terrible to behold.

To some, a saviour. To others, the devil incarnate. To all, now very, very dead.

Cyrano saw the future clearly. He must assume the mantle, take over where the ginger terror had failed.

Become the new master.

Lead the army to victory.

But first, he had to find a way back into his body.

This, thought Marianne Lavalle, linking arms on the right with a middle-aged public relations director whom she recognised from Seven Seven and, to the left, with a pimply youth with ill-fitting facial growth, a sullen growl, and a sword strapped to his back, is not the Sunday morning I had planned.

The tinkling notes of silver that had enticed her to give up the best hours of the night hung in the air like ripe, dripping pears, dangling inches beyond her fingertips. One more task and they were hers to gorge upon. How she longed to feel the precious juices dripping down her breasts, fermenting in sparkling pools around her naked toes. Her fly-half could start there, licking his way to victory.

She eyed Ferret, unsure how in the last few hours he'd managed to simultaneously become shipwrecked *and* join a minstrel show.

Wink.

No, wink.

Annoyingly, her expression remained frozen.

The voice without form gave soothing reassurance, cajoling her along the precipice of a well-manicured dream, manipulating limbs and teasing a battle cry from parched lips.

The banking big shot who'd kicked off the kerfuffle earlier in the evening was centre stage once more, oozing a sprightly mix of charm and venom. Wearing a pure-white toga-style dressing gown with gold trim and a gold cloak clasped at the shoulder, he looked a million times more sophisticated than the almost naked, upside down man-ape who'd bounced along the Piccadilly roofline.

"Oh, my optio," he said. "How will you ever repay me for trashing my luxury riverside apartment?"

"I told you to buy inland."

"Such sweet insubordination! I saw everything. I have a powerful telescope trained on the river."

"Bravo." Ferret wiped his mouth with the back of a hand. "Now, put down the stun gun."

"My friend," the banker laughed, pacing around within the circle, "you take me for a fool?"

Ferret lunged.

The banker danced around the blow. Marianne heard herself roar.

"Pugilism is such a lower-class sport," chortled the financier. "I invoke the right of substitution. The large oaf you were busy putting out fires with on the barge before it was vaporised — he shall take my place."

The crowd parted, letting through a mountain troll of a man, well over seven feet tall.

Marianne's nose twitched.

His hair reeked of damp smoke, his clothes — pocked with rings where once the fire faeries danced — oozed greasy water.

"It's not personal," said the giant, raising an eyebrow.

The banker grinned, narrow eyes sparkling with malice. "I wager a silver crown on the monster to break the vagabond's legs."

"Ass." Ferret crouched low, circling the man-ox.

Marianne felt her brow wrinkle as pernicious thoughts raced around her befuddled brain. She wanted to cry out in support of Ferret, yet the promise of the precious fruit dripping down the insides of her legs in rivulets, gathering in glistening puddles, held her firmly in check.

Damn Old Man Cocks and his refusal to surrender even in the face of oblivion.

This was all his fault, she thought. If only he'd accepted his fate with grace and good manners, she'd be tucked up at home in Cheltenham.

She felt a tingle down below.

But then she wouldn't be with her all-star Ferret.

Except he was about to get his pretty face permanently rearranged.

Who *was* the man-ox?

In response to her question, sounds and pictures leaked from porous thoughts, some as large as icebergs.

Amazing.

All she had to do was close her eyes and listen intently with her inner ears, letting the babbling voices coalesce into a single stream of consciousness.

*Legendary Blackheath scrum-half, fabled for his bone-crushing antics on and off the rugby field.*

Marianne felt her mouth part, her tongue caress her top lip. Perhaps, if he beat Ferret, she'd smash the springs with him instead. That would be a night to savour.

*I'm here for love.*

The thoughts were those of a random stranger, locked arm in arm, across the circle. Jet-black hair and sideburns seduced her attention, his suave manner broadcasting a romance brimming with flowers. Marianne felt drawn to him.

*What about you?*

She didn't dare think it.

The stranger smiled. They all smiled.

*There are no secrets here.*

Secrets.

She tried not to think about the documents in her briefcase and their dull descriptions of sheer thickening vectors, sentient globule frameworks, and combatant debilitation mechanisms.

Jet Black's mouth crinkled at the edges.

She'd been accused of many crimes in her career, but never selling secrets. And yet here she was, openly sharing proprietary knowledge in return for the promise of juicy fruit not of this world.

She was Marianne Lavalle.

She didn't believe in promises.

And yet.

*The cloud will deliver.*

In front of her stupefied eyes, the circle nodded in unison.

In harsh counterpoint to their serenity, the man-mountain grasped at her protégé, coming away with a fist full of shirt, leaving a collar and bow-tie floating free. Ferret kicked out at the giant's ankles. His shoe fell apart on contact.

"Ow." He shook the remains of the leather from his foot.

In time with the circle, she stamped her feet, baying for blood.

Troll-man rushed forward, pinning his adversary to the side of the car, only to have him slip greasily between baseball-bat fingers, courtesy of a coating of slimy olive oil. The big man thumped metal while the wriggly Ferret smacked him in the ribs on the way down, crawled between his legs, turned, and let loose a kick to the buttocks.

The man-ox's spinning kick caught her protégé off guard. He wobbled, trying to regain his balance, allowing the giant to seize him by the throat, except he was far too slick to hold. Sweat and oil clogged his eyes, blinding him. He paused to wipe away the grime, but not quickly enough. A further kick caught him in the stomach.

Ferret clambered slowly to his knees only to be jumped upon by the man-troll, who wrapped an arm around his throat. He wriggled and squirmed, scuttling rapidly away on all fours. In a blink, the giant delivered a kick to the midriff, knocking him into the air. He fell facedown in a heap, winded.

Marianne gasped on the inside, pumping a mixture of astonishment and fear into the silver cloud.

The fly-half twisted around to face the scrum-half, who was swiftly upon him.

"Bravo!" clapped the banker, now sitting cross-legged atop the car. "Pummel his face in."

Smack!

Ferret moved his head to one side.

Smack!

The giant brought his fist down again; Ferret moved his head to the other side.

"You lied about your moviemaking credentials."

"My backers bailed." Ferret's voice cracked.

Smack!

"Then there's the theft of a pair of smalls."

"A misunderstanding of epic proportions."

Smack!

Wriggle.

Smack!

The giant of a man sat on her fly-half, breathing heavily. The skin around his knuckles was bloodied and torn. His dark glasses were perched at an odd angle.

"Finally, there's the small matter of you two-timing Miss Harrington with Marianne Lavalle."

At the mention of her name, Marianne felt her heart jiggle. This fight was about her? Of course it was. How could she be so naïve? The man-troll was fighting for her. Except she hadn't invited him to. So he was fighting for another reason.

Jet Black smiled at her.

*He's doing it to get his sight back.*

A promise that can be fulfilled is one thing, thought Marianne, closing her eyes and feeling her place in the cloud, but one that has no basis in reality is nothing but a lie.

The crowd turned to face her, discontent erupting from every pore.

*It's good to believe.*

And believe she did.

She believed in beating juniors into shape, knocking off the jagged edges. She believed that a sucker should never be given an even break. She believed that fear is the key to not having employees take the piss. And more recently, since her association with the Carlsgrove Group, she'd come to understand that every great business deal requires skin in the game, because otherwise partnerships soon disintegrate into dictatorships.

And yet, despite the logic of her convictions, she still believed firmly in the juice of Eden's fruit, pouring forth from her loins in warm streams of silver.

Once the bone-crusher won, she'd be twenty-five again.


The man-troll cradled Ferret's jaw in his huge hand and moved his face in close. The wriggly fly-half head butted him, causing an explosion of claret. He then pushed away, rolling free, his forehead covered in blood.

"Bravo, my optio." The banker clapped vigorously. "Such spirit!"

Groggily, her protégé rose to his feet, followed by the troll, who erupted from the ground tearing what remained of Ferret's jacket from his back.

"Tim Tim's sister!" he bellowed, swinging wildly, knocking the fly-half to the ground and raining blow after blow across his shoulders. "At her engagement party."

"Everyone was at it," spluttered Ferret. "That's the point of masked balls."

"For these acts, the Old Boys demand you be punished." The man-troll snatched hold of the wriggling mustelid by the ankle and hauled him along the ground. "Pole."

Marianne felt her heart run amok.

The youth to her left reached behind, drooling spittle over wispy whiskers. Presently, he hoiked a length of scaffold pipe forward from the back line.

The banker cackled loudly, beating his thighs with his fists.

"Smash my legs," threatened Ferret, "and it'll cause more trouble than you can possibly imagine."

"Really?" The banker laughed, holding his thumbs aloft.

Suspending Ferret by the ankle, the man-troll reached out with his free hand and took hold of the pole.

"Oh, the horror!" The banker extended his arms and turned thumbs towards the earth.

Marianne felt the rage inside reach boiling point.

Ferret was hers, goddammit!

She'd plucked the cocky junior with a nose for other people's secrets out of the graduate lineup and placed him under her wing, offering a fast-track to stardom. Whatever he'd done to irk the banker, he was still one of her merry band of fighting fuckers for whom no ruck was too big, no bedroom too small. Her signature ran through him, tattooed like a seaside venue through a stick of rock. His loyalty had never been in question; it was the underlying reason for his scalping. Ross had proven to be an untrustworthy bigot. She'd denied him membership of her special club and for that he'd taken revenge on her gang, one by one.

In all her time on this Earth, not one of the fighting fuckers had ever let her down.

Marianne's frown lines cracked the edges of the spell.

But the silver fruit. It hung there, pulsating, offering an eternity of delights.

Undying loyalty, she reminded herself, cut both ways. It was not a sound bite.

*It's good to believe.*

"No!"

Her scream filled the cathedral in her head, growing ever louder, reverberating until it was impossible to hear anything other than the jagged notes of her anger. She felt something tear. The fabric of the cloud ripped, its structure rent asunder, tattered silver edges fluttering in the air.

Marianne let go and fell through an eternal void . . .

. . .into herself.

Every cloud has a silver lining, she laughed. Especially this one. Disconnected from what amounted to a posse, she felt oh so tired. With a system full of vodka, wine, and caffeine.

Not enough vodka, she thought. Or caffeine.

Only fumes.


Ferret wriggled while the man-troll tried to quiet him, metal pole glinting in the morning fire.

She had seconds.

Beyond the outer rim of the circle, standing legs apart, her arms folded, she spotted the young lady from outside Seven Seven, who she imagined to be the orchestrator of this grand event. Even though her brain felt dry, she was certain the girl was the source of the cloud.

Marianne stepped backwards, heel banging into something alien. She glanced down.

Not an orthodox solution by any means.

It had been a few years since she'd graced a court, but back in the day netball was her sport. Goal shooter her position.

"Go ahead, break his legs," she said, the words projecting from her lips, "but know this: You're buying nothing but snazzed-up snake oil, and afterwards, you'll still be partially blind."

From the giant, nothing.

From the banker, a tick of the eye.

Ignoring the queasiness in her stomach and the blood daubed across her patent-leather shoes, Marianne unhooked her arms, leant down, and pulled the grinning ginger head free of its mount. With one hand placed firmly on an ear and the other beneath the projectile, she bent her knees, imagined a hoop just above the girl's head, took aim, and made the shot of her life.

Confident she'd found the target, she unsheathed her nails and with a cry of retribution leapt on the giant's back, located his eye sockets with her thumbs and gouged with her all might, the unofficial motto of her consultancy gang echoing in her ears: *Win or lose, we're in this together — fucking and fighting to the end.*

Ferret kicked out at Tidley-Jones. Once, twice, squirming for his life.

From the moment he wrote that first Bank of Lies cheque and committed fraud against the Old Boys, it was always going to come down to this. Bashing a fellow's head in, ideally in full public view, preferably on the field of play was the only retribution they understood. A full-on crash of limbs was fine by him; scratches and bruises were something he lived for. Every single one he'd ever received made him feel stronger. But shin smashing? No true advocate of the game would do such a thing. Even in the mid-nineteenth century, before the rules were formally ratified, taking a pole to a fellow's legs was frowned upon.

But then so was the introduction of a vicious hellcat.

Touché.

Privately, he'd suspected for a while that Agent TJ was holding something back. And now, despite a valiant attempt to remain retired from the bone-crushing business, he was back doing what he did best.

The lady clinging to Agent TJ looked remarkably like Marianne, but from upside down it was difficult to tell. Her deep-red nails certainly matched those of his ex-boss, although her disregard for her own safety was not the action of a woman he prioritised ahead of his father. He remembered the night he was shot. They'd been out all afternoon, boozing and schmoozing, lining up the drinks.

No wonder he'd been so belligerent.

Tidley-Jones dipped a shoulder; the hellcat dug in.

Ferret hung there upside down, a red mist clouding his vision. Ribs, fingers, toes, collarbone, and skull — they'd all taken a pounding over the years, but never his legs. The thought of being wheelchair-bound filled him with a toxic mix of dread and fury. His rage boiled over, devouring his insides and spreading to the hand gripped tightly around his ankle. In a tidal wave of pent-up emotion, he remembered how it felt to melt into Juliet and, pushing himself into the big man's body, screamed at Tidley-Jones with every fibre of his being.

*Let go . . . NOW!*

He felt the agent's shock as, wide-eyed, the big man unburdened himself of everything, including a rather substantial lunch that now occupied his pants.

The detective fell, taking the impact with his hands. He rolled forward, flipped to his feet, and charged, knocking the giant's legs from under him at the same moment the hellcat jumped clear. Agent Tidley-Jones landed softly on his backside, exacerbating his discomfort.

Ferret cocked his best uppercut and with a whoop he let fly, connecting with the bone-crusher's jaw, setting bells tinkling throughout the big man's cranium. He hit him again and again, adjusting the angle until the faint ringing became a fire alarm, and finally, with a knee to the jaw, a siren signalling a nuclear catastrophe.

"Stop," whispered the hellcat, reaching out to cover his fist. "It's over."

Like a towering chimney brought down by a controlled explosion, the giant collapsed to the ground with a hefty thud and lay there unmoving, gathering flies. A wry smile transited the detective's face. Remarkably, despite their recent experiences, he was still able to see his reflection in the big man's shoes.

Marianne draped her arms around Ferret, held his rear in both hands and kissed him full on the lips. After a few lingering seconds, she pushed him away.

"I have to leave town before the law arrives," she said, a look of steely determination in her eyes, "It's been fun. Call me."

With which Marianne chaperoned the groggy taxi driver towards his dented cab, barking instructions to take her and Juliet's six soiled friends away from the scene at maximum speed.

Ferret took stock. The girl was nowhere to be seen. With her spell broken, the zombie horde was dispersing unevenly in all directions, leaving behind just two of their number who occupied prime spots in a scene of utter devastation. Broken boards, refuse bin lids, bricks, and poles of various sizes lay scattered in a series of concentric circles with a cadaver at the core. For all his bluster, come the defining moment, Sir Edward had lost his head, literally and figuratively.

Some twenty metres away, the detective spotted the missing piece of the ginger terror.

"I feel most queer." The banker slipped down from the roof of the car. "That was the largest Old Boy I've ever seen in my life. Quite a feather for your hat, my optio, if only you still had one."

Flop.

From out of the sky, a grey felt fedora landed on Ferret's head.

Theatrically, he put his arm across his chest and bowed.

The banker huffed and slipped a hand into his dressing-gown pocket. "I await an apology for the destruction of my apartments."

"We need to clear up this mess and scoot." Ferret turned away from his friend. "Eric, gather the head, if you will. Damien, Tristan — your assistance with the body, please."

"I beg your pardon?" said the junior and the banker together.

"You saw what I did to Tidley-Jones." The detective winked at Eric. "Do you want your backside kicked twice as hard, all the way to Soho Square?"

The junior scowled and stomped his feet, looking to Damien for support only to be met with a shrug of the shoulders. Muttering under his breath, he grabbed a carrier bag-for-life and wandered off, while Ferret and the senior junior set to clearing a space in the boot of the car for Edward's body, which they stashed underneath a pile of muddy sheets covered in dog hair. The centurion paced around the car, offering up encouragement but little in the way of actual assistance until Eric's return, whereupon he grabbed the stripy bag from the junior and, making sure that all were watching, added it to the contents of the car's boot.

With the first stage of the operation complete, Tidley-Jones was loaded unconscious into a rear seat and strapped in while the junior removed bricks and placards from the road, before scrubbing half-heartedly at a patch of blood with a rag and a bottle of water.

"I don't suppose you saw where the girl went?" Damien stroked his chin.

"I can't believe she just abandoned us." Truculently, Eric kicked at a hubcap, causing it to fly off.

"Careful with your car," said Damien.

"That heap of crap." The junior stamped on the cap, breaking it in two. "I'm glad it was stolen."

Ferret snorted. "Why didn't you say?"

"It's an embarrassment." Damien covered his mouth, suppressing a snigger.

"Seriously." The junior scratched his neck. "Why would I want a car that's contaminated with dead man's DNA?"

Ferret shook his head. "This is where we say goodbye."

"Grrr!" said Damien, raising his claws.

"Grrr!" echoed Ferret.

Junior Eric curled his top lip. "Break a leg, accursed trouser ferret."

"You too, Junior. And be sure to tell everyone about the fight."

Ferret grinned. Up until the final blow it might have gone either way, and that was the hallmark of a great scrap; one which they'd all remember as a resounding victory for the underdog. Damien and Eric understood that much. Hopefully, it was now the end of the matter.

"To business." The centurion leaned back against the automobile, stun gun on display, baring a fang. "Customary slap first, then you can lick my shoes clean."

Ferret opened the driver's door and fumbled around the steering column. "Where are the keys?"

Tristan patted his dressing-gown pocket. "First, a grovelling apology."

"Seriously?"

"I am a centurion of the First Legion!" The banker stood purposefully erect and jabbed Ferret in the chest with a stubby finger, swollen from riding the rope. "I go where I choose, when I choose, and the law is powerless to stop me. Prime your tongue, legionnaire, and fawn like your life depends on it."

Ferret grabbed his friend tightly by the finger and twisted.

"How dare you!" The banker's face turned cerise. "Unhand me this instant!"

The detective bent the centurion's finger backwards until he let out a muffled squeal, tears gushing from the corners of his eyes. Tristan brought the stun gun to bear, only to have it wrestled from his grip and thrown under the wheels of a passing truck. Reluctantly, the man of finance submitted and handed over the keys.

"Thank you." Ferret released him.

"Tristan's orders were very specific: Find Grandma and screw her until she blabs." The banker leaned against the car, panting. "And yet you chose to defy him. He demands a thousand trouser presses as compensation."

Ferret shook his head and climbed into the driver's seat.

"Furthermore, Tristan is requisitioning your house until his is re-paired," the centurion said as he climbed into the passenger seat. "You destroyed it; you'll foot the bill personally."

"It was hardly my fault."

"As Tristan recalls, he ordered you not to follow the balloon pilot un-der any circumstances. Yet again you defied him."

"Get out."

"Tristan shall do no such thing. The legion has a place for securely disposing of bodies, to which Tristan the Magnanimous will direct you. Afterwards, you'll wash his soiled laundry by hand. Do a good job and he'll buy his dog a collar and kennel."

Ferret's heart sank at the thought of capitulating to his friend, yet what option did he have?

"Do you hear me, legionnaire?"

"I'm done with taking ridiculous orders," said Ferret wearily. "I re-sign."

"You do?" The centurion licked his lips. "I must say, that's rather un-expected."


The detective drove west along the bank of the Thames, carefully avoiding the scrutiny of a line of police vehicles speeding in the opposite direction. He spotted a convenient parking spot near Main Building, the home of the Ministry of Defence, and pulled over. During his tenure with The Consul-tancy, he'd once attended a very drunken, extremely expensive lunchtime event that included a tour of Henry VIII's wine cellars. The vaults lay some seven metres beneath the concrete monstrosity, which was built up-on the foundations of the old Palace of Whitehall.

Ferret climbed out of the car, glad to be away from the chaos, making sure to take the keys. He walked to the first of a line of statues, a memorial to the Chindit Campaign.

Truth be told, he was stunned by recent events.

Had the ginger madman really been in cahoots with his father as part of a drug-dealing circle? Wolfgang's suspicious death and the murder of Edward certainly pointed to an aggrieved third party. True Blue was a large part of the puzzle. There was something else, though, and it involved the singing girl with the silver wash. The way she was able to control oth-ers — except for him and the madman — it was as if she had his recently acquired ability to melt into others, thus influencing their decision-making processes, albeit on a much grander scale.

A pen and paper thrust under his nose broke his concentration.

He recognised the scribing implement from Tristan's trophy wall; it was his friend's Octavian edition Mont Blanc pen. The paper was weighty vellum with three neat folds, a strange accessory for a fellow to carry in his dressing-gown pocket. Seeing his puzzlement, the banker quickly cited his employer's legal department as the inspiration.

"Force of habit," he chortled. "Drunken fellows will sign anything. Inebriated or not, it's still a binding contract."

Ferret applied his paw print to the hastily written note. "That's it?"

"Our *adiutor*, with a little help from my good self, will finish things off."

All that hassle solved, thought Ferret, with a simple stroke of a pen. One of the legion's better-kept secrets, apparently, was that leaving wasn't so difficult after all.

"The boldest measures are the safest," read the banker, examining the memorial.

Ferret headed towards the second statue in the line, lighting up the last remaining red in the packet he'd found earlier. He inhaled deeply. Now that The Network's hierarchy no longer applied, he planned to beat Tristan senseless, leaving him stranded with a bloody nose, a black eye, and a pair of swollen ears. Then he'd head out of town on a wing and a prayer and locate the safe house the agent had mentioned.

Ferret heard the fall of fleet footwork on pavement and felt a sinewy presence approach rapidly from behind. He heard the rasp of a blade being withdrawn from its scabbard, felt the burn of contracting muscle, and realised his pace was way off the mark.

Too slow.

By a metre.

The man of finance was upon him, and this time there was no escape.

# Chapter Forty-One: Starlight

"By great Jupiter's doric column!" Flamen Dialis, high priest to the greatest god of all, jerked open his eyes only to find impenetrable darkness.

They were coming.

He felt it in the air.

The power failure was no accident, the lack of backup generator no horrible twist of fate. The best he might do was light a candle, although truth be told, between the chattering teeth and the aching leg, he felt rather out of breath.

This body was done for.

It was no longer a question of if, more a matter of when. Before he surrendered and let the universe trickle in, there was the troublesome matter of the enemy, who had proven to be tricky, astute, and resourceful. The girl was working for Toad; this much was now apparent. The question was, who was Toad working for?

*The disgusting reptile works only for himself.*

Jupiter's trepanned skull.

He was hallucinating Edward now.

They'd come to blows on the barge, wrestling each other for control of the terror's body, causing a series of horrendous possibilities to stack up. While they fought, many opportunities to escape had passed them by, from a stranded Russian mini-sub to a flock of starving pigeons ready to descend on their assailants, pecking out their eyes. The priest had calculated the possible outcomes in each case.

In every scenario where the ginger crusader walked away unscathed, Wolfgang's son ended up on a mortuary slab, coins resting in his eye sockets. Only one possible option remained: Edward must pay the ultimate price. Even with his sacrifice, the right outcome was still not assured. The boy too must surrender something of great value, for, as the terror was wont to say, a love of all things material is the bane of the turtle.

The priest's thoughts turned to the centurion.

Edward had certainly given *him* food for thought while he clung to the balloon.

He felt a presence in the outer room.

Not long now.

Strange how a delirious mind can wander.

He remembered the imposition of the Millennium Reforms, how The Network cast off the standing orders he and Edward had once held so dear, trashing what remained of The Brotherhood for good. By perverting the Praetorian Guard, the usurpers had silenced all dissent, threatening those who refused to surrender to the new order with dishonourable discharge. To his knowledge, The Brotherhood had only ever issued such a sentence a handful of times. Seeing what was coming, Edward had gone deep undercover. For his part, once their decuria was outlawed, Flamen had quit the country. Disclosure was what the new Caesar wanted, yet it was the one thing they'd sworn never to do.

The decuria had regrouped, far away from the influence of the three legions in a move that suited all parties. As long as they stayed away from civilisation and didn't cause a rumpus, they were safe.

Except this was not the modus operandi of the ginger terror. Given how much trouble he'd caused, it was only ever a matter of time before he attracted the wrong kind of attention.

The priest coughed, drifting in and out of consciousness, feeling chilled to the bone.

He'd seen first-hand what the guard were capable of, drawing their blood rite from the first of the Caesars. They'd form a tortoise of shields around him, delivering thirteen wounds to vital organs with their pugio. After that, they'd hang what was left of his body naked, by the neck, from a public monument.

Flamen heard the sounds of a door being smashed off its hinges. He felt a soft click and smelt the nauseating vapours of diesel and fertiliser.

A vertical band of light split the darkness, backed by the chant of a dozen voices: "*Fortitudo, constantia et victoria!*"

This was it.

The priest laughed out loud.

"Come, centurions. Embrace me."

He heard the shuffle of a boot upon a tiled floor, felt the tightness of a pair of tripwires, and caressed the shaped charges designed to cause injury and collapse in a massive unmitigated fireball.

His teeth chattered.

Oh, so cold.

"I see the brightness of your light, and I raise you."

Click.

With a cracked smile, Flamen cast his arms wide open, felt the power of a million candles scorch his retinas and, embracing the kiss of infinite starlight, offered Lady Fortune his hand one last time.

# Chapter Forty-Two: Missio Ignominiosa

Ferret spun around, expecting to see Tristan bearing down on him dressed in a toga. Instead, he found the centurion had cast aside the regal dressing gown to reveal a costume consisting of a short brown leather skirt with twin scabbards, matching armbands, and etched metal greaves and gauntlets, all trimmed off with the brassiere of the warrior princess. The sight of Tristan in ceremonial garb, commensurate with rank, gave the banker the element of surprise, allowing him to rake his pugio in a downward arc, leaving a grievous injury in its wake.

Click.

The man of finance withdrew a flick knife and, twirling a blade adroitly in each hand, narrowed his gaze. "The twins say die!"

Exhausted and in need of a drink, his right forearm leaking blood from a jagged gash, Ferret demanded one last burst of adrenaline to counter the banker's assault. He'd scrapped with mentalists before, but as he now realised, the madness of an exuberant scrum is very different from institutionalised insanity with a brandy-addled cherry on top.

"Put the knives down," he said. "Let's talk."

Tristan moved in closer, eyebrows knit as one. "That time is long past."

The detective dodged around a statue of Viscount Trenchard, founder of the RAF, listening to the centurion deliver a tirade of abuse. He couldn't deny he'd put the banker's nose out of joint when he was voted in as decanus three years running, thus forcing Tristan to put his aspirations for promotion on hold. That was five years ago, which made it some grudge. The charge that he'd cheated in order to assume command of the decuria was ludicrous. He was simply more popular than the banker.

The irony of the situation, thought Ferret, was that if he hadn't lost his intuition and been deposed by his friend, Tristan would still be a legionnaire.

The detective's mouth ached for water. "While we're airing grievances — you deliberately kept details of my father's death from me in blatant violation of Network etiquette."

"Etiquette schmetiquette. You hated the man."

The banker lunged forward, leading from the left and following through from the right, forcing Ferret to dance around the air marshal's pillar. His left thigh felt weak, his left fist sticky.

Focus.

"While you were being blown up, my optio, I made enquiries regarding our friend the headless corpse." The centurion stifled a smirk. "Information as to his history is now within my orbit. I charge you, by way of contravening a direct order, with aiding and abetting a dishonoured legionnaire."

Ferret half crouched, waiting for Tristan to make a move. He tried to use his intuition to read the banker's intent but came away with naught but meaningless Latin.

"You're not my first kill." A malevolent twinkle blossomed in Tristan's eye. "And I exclude all those balcony-jumping fools whose fortunes I rifled through. They deserved it."

"I don't believe you."

"You really think Rusty is in prison in Angola?"

Ferret inched backwards, careful not to lose his footing. Tom Tom's weekly update clearly stated that Rusty's release from captivity was imminent.

"I gave the order the day he resigned."

Ferret's heart beat a little faster. He mused over Rusty's final few months, careful not to present an opening. Certainly, the banker had treated him like a second-class citizen, demanding unreasonable tributes whenever he stepped out of line. He'd often wondered about the Angola mission but Rusty refused to reveal details, claiming doing so may compromise his well-being.

"You're a liar." The words came as a croak, through parched lips.

The centurion shrugged. "His house is mine. Check the deeds."

A burst of lively chemicals ricocheted through Ferret's tired limbs. Tristan told such epic fibs, it was a wonder his account at the Bank of Lies hadn't been suspended. But then, the banker was borderline crazy, and crazy people believe all sorts of tripe, often going as far as to name it a religion.

"Your property I covet even more. For the longest time I thought you'd never crack."

"Let's do this." The detective relaxed his shoulders, cracked his knuckles, and gazed intently into the banker's eyes.

Although Ferret was no stranger to using his intuition to play financier against legal advisor, partner against chief executive, he'd always done his best to avoid using his gift on his friends. It was easier this way, he reminded himself. As decanus, the accidental discovery of confidential information posed all sorts of moral issues. It was hardly fair to dob in a fellow for holding back, considering how much of his own background he'd glossed over when he swore the oath. The black-hooded fiends surrounding the coffin in which he was bound knew all the intimate details of his lovers, but very little about the supernatural investigations he'd carried out with his dear chum Raffles. His French friend remained mostly clueless to this day. Under threat of expulsion from Millfield for a drug-fuelled misdemeanour, Cyrano's father had avoided a scene by relocating him north of the border.

Solving crimes around Glastonbury had been the perfect opportunity to use his intuition to make a difference. Yet somehow, through a series of choices he hardly remembered making, all the good work went by the wayside. He'd hooked up once more with the Frenchman, boozed and schmoozed his way through university, and aced the exams courtesy of his gift. He'd then spent the last ten years performing the danse macabre with the financial services authority whilst merrily defrauding corporates for personal gain and, at the end of empire, had only narrowly avoided prison.

For what?

To lose everything he had in the world to a liar and a fraud.

Where was the justice in that?

The banker harried him one way then the other. Around and around the bronze viscount they dashed, an unhealthy quantity of blood forming a slippery satanic circle.

He needed a button.

Finding a white one and pressing it at the right time was the key to striking a favourable deal. Hammering on a black one consistently, until an opponent's eyes betrayed deep-seated fear — that was the key to conquering by force.

Ferret held back from melting into the banker, using his intuition to search for the darkest of buttons. He found only greys and whites, red, brown, and amber.

He felt his eyebrows narrow.

Where in Hades was the banker hiding it?

"I know your game, my optio." The centurion grinned. "Do you really think I'm oblivious to what you can do? I have no secrets. Do you know how liberating that feels?"

The detective let go just a smidgeon, melting into the banker, dissolving through layers of obfuscation.

The centurion lunged to the left. Ferret twisted, slipping on blood. He reached out to steady himself, determined to keep his balance but tumbled, banging his head against the pillar. In an instant, the banker was upon him, both blades poised. Desperately he thumbed through the centurion's muscle memories, searching for something — anything — that had previously sent Tristan over the edge. Feeling his way through the index files of the past, he felt his shoulder retract and his hand tighten around a firm cork ball.

"I don't know what you're doing, but it stops now!" Tristan thrust forward, determined to puncture a lung.

Ferret grabbed at the banker's wrists.

"You are weak, my optio."

It was true. He was losing; the needle points moving ever closer.

Deep down in Tristan's dirty underwear pile, he found a pair of soiled briefs with an embroidered name.

"Why did you sack Carmina?" he asked.

"Her name is Babylon!" Tristan pressed home the advantage, spittle gathering at the corners of his mouth.

"She loved you." Ferret felt his leg give.

"Liar!" The centurion leaned forward with all his weight.

Ferret looked Tristan fully in the eye, letting go of his feelings. He felt a deep-seated hatred burning with the heat of a small sun and felt the throb of stubby fingers aching from rope burns, possessing a tensile strength far greater than his own. He grimaced, feeling the tightening of the banker's tendons, anticipating the strain of the stretch. Toes bent, calves hardened.

An unexpected totter.

At last, an opening the width of a credit card. The banker's balance was all skew whiff.

"You do have a secret." Ferret smiled. "And Carmina discovered it."

"Die, quisling."

Tristan pushed hard. Ferret felt his wrist give up the ghost. The switchblade flashed sideways, taking a chunk from his chest. He kicked out at the banker's ankles in a manner that would get him sent off the field of play, catching the centurion roughly above the joint. Tristan wobbled and then recovered, putting his full weight behind the pugio.

"Your secret," said Ferret. "You wear shoe lifts!"

"Lies!" hissed the centurion.

"Absolutely you do!" taunted Ferret.

He hammered repeatedly on the button he'd found, until he felt a series of uncontrollable shudders rack the banker's body. Reaching out with his good leg, he hooked his heel around the centurion's foot and pulled. As Tristan toppled, Ferret evaporated from the banker. The moment Tristan hit the ground, the fly-half broke every rule in the playbook with an exacting kick to the nutsack.

"You should have worn a box," he muttered, gathering up the knives.

Tristan rolled around in agony, clutching his man parts, face red and puffy. Ferret hobbled slowly to the car, turning around at the last.

"I advise an ice pack."

The centurion was on his knees, hunched forward, a portable snorting device thrust up his nose.

"Perhaps not." Ferret reached quickly for the car keys.

"I am five feet eight inches tall!" shouted the banker, raising his head. "And you're a dead man."

"Go home." Much as he savoured the aches and pains of combat, Ferret conceded it was time for a tactical retreat.

The centurion staggered to his feet, each movement accompanied by a wince of agony. "Enough of this nonsense!" he yelled, reaching behind and fiddling with his skirt. Uncoordinatedly, he withdrew a pistol.

Blam!

Hot lead fizzled past the detective's ear. He cocked a moribund smile. He'd given it his all and yet the lunatic kept on coming.

"My pugio . . ." Tristan held out his hand.

Ferret's tongue clung to the top of his mouth. He felt himself shake as he held up his hands.

The centurion lurched forward.

Blam!

Ferret ducked, feeling the projectile pass through his hair, nailing the annoying curl on the side of his head. He staggered away from the banker and around the car, the words of Marianne echoing in his ears: To defeat a maniac, you must become a maniac.

Reaching inside his jacket pocket for the stash of bath salts, Ferret found nothing there.

Through the side windows of the car, he scanned for the centurion.

Too close.

His mind raced.

In a state of delirious panic, he remembered the time he met Sir Edward on the tube and the cacophony of broken notes when the train struck a piano. Then there was the explosion. Edward clenched his fists and mumbled a prayer. Not any old prayer, more of a wish. Expressed with all his might.

Blam!

A side window shattered.

Aping his friend, Ferret wished with every atom of his being for a way out of the crisis.

He became dimly aware of the growl of an engine and the squeal of brakes.

"What perfect timing." The centurion stopped dead, bowing painfully. "My boots are dirty. I command you to hold this irrelevant insect in the licking position."

The motorcycle rider revved the machine's accelerator, rattling the exhaust then, kicking down the stand, killed the engine and stepped away from the bike, facing the banker. "One death is a death too many. I will not sanction a second."

"Tristan the Impervious demands his retribution!"

The driver removed the helmet, placing it on the bike seat and shook, allowing a mass of dark hair to tumble around leather-clad shoulders. "Lower your weapon."

"I shall do no such thing."

Ferret felt liquid lapping at his feet, bubbles burbling with the outflow.

"Come, my friends," sang the girl.

Tristan pointed his handgun at the new arrival, aim wavering. "You promised me he'd die by my hand if I did your bidding."

The girl looked quizzically at the centurion. Sensing he meant it, she reached for her holster.

Blam!

Blam!

Blam!

The girl reeled as each shot hit in turn, striking her in the shoulder, the chest, and the stomach, ripping gaping holes in the crisp black leather.

She slumped to the floor, her weapon clattering to rest by her outstretched arm.

"Two bodies, four bodies, it's all the same to me," said the banker, pointing his gun to the sky, striking a pose. "Now, where were we?"

Ferret dove in the direction of the girl, slipping at the last and coming up short.

Tristan aimed the pistol at his head. "For daring to strike a superior officer I pronounce you *missio ignominiosa*; you are dishonourably discharged from the legion. Your body will swing from Southwark bridge, your eyes pecked out by crows. With your death and Edward's head, my promotion to the Senate is assured. Such a shame you won't be there to see my coronation."

Blum!

# Chapter Forty-Three: Pedagogy

Marcus took a sip of fully-leaded coffee, allowing the brandy to plump his tongue, titillating the insides of his mouth. He swallowed, feeling the sweet burn of infused mocha tango its way down to his stomach and with it, a return to a semblance of normality.

Rajesh had done nothing wrong. His career might yet be saved. His own, however, was damned.

He'd sworn an oath to The Network and made a lifelong commitment to his employer. Now he was being ordered from on high to stuff his friends, screw-up his job, and send all and sundry to hell in a hot-dog van, destroying the directive by which he'd lived his adult life.

*The realm comes first.*

His first boss had stencilled those words into his psyche many years ago. He'd argued at first, citing his network of friends as paramount, but eventually he'd come around. The realm, he'd realised, is a complex creature composed of proud aristocrats, meddling bureaucrats, and the stuffy secret services. The Old Boys had no interest in administration, only the giving of orders, whereas The Network's influence came from its ability to make things happen. Thrown in a cauldron, the elements came together symbiotically to create what he called the "Stool of the Realm".

Take away any one of its legs and the entire structure collapses.

He was able to ignore financial malfeasance and had done so on many occasions. Those with money who wanted power played the game by its rules, or the Old Boys simply called foul and summoned the administrators, who alerted the secret services. The role of City Intelligence was to bury the bodies and hide the evidence. What made this case so unusual was that the Carlsgrove Old Boys didn't need power, influence, or money. They already had all three in abundance.

Marcus sighed and shifted around, occupying a corner of the sofa. He pointed to the spot beside him. "Rajesh, I have something of immense importance to tell you."

The junior took a seat and, reaching out, clasped his hand firmly and made unwavering eye contact.

The *adiutor* smiled, unearthing a pair of dimples that had not seen the light of day for many years.

Perfect.

Exactly as he'd dreamt it.

"The ginger man I told you about the other night."

"Sir Edward." Raj tightened his grip.

"I first met him just after my eighteenth birthday." Marcus's eyes glazed over wistfully. "I was heading into the summer break before the start of university, when out of nowhere this educated, well-travelled man with extraordinary wild hair crashed into my life."

Over the years, the tale of Edward had been through many incarnations, as Marcus looked at it from every conceivable angle, trying to extricate himself from the feelings of guilt associated with their fling. He supposed it was youthful shyness that compounded his sexual frustration, making him an easy target. His plan was to come out abroad where no one knew him. Canada, perhaps. He'd find a partner in Toronto; they'd explore the lakes and forests together.

Young or old, it didn't matter.

"It was like smooching with a whirlwind," he said, breaking eye contact with the junior. "I was smitten. Edward suggested a blind date in a random location, chosen with map book and pin. He was old fashioned that way."

Marcus recalled the vinegary reek of tanned leather mixed with the sweet aroma of mint tea, the hot and sweaty backstreets labyrinthine in layout, the narrow openings full of endless possibilities, licentious depravity lurking around every darkened corner. As he described the scene from memory, he neglected to mention what he'd come to appreciate in later years: his abandonment was not random.

"I was anonymous, with money, surrounded by drugs, prostitutes, and an ever-growing entourage of young male admirers, all of whom wanted me. My father thought I was in Ontario, sailing the lakes, whereas in reality I was holed up in a sleazy souk in Marrakech, immersed in a constant stream of terrible fruits from all the forbidden corners of the world."

Marcus blushed. Under Edward's tuition, he'd gorged himself stupid. Even now, years later, he still awoke in the middle of the night doused in sweat, a smile on his face, as he remembered some heinous act he committed in an intoxicated haze.

It had taken years to get all of his foibles under control and back in the box.

He felt his eyes well up. "Of all the people I met in Morocco, of all the squalid, sensual activities I took part in, Edward was the only one I ever squealed for."

"Come here." Rajesh's words billowed like sweet candy floss.

He laid his head in his protégé's lap. "Edward was my first love. I was so infatuated, I did everything he asked."

Raj ran slender fingers through Marcus's hair, brushing it from his face.

"When that summer came to an end, we bade each other a fond farewell." Marcus sighed from his stomach. "I hoped I might hear from Edward at the end of the following term, perhaps the term after that. Nothing. Not even a card."

"The cad."

Marcus had known from a young age he was destined to serve his country. He'd taken great care to tread a well-worn path through public school all the way to Cambridge, a university with a tradition of supplying men of a certain persuasion to the intelligence services. The only black mark against him was that he wasn't born a full Old Boy.

He rubbed his eyes. "Much like when I found you, Raj, my *beneficiarius* approached me during my final university year. Eventually, I agreed to the terms laid out before me, joining City Intelligence as planned and intending to put the world to rights. On my first day of work, still wet behind the ears, I was invited up to the fourth floor to meet the grand fromage."

The walk to the top floor, heart pounding against his ribcage, represented a bewildering turn of events. Many of his colleagues had been with City Intelligence for years, and they still hadn't formally met the man in charge. From the looks they gave, his career in security services was clearly destined to be very short.

"I was ushered into a dark, oak-panelled room by a fawning PA, the sweat running down my neck. I remember a high-backed chair facing away from me. Slowly, as in a scene from a film noir detective movie, it swivelled around. Imagine my horror when I found the occupant to be none other than the ginger interlocutor."

Raj pulled his hand away. "Whatever did you do?"

"I fainted."

Marcus glossed over the ceremony that followed his recovery, where Edward professed a love that dare not speak its name, conferring upon him the title of Bromeliad.

"Sir Edward isn't his real name," he said, voice a tremor. "City Intelligence has always liked its secrets, but in this case a fellow legionnaire was only too happy to spill the beans."

Marcus gazed longingly into the eyes of his protégé. He was so young, so full of hope.

So unsullied.

He didn't need to know about the fateful day Sir Edward had grabbed a select committee by the throat and brazenly argued that City Intelligence's reach was too limited, bound as it was by the perimeter of the Square Mile. Operational leeway was needed if City Intelligence was to fulfil its mandate. They'd deferred the decision of course, as always. But a few well-aimed bribes and a lost dossier ensured the ginger terror got his way.

Marcus remembered how Edward had turned the whole of London into his personal plaything, his ego swelling to the size of a small moon. The terror declared he was bigger than the department; he actively broke the cardinal rule of spying, seeking public recognition as a counter-espionage superstar. Believing himself a hero of the people, Edward had made everything his business, causing the department to assign two full-time sweepers to tidy up loose ends. Much to their disappointment, he'd still made the front pages of the broadsheets. In desperation, they'd recruited the largest man they knew to wrestle him into shape.

Three years after his reconciliation with Edward, the terror's car had hit a bend at full speed and crashed off the rails. Marcus stifled a sob. He'd pulled Agent Tidley-Jones from the wreckage of the vehicle, damaged but alive, and then watched as Edward's limp body became reanimated, rising from the ashes like a fallen angel. After that day, Edward began blabbering about his special relationship with the universe, making claims of immortality, which put the frighteners on the City Old Boys and caused them to whine loudly to a pet minister. A few days later, without warning, there was a new Sir Edward in town. Except Sir Edward thirty-nine didn't call himself Edward, declaring the title tainted.

Marcus felt the anger boil inside, his eyes welling with tears. After all he'd done for the realm, how dare they strike Edward thirty-eight from the history books! City Intelligence's records still showed him as an incumbent of the title Grand Vizier of Technology, but for twenty years the name T. Granville-Sharpe had not been spoken aloud.

"There, there." Raj offered up a handkerchief.

Marcus did his best to smile, allowing his protégé to wipe away the tears. They lay in silence for what seemed like ages, the chiming of an old, beaten grandfather clock the only punctuation in the steady, rhythmic rise and fall of their chests. The intelligence man felt strangely different, a great weight lifted, setting his inner spirit free. He hadn't told a living soul the story of how he waltzed with Edward thirty-eight. Rajesh was not the intended recipient, but the time and the place were right.

It was exactly as he'd dreamt it.

Down to the promise to keep the tear-stained handkerchief forever.

Thirty-nine, as he became known, set to clearing up the mess left behind by his predecessor, despatching Marcus to a drinking club in Soho. It was frequented by every subversive the security services had ever encountered, including poets, musicians, statesmen, and the odd member of the clergy. The club served many purposes on the information-gathering front, and where hedonism failed, those well-worn intelligence tools called bribery and blackmail kicked in. He was ordered to dismantle his mentor's greatest creation, his information-gathering apparatus. Obliterate the evidence, they said. It's undignified.

He'd played the naïve card, pretending to be shocked at what he found. Had they suspected even for a second that he too was an inductee, they'd have tossed him out of the river door.

The true purpose of Morocco wasn't to get high and have sex, as he'd confessed in the coffin when he swore his oath of allegiance.

It was far more serious than that.

Seven times he'd partaken of the ginger terror's special drugs.

Seven times the universe had inhabited him.

Seven times he'd seen the sands of time shift and part.

It was a miracle substance. And yet, to this day, he had no clue from whence it had come. Edward remained tight-lipped about his source, refusing to name names, even to his Bromeliad.

As instructed, he'd culled the Cult of True Blue, reducing it to ashes and salting the ground upon which it stood. But not before he'd interviewed the members. Men, women, transvestites, transsexuals. There were hundreds of them. Some of them must have been just teenagers when they'd fallen under Edward's influence and been subsumed into his circle of love, built and run with department funding.

He'd wheedled all their secrets out of them, seen all their avatars. Then he'd threatened them with hell's fury if they ever spoke of True Blue again.

"Did the ginger cad even say goodbye?" asked Raj, breaking the silence.

A lump formed in Marcus's throat. "I'd always assumed the security services took special care of him."

Raj hugged his boss tight. "I will never let them treat you that way."

"Let's pray it doesn't come to that."

Marcus had long believed that Edward had fled the country on a false passport. In order to maintain his cover, not a word had passed between them, which was the way it had to be.

"For a long time after he vanished, I thought I still loved Edward," croaked the intelligence man. "But the trust was gone. I came to realise that love without trust isn't love at all: it's a heartless tragedy composed of stalking and jealousy that scars for life anyone who dares to touch it."

"Edward can't hurt you now."

"You can't stop him." Marcus squeezed his friend's hand. "In my premonition he comes through that very door before the hour is up. Our man in the field and our friend in the hat are simply collateral towards that end. He's an immoral, uncompromising bastard like that."

"He still has to come through me," said Rajesh, giving him a long hug he wished to never end.

Across the lounge, a laptop beeped, bringing the moment to a close.

Marcus stirred and lifted his head from the junior's lap. "What are you working on?"

"A hunch. Take a look."

The intelligence man took a gulp of lukewarm coffee and peeled himself from the sofa, ambling over to the desk.

"There's a very faint name stamped into the memory stick's rubber casing," said Raj, suppressing a grin. "I had to use talcum powder to see it."

Marcus donned his glasses and read the screen. "Combat CK. Well, well, what do we have here?"

Raj joined him. "The motherload."

"Registered four years ago, two principal shareholders: MacGregor Cocks and Wolfgang Muller. Thirty-four and thirty-three shares each."

Marcus took another hit of brandy. "Those numbers don't add up. I wonder, who's the sleeping partner?"

Rajesh tapped away at the keyboard. "Let's see what we can find on Cocks."

Marcus felt his glasses steam up.

"Ex-cavalry officer, recognised expert on mechanised warfare," read Raj. "A specialist in battlefield armour. He has a project running with some of our ministry chums called CLAS: Cocks Lightweight Armour System.

The intelligence man closed his eyes, the cogs in his brain whirring away. Before their flight, he'd reached out to all the military specialists in his little black book regarding possible applications for sheer thickening. He'd received just one reply from a department head eager to promote his latest tranche of boffins.

Then there was the break-in at Grrr!

During the debrief, one of the spotters claimed the girl was hit four times. He even thought he'd seen her shot at close quarters, a magazine emptied into her midriff. After the noise died down and the smoke cleared, she'd beaten his bodyguards to a pulp and chased him from the building.

"CLAS exists," he said, eyes wide open. "It's next generation, no thicker than a catsuit."

Raj turned and nibbled his earlobe.

"How perplexing," mumbled Marcus. "If the girl was equipped by Combat CK, why is she working for Carlsgrove protecting the croissant?"

"What if she wants it too?"

"It's possible. How is Combat CK funded?"

Looking to the side, Rajesh hit the keys. "The commerce monitoring database suggests Cocks Associates. It looks like they're in it for a great deal of money."

Marcus closed his eyes, Raj tight against him. "What do we know about them?"

The junior tapped away with one hand, fumbling with the other. "Privately owned family company. Pattern analysis suggests they're currently embroiled in a hostile takeover."

"Oh my." Marcus turned to face his protégé. "Let's hypothesise: Cocks Associates enters into a development deal with Carlsgrove. One party, possibly both, are not entirely honest and the deal turns sour. Carlsgrove take umbrage and goes on the offensive. Cocks retaliates. And we accidentally stumble into the middle of their war."

"I told you I was good." Raj smiled, kissing Marcus on the neck, sending spasms all the way down to his toes.

Outside, tyres screeched on the gravel drive, throwing stones in a wide, clattering arc.

"Bugger," said Marcus, his ardour diminishing. "They've found us. Get down. On the floor. Now, where the hell did you put my gun?"

Damien couldn't say for certain who pulled the trigger.

The mind plays tricks like that.

He and Eric were sitting in the back of a taxi playing follow the leader along the Embankment, when they spotted the embarrassment wagon parked up. Seconds later they heard the girl's siren song.

The senior junior listened intently to the nuances within the notes, picking out a cry for assistance. Judging by the urgency with which Eric paid the cabbie, he'd heard it too. They hurried across the road, only to discover the nutter in the toga from earlier, now sporting the garb of a transvestite gladiator, waving a gun in the air and threatening to stiff the detectant moviemaker. Events moved quickly. Before they knew it, the girl of their dreams was peppered with holes.

Damien screamed out in anguish, diving in the direction of her slumped body, pipping Eric's instinct for retribution by a tenth of a second and that of their gaming pal by a full tick of the clock. Up close, the senior junior realised he had no idea what make of gun the girl's weapon was, so he improvised. Safety catch off. Load the chamber. Squeeze the trigger.

Blum!

"Oh, crap!" mouthed Eric, watching the projectile fly wide of the mark.

"Balls on toast," muttered Damien. The words came out as a jumbled mumble, through a mouth full of cotton wool.

"Boys." The gladvestite pointed his weapon at their heads.

The junior let out a blood-curdling shriek, screaming at the top of his lungs: "Give me the gun!"

He had the right of it.

They were about to be topped quarrelling over a pistol, a squelch mark in each of their foreheads. Damien imagined rumour and speculation running riot. He closed his eyes tight and prayed to the Blessed Virgin, wondering how the fisticuffs at the funeral might play out between their families. His demented ogre of a father versus Senior Eric Senior, who by all accounts was a bellowing ox with a fuse shorter than a seahorse's cock.

Click.

"The nutter's got a log jam!" shouted the junior, wrestling hold of the girl's weapon.

Damien opened his eyes, mumbling thanks to the Mother Mary.

Blum!

Their second projectile hit Toganuts in the thigh.

Confused, the gladvestite wiped the gooey remains of a projectile from his leg. Lips pursed, he released the magazine from his faulty weapon, cleared the chamber, and reloaded. "Who's first, ladies?"

The senior junior closed his eyes once more. If he was truly destined to die, then he'd die kissing the girl. He crawled up close to her, feeling the way with his fingers, determined to press lips.

Eric tugged at his trouser leg.

Damien blinked, orienting himself.

Toganuts was busy trying to swat a swarm of incredibly annoying invisible insects. The senior junior watched an array of miniature tongues snake out from the projectile's point of impact, amalgamating to form creeping lapis dragons that covered legs, torso, and arms, and finally the nutter's face, leaving his entire body glowing a deep iridescent blue. Eyes as wide as old Ford headlamps, the whites flashed over.

"You'll pay for this!" Toganuts gouged frantically at his eye sockets, staggering blindly. Tripping on a raised paving slab, he crashed painfully to his knees.

The moviemaker shuffled away. His enemy rolled over onto his back, panting, staring into space. His breathing slowed; the muscles at the side of his mouth contracted, parting lips to reveal a pair of perfect white teeth.

"Bitchfucker!" Eric was the first to his feet. He ran towards Toganuts and kicked him in the side. "How DARE you shoot her."

Emboldened, Damien put his ear to the girl's chest, pressing his head tightly against the dark leather.

"She's alive," he said, aware that all eyes were upon him. "We need to call an ambulance and not move her."

"Good luck with that." The detectant grasped his right forearm. "Eric, Damien — I owe you both."

"We didn't bloody do it for you!" screamed Eric, kicking Toganuts once more.

"Carry on," said the moviemaker, tearing a strip from his tattered trousers and tying it around his arm. "He deserves it."

Damien nodded.

The detectant grimaced. "Who's going to assist me with this pressure dressing?"

In the end, the senior junior obliged, albeit reluctantly. Like Eric, he'd been introduced to blood sports at a young age and claret-covered arms were nothing new to him. He was loathe to touch the stuff, not because it gave him the jitters, rather that he didn't know where the filthy trouser ferret had been. While he assisted, Eric continued to kick at Toganuts, avidly reciting phrases from the catalogue of Old Boy insults.

Once the moviemaker was comfortable, Damien removed his jacket, diligently folded it into quarters and inserted it between the girl's head and the floor, taking time to examine the ragged entry holes around her torso where the trio of projectiles had struck, messing up the fine Italian leather.

No blood.

Delicately, he brushed a finger across her cheek, allowing the tip to touch the crevice formed by her full lips. Based on the freshness of her complexion and the clarity of her voice, he was sure Eric was right: She must be a filly. What he really wanted was to play the role of Prince Charming and wake her from her slumber with a delicate kiss, but Eric kept on coughing whenever he got close.

He stretched his arms, stifling a yawn.

London answered with a reveille call of rattling exhaust pipes and horns. Drivers gawped at them. Between the prostrate girl, the bright-blue, cross-dressing gladiator, and the blood-covered tramp, they had no idea what to make of it. A rogue car pulled over. The moviemaker improvised, claiming they were shooting a scene for a film using hidden cameras. He signed up the driver as an extra. With a cry of "action!" Toganuts was re-acquainted with his dressing gown, lumped into the back seat of the embarrassment wagon and strapped in beside the bone-crusher. Remarkably, the blue tinge, which looked akin to eggshell close-up, faded to a fine sheen then vanished completely. Ferret tried to move the girl. The stiff resistance he met soon persuaded him of the futility of the operation.

As soon as the extra departed, the junior turned on the detectant. "You're a fraudster, you really are. We can't find any of your movies online, and your website's been torched."

The moviemaker grinned. "Where's your sword, Eric?"

"In the Thames," spluttered the junior. "I was minding it for a friend."

"Like you're minding my gun." Ferret held out his hand. "I don't know how the girl got it, but it belonged to my deceased father."

The junior glowered from beneath a knotted brow. "I could just shoot you."

"And make another body?" said Damien. "Don't be mad."

Brring!

Eric and Ferret both moved for their phones at the same time. Eric drew a blank; Ferret found his pocket empty.

"Hello?" said Damien, his greeting tinged with suspicion.

"Finally," purred the voice on the other end of the line. "Someone real, who isn't an answerphone."

"Miss Harrington . . ." The senior junior heard his whispery words splinter.

What followed was one of Miss Harrington's classy but inappropriate late night-dumps, which consisted of a string of bitchy superlatives without the option to participate. Her boyfriend was a triple jerk; she hated him. Something about a terrible mistake involving a granny. Then he lost concentration, his eye wandering to the girl. He imagined their lips meeting in a cascade of salty foam, his hand firmly on her well-proportioned bottom. Something about a premonition, an accident on the river, parentage called into question. And sobs. Lots of sobs.

"Be strong," he said. "He's not worth it."

"Have you listened to a word I said?"

"Every single one."

"Then tell me, why am I screwing Grant?"

"Who's Grant?"

"Pay attention. The man in my bedroom."

Damien's mind wandered back to the girl. How was it Miss Harrington always knew exactly when not to phone? She was crying buckets over the moviemaker, who she thought was sleeping with the fishes.

"Your geek detectant is very much alive," he stammered. "In fact, he's standing right next to me."

Ferret took the phone without hesitation. Despite his injuries, he smooched in front of an invisible mirror, seducing Miss Harrington with his voice, the tones sparkling with mischief and desire. Damien turned away, determined not to listen, yet he found himself drawn into the conversation, which, despite his misgivings, turned into the best phone sex he'd never had.

He brushed the girl's hair to one side, winding a lock around his finger. It would look fantastic clipped up, creating such anticipation for later. Perhaps some designer frames.

Damien felt a hand on his shoulder.

Ferret winked and handed back the phone.

"Are you listening?" said Miss Harrington. "Grant has to go. I want you to call reception and report a fire. Here's the number."

He scribbled down the details on the back of his hand while Ferret and Eric argued over the weapon. After much arm-twisting, the junior handed it over. He bade the moviemaker a dispassionate goodbye, kicking the embarrassment wagon for luck.

"When you're done, torch the car."

"After I meet my friend." The detectant tipped his hat. "We had a saying in a place I once worked: Don't count your chickens until the fat lady sings."

As the car pulled away, Damien thought he heard something banging in the boot. Evidently, from the curious crook in his eyebrow, Eric heard it too. They were both tired after a long, hard night — that was it.

"Have you figured it out yet?" asked Eric, a mischievous canter to his voice.

"Figured out what?"

"Her identity, dummy." The junior reached down and gathered up the girl's hair into a top-knot. "Now imagine she's wearing thick black frames, a truckload of makeup to hide the pock mark, and some geeky clothes . . ."

"My god . . ." Damien's jaw dropped progressively lower with each passing second.

Xara.

Miss Harrington's intern.

What in God's name was she doing here?

Of all the irritations that scratched at Ferret's bum, there was one above all others that truly irked him.

Backseat drivers.

His French friend, for instance, was a critical fidget who always knew which lane to be in despite the fact that he'd steadfastly refused to take a driving test.

*One is a terrible chauffeur*, said a voice in his ear. *Edward's decuria?*

"One nine seven six."

*Again.*

This was long past tedious.

He'd tried to emulate the ginger troublemaker using the same set of imagined visuals, but the great brass reels on the machine he'd made spun without ever stopping, reducing the operation to sheer guesswork.

*Next left. By Jupiter's gouty toe! Right.*

Ferret slammed his foot on the brakes, skidding to a halt. Thankfully, once outside London there was little traffic on the road. Heading north-west, he'd pondered how he might outrun a high-powered police pursuit vehicle in Eric's knackerwagon, what he might say regarding his clothing, and how to explain away the body in the boot, which fingered him as a trainee serial killer transporting a cache of freshly anaesthetised victims.

He caressed the gun he'd taken from Junior Eric, questioning his sanity. The voices in his head made a murder trial more, not less, likely if he was apprehended.

Looking over his shoulder, he reversed back the way he'd come and turned into The Old Mill. The gate to the sprawling complex was pinned open, revealing a broken Tarmac track pitted with holes. Slowly, he picked his way around them and, once clear, floored the accelerator, hurtling down the driveway at breakneck speed. He pulled the handbrake hard at the last, squealing to a halt in a screech of burning rubber and kicking up a tsunami of gravel.

*Bravo. Now, as agreed.*

In between shouting conflicting directions, Edward's head had explained at length how the universe has a will of its own, a way with events, and how thwarting that will brings unpredictable consequences. Ferret had pulled the car over halfway through the monologue and rummaged through the contents of Eric's boot. Finding a holdall of S&M gear, he'd chosen something with which to silence the chattering. Shortly afterwards, the disembodied voices in his head started in earnest.

He knocked on the door of The Old Mill using a tell-tale pattern of taps and stepped back, hands held high.

Hinges squeaked.

A letterbox jangled.

And there in front of him, pistol in hand, was the most welcome sight he'd seen in weeks.

"My, what a fabulous fedora," said Marcus with a wry smile. "Come inside before anyone sees you."

Ferret doffed his hat, and with a slight bow, handed his friend a carrier bag.

"What's this?"

"The most bizarre present you're ever likely to receive."

Marcus took the gift and ushered him in, double locking the door. As an extra precaution, he inserted a steel bar into a pair of horizontal slots. Content that nothing was coming or going without consent, the intelligence man took a peek inside the bag.

He recoiled in horror, nostrils flaring at the stench of blood, mucus and singed hair. With great deliberation, the bag was placed atop a plant stand and the plastic peeled back.

"Nice ball gag," said a voice from behind.

Ferret turned around, heart pounding, to see Rajesh standing in the doorway to the kitchen. He greeted the junior, all the while suppressing a smirk. The newest member of the decuria and his old friend were wearing matching dressing gowns. With a smile, the detective removed the gag and tossed it to Raj, who stepped aside with a shriek, allowing it to fall by his feet.

The head smiled, its mouth full of cracked teeth.

"It's good to see you." Marcus hugged Ferret hard. "We feared the worst."

The detective looked his government friend up and down, a million thoughts colliding in a cerebral supernova. There was so much to say, so many questions in need of answers. His mouth, dry to the core, did its best to interpret the jumble of desires, gave up, and converted the mess to a single word.

"Drink."

"My apologies," said Marcus, pointing towards the liquor cabinet. "How rude of me."

"One is dying for a cup of tea," said the head. "White, one sugar please."

Rajesh stood rooted to the spot, mouth agape, catching flies.

"It's disconcerting at first," said Ferret, sorting through the cabinet. "After the novelty wears off you'll soon find it becomes very annoying. That's why the gag, which is really rather pointless as all it does is talk straight into one's head."

The detective poured himself a double Macallan, knocking it back in one gulp. Then he fixed a second. Marcus, meanwhile, despatched the confused junior to the kitchen to produce a round of non-alcoholic beverages. Ferret sat down while his friend set to with a security services field kit, staunching the flow of blood and sewing up holes.

The junior returned, struggling to balance a tray packed with tea and toast.

"I've left quite a mess outside," said Ferret.

"Such as a headless corpse?" Marcus waved his hands excitedly. "Rajesh, will you please move the body into one of the outhouses."

"Bodies. Agent Tidley-Jones and I had quite the fight. I apologise for giving him the hiding of his life, but I was left with no other option."

"I'm so sorry," said Marcus, fluffing his fringe. "He's usually so reasonable. I assigned him to the case because he has previous experience of controlling Edward. Rajesh, please move TJ too."

"And our banking friend."

"You kidnapped the centurion?" Marcus breathed in deeply. "Oh my."

The detective hurriedly described their friend's assault with knives and a gun for the offence of pursuing and assisting Edward. The banker was unconscious, incapacitated by noxious chemicals.

"He was shot by a random girl who appeared from nowhere on a motorcycle." Ferret produced a pistol. "I recognise this as belonging to my late father."

Marcus's face clouded over. "Did she follow you?"

"Last seen out of it, on the Embankment."

"Thank god." Marcus motioned towards the door with his hand. "Raj."

"Yes, yes," complained the junior loudly. "I get it. I'm demoted to dogsbody."

Raj took the car key and let himself out, muttering loudly about the horrible lot of the underling. The intelligence man relocked the door, then turned to address the head.

"The trail of destruction you've left behind matches the work of the ginger terror." Marcus drew his gun. "However, despite many physical similarities, you're not him. So who the bloody hell are you and what are you doing here?"

Ferret stared hard at the broken head dribbling goo down the front of its perch. He shot a glance in the direction of his government friend, then settled his gaze back on the grizzly ginger trophy.

"By Jupiter's posthumous vasectomy, I apologise for Edward's reckless behaviour," it said croakily. "As you correctly noted, the head is not his."

"Talk faster." Marcus brought his handgun to bear.

"The owner's name was Gerald. When I first returned to England, I sought out an Edward lookalike and struck a Faustian bargain to borrow his body, should the need arise, in exchange for earthly riches." The head looked on, with its one good eye. "For this mission, it was imperative to have Edward at his most virile. Gerald made a fine avatar, but once the heat was turned up, he ceased to be reliable."

"If this was Edward's avatar," scowled Marcus, "then Edward it is not. Where is he, and who are you?"

"My name is Flamen Dialis," replied the head. "Like your good selves, I am a humble servant of Rome."

"How did you know where to find me?" His voice tinged with suspicion, Marcus clicked the weapon's safety catch to off.

"Steady on." Ferret stepped between his friend and the target. "Agent TJ divulged the address."

"Out of my way."

The detective folded his arms and stood his ground. "The head knew my father."

"The device you acquired from Soho Square," said the head. "Do you have it here?"

"You stole the Precious?" Ferret bit his lip. "Then all this trouble is your doing."

"I had no choice." Marcus glared at the soot-blackened face of Gerald, lowering his weapon by forty-five degrees. "It poses a threat to the realm."

The detective felt an odd set of tremors traverse his hands.

The Precious, he thought. It's here.

"Tea," said the head. "By Jupiter's furry chestnuts, I must taste god's brew one last time. Then we will piece this puzzle together."

Ferret had long considered Marcus to be one of only a few genuine, trustworthy allies. His old boss Marianne was number two, his father's ex-handyman Bob number three. The Frenchman, although entirely predictable, he classed as untrustworthy.

Having an ally turn against him was not something he'd previously considered. He felt the hole in his heart where the Precious belonged, felt a perverse leer traverse his face. All this time Marcus had been playing DeathWorld: Apocalypse, keeping it for himself.

A dribble formed at the edge of Ferret's mouth. He'd discovered the Precious. It was his by right of conquest.

What he wanted to do was search the place from top to bottom, turning over tables and pulling out drawers but, having discovered a dislike of guns pointed in his general direction, he made his apologies and ambled over to the tea tray, helping himself to a mug of tea and a buttered triangle of toast, which he folded in half and demolished.

What remained of Gerald slurped tea through a straw from a mug held aloft by Marcus; the liquid promptly slopped out of the head's neck and gathered in a puddle on the carpet. Revived by the transfusion, a mischievous sparkle flashed across the head's functioning eye.

"Dead one is not!" it yelled, causing the plant stand to shudder and a shiver to run down Ferret's spine.

"Edward?" Marcus dropped the mug and raised his weapon.

"Bromeliad . . ."

Ferret laid into a second triangle of toast, then a third, keeping an ear on the conversation developing between his dear friend and the certifiable remains of Gerald. Judging by the raised, emotive voices, Edward and Marcus were once very close.

The head began to sob. Slowly at first, then uncontrollably.

The detective raised an eyebrow. He'd known Marcus for nearly ten years and in all that time he'd never once mentioned a paramour named Edward. Hopefully, they had a lot of catching up to do. With the pair otherwise engaged, Ferret jammed the last of the toast into his mouth and scanned the room.

A large wooden farmhouse table occupied one wall of the living space, flanked by two high-backed chairs each facing a laptop computer. Between the two portables lay an array of black equipment strung together by a series of black wires. A black four-way power strip connected the hardware to the mains. He identified a black printing mechanism, a black oscilloscope — undoubtedly the big brother to the SniffPhreak 2000 — and an array of indefinable black boxes, each with an impressive number of switches and dials.

In floods of tears, Marcus seized the head and cradled it in his arms. Ferret turned away in embarrassment. As he did so, a faint pulse of golden light caught his eye. It was almost imperceptible, tucked away beneath the table, hidden under a solid-black drape.

A quick look at his government friend.

Was he really going to snog the head on the lips?

Without waiting for the outcome, yet secretly imagining tongues, Ferret dived under the table, lifted the cloth, and came face to face with the captive Precious. He unlatched the cage in which it was locked and removed it to stroke its contoured grip.

"Noooo!" cried Marcus.

Ferret flinched, surprised at the sudden outburst, banging his head on the underside of the table. His fingers came to rest on an exposed glob of golden jelly embedded in the heart of the controller.

He felt woozy.

A great bottomless pit formed. He fell, feeling the walls collapse behind him. The raw energy of the Precious flowed through him, forcing the flesh of his face back around the ears. Faster and faster he plummeted, buffeted by tempestuous eddies, fully expecting to be spat out like a human torpedo into the streets of DeathWorld and immediately fired upon by a bevy of bad guys armed to the teeth with RPGs.

Instead, he found himself standing on a staircase in a familiar, book-lined study.

"*Mein Sohn.*"

Ferret recognised the voice immediately. "*Vater?*"

"I am so sorry for ze vay sings turned out."

Was he having a deranged vision of the past, or was the past somehow colliding with the present? It mattered not. What was important was that it was happening, in a Wonderland sort of a way, for his father had never issued an apology before in his life.

Sensing this world was coherently different to his own, Ferret reached out to embrace his father.

"But of course." Wolfgang held him tightly. "Ve must get ze pleasantries concluded before your friends arrive."

"You're not exactly the father I remember," whispered Ferret, savouring the moment.

A flash to the left, a flash to the right, then one more.

He sensed Marcus in his dressing gown, side by side with a well-built ginger chap sporting crazy sideburns, a cavalier goatee, and a deer stalker hat. A skinny older gent dressed in a white priestly robe, bald pate aglow, brought up the rear. Ferret knew immediately that this was Flamen Dialis.

"Gentlemen," said Wolfgang, with a bow. "Zer is much to know und time ist short, for ze device ist already dialling home. Fortunately, in zis universe, ve operate at ze speed of thought. Hold on to your hats."

Ferret saw the last few months of the lives of all present spread out like the pages of a 3-D graphic novel. He found himself, along with Marcus, in a monastery in northern India undergoing a ritual to save his father. The nonsense with the devil dog at Erin Breweries unfolded before their eyes; Bob appeared on the doorstep with an accompanying video and a package. Escape from purgatory came assisted by the cobalt liquid; the plan to send him to Grrr! acquired motion. Fast forward: in Porton Down, metal scraped against concrete, the skinny gent pushing hard with a shoulder against a sealed blast door.

Marcus gasped out loud.

"Ours was not the first team to explore D-XIII," mused Sir Edward, "for it truly is the strangest of chemicals, one whose states differ depending on volume. In the dash for intellectual treasure at the end of World War Two, the Americans spirited away the Nazi burrowers and rocketeers, while the realm looted Kiel and pocketed Project XIII along with the rest of the German drugs program."

Ferret opened a hat box; later he performed naked to the camera, wearing the contents. Edward guffawed, having watched it all. Marcus's thoughts spiralled around the logistics of a raid. Soho Square spun into view, flipping and flopping. Ferret observed the girl who'd tried to reason with the banker slithering snugly through an open window. She coshed his friend Raffles, still a dab hand at breaking into safes, pulling the Precious from his limp hand.

Outside, an explosion.

With the girl distracted, Marcus snatched the Precious from her grasp and ran for it; his bodyguards opened fire, hitting her multiple times. Sir Edward and Flamen intercepted him. The girl followed, depositing a trail of silver sparks in her wily wake.

"Zis is Cocks's doing," muttered Wolfgang. "His only interest in ze chemical ist its ability to sheer thicken ven struck und dispel ze resulting heat quickly."

Images of flexible armour floated into view. Double-layer sports monofibre webbed with molecular filament Kevlar, holding a layer of silver liquid close to the skin.

"For years, perfecting ze armour vos his only interest."

"The girl is an associate of Toad," flapped Edward, naming him parasite in a dozen languages.

Wolfgang chipped in, much to Marcus's delight, confirming Walter was indeed the third man in Cocks's enterprise. A downdraft of recriminations from Edward and Flamen followed.

Ferret felt the icy bile of betrayal rise in their stomachs.

"When ze ministry sold off its estates und privatised Porton Down, an offer vos made und accepted for some of ze stores," said his father. "Walter, for all his cleverness, upset anozer party, who later came knocking."

Marcus's thoughts turned to the Carlsgrove Group's complicated structure of international shell companies designed to obfuscate their holdings, projected for all to see. Ferret knew of the private equity firm by reputation. It was a company one did not tussle with.

"They own RockSlut hardware, who in turn own the croissant," said Marcus.

"Apart from ze insert of golden goo, vich zey must get from us." Wolfgang danced from side to side, a smirk upon his face. "Only vonce ze armour vos complete did Cocks concede to zer fabrication."

Ferret was stunned.

His father had helped to create the Precious.

He found himself sliding backwards through the pages of the novel once more, passing through the doors of Grrr!, feeling the pain of losing Wolfgang's files. Around the group, in the shadows, incomplete shades of Junior Eric, Damien, Hartley, Clifford and Malory, and a hundred other Old Boys stirred, ruffling the fabric of the makeshift universe. Slipping through a hole in the novel's spine, he and Marcus became privy to an animated discussion between his father, Sir Edward, and a third party, whom the pair were busy ridiculing.

"You vish to pass a digital file through ze liquid?" Wolfgang ran a hand haphazardly through a mane of swept-back, tangled black hair. "Impossible!"

"A waste of valuable resource." Edward banged his fist into an out-stretched palm.

The rabbit hole squeezed tight, spitting the companions back out, accompanied by a thought commentary from the chemist: ve argued vis Albright vor veeks. As it turns out, it vos ve who ver wrong.

Edward and the skinny chap rode a wave of pent-up emotion imbued with doubt, offering up the only possible solution: The Precious was Albright's battlefield globe resurrected, given a new overcoat, then enhanced with cutting-edge technology. Thoughts tripped over thoughts, poleaxing one another. Edward had discussed Albright's exuberant theory many times in the search for an explanation for his peculiar powers. The psychologist claimed that every object in the universe is composed of visuals, sounds, and feelings, even though not all traits are always observable. Spoken wishes contain embedded subconscious information that the universe decodes.

Sir Edward huffed. He preferred to credit God.

"I am proof he voz at least partially correct," declared Wolfgang. "My computer files, zey appear to be a binary mishmash of vons und zeros. Unseen are ze feelings I had ven I vas typing, ze sings I voz saying to myself. Von talks to ze unseen elements of ze files, transformed by ze magic liquid."

"Extraordinary!" exclaimed Edward. "How many battlefield globes did one create?"

Five hundred und zirty-two, thought Wolfgang. Delivered to Toad, vonce ze twelve suits ver complete.

"Come, oh my friends . . ." sang a voice from the pages of the book.

The polished words echoed into eternity, carrying images and feelings, jettisoning their glowing payload into the ears of all present. An explosion of thoughts circled like mechanised hornets. By Jupiter's clandestine man-cave, sighed Flamen, in my old age I have become a buffoon. Albright's original work focused only on the chemical's ability to absorb and mirror emotions in its golden state. The girl's powers are the unforeseen consequence of deploying the liquid in its silver state over the entirety of a human body.

The circle of thoughts became a speeding merry-go-round of creativity as the group reacted to this new information. Working together, they fleshed out in a millisecond a working hypothesis that might otherwise have taken many hours. Given the fervour with which the girl sought the Precious, it must be the only fully functioning device in existence.

Carlsgrove is playing for the lot, thought Marcus, joining disparate facts like dots to form a picture in the collective mindspace.

Seeing the inner workings of his friend's head exposed, the detective marvelled at how Marcus's mental processes worked. So different to his own. He felt the sense of panic that Cocks and Troutman felt when the hostile takedown of their business venture began. No wonder they'd employed a talented assassin to protect their investment.

"We must assume Carlsgrove has procured copies of all the classified research notes," said the skinny chap.

Wolfgang nodded. "But until ze inserts ver delivered, zey had no liquid."

"And the secret of secrets?" asked Flamen.

Wolfgang smiled.

"By Jupiter's teeth!" The skinny chap laughed out loud. "They don't know."

Know what? Thought Ferret and Marcus as one.

The detective felt the pages of the novel turn once more, sucking them in and spitting them out through the spine. They heard Edward and Wolfgang conversing in German with a group of older men dressed in white lab coats. Ferret translated, marvelling at how his mind made words into pictures. He saw the four stable states of D-XIII. In large quantities it remains transparent. Nine hundred and ninety-seven millilitres produces the silver state. Fifty-nine millilitres produces the golden state. Thirteen millilitres or less, and what one sees is the beautifully complex cobalt state.

"The Germans named that state *Spezial Kobalt Dreizehn*," said Edward. "We called it True Blue."

Wolfgang grinned. "Ze official records describe only Albright's vork. Such a secret ve kept, hidden in plain sight. Latterly, Cocks suspected zer vos zomezing I vos not telling, zo I confessed zat SK-13 could incapacitate und persuaded him to fabricate a pistol for my defence."

The unique properties of True Blue danced before Ferret and Marcus. The detective saw how his father had secretly deployed the liquid onto his skin during his youth, taking meticulous notes of the mathematical patterns behind the effects and, later, once he had analysed the results, burnt the evidence.

"Is this what I am?" he scowled. "An experiment?"

"*Nein*," said Wolfgang. "You are my *Sohn*."

"How could you do this to me?"

"Ve needed successors. Ve ver in fear vor our lives."

"For which one chose one's Bromeliad," said Edward. "Before we proceed further, one must name Edward's decuria."

Ferret felt the cold worms of despair burrow into his belly. Earlier, he'd thrown everything including the kitchen sink at the problem. He'd even tried inserting pictures on the legion reel: the bull, Hercules and Pegasus. The cohort reel was configured to ten, the centuria reel, six. Decuria might be ten or possibly twenty. He'd tried both. Whatever he did, however he formatted the numbers, the reels spun and spun, always without purchase.

Here in the realm of thought and feeling, things were different. Here he might employ his government friend's brain, which was much better suited to solving puzzles.

Marcus smiled.

Already he was on the case, thinking in the abstract.

Ferret and Marcus worked quickly, swapping in Roman numerals, then adjusting the maximum value on each reel to infinity and finally, as an experiment, the minimum value to nothing at all. The reels spun. This time they ground precariously to a halt, one by one, in a juddering screech of brass and metal.

"Zero!" said the detective and the government man together.

"Bravo." The sound of Edward's clapping filled the room.

"Ve can finally tell you," said Wolfgang, a tear running down his cheek, "vy I vas missing for so many of your childhood years."

Ferret felt sick to the stomach.

As a boy, he venerated the presents his wandering father brought home. Later, as promises were broken and his disappointment grew, he took to destroying the intermittent gifts with a hammer. Liberated by the carnage, he'd come to love the freedom of boarding school and the lack of parental supervision. Shortly after his mother went doolally, the frequency of his father's visits increased, culminating in a series of shouting matches each longer and louder than the last. The final straw came with his acceptance of The Consultancy's offer, an event that created an insufferable family wedge. Over the years, he'd accepted his fellow legionnaires as surrogate siblings and, with his French friend's assistance, demoted Wolfgang to the role of despised pantomime villain.

And yet here he was, getting on rather well with a confusing pastiche of his father. He'd known this version of Wolfgang for perhaps a second and yet he felt he'd known him for his entire life. It was such a shame he hadn't seen this side of his father when he was alive.

"I am dead?" said Wolfgang. "Oh dear."

The detective felt his father's fears rear up like a skittish mare taunted by candy-apple goblins. He was at home in London, albeit briefly. Always he was looking behind, searching the shadows for mean men with bayonets in their eyes. Only in the Middle East did he find absolution, in ministry compounds and military bases, surrounded by armed guards and special forces. If he avoided his family, pretended not to care, only then might they stay safe.

Always running.

"It vos your sirtieth birthday und you turned up late, drunk, und belligerent," said Wolfgang. "So I shot you mit True Blue for abusing your spezial powers. Ven you apologised, only zen vos I going to give zem back.

Ferret felt his father's fear once more. Someone was after him. His laptop and satellite phone remained hidden; the files he'd prepared were of little value as ones and zeroes, only the ethereal content, buried deep within invisible structures was of consequence. Edward would piece the puzzle together. They had a long understanding. No earthly communication was safe. An omen must be sent by dream carrier.

Before that, a precaution.

Bob, the unknown soldier. Unwitting, untraceable.

Then a life-threatening act, something completely out of character to generate a premonition.

Flamen smiled. "A valiant effort, my friend."

"Who were you avoiding?" asked Ferret. "Not Carlsgrove; that came much later."

Already, he knew the answer.

With what he'd learned, it was obvious.

The legion.

He wanted to cry "bullcrap!", but at the same time it was entirely coherent, bringing perspective to the ongoing veil of secrecy, the late-night calls, the missing birthdays. The legion was a vast singles club, after all; hardly the place for a family man.

Marcus put a finger to his lips. "The croissant device is recording everything we say and think. We must discuss such matters outside of here."

The detective hugged his father. "It's good to finally understand you."

"Come back zoon, *Sohn*. Und zay hello to your lovely sisters. I miss zem zo much."

Ferret imagined being unborn, pulled backwards through space and time by a giant umbilical chord. He awoke with a jolt, gasping for air. Rolling onto his side, he pulled his finger from the golden goo. Next to him lay his government friend, finger also pressed into the sparkling jelly, and between them, Gerald, tongue inserted into the Precious' exposed innards. Marcus opened an eye and, without pausing for breath, disconnected the head and pushed the croissant back inside its cage.

There was so much Ferret wanted to say, yet given what they'd shared of each other's feelings and experiences, no words were appropriate. Instead, he waited until they'd extricated themselves from beneath the table, then issued a kiss to the cheek.

"Thanks for the hat."

Marcus blushed.

Back on top of the plant stand, the head grinned, its cracked teeth reminiscent of Stonehenge.

"Why did you keep Decuria Zero from me?" asked the intelligence man.

"To ensure one's safety," said the head in Edward's voice.

"And my father?" asked Ferret.

"He was legion, this much one has deduced," said the head, switching to Flamen's voice. "We dare not induct him into Decuria Zero, the *Collegium Pontificum*. He was under constant observation by the security forces, the Americans, the Russians, and the Chinese. Only after he took a moral stand and avoided the millennium vows did The Network follow him too."

Ferret and Marcus listened intently as the head, speaking in tongues, explained how the secret society they knew as The Network had undergone many rebirths in its long history, which some suggested stretched all the way back to the great republic. Edward and Wolfgang had signed up to a society called The Brotherhood of Light and Reason, founded on mutual respect and goodwill to all, which then morphed into The Brotherhood and later The Network, adopting the Nietzschean philosophy of Will to Power.

The detective rubbed his chin.

With all those changes of name, it was no wonder he'd never been able to find any references to the society in the conspiracy books he'd pored over.

As with Rome itself, a series of checks and measures were put in place by the founders to ensure that no one man was able to usurp control of the three legions. Flamen took up the talking stick, describing how, with the disbanding of the *Collegium*, those balances lay in tatters. Ferret stifled a yawn. At The Consultancy they used to refer to this sort of meeting as a hedgehog curry: too little meat and what there was got stuck in one's throat. Flamen droned on. He talked about the cryptographic obfuscation of decuria records and the parallels of the *Collegium*, which had no official charter or member list. Only a single name was declared in the records: the holder of the title Flamen Dialis.

"By Jupiter's spurting phallus!" exclaimed the head. "They tortured my predecessor for days to winkle from him the names of his co-conspirators. Once he expired, they placed The Network on lockdown and began a witch hunt that lasted for twenty-four years, so determined were they to root out and forcibly extirpate fifth columnists affiliated to Decuria Zero."

"And yet this is the first I've heard of it," said Marcus suspiciously.

Ferret's arm throbbed where his friend had applied a suture. He chanced a scratch, listening to the conversation hum along like a well-tuned engine, learning how those who ask the wrong kinds of questions are now referred to a Senate security commission. As a religious institution, the job of the *Collegium* was to advise the Senate on godly matters, keep the sacred texts sacred, and interpret and enforce the Constitution.

Until a revolt led by the Second Legion, to install their Caesar.

*As a citizen of Rome, I have no secrets before The One.*

The detective flicked a thumb across his bottom lip.

That explained the first of the vows.

"Thankfully I'm out of all that," he said flippantly.

"Excuse me?" said Marcus and the head together.

"I've been meaning to tell you: Our friend the centurion dishonourably discharged me from service. It won't stick, obviously, as I resigned first."

"You did what?" shouted Marcus.

"He left me no choice. It was that or have him move into my home for inadvertently trashing his apartments. Once installed, he'll never leave."

"Ferret, you're a bloody fool."

"I'm sure we can sort it out."

"It's not as simple as that." Marcus held his head in his hands. "When Rusty resigned, Tristan had him bumped off before I was able to intervene and talk him out of it. Officially, Tom Tom will learn shortly that he died in a botched escape attempt."

Ferret felt a great rush of fear envelop him.

Since getting his intuition back, he'd come to despise what The Network stood for: its worship of Plutus, its stupid rules, and its rigid hierarchy. He was so glad to be out.

Except.

He gulped.

They were going to stalk him, just like they had stalked his father. He'd be looking over his shoulder for the rest of eternity. There was only one thing for it: run away. To Antarctica.

"Are you listening to me?" Marcus waved a hand in front of his face. "Did you sign anything?"

"Our friend has my resignation letter in his pocket."

"I'll say this once only. You didn't resign. There is no letter. The word of a centurion may carry great weight, but the word of an *adiutor* is weightier. I'll deal with your dismissal while our banking friend's out cold."

"But my house."

"You wanted an adventure. This is the price, detecting consultant."

Ferret felt a great albatross fall from around his neck. Everything he'd acquired through illicit means he'd lost, forfeited to The Network. The Maserati. The Regent's Park house. Trouser presses by the score. For the first time in a long time, he was a free man with nothing left to lose. Any threat the centurion tried to wield was null and void.

He laughed.

In the last few days he'd been through hell. But now, after meeting his father and sorting out their relationship, a familiar warmth rippled through his body. During their maltreatment session, the police tag team had loosened up all his muscles nicely. Shrew-face and Strauss had helped to hone reaction times. The rumpus on the bridge had tested his stamina, the explosion had cleared out his ears. There were a few square centimetres of flesh around the ankles that hadn't been beaten into shape until the rough-and-tumble session with the legendary scrum-half. All he'd been missing was a team tattoo to mark the occasion. Thanks to the centurion, he had one, in the shape of a snaking scar.

Finally, the pre-season tour of Hades was over.

At last, he was match-fit. Not quite the fly-half of old yet, but a lean, mean kicking machine nonetheless.

Posturing and chasing deals; backstabbing for money and inserting friends as middlemen; playing boo with the FSA and avoiding jail time because of who he knew. He was over it all. At the time, it was exciting but compared to the fun he'd had over the past few weeks, it was now meaningless twaddle.

"We're not done yet," he said, thinking of the great detective Sherlock Holmes, knowing he wouldn't let it end here.

The head tried to nod but lost its balance. Instinctively, Ferret dived and caught it by the ears.

"By Jupiter's knockers, I feel faint."

Ferret placed the head back on its pedestal. "The Network has lost its moral compass. I don't know what hare-brained scheme you have in mind to right things, but count me in."

The head chewed its bottom lip. "Prior to the coup that installed Caesar, a complex series of magical operations were performed by rogue members of the college, spells that persist to this very day. In order to strike at The Network, we must attack its very foundations. Your father's task was to crack the chemical formula for D-XIII to enable the production of unlimited quantities so we might create an army with which to annul the magic. At this task, he failed."

The detective nodded. "Then we must collect what remains."

"That pitches us against Carlsgrove," said Marcus. "I don't need to tell you how dangerous they are — they murdered Wolfgang. They pose a threat to the realm. They must be stopped."

Edward coughed. "One must do this the old-fashioned way."

Ferret put his right hand on the head; Marcus joined him.

"From the old flame to the new," it croaked. Speaking in a tremulous voice that rattled the lamp shades, it continued: "By Jupiter's wedding tackle, I swear you are the chosen light of The Brotherhood. *Fortitudo, constantia et victoria*."

"*Fortitudo, constantia et victoria*," said Ferret and Marcus together.

"Do not let the croissant fall into enemy hands."

The head closed its functioning eye. A wisp of pale-blue smoke drifted from each of its nostrils, briefly taking the shape of a skinny old man and a wild, untameable force of nature before dispersing in every direction, throwing open all the ground floor doors and windows, and leaving behind a motionless lump of flesh.

Ferret's head felt full.

It was going to take time to process all the experiences he'd had that weren't his own. He'd seen and heard all that his friend Marcus knew, and vice versa, which was a massive boon. One thought troubled him, nagging away like an hirsute northern fishwife.

"DeathWorld: Apocalypse launches in less than two weeks. We must discover Carlsgrove's plans and thwart them."

Marcus made his way over to the liquor cabinet and withdrew the bottle of scotch, pouring out a pair of doubles. "Let's drink to that."

Ferret clinked glasses. "My old boss Marianne is up to her neck in it. I'm heading to Bath."

"Perfect. I'll take Toad and Albright."

"There's someone else." The detective grimaced. "When my files were being crushed to death, I saw a figure operating the controls. He was silhouetted in darkness, with the wings of a crow. After all we've been through, I'm certain he's one of us. A turtle."

As his friend considered an answer, in stumbled Raj.

"That was very hard work. Those bodies kept on moving back and forth of their own accord. So c'mon chaps, spill. What did I miss?"

# Chapter Forty-Eight: Restitution

Flamen felt woozy all the way to his core.

He'd been party to two deaths, for which restitution must be paid.

The universe forgave him for the bald, skinny chap with the terminal illness. The deal was straightforward: Charlie Muggins, ex-paratrooper, wanted to live and breathe adventure one last time before he passed away. Flamen in turn needed an avatar with which to travel abroad and engage the enemy. Both parties were winners. It was Gerald's family he felt bad for. They were destined to never know the part he'd played, nor would they ever bury the body.

Flamen sniffled, thinking of the vengeful one-eyed giant who'd struck the fatal blow. Edward's exuberance behind the wheel had brought a premature end to Tidley-Jones' promising rugby career. Although he was seeking justice, it had hardly been served.

The old man shifted his bony bottom.

In the last few weeks, shut off from the monastery in a private meditation cell secreted away at the top of a tower, he'd lost twenty pounds and aged thirty years.

Such was the cost of dying twice and taking little in the way of sustenance.

He'd put so much of himself into re-creating Edward that he hardly had anything left for Muggins. Edward's force of will was that of a rampaging elephant. Eighteen hundred and twenty-three times he'd taken True Blue, attaining a level of initiation far beyond anything they'd imagined possible. It was those final four doses, the ascent to level two hundred and eighty-two that had changed everything.

During that final session the gates to the divine opened to the width of the universe, allowing it to gush through him like a fat, overburdened river in flood, rewriting who he was forever. No longer was he Thomas Granville-Sharpe; no more did he play the role of Sir Edward. He was Flamen Dialis, High Priest of Jupiter, servant of God. All that he'd been was washed away, detritus of no consequence.

In shock, his beautiful ginger locks fell out.

On the plus side, Wolfgang's son was redeemed and Bromeliad was still alive!

Mission accomplished.

They both had a long way to go to reach their full potential. Ferret was only level eight, Bromeliad level four. The future of The Brotherhood was in their hands now. They must not fail.

Bromeliad knew what must be done.

Privately, they'd discussed the matter.

Attain level five, come out from the shadows, grab the reins of power, and formally name himself Sir Edward forty-two.

Forego the realm.

Strike terror into the hearts of their foes.


What kind of Edward might Bromeliad become?

Not a self-made sex beast like number thirty-eight, that was certain.

A new millennium required a new kind of Edward. Smart and astute, not a blunt force with a permanent erection.

Flamen's thoughts turned to The Dark One.

He'd sensed Him briefly during the escapade in Soho Square. Edward reported His presence during the rooftop escape, overseeing His cronies who stole the inert body of the Frenchman. Finally, they'd both sensed Him during the centurion's attack. Ferret had tried so hard to summon help from the universe, but he was not yet at a level to do so. The girl's arrival was Edward's doing. From what they'd learned, her armour was easily able to withstand three shots, yet she fell so easily.

Undoubtedly, her incapacitation was His doing.

All a part of His dark plan.


The priest staggered to his feet, aided by his staff of office. In the last few weeks, he'd hardly used his legs at all. His head spun. So little energy.

Something wasn't right.

There was an ache in his limbs he hadn't felt before.

He coughed.

Black blood with a taste like stale iron.

Not good.

His head spun faster, his legs gave way.

Intoxicant.

Systemic in nature.

The priest lay motionless, staring into space.

How?

He'd trusted his friend the haruspex with preparing his meals.

Only the haruspex.

The door to the cell scraped against hard flagstone, grating as it opened.

By Jupiter's damned children, now it made sense.

During their time in the Precious, Bromeliad had thought about the reports of Wolfgang's death. The scientist's head had been ripped off, his body split open, and his ribcage spread wide. Officially, he'd been cut to death by a propeller. And yet his injuries matched those the seer had inflicted on the sacrificial hen.

Carlsgrove may have pushed his friend, thought Flamen, but Wolfgang was dead before he hit the water.

"Now he sees it," said a gruff voice from above.

The priest felt a hand around his scrawny neck; cold steel slipped beneath his ribs, puncturing a lung. Then his belly, rupturing his liver and spleen. He coughed, unable to breathe. Finally, the point slipped between bones, piercing his heart.

"Tell mighty Jupiter that Plutus sends his regards. Old man . . ."

# Acknowledgements

With gratitude to: my family and friends, for being there & participating in many years of nonsense; The Valhalla Club, for those legendary late night booze-ups; Carolann and Mel for editorial assistance; Amber Barry for proofreading and editing; my Criminal Case chums, for the laughs and great banter; Muse, Nightwish, Ghost BC & the Ramones, for providing musical inspiration when I ran out of ideas; the CAPITAL programme, and a number of consultants in particular (naming no names), whose antics gave rise to Ferret, Cyrano, Marcus and the centurion – I owe you a beer or ten...

I raise a glass to the people of influence who left us during the writing process, especially Christopher Lee, Lemmy, Alan Rickman, David Bowie, and last but not least Sapphire and my mum.